COLD IRON KILLS

A DCI ROBERT KETT NOVEL

ALEX SMITH

RELENTLESS MEDIA

COLD IRON KILLS
Published Worldwide by Relentless Media.
This edition published in 2025.

Edited by Hanna Elizabeth and Jacqueline Beard

ISBN: 978-1-913877-20-0
18.0.1

www.alexsmithbooks.com

ALSO BY ALEX SMITH

The DCI Robert Kett Thrillers

Paper Girls

Bad Dog

Three Little Pigs

Whip Crack

Run Rabbit Run

Stone Cold Dead

Every Mother's Son

Sweet Briar Rose

Jaw Breaker

Knock Knock

King Rat

Knuckle Bones

Lucky Number Seven

Unholy Saints

Truly Madly Deadly

Every Last Devil

Red Line

Cold Iron Kills

The DI Harrison Baird Thrillers

A Long-Dead Thing

Other Books

Six Days, Six Hours, Six Minutes

The Harder They Fall

For Bunny

PROLOGUE

Wednesday

THEY MOVED IN LIKE A BLACK TIDE, QUICK AND QUIET.

Sergeant Julia Gorski took point, clutching her SIG MCX rifle to her chest as she wove a path between the trees. Behind her, fanning out through the sparse woodland, was her team. Eight men and women, all kitted out in tactical black, all armed. She trusted every single one of them with her life because they had proven themselves time after time. In the heat and the hell of battle, these were her guardian angels, and she was theirs.

She reached the treeline, lifting a fist in silent command. As one, the unit stopped dead, blending like phantoms into the shadows between the trunks. Gorski lifted her monoscope, scanning the short stretch of barren scrubland ahead. It led to a chain-link fence, and past that was a war zone. A dozen buildings lay in various states of ruin, chunks blown off, roofs caved in. Enormous tank busters blocked the roads, twisted sculptures of metal covered in barbed wire. Around these, cars and trucks were scattered like broken toys, their bodies rusted, their windows shattered.

There was no sign of anyone alive.

She scanned the perimeter again, just to be sure. The sun was behind them, throwing liquid fire on the scene ahead. In a perfect world, they'd have struck two hours ago under the cover of darkness.

But she didn't live in a perfect world.

"Everything okay, Sarge?" came a whisper from beside her. Gorski didn't need to look to know that it was Joe Carmichael.

She nodded, pocketing the monoscope and turning to her second in command. Carmichael rested on his haunches by a tree, his rifle stowed but ready. Through his visor, his eyes were dark, his expression tense. Behind him, the rest of the team was almost invisible.

"We move fast, we move hard," Gorski said. "Intel is pretty sure Maynard's alone in there, and we want him alive."

She'd relayed the same orders half a dozen times since the briefing an hour ago, but it never hurt to hammer it home.

"But this is Joseph Maynard. This is the guy who used to head up Hollenbeck. He's going to be heavily armed and extremely dangerous. If in doubt, light him up."

In truth, nothing would give her more pleasure. Maynard was a monster, a man who'd carved a trail of misery and cruelty and torture and death for years. *Decades.* She pictured his old face, chiselled by a lifetime of hate, of wickedness. She wasn't a judge, or a jury, but she was all too aware that sometimes her job was executioner.

Maynard was coming with them today in handcuffs.

Or he was coming in a body bag.

Gorski faced front, counted down from five the way she always did before a raid.

Five.

She'd been here a hundred times before, but her body was still fizzing, a live current running through her.

Four.

Her heart machine-gunned against her Kevlar breastplate, her skin prickling.

Three.

She took a long breath. Calming, cooling.

Two.

She lifted the crucifix around her neck and kissed it, thinking of her mum, of her sister. Of Ben, and what they had created together.

One.

"Go, go, go."

She broke into a jog. The scrub was uneven, a minefield of dents and craters that did their best to trip her up. She moved as urgently as she could, aware that she and her team were easy targets if anyone happened to be watching. But other than a startled pigeon that exploded from a bush—almost stopping her heart dead—there was no sign of life in the twenty-three seconds it took them to cross.

Gorski dropped down next to the fence, scanning the landscape on the other side. This close, she could see a layer of ancient paint on the vehicles and the buildings, the floor littered with unexploded paintballs. Another veteran officer, Chester Andilet—who'd served with her for years now—snipped through the links with a pair of bolt cutters, pulling open the makeshift gate.

She eased through the gap, on high alert. More birds took off from the artificial scenery, their wings clapping out an applause as the team advanced. The paintball facility hadn't been used in years, the weeds waist high. Gorski waded through them, aware, without even looking, that her team had spread out in a line. She watched the world over the barrel of her gun, sweeping it left and right as if it were part of her, seeing the main building fifty yards ahead. It was an immense warehouse, brick walls and a corrugated iron roof. Intel had shown that the front of this building was heavily secured, but the single door in the back wall wasn't chained shut.

It wasn't even closed, Gorski saw as she reached the building. The door was open a crack, leaking darkness.

She activated the torch on her rifle while her team caught up—six facing the door, two aiming their weapons back the way they'd come in case anyone was planning to sneak up on them. She nodded to Andilet, who stowed his rifle in order to take hold of the door.

He nodded silently.

One, two, three.

Then he wrenched the door open.

Gorski moved inside, fast and hard, her torch lighting up a short, dark corridor—concrete floor, breeze-block walls. There was only one other door and she jogged to it, trying the handle to find it unlocked.

A hand rested on her shoulder, Carmichael telling her they were ready. She opened the door, entering a much larger room. Her torch lit up more artificial scenery—buildings and barricades and barbed wire. The ceiling was lost in shadow overhead.

A solitary figure stood in the middle of the space, dressed in overalls, facing away from them.

In his hand, he held a rifle.

A surge of adrenaline tore through Gorski as she moved

towards him. Beams of torchlight cut through the dark, a vortex of light and shadow that made it feel like the room was full of people.

But there was just the one man, slowly turning.

Twenty yards away. Gorski took a breath, called out.

"Armed police! Do not move!"

The man continued to turn, like a ballerina on a musical box. He was wearing a paintball mask, his face concealed behind the glass visor. He was definitely holding a gun of some kind, but there wasn't enough light to see what.

"Drop the weapon!" Gorski roared.

Ten yards, and the man lifted his rifle.

A split second to make the decision. A split second to decide between this man's life, or the life of somebody on her team.

Or her own, of course.

Gorski lifted her gun, mirroring the man as he raised his. She saw the long, black barrel, the magazine—and the bulbous compartment on top where the paintballs were stored.

It wasn't real.

"Hold fire!" she called out, breaking into a sprint. "Drop the fucking gun!"

The man squeezed off a shot, something thwacking into her shoulder. She didn't stop, reaching the guy in a heartbeat and driving the butt of her rifle into his masked face. He dropped like his strings had been cut, the gun clattering to the floor. His mask had been shattered, and through the mess of plastic she saw the face of a teenage boy, blood streaming from his broken nose.

"You okay?" said Carmichael, touching her shoulder. "You're hit?"

He pulled his fingers away, the tips bright pink.

"Paint," she said. "Sutagon, check on the kid. The rest of you, clear the room!"

The tactical officers separated, staying in pairs as they crossed the cluttered space. The sound of their shouts echoed off the walls, floated up to the high ceiling. Gorski kept her rifle ready, glancing at the medic who crouched next to the boy.

"He alright, Chris?"

"Yeah, Sarge," said Sutagon. "Unconscious. You want me to secure him?"

Gorski nodded, watching the team converge by the only other door—which led off from a walkway at the top of a short flight of steps. One of them flicked a switch, the overhead lights coming on with a crunch, blindingly bright after the dark. Everyone turned to her, waiting for a command.

She didn't give one, because something didn't feel right. They'd surveilled this building for five days straight, seeing nobody come in and nobody go out. The thermal imaging cameras had revealed signs of life, but not much—maybe one or two people, moving from room to room over the course of the day. They'd assumed it had been Maynard, oblivious to the people who watched him.

So who's the kid? she asked herself.

And where was Maynard?

She moved through the scenery, climbing the steps and filtering past her team. There was no point being quiet any more, because half the county must have heard them breach. She nodded to Carmichael, watching him open the door. Then she pushed through, her torch peeling open the dark.

Another man stood at the end of the corridor, dressed in identical clothes to the first. He, too, held a gun.

"Armed police!" Gorski cried out. "If—"

The man jerked the gun up. A rifle, like the first, but this one had no compartment for paintballs.

A split second to make the decision, and she did.

She pulled the trigger, the SIG barking, the gun recoiling as it fired. The man jolted, falling back, the barrel of his gun swinging earthwards. It spat fire, the sound of it deafening in the contained space. Bullets chewed their way through the walls as he tried to lift the weapon again.

Gorski lined up her second shot, pulled the trigger.

The man's head snapped back like he'd been hit by an invisible sledgehammer, and he crumpled to the floor. Carmichael ran past her, keeping his rifle trained on the body until he'd kicked the gun away. He ducked down, lifting the mask away. He didn't even have to put his fingers to the man's throat before shaking his head.

Dead.

No time to think about it, no time to acknowledge that the face of the man she just shot looked young. Looked almost like a *kid.*

"Keep moving," she said.

There were two doors here, one to Carmichael's right, the other at the end of the corridor. He put his hand to the first, waiting for Gorski and the team to catch up before pulling it open.

A cupboard: shelves, a mop, a breath of cool, damp air.

"Clear," he said, closing it.

He grabbed the handle of the second door, waiting for Gorski's nod before opening it for her.

She stepped over the body of the dead man and charged through, acid in her throat. It was another large room, the ceiling lower. It was pitch black in here, too, but the constellation of torches cut through the shadows, revealing walls lined with arcade machines. Half a dozen pool tables blocked the way like street barricades, the balls littering the carpeted floor. The place stank of stale beer and incense.

"Armed police!" yelled Gorski. "If anyone's here, make yourself known!"

They fanned out, funnelling through the gaps between the tables. Pool balls clacked as they were kicked out of the way. Gorski counted the doors, two at the far end of the room, one to their left.

"Armed police!" she shouted again. "We will not hesitate—"

The power came on, the room suddenly drenched in light. As one, every single arcade machine came to life, a madness of bleeps and chirps and jaunty music.

"Fuck's sake," said Gorski. "Be alert!"

The door on their left crashed open and somebody ran through it—overalls, a mask, a gun in their hand.

A split second... but this time she didn't have to make it. One of the team—Paxton, she thought—opened fire. Two rounds, both finding their target. The masked man doubled up with a grunt, toppling sideways.

"Ahead!" yelled Carmichael.

One of the doors in the far wall had opened, nobody in sight.

"Show yourself," shouted Gorski, moving slowly towards it. "Come out slowly, or I swear to God."

A flash of movement, and a cylinder flew out of the door. It hit the floor, bouncing twice before rolling to a stop.

Fuck, thought Gorski.

"Gren—" was all she had time to say before the cylinder detonated, a blaze of light that felt bright enough to punch a hole clean through her. Thunder ripped through the air, shaking her bones to dust.

But no heat. No shrapnel. No blood.

She was alive.

"Flashbang," she said, the word pulverised by the ringing in her ears. She tried to see the door, but the echo of the light was too bright.

Somebody fired a shot, but she couldn't tell who. It was answered by more gunfire, the air rupturing. Gorski grabbed the edge of a pool table, using her shoulder to flip it onto its side. She ducked behind it, hearing the thump of bullets against wood, hearing the shouts of alarm from her team as they scattered for cover. Something sliced across her cheek, ice cold, razor sharp. Carmichael skidded down beside her, his face warped by panic.

"One shooter, inside the room," he said, as another round of gunfire erupted. "On three."

Gorski was still blinking blotches of light, so bright that the room could have been on fire. She nodded, waiting for Carmichael to lift three fingers. They stood up together.

A man stood in the open door, clutching a small, black pistol. He wasn't wearing a mask, and his face was twisted into such an expression of terror and rage that it was easy to pretend he wasn't just a kid. He spotted Gorski, swinging his gun towards her.

"Wait," she said, and she wasn't sure whether she was talking to him, or to Carmichael.

A deafening crack from beside her, and a wound opened up in the young man's throat. A fan of blood blossomed on the doorframe as he spun around, the gun still in his hand.

A second shot from Carmichael knocked him flat.

"Sound off," said Gorski. "Anyone hurt?"

She skirted around the pool table, aware that the second door in the far wall was open now too—nothing but darkness on the other side. She jabbed a finger towards it, seeing one of the team peel away.

"Carmichael," came a reply, echoed through her earpiece. He was right there, by her side.

"Goss."

"Andilet."

Gorski approached the door, kicking it all the way open. The kid on the floor wasn't dead, but it wouldn't take long. He clutched at the wound in his neck, his eyes blindly roving the ceiling. He looked young, late teens, maybe, his dark hair plastered to his face, his tongue flexing inside the bloody pit of his mouth.

"Christ," said Gorski.

"Robinson," came another voice in her ear.

"Sutagon."

"Harris."

Gorski swung her rifle around the small room, lighting it up to see a couple of battered leather chairs, a desk, a whiteboard. Other than the man at her feet, it was empty. She kept listening, aware that she was one name down.

"Anyone got eyes on Milford?" she said.

She crouched by the kid, stowing her rifle in order to put a hand to the boy's throat. Even through her glove, she could feel the heat of his blood as it spilled through her fingers. The sight of it reminded her of rats fleeing a sinking ship. She pressed hard, shouting.

"Sutagon! Get in here!"

The boy turned his face to her, gulping. He put a hand on top of hers, almost tenderly.

"You're going to be okay," she said, grateful for her visor so he wouldn't see the lie on her face. "What's your name?"

He opened his mouth to answer, but death came for him before he could speak. His eyes rolled up, staring at something through the roof. He squeezed her hand, just once, then his arm flopped to the ground, splashing in a puddle of blood.

For a split second, and only that, the horror of it overwhelmed her.

Then she forced it down, forced herself to stand, forced her hands to grip the rifle. There was a lifetime ahead to think about this boy—and it would be a lifetime, she knew—but they still had work to do.

And they still had one man down.

"Milford?" she said into her radio. "Ben, you alright?"

No reply.

"Anyone got eyes on him?"

"No, Sarge," came a serenade of voices.

She walked through the door into the light of the bigger room, into the incessant noise of the arcades. Her unit had composed itself, two gathered around the second door, the rest positioned to continue the assault. It wasn't hard to see they were rattled. They were all seasoned officers, but firefights like this were few and far between—especially in Norfolk. They looked to her for an order, and she gave it by moving to the head of the pack, checking the magazine of her rifle.

"Anyone see where he went?" she asked.

But with no sign of Milford behind them, the answer was obvious.

Gorski took a steadying breath as she walked through the last open door. Another corridor, the walls bare blocks daubed with symbols that looked like they might have been painted in blood. The bulb in the ceiling was on, but it was flickering—a strobing light that made everything move like a cheap animation. A single door waited for her at the end and she moved towards it, hating the way her body had started to tremble, the way her gun rattled in her grip.

She'd managed three steps before the first scream ripped its way out of the door.

Shit.

Gorski increased her speed, adrenaline warping reality, making the corridor far longer than it was. Her team ran behind her, but she no longer felt the reassurance she normally did with Carmichael and the others at her back. Something was seriously wrong, she felt like she was losing control.

But what choice did she have? A second scream tore out of the room ahead, a concussive blast of sound that almost stopped her in her tracks. She slowed to a walk, reaching the door, shouldering through it, her gun raised.

In front of her was a scene that belonged in a nightmare. The room was the size of a school classroom, almost every inch of the walls daubed crimson with arcane symbols. The floor was covered in a carpet of sawdust that had been stained red, like a butcher's workshop.

There were two men in the middle of the space.

One was Ben Milford, on his knees, his helmet off and his earpiece ripped away. His rifle was nowhere to be seen. His nose was swollen, his face crimson. He groped at his own throat, his fingers slick with blood. His eyes were wide and white with terror, and it wasn't hard to see why.

The second man stood over him, wearing a heavy robe of black and gold cloth. His face was concealed by a mask the likes of which Gorski had never seen before, bone-yellow with dark, wicked eyes—something that belonged in a carnival of the damned. Curving up from it was a heavy crown of metal thorns that almost scraped the ceiling.

One of the man's hands held a wire noose around

Milford's neck, hard enough to cut into his skin. The other gripped a rusted blade that had to be two feet long, the tip resting against the back of Milford's neck.

"Drop the weapon!" said Gorski, almost a scream. "Drop it now, or I will shoot."

She advanced into the room, stepping to the side to make space for the team. They funnelled in behind her, spreading out—every single rifle pointing at the masked man's head.

"You alright, Ben?" she said, giving Milford a nod.

He tried to reply, but the man pulled the metal noose tighter, reducing Milford's words to a gargle. He scratched desperately at his own throat, tearing his skin.

"Drop the knife," Gorski said, her finger tight on the trigger. "And let go of him. You've got to the count of three."

She wasn't sure why she was hesitating, other than the fear of a death reflex that would drive the blade through Milford's neck—rare, but not unheard of.

"One."

The masked man cocked his head to the side, something unnatural in the movement that made the goosebumps boil on her arms. His eyes were pitch black, the eyes of an insect. He pushed the blade harder against Milford's neck, making him scream again.

"Two, motherfucker," said Gorski. "I am not joking."

She stepped closer, the team moving in, contracting around him like a fist.

"You will die," said Gorski. "I swear to God."

The sweat ran into her eye, threatening to blind her. Her finger tensed without her permission, and for a moment she actually thought she'd taken the shot.

"Thre—"

The man dropped his knife into the bloodied sawdust,

but he didn't let go of the noose around Milford's neck. Milford was making a noise that belonged to an animal, a choked whine of desperation.

"Back off," said Gorski, stepping right up to them. "Let go of him."

"Are you sure?" asked the man, a dry whisper that seemed to fill the room.

Milford tried to speak, but he couldn't get a word out.

"Now!" Gorski said, just five yards away—close enough that it would be impossible to miss him.

"As you wish," said the man.

He reached behind Milford's neck with his free hand and something clicked. Then he stepped back, letting go of his victim. Milford tumbled to the side, still fumbling with the noose around his neck. Over the hammer of her pulse, Gorski could hear a soft whine.

"Help him!" she screamed. She aimed the rifle at the masked man. "On your fucking knees, now!"

The man did as he was told, obviously struggling to kneel. Three of her officers crowded around him, all shouting at once. Gorski stowed her rifle, grabbing the man by his shoulders and shoving him to the ground. He hit the sawdust hard, the crown of thorns coming loose. She dropped onto his back harder than she needed to, her knee in his spine—his scream of pain giving her a pleasant jolt of satisfaction. She twisted his arm up, snapping a pair of cuffs on one wrist, only managing to breathe again when she'd secured the other.

Her relief was short-lived.

"Cutters, hurry!" yelled Carmichael.

He was on his knees by Milford, grappling with the noose around the man's neck. Milford was rolling back and forth, his hands to his throat. He opened his mouth and vomited a gout of blood, choking on it.

"Fuck!" said Gorski, crawling over the blood-drenched floor. "Ben? What's happening?"

"It won't come off," said Carmichael, stumbling over his words. "Fucking thing's getting tighter. Some kind of..."

Milford bucked so hard his whole body almost came off the floor. His eyes were bulging out of their sockets, one of them bright red. More blood-flecked foam sprayed from his mouth.

Gorski tried to get her fingers beneath the metal cord that had been wound around his neck, but it was too tight, already deep inside his flesh. The whining noise was coming from behind his neck, the dull whine of a motor.

"Turn him over!" Gorski said, her panic a living thing inside her. "Now!"

Together, they managed to roll Milford onto his belly. He writhed madly, his legs kicking up a ridge of sawdust, a boot cracking Robinson in the face. The noise he was making was unholy, a demonic growl. Carmichael sat on his lower back, planting his hands on his shoulders to keep him still.

Only then did Gorski see what was making the noise.

There was a contraption on the back of Milford's neck, a sturdy motor the size of a hardback book, connected to the metal noose. It was cranking slowly, each beat twisting the cable, drawing it tighter.

"What the hell?" she said, barely a whisper. "Get it off!"

Goss ran across the room, handing her the bolt cutters. Her hands were almost too numb to take them, too weak to keep them steady. Carmichael planted his hands over hers, working with her to clamp them around the noose.

It didn't work. It was too embedded in his flesh, there was too much blood.

"Come on!" she shrieked. "Cut it!"

The motor continued to twist and tighten, relentlessly. Milford's movements were growing weaker. Gorski tried again, the cutters slicing through skin and muscle, slipping on the metal cable. She couldn't get purchase.

"Sarge," said Carmichael.

She pushed the cutters deeper, but Milford's throat was a ruin. Blood gushed from a severed artery, soaking into the sawdust. Two of her officers had dropped down beside her, all of them working their fingers into the soup of Milford's neck.

Still she tried, moving the cutters, searching for the cord.

"Sarge, he's gone," said Carmichael.

Milford had fallen still, a single, gasping exhalation bubbling from his throat. Even though he was dead, the motor continued to tighten. It wasn't going to stop until it decapitated him.

Carmichael put his hand on Gorski's arm.

"Jules, he's gone."

Her head was fizzing, a screaming whistle filling her skull. She used the bolt cutters like a crutch to push herself to her feet, the world careening around her, a madman's dance. She couldn't bring herself to look Carmichael in the eye—she couldn't face looking any of them in the eye, because she could sense them all waiting for her to tell them what to do.

And the truth was, she didn't know.

Instead, she turned to the other man who lay at her feet. His mask was turned her way, those dark eyes emotionless.

But he was laughing. She could hear his joker's chuckle

behind the porcelain mask, she could see his body shuddering with the force of it.

She stepped up to him.

"Gorski, don't—" Carmichael started, but she ignored him, swinging the bolt cutters like a golf club. They hit his mask, shattering it, sending pieces of porcelain spinning across the room.

Beneath was a face she'd seen too many times in photographs on the briefing room wall, in case files full of madness and murder—gaunt, haggard, his hair and his beard pure white, his face twisted into an expression of deranged glee.

Joseph Maynard.

"What did you do to him?" said Gorski, pushing the tip of the bolt cutters into the man's face, hard enough to slice his cheek. "What the fuck did you do?"

Maynard stared back at her, wild-eyed with defiance.

"You told me to let go," he said, and he howled his laughter in her face.

A split second. It was her choice to make.

She dropped the cutters, swung her rifle up, thumbed off the safety.

"Sarge, no!"

She pulled the trigger just as somebody smacked her elbow. The gun jerked, the shot causing an eruption of bloody sawdust just inches from Maynard's head.

Carmichael grabbed her, pulling her away—one hand on her arm, the other wrestling with the barrel of her gun. She fought him for all of three seconds before her strength failed her.

"Alright," she said, shaking herself free. "I'm done, Joe, I'm done."

The shot had missed, but it had served its purpose. The

smile had been wiped from Maynard's face, his eyes lizard cold as he watched her. Gorski let go of her rifle, taking three deep breaths and staring at the ceiling. Only now did she notice the hooks that had been set there, five of them in the shape of a pentagram, brown with rust—or maybe blood.

"What?" she said, more to herself than anyone else.

"You wouldn't understand," said Maynard.

She looked back at him.

"You'll rot in hell for this," she said. "But before that happens, you'll rot here. Every second you have left. Nothing but misery and pain. You hearing me?"

Maynard's face split open into a grin of delight.

"Oh, so you *do* understand," he said.

Gorski closed her eyes for a moment—but only for a moment, because the vertigo almost took her. She put her hand to her radio, calling it in.

"We have Maynard," she said.

"Received and understood," came Superintendent Colin Clare's reply—sounding miles away, even though he was only on the road outside. "We heard gunfire. Ambulances are on standby."

Gorski dropped the call.

"Get this prick up."

Goss and Andilet hauled Maynard from the floor, the older man wincing as he was manhandled. They opened his robes to check for weapons, revealing a white linen suit and bare feet. He never took his eyes off Gorski, licking his lips as he studied her.

"It's over," she told him. "You're done."

And he smiled again, shaking his head.

"How wrong you are, my dear. It's only just begin—"

Gorski drove the butt of her rifle into Maynard's face, jolting his head back so hard it might have come clean off.

Goss and Andilet lost their grip and he slumped to the ground. She was almost tempted to give him another strike for good measure, but once again Carmichael was there, an infuriating hand on her arm.

"There will be other chances, Sarge," he said quietly. "When nobody's looking. He'll get what's coming to him."

She left him where he was, bracing herself. The last thing she wanted to do was look at Milford, but she did. She owed him that much. From here, she couldn't see his face. It was a small mercy.

I'm sorry, she told him. *I should have done better.*

"Go," she told the officers that remained. "Make sure this place is definitely empty."

One by one, they walked out of the room, offering quiet salutes to the man they left behind.

"You gonna be alright, Sarge?" asked Carmichael, the last to go.

She shook her head, because she didn't want to lie.

He gave her a nod, heading for the door. Gorski kneeled beside Milford's cooling body, resting her fingers on his shoulder. She called out again, just as Carmichael was leaving the room.

"Oh, and Joe."

He turned back, waiting.

"You'd better let Kett know we got him."

CHAPTER ONE

"Dad! Moira's naked again!"

DCI Robert Kett stood in the hall of their house, his forehead resting against the cool front door—the only thing keeping him up. Somewhere overhead, his children thundered like elephants as they got ready for school. He didn't know how they were *still* getting ready, because they'd been awake for three godforsaken hours. There had been all the time in the world to get dressed, brush their teeth, eat breakfast, and finish off their homework.

And it still hadn't happened.

"Dad!" Evie screamed again. "She's *naked*!"

Kett was too exhausted to look. He hadn't slept, although he couldn't blame the kids for that. Yesterday, Superintendent Clare had pulled him into his office and told him that—just eight days after they'd discovered the likely location of Joseph Maynard at the end of the last case—they were going to raid his hideout.

"I need to be there, sir," he'd said.

"No, you don't," Clare had told him. "You're the last person who needs to be there. And if you even think about turning up, Kett, I'll tie your scrotum in so many knots even Alexander the Great won't be able to undo it."

He hadn't got the reference, but he'd got the meaning.

So the night had been endless, and unbearable. He'd tossed and turned so much that Billie had kicked him out of the bed sometime after two, and he'd dozed fitfully on the sofa until Moira had thrown herself on him three hours later—his phone clenched in one hand, his dreams full of Maynard's grinning face, full of the Pig Man, full of the horrors of Hell House, where Hollenbeck had almost killed him two years ago.

"Dad!" Evie cried out, desperate now.

He turned with a groan, seeing his seven-year-old daughter at the top of the stairs. She was wearing her uniform, but her hair looked like something had been nesting in it—something the size of Big Bird from *Sesame Street*. For some reason, even though she'd definitely had both socks on ten minutes ago, one foot was bare.

"She's naked!" Evie said for a third time.

"I'm not naked!" Moira roared, running up beside her sister.

She was, as reported, completely naked.

"Moira, what are you doing?" said Kett, checking his watch. "We were supposed to leave for school fifteen minutes ago. Why did you take your clothes off?"

"I didn't!" she screamed, stamping her foot. "I'm wearing clothes!"

Kett lifted both hands in the air in a confused shrug, wishing Billie hadn't left for work an hour ago.

"What?" he managed.

"It's fancy-dress day," said Moira. "We're going as people from old stories, remember?"

"Yeah, I remember. You're going as Puss in Boots, we

got the costume. You were *wearing* the costume. What happened to it?"

"I changed my mind," said Moira, scratching her bare bum. "I'm going as the Emperor."

He had no idea what she was talking about, but Evie must have got the joke because she dropped to the floor, howling with laughter.

"What?" Kett said again, just a croak.

"The Emperor's New Clothes," said the five-year-old, turning on the landing like a model on the catwalk. "You know?"

Please give me strength, said Kett, rubbing his face before looking back up.

"You can't go as the Emperor," he said.

"Why?" said Moira, stamping again.

"Because if I drop you off at school like that, I'll get arrested," he said. "Also, it's October, you'll freeze."

"I won't!" she yelled, stamping both feet this time in a goblinesque kind of jump. "I've got clothes, they're just invisible. Look!"

She proceeded to jiggle herself back and forth along the landing.

"Right," said Kett, losing his temper. "I'm going to give you ten seconds to get your cat outfit back on."

"Or what?" said Evie, who wasn't helping the situation.

"Or... or *I'm* going to take *my* clothes off and be the Emperor, and I'm going to drive you to school like that."

The two girls looked at him in wide-eyed horror, then they bolted, laughing their heads off.

"Please don't do that," said Alice from the living room, her face lit up by her phone as she scrolled endlessly through TikTok—it was all she seemed to do these days. "You'd scar the whole school for life."

He ignored her, taking out his own phone to see if there had been any contact from Clare or the firearms unit. He hadn't been told the exact time of the raid—another of Clare's tactics to keep him away, he was sure of it—but he knew it would have happened by now. If they hadn't called to give him an update, it probably meant it had played out without a hitch.

Either that, or it was *FUBAR*.

"Hurry up, girls!" he yelled, opening the front door. A fist of cold wind and rain entered the house like a home invasion. "I'm leaving!"

"Wait!" yelled Evie, galloping down the stairs. She'd put her sock back on, and she sat to pull on her shoes.

"Where's your bloody sister?"

Moira appeared at the top of the stairs, *still* naked, although now wrapped in what looked like a blanket. She stared at him defiantly, and he flapped his arms again, too tired to ask her for an explanation.

"I'm a Roman," she said. "This is a taco."

"Toga," said Evie.

"No! Taco!"

"Have you got pants on under your taco?" Kett asked.

She lifted the blanket to show that she did, and a vest too.

"Then I don't care. Just get in the car."

Grinning smugly, Moira walked down the stairs, almost tripping on her outfit. Kett closed the door for a second, walking up to his youngest and fixing the blanket properly, tying it in a knot over her shoulder. He fished a pair of leggings from the wicker laundry basket in the utility room and held them out.

"These are purple," he said. "Roman emperors all wore purple leggings."

She didn't look like she believed him, but the cold air still lingered and she shivered her way into them. Evie passed her some shoes.

"You ready?" he asked them, checking his watch again. "Because school started, like, five minutes ago."

"Ready!" said Moira.

"Ready," said Alice, walking out of the living room with her bag over her shoulder.

"Ready!" said Evie, who was squirming for some reason.

"Then let's go!"

Kett opened the door again, only to hear Evie call out.

"Actually, Dada, I think I need a poo."

THANKS TO TRAFFIC, it was after nine by the time they reached the school. Kett apologised to the secretary for being late, then to the teacher for Moira's costume, and then again to the line of cars that had queued up behind his Volvo because he'd blocked the road.

By the time he'd crunched his gears and pulled away from the school, he felt like there was a wind-up monkey with cymbals crashing its way around his skull—loud enough that he didn't hear his phone until it had almost rung off.

He swore, breaking the cardinal rule of driving by answering it while on the move.

"Kett," he said, pinching the phone between his ear and his shoulder as he tried to find a place to pull over.

"Sir, it's Carmichael," came a voice, battered by static. "Tactical."

Kett felt, for a moment, like his heart was made of glass and somebody had struck it with a hammer. He bumped the

Volvo onto the kerb, earning a blare from the car behind as it thundered past.

"Joe," he said. "You get him?"

He knew, as soon as he'd spoken, that it was the wrong question. He could hear it in the breath Carmichael took before answering, and the anger that simmered in his words.

"Yeah, we did. Maynard's out cold. He was waiting for us, sir. He knew we were coming."

"Everyone alright?" said Kett.

The right question, but too late.

"No," said Carmichael. "Intel was wrong. It wasn't just Maynard. He had four other men on site, all armed."

"Shit," said Kett. "You all made it out, though?"

"Milford's dead, sir."

Kett closed his eyes, the rush of blood loud enough to drown out the horns of passing traffic. He felt a stab of shame when he realised he couldn't picture Milford's face—he knew several members of tactical, but not all of them.

"He was shot?" he asked.

"No," was the reply, and nothing else. "I've got to go. Gorski wanted you to know. The Superintendent's on site. He told me to pass on a message, too."

"Don't bother," said Kett. "I know what it is."

"Good," said Carmichael. "Because I'd have to hit the confession booth if I repeated it word for word."

Nobody laughed.

"Look, I'm sorry about Milford," said Kett.

But the line was dead.

He threw his phone onto the passenger seat, rubbing his face as if it might slough off the exhaustion, the misery, the horror of knowing that Maynard had taken another life.

Then he put the car in gear, checked his mirror, and pulled onto the road.

CHAPTER TWO

DC Kate Savage felt like she hadn't taken a breath since she'd watched the tactical unit breach Cold Iron Paintball—nearly fifteen minutes ago.

Fifteen minutes of gunfire, of shouting, of screams.

Fifteen minutes of forgetting how to breathe.

She stood well back from the gates, a line of tactical vans, IRVs and ambulances blocking the road between her and the building. Superintendent Clare loomed beside her, dressed in his camel-coloured Big Tossing Jacket, his body locked tight with worry. She couldn't remember him ever being this quiet for this long before. On her other side was DI Porter, fidgeting relentlessly as they waited for news. His expensive shoes scuffed the pavement, his hands rooted in his hair, his watch glinting in the meagre daylight.

Nobody spoke. Nobody wanted to jinx it.

Cold Iron Paintball was a large, single-storey warehouse capped with a metal roof, the name emblazoned in blue flames on its black wall along with the bloody maw of a tiger. It sat on the far edge of an industrial estate in Thetford, planted in the middle of a weed-strewn yard and surrounded by barbed wire fences. The windows had been boarded over, and the front door had been bolted from the inside—hence Gorski and her unit breaching from the rear of the building fifteen minutes ago.

Savage checked her watch.

Sixteen minutes.

There had been no more gunshots, but she could still hear shouting from inside. The panic was enough to overwhelm her, gripping her lungs like a fist, making the bright morning feel like midnight.

Come on, she thought. *Come—*

The door at the front of the building opened, the sound of it like another gunshot. Savage jumped, the adrenaline like shards of glass moving through the soft tissue of her veins.

"Contact!" yelled one of the PCs who crowded by the chain-link fence. The call was repeated, carrying like a Mexican wave.

Everybody tensed, then collectively relaxed when an officer in tactical uniform appeared. Savage hauled in a breath that detonated explosions of light against the sky, her entire body electric.

"We've got a man down!" the firearms officer yelled, lifting his visor to reveal a face creased with fear. "Hurry!"

The waiting police surged forward as one, PCs storming the gate and crowding the yard. Four paramedics moved with them, like green fish startled by a shoal of sharks. The firearms officer held the door open, ushering them inside.

"Let's go," said Clare, striding across the road.

Savage glanced at Porter, meeting his eye. Then they followed the Super through the open gate, jogging to keep up with him. The building loomed above them, the painted tiger watching with hungry eyes and baring sharp teeth.

The firearms officer was still by the door, and he nodded to the Super as he reached him. It was Joe Carmichael, Savage saw, Gorski's wingman. He looked a hundred years old.

"Who's down?" said Clare.

"Milford, sir," said Carmichael.

"Dead?"

Carmichael nodded, his eyes dark. He stank of gunpowder and sweat, the sharp tang of violence that followed the unit everywhere. He glanced at Savage for a second, then at Porter, before turning back to Clare.

"It was an ambush, sir. Four guys, all armed with rifles. We took them out, but Maynard was waiting for us. He got Ben, he..."

Carmichael shook his head, unable to find the words.

"You have to see it for yourself, sir."

"Where is he?" said Clare.

"You'll find him. Paramedics are in there. There's a chance..."

He didn't finish, the words dying on his lips. There was no chance, Savage knew. She could see that written into every line of his face.

"And Maynard?" asked Clare.

"Same room."

"Alive?"

Carmichael gave the Super a look that said it all. Clare moved through the door, swallowed by the darkness of the building. Porter went next, and Savage was about to follow when Carmichael took her arm.

"Just a head's up, Kett's on his way."

She nodded a thank you, walking into the cool lobby. It was a decent space, a small desk in the far corner and a couple of leather sofas forming a waiting area. The walls were laden with posters, most of them mock-military recruitment images with paintball guns instead of real ones. She could hear a chaos of sound coming from nearby, artificial tunes and irritating bleeps that had no place here.

There was only one other door leading from the room, and a dead man lay there.

A paramedic crouched over him, searching for a heartbeat that Savage knew she wouldn't find. The man lay in a puddle of blood, his overalls shredded by gunfire. A paintball mask lay beside him, the visor shattered. His face was turned to the ceiling, those open eyes searching for answers amongst the cobwebs.

Not a man, she thought as she walked closer. *A boy*.

He was a teenager, his hair cropped at the sides and curly on the top, a coating of bum fluff on his cheeks. His small hands were curled into claws, his fingers filthy, his nails chewed to the quick. Beside him was a black pistol, not too dissimilar from the ones the tactical unit carried.

"The hell?" said Porter, leaning over her shoulder. "He's a kid."

The paramedic had given up, her face gaunt. She looked at Savage.

"Two shots, one went right through his heart." She wiped her cheek on her shoulder. "Would have been dead before he hit the ground, if that's any consolation."

It wasn't.

Savage walked past the body, careful not to step over it—that superstition, never crossing the dead, had been passed down to her from her granddad. Ahead was a much bigger room filled mainly with pool tables—two of which were upended and riddled with bullet holes. Arcade machines crowded the walls, and it was from these that the jaunty music was playing. Two constables were trying to turn them off, but they weren't having much luck.

The air reeked of gunpowder and blood and something worse that festered under it all.

"Christ," said Porter, watching his feet as he stepped into the room. "Looks like a warzone."

He nodded to the left of the room, where two doors stood open. Another paramedic worked inside the shadows of the first room, watched over by a uniformed PC.

"Body," said Porter.

Savage moved towards the second door, kicking her way through a carpet of shell casings. Beyond was a short corridor, three tactical officers leaning against the wall like they were queuing up for a wake. They watched her as she passed, their mouths grim lines.

She'd almost reached the door at the end when Superintendent Clare walked out of it, and the expression on his face stopped her dead. He looked afraid, his skin waxy and pale, his eyes liquid. He lifted the hairy sleeve of his jacket to his mouth, as if he might be about to throw up. Only then did he notice her standing there.

"Don't, Kate," he said, shaking his head. "You don't want to see."

"Sir?" she replied, her pulse drumming in the back of her throat. She felt Porter step up behind her.

"Just don't," said Clare. "I'll deal with this."

She looked past the Super to the door—catching a glimpse of a red room, symbols painted on the walls, metal hooks in the ceiling. She could hear Julia Gorski in there, shouting at somebody.

"Toss off!" Clare barked. "Both of you."

His command made her jump, and she backed away, colliding with Porter. Together, they retreated into the arcade room, where she perched on the edge of a pool table.

Her legs felt like they'd been filleted, like there were no bones to hold her up.

"Crikey," said Porter. "What was that about?"

She didn't have time to answer before the clatter of a stretcher rose from the corridor they'd just left. Two paramedics appeared, pushing a body. Dead, of course, because you didn't pull the blankets over the face of somebody living. They were rattled, that much was clear. One of them stared at Savage as she walked past like she was trying to telegraph a secret message.

Gorski followed the stretcher as far as the middle of the room, then stopped, her jaw set tight as she watched it go. Carmichael met the paramedics at the far door.

"I'll ride with him, Sarge," he said. "Least I can do."

Gorski nodded, wide-eyed and stone-faced as she walked back the way she'd come. She didn't even seem to notice Porter and Savage.

"Never seen her look like that before," said Porter. "Must be bad."

Understatement of the century, thought Savage, but she didn't have time to say it. There was a cry from deeper in the building, one that echoed off the walls.

"We've got a live one!"

"You go," said Porter.

Savage pushed herself off the pool table, crossing the room and entering another corridor. This one led past a small cupboard into what looked like an indoor village: painted buildings, old cars, roads blocked by barricades. A handful of portable lights had been rigged up by the police, but the ceiling was so high that she felt like she'd stepped into the night—the disorientation making her even less steady on her feet.

A cluster of uniformed officers stood in the middle of

the room, on a section of floor that had been painted to look like a road. One was a tactical officer—Savage recognised Christine Sutagon, the medic—who stood back, her rifle stowed against her chest. She'd taken her helmet off, her face taut with concern. Beside her were two constables.

One of them was Duke, and he must have sensed her coming because he turned around and looked at her. She'd been with him long enough to read his expression like an open book.

He was scared.

Two paramedics crouched on the ground, one either side of a man who sat there.

No, she thought when she saw his face. *Another boy.*

The kid was wearing paint-spattered overalls, and Savage thought that his face had been painted too until she got close enough to realise it was blood. His nose was a swollen mess, a gash stretching from the bridge all the way down to the left nostril. He'd been cuffed, but he was doing his best to stand up. Duke's hand on his shoulder was the only thing keeping him down.

"Let me go!" he said, flashing bloody teeth. He had the look of a wild animal, his bright eyes blazing in the LEDs. "Just let me go!"

"Not a chance, mate," said Duke. "Sit down, or we'll cuff your feet, too."

He gave the boy a shove that knocked him over onto his back.

"Hey," Savage told him, no malice in her voice. "Easy, Aaron."

"Easy?" said Sutagon. "You not seen what these pricks did to Ben?"

The boy had managed to sit up again and Savage knelt beside him, lifting her hands to show she meant no harm.

He really was young, still a teenager. He was scrawny, his face decorated with spots and uneven stubble. He looked at her, still struggling to get to his feet.

"Easy," she said. "If you get up, they're only going to knock you back down again."

"Let me go," he said, baring those crimson teeth. One of the front ones had been snapped clean in two. "I didn't do nothing, I wasn't here, just let me go."

"You weren't here?" said Savage.

"He was here," said Sutagon, nodding down the artificial road. "He had a paintball gun rather than a real rifle. Only reason we didn't take him out."

Savage spotted the gun. In the lights, it was easy to tell it was fake. But in the dark, in the chaos and confusion of a raid, it easily could have been real.

"I wasn't here," the kid said again. He was writhing, his legs kicking at the ground, the cuffs rattling as he tried to shake them off. His eyes were so enormous that she wondered if he was on something.

"What's your name?" she asked.

"Ian," he replied without hesitation.

"You got another name that goes with that one?"

This time, he didn't reply.

"How old are you, Ian?"

He didn't seem to be able to answer this, either. He stared past her at the artificial scenery.

"He's got nothing on him," said Sutagon. "Checked him for weapons, couldn't find any ID. No phone."

"You local?" Savage asked. "You live around here?"

Ian nodded.

"Thetford?"

Another nod. She didn't think he'd blinked once. He

was muttering something, and when she leaned in she heard the same three words over and over.

"I wasn't here, I wasn't here, I wasn't here."

"Hey," she said, clicking her fingers, bringing him back. "Ian, I need you to listen to me. Far as I can tell, you haven't done anything wrong, okay?"

She ignored the noise that Sutagon made.

"You didn't have a real gun, right?"

"He had a gun, he took the shot," said Sutagon. "Hit Gorski."

"With a bullet or a paintball?"

Sutagon didn't answer.

"So you didn't hurt anyone," she said to the lad.

Ian stopped whispering and looked at her, shaking his head.

"You must have been terrified, all these people running through the door. Can you tell me what you were doing here?"

The kid shook his head again, like he didn't know the answer.

"Playing paintball? You and a few others?"

"They don't play," he said, his movements calming. "They never play."

"The other men here? You know them?"

He nodded, trying to sniff with his broken nose, gagging on the blood that dripped down his throat.

"You know the older man who's here?" Savage pressed.

The nod continued.

"You know his name?"

"He doesn't have a name," said Ian. "Not one, anyway. He says he has lots of names."

"Yeah?"

Savage rocked back to relieve the pain in her knees. Ian sniffed hard, his face screwing up.

"My head hurts," he said. "I want to go home."

"You tell us where you live, we'll take you home," said Savage. "It's near here?"

He pointed to the door that led outside, but didn't say much more than that.

"The man who was here with you," Savage continued. "What else do you know about him?"

The shutters seemed to drop over the boy's face, and he stared at the ground.

"Because he's just a man, Ian," Savage said. "Whatever he's told you. He's an old man, and he can't hurt you any more. You hear me?"

If he did hear, he didn't show it. He was muttering those same three words again.

"I wasn't here."

"He can't hurt you, because we've arrested him," she went on. "He's going to prison, Ian, for years. For the rest of his life, probably."

She heard footsteps behind her, and turned to see a couple of constables creep into the room. She could hear chatter from their radios, muted by the enormous space. Ian was still speaking to himself, rocking gently back and forth, his cuffs clinking on the concrete floor. Whatever he was seeing with those moon-bright eyes, it wasn't in this room.

"Can you get him to hospital?" she asked the paramedics.

One nodded, heading for the door.

"I'll get a stretcher," he said. "Don't trust him to make it all the way on his feet."

Savage watched him go, then turned back to Ian.

"You don't have to be afraid," she said. "Maynard's just a man, he can't hurt you."

The boy stopped muttering. He ran his tongue over his lips like he was tasting his own blood.

"I know," he said. "I know what he is. And he *can* hurt me. He can hurt anyone. He can hurt *everyone*. That's what he said he wanted to do."

"Hurt everyone?" asked Savage.

"Yeah, he said he was planning the end of the world."

Savage met Duke's eyes, just for an instant.

"But it's not him who's going to end it," Ian went on. "It's not him who's going to hurt us."

"No?" said Savage. "Then who?"

Ian's eyes swivelled in their sockets, taking a moment to find her.

"The other man," he croaked. "The master."

CHAPTER THREE

As usual, the traffic gods weren't kind to him.

It was over an hour after he'd received Carmichael's call that Kett pulled his car up to the swarm of police vehicles and ambulances that surrounded Cold Iron Paintball. There were so many of them that he had to park right at the end of the road, jogging the rest of the way as much as his permanently aching back would let him. By the time he reached the building, he was out of breath and panting hard.

"You alright, sir?" asked one of the constables guarding the door. "You run all the way from Norwich?"

Kett glared at her, resting his hands on his knees.

"Superintendent about?" he said.

"Inside," she said. "He told us you'd probably show up, said you weren't allowed anywhere near the place."

"But then he said you wouldn't listen to us," said the second constable. "So just to let you in anyway."

"That wasn't exactly how he phrased it," said the first PC. "He mentioned something about twisting your, uh..."

"Your dangly bits, is what he said."

"Right, twisting them into a balloon animal of some kind."

"Monkey," said the second PC. "He definitely said monkey. More precisely, a capuchin monkey."

"Noted," said Kett.

They stood to the side, waving him through into a small reception area. A couple of forensic technicians stood behind the desk, chatting quietly to each other, and another PC pointed through the open door. Kett walked into a bigger room filled with arcade machines, spotting Porter and Duke leaning against a pool table. They both looked around when they heard him.

"He won't be happy, sir," said Porter. "He said if we saw you, we needed to tell you he's going to weave your nutsack into a rug, and put it outside his office door so everyone in the force will have to step on it in order to talk to him."

"That man has an unhealthy obsession with my genitals," said Kett as he walked over.

But he wasn't laughing. The atmosphere in the room was oppressive, the air rank with smoke and blood. There were no bodies, but it didn't take a genius to identify the stains they'd left behind. People had died here.

"Gorski about?" he asked.

Duke nodded through one of the doors at the end of the room.

"Through there, sir, with the Super."

"Savage?"

Duke shook his head.

"She went to the hospital with one of the kids they found here, to keep an eye on him."

"Kids?" said Kett.

"Young lad," Porter added. "Sixteen, maybe. He's not all

there, shot Gorski with a paintball gun when she breached the compound."

"She shoot back?"

"No, but she put a pretty big dent in his face with the butt of her rifle."

Kett swore beneath his breath, looking at the door, seeing a glimpse of a corridor beyond—the light strobing.

"Maynard through there?"

Both Porter and Duke nodded, but it was the DI who spoke.

"Out cold, still. Given what happened, he's lucky to be alive."

"Maybe," said Kett, the furnace in his stomach igniting. "Maybe not. He hasn't met me yet."

He walked through the door and along the corridor, hearing voices in the room ahead. He recognised Superintendent Clare and Julia Gorski, and sure enough, when he peeked inside, he saw them both in the far corner. For some reason, the Superintendent was wearing his atrocious furry jacket.

Maynard lay on the ground, draped in heavy robes, his hands cuffed. His face was obscured by a paramedic kneeling next to him on the bloody sawdust floor.

Gorski spotted him, her face drawn, her eyes red as if she'd been crying. Clare didn't even have to turn around to know who stood there. He looked up at the ceiling—which was studded with metal hooks, Kett saw—and groaned like a yak.

"What a tossing surprise," he said. "I made it abundantly clear that if you showed up here, Kett, I would macrame your fleshy treasure chest and hang it on my bedroom wall as a dreamcatcher. And yet, here you are."

Clare turned around, and Kett was startled by how tired

he looked. His skin was yellow, and his eyes seemed to have receded inside his skull, dark hollows that made him look half-dead. He was stooped, as if he carried the weight of the world on his shoulders, and when he lifted a hand to his mouth, it was trembling.

"Sir," said Kett, not moving from the door. Now that he was here, he didn't want to take another step into that infernal room. The walls had been inscribed with arcane shapes: pentagrams, and other things he didn't recognise. Maynard's trademarks. "Julia. I'm so sorry."

Gorski stared at the floor, at a blossom of red as bright as a rose petal. It was where Milford had died, he realised. He could almost see the shape of him in the sawdust. The butcher's shop smell of the room filled Kett's throat, the reality of it making a shudder rip through him, top to tail.

He turned to the paramedic, and the man she concealed.

"Maynard?" he asked.

Nobody replied, but the answer was clear enough in their silence.

"He's going to be okay," said the paramedic, her knees cracking as she stood up. "He's stable, but we really need to get him to the hospital. I'll get a stretcher."

She moved away, and Kett saw the face of the man who lay there. He'd seen it before, of course, in the few photographs they'd managed to capture of Maynard. He'd always looked like a villain from a cartoon, or maybe a Bond film. Sharply dressed, his expression arrogant, boasting the inexplicable charisma that bad men—*truly* bad men—often seemed to carry.

He deserved his reputation. As part of Hollenbeck, Maynard had been responsible for countless deaths—not to mention the assaults, the kidnappings, the torture, the rape.

For decades, he'd left a river of blood behind him, even after they'd taken down the other members of his murderous cult.

Now, though, lying prone on the floor, his face slick with blood, his mouth hanging open, his eyes closed...

Now, he just looked like an old man.

Kett felt the furnace inside him roar, that old and familiar fury, the injustice that Maynard was alive when so many others had died at his hands. How easy it would be, he thought, to take Gorski's sidearm and blow a hole in his head, or stamp on the man's face until he would never wake up. The force of it made him double over, a wave of sickness drowning out the rage.

"Can I leave him here?" said the paramedic, studying Kett's face, seeing the emotion. "With you?"

"He's safe," said Clare. "Nothing's going to happen. Right, Kett?"

"Right," he replied, his voice hoarse. "We won't touch him."

She hesitated a moment more, uncertain, then walked out of the room—jogging down the corridor.

Kett met Gorski's eyes, and he saw it there, the same hatred, the same nausea. He wondered how she'd managed to restrain herself, after watching one of her team die.

He wondered if he would have been able to do the same thing.

"Tell me what happened," he said.

"What happened is a monstrous balls-up," Clare answered, rubbing his dry lips. "I take full responsibility. We were watching this place for days. Nobody came, nobody went. I assumed Maynard was alone. I made the call. This..."

His eyes darted to the man on the ground.

"This is my fault."

"No, sir," said Kett, pointing to Maynard. "It's *his*."

The words rang hollow, but Clare nodded anyway.

"We came under fire as soon as we entered," said Gorski, tapping the bright pink paint splodge on her shoulder. "Four assailants, all in paintball gear with masks. First took a shot at me with a fake rifle. The rest were armed to the teeth. MP5s, older models, but in good working order. They had flashbangs, too, and a couple of actual grenades that thankfully they didn't use. We found a stash of weapons and ammo in a room down the hall. It's big enough for a coup."

She stopped for breath, checking her rifle instinctively.

"Dropped the other three assailants. They're all boys, in their teens, maybe early twenties. Too young for this shit."

Her eyes had turned liquid, her jaw set.

"They were waiting for us. I don't know how, but they were ready. We lost sight of Milford in the firefight, he must have come down here. Heard him screaming, and by the time we got to the room, Maynard had him. He had this..."

She stopped, her mouth flexing as she tried to find the words.

"A contraption," said Clare, taking over. "A mechanical garrotte. The noose was strapped around his neck. It was connected to a motor, and a ratchet. The wire contracted, strangling him."

"It didn't strangle him," said Gorski. "It near enough cut his fucking head off."

"What?" said Kett, shaking his head. "*Why?*"

"Why what?" Gorski spat.

"Why use something like that? Why not shoot him as soon as he came in?"

The answer was so obvious that Kett spoke it himself.

"Because he's Maynard. But it doesn't make sense. You said they were waiting for you?"

Gorski nodded, wiping a bloodied hand over her nose.

"They were armed, and positioned where they could do the most damage. They knew we were coming."

"I kept this as tight as I could," said Clare. "But somebody like Maynard will have eyes and ears everywhere. It's not out of the realm of possibility that he got a tip-off."

"Not from any of my men," said Gorski, giving Kett a look like this might have been his fault.

"So why was he here?" said Kett. "If he knew we were coming, why wait? Why not run? He had those kids to keep us busy, he could be halfway across the country by now, or out of it completely."

As if answering, Maynard groaned. He arched his back, his mouth opening to reveal the bloody mess of his gums. He'd lost his top two front teeth, Kett noticed. He tried to move his arms, but they were cuffed behind his back. He inhaled, then a hacking cough erupted out of him, spraying a mist of blood into the air. He rolled onto his side, still coughing. His eyes finally opened, swimming in and out of focus as he came around.

"Welcome back, you piece of shit," said Gorski, swinging her rifle into position. "Stay down. Don't give me an excuse."

"Gorski," said Clare, the warning in his voice clear enough.

Maynard found his way back, looking at Gorski, and Clare.

Then seeing Kett.

His mouth split open again, but this time there was no mistaking it as anything other than a grin. He stayed on his side, drowning in his robes, breathing soft, hoarse laughter.

"Finally," he said, his words distorted by his missing teeth. "The legend that is Robert Kett. Last time I saw you, you were playing a little game of cat and mouse in Hell House. Remember?"

"Shut up," said Gorski.

"We almost had you then," Maynard went on, ignoring her. "You were so close to breaking, so close to becoming one of us."

"Shut your mouth," Gorski went on.

"But you played the game, Robbie. You played it well."

He broke into another round of coughs, his face covered in sawdust and blood. Kett could hear a stretcher rattling up the corridor as the paramedic returned.

"You handled it well," Maynard said again. "And now you're going to get another chance."

"What?" said Kett. "What are you talking about?"

Maynard grinned that toothless smile, meeting Kett's eye. He looked deranged.

"You're about to have another shot," he said. "So be a good—"

Gorski lost it, stepping forward before anyone could stop her and launching a kick at Maynard. Her boot connected with his cheek hard enough to snap his head around, his body rolling from one side to the other.

"Enough!" bellowed Clare, grabbing the sergeant by her uniform and hauling her back. "That is not how we do things!"

"Hey!" said the paramedic as she walked through the door. She glanced at Maynard—who was unconscious again. "What's going on?"

"Nothing," Kett told her, and they all turned to Clare. He chewed on it for a few seconds.

"Nothing," he echoed. "They're just leaving. And get that tosser out of here before *nothing* happens again."

The paramedic studied them all for a second more before tugging one end of her stretcher through the door, struggling with it on the thick carpet of sawdust. Another paramedic pushed the rear end, ashen-faced as he sensed the atmosphere.

"Move," said Clare.

He steered Gorski across the room, grabbing hold of Kett's sleeve and manoeuvring him as well, like a parent with a couple of squabbling siblings. He pushed them both into the corridor, giving Kett another shove to keep him moving.

"Out," he said. "I knew this would happen as soon as you showed up."

"I didn't do it, sir," said Kett. "*She* did."

"It doesn't bloody matter," said Clare as they stepped into the bigger room. "I can't have anyone taking this into their own hands. We're police, Julia, not vigilantes."

Porter and Duke had both pushed themselves up, alert.

You okay? Porter mouthed to Kett, and he nodded.

Gorski walked to a pool table and braced one hand on it, breathing deeply. She put the other to her belly, as if she'd been injured. She was crying again, wretched sobs that made her body contract. Clare put his hands to his hair, shaking his head.

"I want you out, Kett. You can't be here. This whole thing was a powder keg before it even started. Now it's nuclear."

"I need to be here, sir," said Kett. "This doesn't feel right. You know Hollenbeck as well as I do. It's all about the spectacle, all about the game. Maynard's planning something."

"Maynard's a dead tossing duck," said Clare, slapping his hands to his side. "He's an old man who messed up and got caught. He's going away like everyone else from Hollenbeck, end of story."

"No," said Gorski, sniffing. "Kett's right, sir. There's something going on."

She turned around, using her sleeve to scrub her face.

"Right before I knocked Maynard out, he said something."

"The first time you knocked him out, or the second?" said Clare.

"He said it was only just beginning," Gorski went on. "I don't know what he was talking about, but that's what he said."

"Kid in the back room was going on about that too, sir," said Duke, walking up, one hand on his Taser. "The paintball guy. Said Maynard was planning something."

"Did he say what?" asked Clare.

"End of the world," Duke replied.

"Well then, none of us have anything to worry about," said Clare. "If the world's ending, we may as well go home, drink a beer, and make love ferociously to my wife."

"*We*, sir?" said Kett.

"Or you can pull your thumbs out of your tossholes, all of you," Clare went on. "Maynard's done. He's going to prison. And as much as I detest the idea, as much as it goes against every grain of moral fibre in my body, I know that at some point he's going to walk into his cell and find a noose around his neck. Or somebody's going to shank him in the shower. Right, Gorski?"

She didn't reply, staring defiantly at the floor. One hand still rested on her stomach.

Ket heard the stretcher again, and a few seconds later it

rolled out of the door. Maynard lay on it, wrapped tight in a blanket, still unconscious. His jaw was already starting to swell. Both paramedics eyeballed Kett as they headed for the exit.

"I didn't bloody do it!" he muttered.

They all watched Maynard go, the stretcher passing through a puddle of blood on its way out of the door.

"It's over," said Clare, but even he sounded doubtful.

"It's not," Kett replied. "Because that's what's weird, right? Maynard chose not to run, he chose not to escape. He chose to be here when we arrived. That means he wanted to be caught."

"Why, though?" said Porter. "Even a monster like him knows what we'd do if we caught him, especially after Milford. Prison's the least of his worries."

"Because it's a game," said Kett, trying not to let the fear and the sorrow back in—the memories of everything Hollenbeck had done to him, to Billie, to the kids. "And now we're all playing."

CHAPTER FOUR

It was the last thing he wanted to do, but the first thing he did after Maynard had been rolled out of sight.

"Robbie?" said Billie as soon as she answered his call. She sounded like she was out of breath. "You okay? The girls go in without a fuss?"

"Yeah," he said, leaning against an arcade machine in the corner of the room. Technicians and coppers bustled past, examining the bloodbath. "Well, Moo-moo was naked, but that's not what I'm calling about."

"Our five-year-old being naked at school is *not* what you're calling about?"

He took a breath, and in that moment his wife seemed to understand everything—how could she not? Hollenbeck was as much her story as his.

More, maybe.

"What?" she asked, the word like a cold breath on his cheek.

"They got him," said Kett. "Maynard. The raid was this morning. I didn't want to mention it because I didn't want you to worry."

"*What*?" she said again, and he heard her walking. There was the crunch of a door opening. "You got him?"

"Yeah. He's on his way to the hospital now, under police protection. He was caught red-handed, Billie, he's going to prison."

"That's good," she said. Her voice sounded fainter, as if she'd stepped outside. "That's great."

Kett didn't reply, chewing on what he needed to say.

"Robbie?"

"I don't want you to worry," he started. "But something's wrong. It was too easy."

"He didn't fight back?"

"No, he did. He fought back hard. Gorski lost one of her men. But Maynard didn't run, and he had plenty of time to. He's... I think he's planning something."

Billie didn't say anything, but he heard a reply in her silence.

"He mentioned me by name as soon as he saw me," Kett explained. "Mentioned Hell House, told me I'd have another shot at whatever sick game he was playing."

"But he can't hurt you if he's in custody, right?"

"He can hurt me anywhere, I think, if he wants to. He's not alone. He had four young lads, teenagers, armed to the teeth. They were willing to die for him. Three of them *did* die. That's how they work, Hollenbeck. They recruit people to do their dirty work. They brainwash them. They train them up into killers. Into..."

He didn't want to say it, because he didn't want to throw her back into the horror of her kidnapping, of the Pig Man. But she knew.

"Monsters," she said.

"Right. We don't know who else is working with him, and what they're planning."

"What are you telling me, Robbie?" she asked.

Kett waited for a couple of PCs to pass, including Felicity Niven, who gave him a wave.

"I'm saying it might be good for you to get out of the city for a bit," he said. "You and the girls."

"Robbie, no."

"It's happened too many times. First you, and then them, and then me. They want something from me, and I don't know what. There's nothing to say they won't come after us."

"Then you come too," she said. "We can all go."

He shook his head, even though she couldn't see it.

"I have to finish this," he said. "Maynard's the last of them, and this—whatever it is—is his swan song. I might be wrong, it might be nothing. But if he's planning something, I have to be here to stop it."

She knew better than to argue with him.

"Please, Billie. Just for a few days, until we know it's safe."

"But that's just it," she replied. "We're never going to be safe. When you finished Hollenbeck, after Hell House, when you put them all away, they promised they weren't after you, they promised they were done with us. Now this? No, Robbie. They only win if they scare us into running, if they stop us from living our lives. Right?"

Or if they kill us, he thought.

"I'm done with them. They've come after all of us, but we got through it every time. We won every time. You're right, this is their swan song, this is their last shot, their... their Hail Mary. It's pathetic. I'm not going anywhere."

Kett sighed, pushing himself away from the wall as another uniformed constable entered the room. This one shouted over to him.

"Sir, you probably want to take a look at this."

"Give me a sec," he told him. "Can you at least stay at Mum's?" he said into the phone. "Just for tonight?"

"God, Robbie, that's worse than being kidnapped again," she said, and he surprised himself by laughing. She laughed too, softly. "I'll pack a bag when I'm home from work. Just a night, okay?"

"Just a night," he said. "Look, I'd better go."

"Be careful," she told him. "But Robbie, no more running. You've got Maynard. You just have to make sure he never gets out."

"I will," he said, thinking about Gorski kicking the old man in the head, thinking about how much easier this would be if she'd shot him. "He's done. I love you."

"I love you too," she said, and she hung up.

Kett followed the constable through the open door and halfway down a hallway, where he stopped and gestured into a tiny cupboard. There was enough space for some shelves and a mop, but that was about it.

"It's a closet," said Kett, peering in.

"It's not, sir," said the PC.

He looked again.

"No, it really is. Look, there's a mop."

"It's not a closet," said the PC.

Kett was about to put a hand to the man's forehead to see if he was feverish when the shelves began to move, swinging inwards with a screech of grating metal. Porter appeared in the crack, a grin on his face.

"Boo," he said, shining his torch into Kett's face.

"Watch it," said Kett, covering his eyes as the pattern of his retinas exploded. "What's in there?"

"Come and see, sir. But be warned, it's not nice."

"When is it ever?"

Kett entered the closet, pushing through the secret door into a short, featureless corridor lit by Porter's torch. It was freezing in here, a draught blowing from the open door at the other end. More beams of light moved frantically back and forth through the dark.

"How'd you find this?" Kett asked.

"Duke did, sir," said Porter.

"Impressive."

"It really wasn't. I told him to check the cupboard and he tripped and fell into the shelves, went straight through them. Arse over tit. It was brilliant."

Kett reached the door, leaning in and immediately recoiling. The room beyond reeked of rotting meat, an aroma of death that scoured his sinuses and planted a dull ache inside his head. He looked at Porter.

"Body?"

"Yeah, but not what you're thinking."

Kett took as deep a breath as he could, put his sleeve over his face, and walked inside. The sizeable room beyond was lit by a couple of torches, although they didn't do much. It was absolutely freezing in here, as cold as a fridge, and when Kett clicked on his own torch he saw another open door at the far end, spewing cold air.

He swept the light around, spotting Duke standing beside one of the tactical team. Both were looking at something that hung from the ceiling—a lump of heavy flesh about the size of a small person.

Or a child.

"Told you," said Porter, setting off across the room. "Not nice."

Kett walked with him, lifting his torch. The lump of raw meat glistened, rubbery strands of sinew and streaks of fat dissecting the mess. A hook had been rammed into the ridge of its spine, connected to a metal rung in the ceiling. He could just about see the stumps where there had once been limbs, lumps of yellow bone protruding from them. A bucket sat beneath the animal, the blood inside congealed into a solid mass.

The smell of it was awful, but it hadn't started to turn—the cold air had kept the worst of the rot from setting in.

"You said it wasn't a body, Pete," said Kett.

"It's not, sir. Not human, anyway."

"Sheep," said Duke.

"Huh?" said Kett, aiming his torch at the PC. The man beside him was Chester Andilet, one of Gorski's long-serving tactical officers. Both looked like they'd woken from a nightmare to find themselves still inside it.

"Sheep, sir," Duke said again, pointing to the head of the cadaver.

Kett walked past him to get a better look. Sure enough, it was a sheep.

"Poor bastard," said Kett. "Any idea why?"

Both Duke and Andilet turned their torchlight to the corner of the room, revealing a wooden table laden with metal trays. Kett had to take a few steps towards it, giving the dead sheep and the bucket a wide berth, before he understood what he was looking at.

At least six or seven wide, flat steaks had been trimmed from the animal and laid out on a platter, smaller ribbons of flesh laid out around them. There was a green sheen on all of it. A dozen blades of different shapes and sizes were scattered across the table, from a brutal meat cleaver to a collection of scalpels that would have been more at home in a hospital. All were crusted with blood. There were bones, too, polished to a shine. One had been carved with a set of symbols, maybe runes.

Kett put his sleeve to his mouth again, feeling a stew of acid rising from his unhappy gut.

"Not nice at all," said Porter.

"King of the understatements today, Pete," Kett told him. "This is Maynard's MO, for sure. We saw all this stuff on the Aggie Clegg case."

There was a notebook on the table, sunflowers on the cover. It was battered with use and smeared with blood. Kett patted his pockets until he found a pen, using the tip to open the cover. The first page was covered in dense writing and scribbled illustrations that looked vaguely anatomical.

"Maybe whoever did this was training to be a butcher, sir?" said Duke. "My uncle's sister's brother was a butcher, back in the day. He always had stuff like this lying around his shop."

"Your uncle's sister's brother?" said Porter. "Isn't he your uncle too, then?"

"No," said Duke, without further explanation.

Kett flipped through a few more pages, although it was hard because they were glued together with blood. He stopped on one where a pentagram had been drawn in black ink, so hard that it had ripped the paper. A skull filled the centre of it, its right eye coloured with a smudge of blood.

"Bet your uncle's sister's brother's nephew's dentist's budgie didn't have those in his butcher's handbooks," Porter said.

Kett let the book close.

"This thing's covered in prints. Anyone heard from Cara yet?"

"She's on her way, last I heard," said Porter, heading for the door. "I'll check."

"Far as I know, butchers don't use scalpels," said Andilet.

"Right," said Kett, looking at the strips of flesh on the table. Some were two-foot long, maybe more, wound into spaghetti-like tangles. It would have taken some care and patience to remove them from the body. "So what the hell are we looking at?"

"A sheep," said Duke.

"I know, Aaron. I mean... Never mind. Is Franklin here yet?"

"Not sure, sir," said Duke.

"Can you go find out? We need to know if this is just somebody preparing their lunch, or something else."

Duke clomped out of the room, humming something jaunty beneath his breath. He must have hit the secret door on his way out because it clattered into the wall, the deafening clang of it almost turning Kett inside out. He shot a murderous look after the PC.

"I mean, it's got to be something else, right?" said Andilet, adjusting his rifle. "You don't hang a sheep up in a secret room, then dissect it, if you're planning a barbecue. Not with scalpels. And you certainly don't let it go green."

"No," said Kett. "You don't."

"You know what I think?" the tactical officer went on. "I think this is somebody practising. You know? Same way we do when we start out. You get blanks before they trust you with live rounds. This is his training run."

Kett turned back to the ruined carcass that hung from the ceiling. He didn't know how, because nobody had touched it, but it was swinging gently on its hook—like the bloody thing was coming back to life. More acid gargled up his throat and he swallowed hard. The desire to run from the room and head outside for fresh air was almost overwhelming.

"What's he training for?" he said.

"You don't need me to tell you that, sir," said Andilet. "You're the detective."

"A person," he said, nodding. "He's working up to a human being. I hope you're wrong, Chester."

"To be fair, I usually am," said Andilet. "Too much YouTube."

Kett turned his attention to the door, enjoying the cold air that washed through it.

"Cellar?" he asked.

"Better," said Andilet. "Tunnel. Goes for about fifty metres, comes out in the woods. Old air raid shelter maybe, I don't know. Explains why we didn't see anyone coming and going."

"Shit," said Kett.

He took a breath.

"You alright, Chester. After what happened?"

Andilet didn't answer immediately, staring at the floor like he was watching Ben Milford die all over again.

"Who does that?" he said after a moment. "Who kills somebody like that?"

He looked up, his eyes like pools of shadow in the dark room.

"Gorski still about?" he said.

Kett nodded.

"You know about them?" Andilet went on. "Her and Ben?"

"They were together?"

Andilet nodded.

"They kept it quiet. Workplace romance and all that. Two years, nearly. And..."

He blew out a breath, looking over his shoulder to make sure nobody else was listening.

"I wouldn't say anything, but I think you need to know. She's pregnant."

"What?" said Kett.

"They're not long in, and only a few of us know. They were going to make it official at some point. I guess they'd have to, when she started waddling around. Not like you can do this job with a baby in your belly."

He sucked in a sigh.

"So yeah, there's that."

"God," Kett said, picturing Gorski's rage, understanding it.

"Just saying, maybe don't leave her alone with Maynard," said Andilet. "Not until you've got what you need from him, anyway."

"Noted," said Kett. "He's gone, on his way to the hospital."

Andilet spat out a bitter laugh.

"Yeah, I know," said Kett. "Believe me, I know."

He rested his hand on the man's shoulder for a second.

"I'm sorry."

Then he made for the door.

CHAPTER FIVE

Savage stepped out of the Norfolk and Norwich University Hospital, receiving a slap of icy wind from the obnoxious morning. She pulled up the collar of her jacket, shivering her way across the car park and practically diving into her Audi.

Ian, the teenage boy they'd found in Cold Iron, was safely inside, handcuffed to a private bed and watched over by two nurses and three constables. He'd calmed down a little, but he'd still not said much more than those same three words—*I wasn't here*—over and over and over, like he could make it true by the sheer force of repetition. As much as she'd tried, she hadn't managed to get a surname out of him.

Or anything more about the man he'd called the master.

She fired off a quick text to Kett: *Ian dropped off, you need me back?* Then she started the car, twisting the heat up to high. She drummed the steering wheel for a moment while she waited for a reply. When it didn't come, she called DS Alison Spalding.

"Is it as bad as they're saying?" Spalding asked as soon

as she'd picked up, her voice booming through the Audi's speakers.

"Worse, Sarge," said Savage. "You heard about Milford?"

"Yeah. Bastards. Tell me what you need."

"One of the kids who was shooting at the tactical team survived. His name's Ian. No surname. He's about seventeen, eighteen. Maybe younger, I don't know. He says he's local to Thetford."

"Please don't say you want me to find a random teenager called Ian in a town of twenty-five thousand people," said Spalding.

"I mean, if anyone can do it, you can, Sarge."

"Buttering me up won't help, Kate."

"I think we can narrow it down," Savage went on. "He doesn't look like he drives, which means he cycles or walks to the paintball place. It's right on the edge of the estate, so we're probably looking somewhere to the north of the station, off Croxton Road. I don't know."

"I'll see if there are any matching mispers or suspects," Spalding said. "But don't hang anything on it."

"Big ask, Sarge, thank you."

"Big arse Sarge?" came the reply.

"What?"

"Whose arse? Mine?"

"*What?*"

"Is that a *nickname?*"

Savage was distracted by a text message. When she glanced at her phone she saw that it was Kett.

If Ian's a lead, follow it. If not, come back.

"I'd better go, Sarge," she said. "Thank you."

She ended the call, tossing the phone onto the passenger seat and reversing out of the parking space. It was a quick trip to the A11, and five minutes later she was heading south-west past HQ. Five minutes more and she heard her phone ring, answering it on the hands-free.

"It's your old pal, Big Arse Sarge," said Spalding.

"I don't understand what you're—"

"You got lucky, Kate," the DS went on, sounding a little frostier than normal. "No missing person by the name of Ian, but I checked in with the high school and they've got a vulnerable student called Ian Hipkin who's been absent for a few days. He's fifteen, and he's in their unit for kids who're struggling. They tried calling his home but no answer, though the woman I spoke to said that was pretty normal. You want his address?"

"That's amazing, Sarge, thank you."

"Woodlands Drive. I'll text it. You were right, it's just off Croxton Road."

Savage felt a glow of satisfaction, but it was short-lived.

"You know, Kate, I'm aware you all think I have the easy job here in the office, but you should be grateful for this fat arse, because if I wasn't sitting here doing all the hard work, you wouldn't have a clue about anything."

"I'm really sorry," said Savage, overtaking a lorry. "I have no idea why you're saying that. You have a lovely... bum."

No reply.

"Sarge?"

Spalding had hung up. Mystified, Savage used the Audi's touchscreen to call Duke, dialling up the volume as she overtook a couple of HGVs. It took him almost nine rings to answer.

"Kate, you okay?"

"Yeah. You still at Cold Iron?"

"Yeah. Absolute nightmare."

"I know," she said. "I can't believe it happened."

"You heard?" said Duke. "About me falling through the secret door?"

"What?"

"Landed on my arse. Porter had to help me up because I was wedged in the corner. Like I said, absolute nightmare."

"Oh, right," she said. "That does sound... stressful. What are you doing right now?"

"Just waiting for forensics."

"Then they won't miss you. Grab a car and meet me up the road, yeah? Woodlands Drive."

"Sure," he said. "I'll check it with the guv."

"He won't mind," she said. "Tell him it's a lead, and that given what's just happened, I don't want to be on my own."

"Sure," said Duke. "Woodlands Drive. I'll be there."

TRUE TO HIS WORD, he was waiting for her when she pulled the Audi off Croxton Road, leaning against an IRV fifty yards away from the junction. She parked behind him, stretching like a cat as she got out. It was still raining, but only just, the wind swirling the drizzle into dancing patterns. There was a weird smell, like she'd stuck her head in a wheelie bin.

The street was made up of small, neat, semi-detached houses, most of which were perfect clones of each other. She found the one she wanted, seeing an untidy garden piled high with black bin bags, and a driveway that was almost obscured by the weeds that had grown there. She wasn't sure, but she thought the stench in the air might be coming from there.

"You smell that?" she said as she walked over to Duke.

He sniffed his armpit.

"Is it me?"

"Why would it be you, Aaron? Have you been rolling around at the dump?"

"No. But I did roll around in that room with the dead sheep."

Savage frowned.

"You did what? With *what*?"

"The secret room I found, it had a sheep hanging from the ceiling. Butchered. There were scalpels, notebooks full of weird drawings, proper occult shit." He shuddered. "I don't know, it was weird. Reminded me of all the stuff from the Clegg case, you know?"

"Because that's what Maynard does," said Savage. "That's what he's obsessed with. The Devil, all that Satanic ritual stuff."

"You think it's real?" said Duke, leaning in and speaking quietly.

"Do I think Maynard's in league with Lucifer?" She lifted an eyebrow. "No, Aaron, I think he's a sad old man with a dead sheep fetish."

Duke nodded, although he didn't look sure.

"By the way," Savage went on. "Did you say anything to Spalding about her... about her rear end?"

"Rear end of what?" said Duke.

Savage spotted movement from the Hipkin house, the net curtains over the upstairs windows rippling.

"Doesn't matter, let's go."

They crossed the street together, weaving a path through the swamp of bin bags. This was definitely where the smell was coming from. The air was heavy with rot, making her eyes water. Most of the bags had been ripped open, probably by foxes; furry, month-old food waste and open bags of dog shit scattered everywhere. By the time she'd pounded on the front door, she felt giddy.

"That's so bad," groaned Duke, covering his face with both hands.

Somewhere inside, a dog started barking. Savage knocked again, and this time an upstairs window opened—not in this house, but the next one over. The man who leaned out of it was so enormous that he was in danger of toppling into the garden below. He was completely bald, the features of his face almost lost in the middle of his giant cheeks and his Neanderthal-like forehead—reminding her of a Danish pastry, for some reason. He wasn't wearing anything on his corpulent top half, and thankfully she couldn't see anything lower than his sagging bosom.

"You here for that shit?" he said, raising his voice to be heard over the barking dog. "I've had it with that woman. Look at it, fucking rank!"

Before Savage could answer, the upstairs window in the Hipkin house opened. Savage stood well back, in case anything came flying out, but the only thing that appeared was a woman. She was in her forties, her face almost completely covered by a tangle of greying brown hair. She wore a bright green and yellow Norwich City shirt, and when she jabbed her finger towards the man next door, Savage saw her nails were painted the same colour.

"You can suck my cock, Terry," she yelled, flapping the net curtain out of her way.

"Yeah?" roared the man. "You'd probably like that, wouldn't you? You fucking... fucking big cock lady."

"*You'd* like it, you big cock-lady-loving cocksucker," she screamed back. "No wonder you love a lady cock, given your wife has a bigger cock than you do. Bet you love that right up your arse."

"Hey!" yelled Savage. "That's enough!"

They ignored her, screaming insults from their upstairs windows like a Punch and Judy show.

"You know what you can put up your arse, Helen?" Terry shouted. "All that fucking rubbish. Why don't you stick it up there now? Plenty of room I bet."

"Why don't you eat it, you fat fuck?" the woman blared. "Or do you not want to, because it's not a big lady cock?"

"Enough!" roared Savage. "Pack it in right now, both of you, or you'll be coming with us in cuffs."

She pointed to the man.

"Inside, now. Not another word."

Then she swung her finger to the woman.

"And you, open the bloody door."

The woman looked like she was going to start slinging insults at them, too, but with a grumble of half-audible swear words, she slammed the window shut. The man hesitated, his face dripping with sweat despite the chill.

"Fucking menace, that woman. Her and her son and her dog."

Then he snuck back inside.

A lock turned, and the Hipkins' front door opened. A streak of black lightning exploded out of it, fast enough to make Duke scream. Savage's first thought was that it was a rat, but when it stood on its back feet and licked her knee she realised it was a tiny dog—a Pomeranian, more hair than body. It propelled itself off her and ran to Duke, leaping up his leg with surprising strength. He grabbed it with both hands, holding it in front of him while it squirmed and barked.

"Help," he said.

"He won't hurt you," said the woman, pushing her hair out of her face. "Worst he'll do is lick your face."

"I don't want to be licked," said Duke.

"Maybe jizz on your leg," she added.

"Help!" Duke said again, thrusting his arms out even further.

"You're Mrs Hipkin?" asked Savage. "Helen, right?"

The woman swept her arm through the air so violently that Savage leaned back, but she was just gesturing at the garden.

"I told you before, none of this is my fault. If the bloody council did their job then all this shit would've gone. Half of it's his next door, though he won't admit it."

"Lies!" came a roar from the direction of the neighbour's house.

"I didn't even put all that dog shit in the bin, it wasn't me, so screw 'em for punishing me and nobody else on the—"

"Mrs Hipkin, this isn't about the rubbish," said Savage. "It's about your son."

She rocked back like she'd been slapped, then immediately came on the attack again.

"Well what he's done has nothing to do with me, or with him," she said, pointing a painted nail next door. "Everyone gives my lad shit, but he don't do nothing."

"Is he home?" asked Savage.

Helen licked her teeth, then shook her head.

"At school, isn't he? Like a good lad."

"Can I see a photo of him?"

"Why?" Helen asked.

Duke was struggling with the dog, even though he was about a hundred times bigger than it. It was straining its floofy head towards him, a tiny pink tongue lapping at the air.

"Because I asked," Savage wheezed. The smell of the

rubbish was like a dirty blanket held over her face. "And can we do it inside?"

"Fuck's sake," said Helen, retreating into the house. "But make it quick, yeah? I've got jobs to do."

Savage walked inside, Duke following with his new friend. Helen closed the door behind them, making her way through the closest door into the front room. Savage moved down the short corridor to the kitchen, which was surprisingly ordered given the mess outside. Through the window was a small garden, a swing set and a slide taking pride of place. There were explosions of colour all over it and the wooden fence—paintball pellets.

"You've got other kids?" Savage asked.

"What?" yelled Helen.

Savage glanced up the stairs, studying the photos on the wall. Instead of showing friends and family, they were all pictures of Val Kilmer in a variety of films. She glanced at Duke to see if he'd noticed, but he was still wrestling the Pomeranian.

"You can put it down, mate," she said.

"Oh, right."

Duke lowered the dog to the floor, where it immediately began to climb his leg again.

At least she *thought* it was climbing. It was mainly just grinding.

"Are you cheating on me, Aaron?" she asked.

"Not willingly," he replied, using a giant foot to gently push the dog away. It wasn't working, the animal returning to his leg with a worrying series of grunts.

"Here," said Helen, walking out of her living room. She thrust a photograph at Savage so hard it glanced off her face.

"You need to calm down," Savage said as she took the

photo. Her cheek was stinging. "Or this is going to get a lot less friendly. Understood?"

Helen folded her arms over her sizeable chest, undaunted.

"There he is. What do you need that for anyway?"

The photo showed a teenage boy in the exact same top Helen was wearing now—although it hung off his skinny frame like a sail from a mast. It was a couple of years old, but the boy who stared miserably at the camera was instantly recognisable.

"Does Ian hang out at a place called Cold Iron Paintball?" she asked.

"What does that have to do with anything?" Helen shot back. "You try having a kid like him, yeah? School don't want him because he's not like all their robots. Says he's got neurodiversity or some shit, says I should get him diagnosed. So I try, but nobody's got time for us. Doctors won't see him, fucking council won't do a thing. He's been on a waiting list since he was eight years old. He's fucking fifteen now, all them years of waiting, and for what? He'll be leaving school in a year, and they haven't done shit."

She paused for long enough to suck in a breath.

"So what if he hangs out there, eh? At least he's happy. He's never going to be a doctor, so who fucking cares what he's doing so long as he's happy? You tell that school of his, and that fat wank next door—"

"Hey," said Savage, her patience paper thin. "I said calm down. Did you know that Ian was at Cold Iron this morning?"

Helen sniffed, shrugged.

"Yeah. Got him his own gun for his birthday, he's been practising with it. If he's not in the mood for school, I just let him go. No harm in it, whatever you lot say."

"Did he ever mention who he spends time with there?"

The dog was really going for Duke's leg, its eyes bulging, its tongue flopping. Duke was doing his best to shake it off, but it kept lunging back for more.

"No," said Helen. "Other lads like him, I guess. He talked about one called Liam. I never asked."

"He didn't mention an older man there? Somebody who went by the name Joseph Maynard?"

"What old man?" she said, and for the first time a hint of concern broke through the wall of anger. "He never mentioned nobody. What, has somebody done something to him?"

"Not in the way you're thinking," said Savage. "But he's never spoken about what goes on there? Anything weird?"

"No," she said. "There was nothing weird going on, that's why. I wouldn't leave Ian somewhere he was in danger, so whatever you're thinking, stick it somewhere the sun don't shine."

"Does he have a phone?"

"He's fifteen, course he has a phone. Never off it. Always on that YouTube, TikTok, WhizBang, whatever, like a zombie. Always watching those influencers and their cars. Influencers. What kind of job is that anyway? They're *bad* influences, all of them. Only thing they've taught Ian is how to be an arsehole, and he had his father for that. That's one of the reasons I thought the paintball was good, got him away from the screen."

"He's got it with him?"

"Not much fucking good if he doesn't, is it?"

"Any chance we can have a look at his room?" asked Savage.

"Yeah," said the woman. "When you come back with a warrant."

"We can," Savage told her. "And we will."

"Then go do it," she said, leaning in. "And until you do, this conversation's fucking over."

She eyeballed Savage for a second, then opened the front door and stomped outside. She slammed it behind her hard enough to make the whole house shake.

"Did she just storm out of her own house?" asked Duke, still trying to dislodge the dog.

"Looks like it," said Savage. "I'm going to take a peek upstairs. You okay?"

"I'm really not okay," he said as the Pomeranian began its undulations again. "Can I come with you?"

"I'd hate to break up this new relationship," she told him. "Cover for me if she comes back."

She bounded up the stairs, finding Ian's room at the back of the house. It was small, just enough space for a single bed, a desk with a computer, and a wardrobe that looked like it was coming apart at the joints. The walls were plastered with posters of soldiers, all wearing camouflage with painted faces. A few adverts for paintball guns finished the display, cut from magazines. A collection of dusty toys crowded precariously on a shelf over the desk, along with a few ancient DVDs.

Downstairs, somebody hammered on the door.

"Hang on," she heard Duke shout. "I can't get past the dog."

Savage opened the desk drawers, finding nothing but more magazines and a lot of crusty-looking socks.

"Nope," she said, turning to the wardrobe instead.

More knocking, and Duke hissed a warning up the stairs.

"Kate! Hurry up!"

There was nothing inside except for a heap of clothes

and some more DVDs. She ran her hand along the top, her fingertips bumping against something. Stretching as high as she could, she worked a box over the edge, lifting it down. It was the size of a shoebox, but it had once contained a pistol of some kind—bright orange, with a compartment for paintballs. She dumped it on the bed and opened it up, seeing a notebook, a thin, sharp kitchen knife, a silver ring.

And a small glass jar of what could only be blood.

"Hang on," she heard Duke yell as the knocking continued. "I think he's nearly finished."

Savage picked up the box and ran back downstairs. As soon as Duke saw her coming, he opened the front door. Helen Hipkin marched in, apoplectic with rage. The dog finally abandoned Duke as it ran over to her.

"I suppose you think that's funny, don't you? Locking me out of my own house."

"Technically, you did it yourself," said Savage, and before the woman could get a breath in to reply, she kept going. "Listen to me, Mrs Hipkin. Ian was involved in an incident this morning, a serious one. He was hurt."

The woman lurched to a halt, breathing like an ogre.

"He's okay, but we've taken him to the hospital in Norwich for treatment."

"*Now* you tell me?" she said, grabbing her coat from a hook by the door. "He's alright?"

"He's alright. But it was serious. I need you to listen to me, and then Aaron can drive you there. Okay?"

The woman nodded, her hair falling over her face.

"We think Ian was caught up in something at Cold Iron. Something very serious."

"He wouldn't—"

"He might not have even known it was happening," Savage interrupted. "But he was there. This could get bad for him, and for you. But it doesn't have to. The more we can find out about the man Ian was spending time with, the better his shot at getting out of this painlessly. He never mentioned an older man, Joseph Maynard?"

"No," said Helen, her chins swaying as she shook her head.

"He never talked about somebody called the master? Someone he was scared of?"

She continued to shake her head.

"He never said nothing about anyone, other than that kid, Liam."

Savage lifted the box.

"You've seen this before?"

"The gun? Yeah, I bought it for him."

"Not the gun," said Savage, opening the lid. The woman's eyes just about burst from their sockets. "This was in Ian's room."

"That's not his," she said. "It can't be. Is that *blood*?"

"I'm going to take it with me," said Savage. "I'm going to find out. Is that okay?"

She was too stunned to do anything but nod.

"I met Ian," Savage said. "He's a good kid. I don't want him to get into trouble."

"Yeah, he's a good kid," Helen echoed, but it was just a whisper.

Duke stepped outside.

"I'll take you," he said.

"Can I bring my dog?" Helen asked, scooping up the Pomeranian. It panted lustfully in Duke's direction.

"Definitely not," he said.

Helen locked the dog in the kitchen and hurried outside. Savage followed her onto the rubbish-strewn drive-way, closing the door and watching her climb into the IRV.

She looked like a ghost in the passenger seat as Duke drove them away, all of her bluster gone.

Savage crossed the street, hearing a shout from the neighbour's house. Terry was halfway out of his upstairs window again, still half naked.

"You gonna make her sort out that shit or not?" he bellowed.

"Shut up, Terry," Savage replied, *probably* too quietly for him to hear.

She dumped the box on the passenger seat of the Audi and pulled out her phone, texting Kett.

Sir, I think I might have found something.

CHAPTER SIX

THE BUTCHER'S ROOM WASN'T THE ONLY NASTY SECRET lurking in Cold Iron.

An hour or so after they'd found the sheep, Kett heard the unmistakeable sound of vomiting from the large room at the back of the facility. He was standing in the corridor outside the cupboard with the secret door, talking to Porter, and he stopped mid-sentence as somebody unloaded over the floor.

"Tell me you didn't make tea, Pete?" he said, but his attempt at humour dropped dead when a uniformed constable staggered through the door, his hat in his hands. He opened his mouth to speak but couldn't seem to find the words, gesturing back the way he'd come like a talentless mime.

"Dibs not going, sir," said Porter.

"*Dibs*?" Kett said. "This isn't the Famous Five, Pete."

He set off, passing the PC and entering the room. It had to have been a warehouse originally, because it was enormous. Now it was used as an indoor arena, the fake scenery and numerous buildings spattered with explosions of paint in a multitude of colours. The door at the rear of the room was open, weak daylight exploring the short corridor and pooling on the sawdust floor. A collection of coppers milled outside, gathered like crows.

Another constable stood in the middle of the room, and she had her hat in her hands as well. *Not a great sign*, thought Kett. Two members of the forensic team stood beside her in their crisp overalls. One was a young woman who was bent double and dribbling sick. The other was Cara Hay, her hand on her colleague's back, her hairless head slick with sweat. When she looked at Kett, he saw more than a little fear in her expression.

He almost stopped right there, because whatever this was, he didn't want to see it.

But he kept moving. Step by step by step, the way he always did. The way he had to.

Hay and the others were standing next to a wooden shed, maybe twelve feet by ten feet with a pitched roof. It had been painted in a camouflage pattern and decorated with plastic barbed wire and dozens of metal signs, all of them warning of danger—electric currents, mines, explosives.

Kett had the idea that whatever lay in there was much worse.

"Cara," he said, giving her a nod. "She okay?"

Hay didn't dignify the question with an answer. The young woman retched again, wiping the drool from her mouth.

"I'm so sorry," she groaned.

"No need to apologise," said Hay, her Trinidadian accent thicker than ever, the way it often was when she was truly shocked. "Go, I will handle this."

The technician ran off, almost hitting a sprint by the

time she was outside. Kett watched her go, wondering how fast he could get to the doors if he really tried.

Wondering if he'd just keep on running.

"It's in there?" he said when he turned back to the shed.

"It is," said Hay. "You'll need a light."

Porter clicked on his torch and handed it over.

"Age before beauty, sir," he said.

Kett took a deep breath. The air was stale and laced with chemicals from the paint, but he couldn't smell blood or rot the way he had back in the sheep room. He couldn't smell death.

But when he opened the door and beamed the torch inside, he saw how wrong he was.

The shed was empty except for a short bookcase at the far end, painted white and adorned with bright red flowers. It was the kind you might see in a child's room, but there were no books here, just several glass jars neatly arranged on the shelves. They looked like they were filled with black fluid, until Kett lit them up and saw the ruby glow.

"Right," he said, ducking beneath the door and walking inside. The floor was covered with the same sawdust as the rest of the building, stiff with old paint that crunched beneath his boots.

"What is it?" asked Porter, leaning in after him.

"Not sure yet," he said, reaching the shelves.

There were five jars in all, each one roughly the size of a toilet roll, capped with a glass lid and a lever arm clasp. They had a name, these jars—his mum had dozens of them for pasta and lentils and stuff—but he couldn't for the life of him remember what it was.

He angled the torch so the glare wouldn't reflect in the glass of the top left jar. It was filled roughly halfway with what had to be blood, congealed with age, furry with mould.

"Sheep?" said Porter, right in Kett's ear. He jumped so hard he almost thwacked the DI with the torch.

"How the bloody hell am I supposed to know that?" he snapped, feeling his heart thrashing all the way up to his temples. "It's not exactly woolly, is it?"

"Looks a *bit* woolly," said Porter. "With the mould."

Kett moved the light to the next jar and immediately recoiled—backing into Porter, their heads cracking off the low ceiling in unison.

"Ow, sir," Porter said, rubbing his scalp. "Little warning."

"Give me a bit of bloody space, then," he snapped.

Kett swung the light back, illuminating the second jar again, seeing the blood, seeing the very human ear that floated in it.

"Probably not a sheep, then," said Porter.

"You think?" he replied, swallowing dust.

In the third jar, poking from the coagulated blood like an iceberg in the ocean, was a finger—slightly crooked, as if it was beckoning them. There was another finger in the fourth jar, or maybe a toe, he couldn't be sure.

By the time he spotted the eyeball staring back at them from its pool of jellied blood inside the fifth jar, Kett was ready to hurl.

"Move, Pete," he said, pushing past the DI, cracking his head again as he walked through the door. He gulped down paint-scented air until the worst of the nausea passed, although the little puddle of vomit by his feet didn't help. His skin was slick with cold sweat despite the chill.

"Grim," said Porter as he ducked out of the shed, still rubbing his head.

"You think it's real?" Kett asked Hay.

"If it isn't, then somebody has gone out of their way to

make it look authentic. And then I have to ask, what is easier: creating jars of fake blood painted and decorated to seem old, or just filling jars with real blood and letting it rot?"

"And adding some body parts," said Porter. "An ear, an eye, a finger, a toe."

"Not a toe," Hay asked. "A tongue. And you saw the last thing?"

Both Kett and Porter shook their heads.

"Can't be worse than an eye," said Porter.

"That depends," said Hay. "Would you rather lose an eye, or your..."

She left the question unfinished, and it took Kett a moment to catch on.

"Seriously?"

"On the middle shelf," she said, nodding. "Severed male genitalia."

Kett and Porter squirmed.

"I'm going to wait until Emily arrives before I open them. But I'll check for prints on the Kilner jars now."

"Kilner," said Kett, clicking his fingers. "That's it, thank you. You think you'll get much from them?"

"The jars? They're a dime a dozen, you'll find them in every kitchen. But I will do my best. Are you finished in there, or do you want another look?"

"Another look at the severed male genitalia?" said Kett. "No, thank you, I'm done."

He moved out of her way, stepping over the vomit and heading for the back door. It was a blessed relief to be outside. He could feel his entire body drinking in the weak daylight, relishing the light drizzle on his skin.

"You think you've seen it all, sir," said Porter, following him out. "Then you stumble onto a jar full of willies."

"Just one willy," said Kett. "I hope."

"Quite a collection though. Has to be Maynard, right? This is him all over."

Kett nodded, kicking a stone across the courtyard. It clanged off a metal hut, bouncing into the overgrown shrubbery. There were dozens of buildings out here, just like inside. How many of them held similar horrors?

"Poor bastard, whoever it is," Porter went on. "Bad enough being murdered. But then you get chopped up and stuffed in some cookware like in my nan's kitchen. What was he going to do with them?"

Porter took aim at a stone of his own, punting it. It went flying, but so did his shoe—soaring through the air and landing in the scrub.

"Bloody hell!" he said, hopping gracelessly. "Sir, can you grab that?"

"No!" exclaimed Kett. "You get it."

"Then I'll have a wet sock," Porter protested. "I hate wet socks. Please, sir?"

Kett scowled at the DI before heading into the enormous paintball yard. It took him an age to find the bloody thing because it had rolled into a bush, and his jacket got drenched as he pushed himself into the tangled vegetation to try to retrieve it. He walked back, tempted to use the shoe as a weapon.

He didn't get the chance. Clare stomped out of the back door, raging so hard his face was puce. The Super looked at Porter, still balancing on one leg.

"What in the name of Godfrey's toss are you doing, Pete?" he roared. "Where's your shoe?"

Porter blanched.

"Uh..." he started.

Kett lobbed the shoe at the DI and he dived for it, losing

his balance and planting his stockinged foot right in a puddle.

"No!" he groaned. "My sock!"

"You're going to be eating that sock in a minute, you diseased rectum," roared Clare. "And the shoe as well. Put it on and stop tossing about."

He turned to Kett.

"A jar of cock?"

"No thanks, sir," Kett replied.

The Super's face turned from puce to plum.

"Sorry," Kett added. "You've seen it?"

"I've seen it," Clare said. "I wanted to make sure it was what Hay said it was."

"It's definitely a willy?" said Porter, who had successfully put his shoe on. He grimaced as he took a step. "It's bloody soaking."

"It is," said Clare. "An eye, an ear, a finger, a tongue, and a Beef Johnson."

"Beef Johnson?" said Kett.

"Yes, Kett. A Beef Johnson, a ding-a-ling, a doinker, a little buddy, a chubby bingbong, a fleshy popsicle, a floppy noodle, a skin flute, a—"

"Enough!" Kett said, too many images flooding his head. "I get it."

"Franklin's on her way, she's going to start with the jars," Clare went on, and Kett missed what he said next as his phone buzzed. He pulled it out, seeing a text from Savage.

Sir, I think I might have found something.

"Hang on," he said, calling her back.

"Sure," said Clare, flapping his hands. He was almost maroon now. "I've got nothing better to be doing. I'll just stand here with my devil's bagpipe in my hand while you piss about on the phone."

"Sir," said Savage, who had answered. "What on earth is a devil's bagpipe?"

"You don't want to know, Kate," he said. "What have you got?"

"Spalding found an ID for our paintball shooter. Ian Hipkin. He's fifteen. I paid a visit to his house, found something in his room. A box of... of weirdness."

"What kind of weirdness?"

"A notebook full of arcane stuff, a silver ring that's got some kind of eye on it, and a jar full of—"

"Do not say willies," said Kett.

"What? No, sir, a jar full of blood."

"Kilner jar? Small one?"

"Yes," said Savage. "How did you know?"

"You'll find out when you get back here," he said. "You on your way?"

"Can be, sir, unless you need me elsewhere?"

"No, meet us back at Cold Iron."

"Sir," she said, and hung up.

"Kate found another jar of blood in the house of the kid who shot Gorski with a paintball," he said.

"Willies in it?" asked Porter.

"I don't think so. She's on her way."

"That's what I came out here to say," muttered Clare. "Before you lot distracted me with wet socks and whompers. A 999 call came in a few minutes ago. Somebody's reported a kidnapping."

"Shit," said Porter.

"Young lad," Clare went on. "A trainee mechanic. Went missing at work this morning. Nobody thought anything of it until they checked the CCTV. Somebody bundled him into the back of a vehicle."

"Probably a coincidence, sir?" said Porter. "Right?"

"It was a hearse," Clare added.

It was like somebody had slipped a needle into the soft meat of Kett's heart. The goosebumps crinkled his arms, pulled his scalp painfully tight.

"A hearse?" he said.

"Right," said Clare, studying Kett. "Not the first time we've seen that, is it?"

Kett could still remember the horror of being nailed inside a coffin and slid into a hearse, the endless dark. There were nights when he woke up screaming from dreams of his own funeral—nightmares of what Hollenbeck had put him through.

"This is them," he said.

"It might not be," said Porter. "Maynard's in hospital. He's out of the picture. How would he be able to throw anyone in the back of a hearse?"

"Because this is what he does," said Kett. "This is what he was talking about. '*It's just beginning*.' When did it happen?"

Clare checked his watch.

"A little over an hour ago," he said. "Up in Fakenham."

"Fakenham?" said Porter. "Bloody miles away. I'm telling you, there's no connection."

Clare turned to Porter, baring his yellow teeth like an angry horse.

"Then explain this to me, you cockless, sockless wonder."

"Not *sockless*," said Porter, miserably.

"If this isn't Maynard, if this has nothing to do with all the shit we've found here, then why did somebody draw a tossing pentagram on the floor in the missing lad's blood?"

CHAPTER SEVEN

It took an age to reach Fakenham, the back roads jammed with tractors that seemed to make a sport of blocking Porter's Mondeo. The garage in question sat on the edge of town, already mobbed by IRVs. At least half a dozen constables occupied the small forecourt, none of them looking very busy.

Kett and Porter climbed out together and walked to the building, the constables making way for them. The garage was made up of two parts, a larger section on the left with 'McGarvey's' painted in neat letters above the door, and a smaller one on the right, its shutters open to reveal a parking bay.

"Literally the worst thing in the world," said Porter as they went.

"Getting kidnapped?" said Kett. "You're not wrong."

"No, sir. Wet socks."

Kett stared at him.

"I mean, I'm not saying kidnapping is fun. But wet socks are just awful. The worst. Ruins your whole day."

"You're ruining my day, Pete," he muttered.

A constable held the door open for them and they entered the main body of the garage. It was bigger in here than it had looked from outside, as deep as it was wide. A couple of cars occupied the middle of the space, one lifted on a jack. A third was suspended over the mechanic's pit. The place smelled of exhaust fumes and oil and rubber. Other than the four constables who idled by the desk, it was empty.

"Where'd all these Uniforms come from?" asked Porter. "Half the bloody Force is scratching their bollocks in here."

"Where'd it happen?" Kett shouted, his voice echoing off the stark walls.

One of the PCs walked over, pointing to a door leading to the smaller building.

"In there, sir. We've got some CCTV on the computer. Owner's out back, I'll go grab him."

Kett walked through the door into the smaller space, which was just about big enough to hold a single car. The concrete floor was covered with scuff marks from countless tyres, but right at the back of the room, maybe two feet across, was a crimson pentagram. It had been drawn quickly, but the artist had been careful to make sure the lines were unbroken. In the middle of it was another symbol, a skull. This had been done in chalk, although the skull's right eye was daubed with blood.

Kett took a photo of it, spluttering out a sigh.

"You ever remember anything like this happening in London, Pete?" he asked.

"Satanic shit?" Porter shook his head. "Oh, except that cult in Shoreditch. You remember them?"

"That wasn't a cult. That was four old ladies crocheting a blanket who got their pentagons and their pentagrams in a muddle."

"Four old ladies and their evil cat," he said. "Remember the cat?"

"No," he said.

"Evil."

The roller door was open, leading directly onto the forecourt. There was a CCTV camera mounted in the corner, facing the door, but the light wasn't on.

Kett returned to the main section of the garage, Porter slouching along beside him. Every time the DI put his right foot down, his shoe squelched. This, at least, brought a smile to Kett's face. There was another man waiting for them by the desk, struggling to hold up his own weight. He was immense, maybe six-two and twenty-five stone—most of that in his belly. He wore a pair of green cords held up with suspenders, and a sleeveless vest that seemed on the verge of giving up life completely. He whisked his flat cap off as they approached, using it to fan himself even though the building was as cold as the world outside. He was wheezing like he'd been kicked in the knackers.

"This is Bob McGarvey," said the constable. "Owns the place."

"Old Bob," said Bob.

"You what?" asked Kett.

"Call me Old Bob. Everyone else does." The man's accent was as local as they came, although he was so out of breath he was struggling to speak. He held out a sweaty hand, but Kett ignored it.

"Take a seat, Bob," he said. "Before you keel over."

The man was happy to oblige, the ancient swivel chair by the desk issuing a screech of distress as he dumped his bulk into it.

"You don't look old enough to be called Old Bob," Kett said.

"Son's Young Bob," he replied, his voice full of phlegm.

"Makes sense." He pulled out his warrant card. "I'm Middle-Aged Bob. DCI Robert Kett. This is Not-Bob, DI Pete Porter. Can you tell us about the lad who's missing?"

"Not missing," he said. "Taken. Name's Dennis Lynn. Son of a friend of mine. He's here on work experience, but paid."

"For how long?"

"Few weeks. He's good. Only seventeen, but knows his stuff. Better than the other pricks who work here."

"They around?"

"Sent them home," said Old Bob. "I can call them back?"

"In a bit," said Kett. "They were here this morning, though?"

He nodded, his neck bulging. His face was clean shaven, but there was a dense patch of hair beneath his chin, out of sight unless he lifted his head. Kett wondered if he even knew it was there.

"Three others here," said Bob, still struggling to get the words out. "They went out, though."

"They left?"

"They get lunch most days from Gregg's."

"You were here, though?"

His head swayed left and right.

"Haven't got it in me any more," he said. "One bad shit away from another heart attack. Kyle runs it for me now. Dennis is new. His dad's a mate of mine, fucking minted, he is. It's just a trial. Good head on his shoulders."

If it's still on his shoulders, thought Kett.

"Be even better if he managed to stay off his phone. Kids, they're addicted to them."

"His phone here?"

The man shook his head.

"You've got cameras? I saw one next door."

"One outside too," said Bob.

He coughed out a rattling breath as he leaned over the desk. The CCTV feed was already on the screen, and he used a sausage-shaped finger to press play. Kett put on his glasses and leaned in, engulfed by the cigarette and armpit smell of the man. On the small screen was the forecourt outside, deserted. The time stamp in the corner said 12:15.

"That right?" he asked.

"Hour out," said Bob. "Can't figure out how to change it when the clocks go back. It's right half the year."

"So quarter past eleven," said Kett. "Sound?"

"Not on the outside one."

It was no surprise. There was barely even a picture, the camera caked in dirt and grease, turning the forecourt into an impressionist painting. Still, it was clear enough to see the three young men who walked out of the door, swaggering their way onto the street and out of sight.

The time stamp clicked another minute, and then another. The only sign of movement was a handful of cars moving down the street.

"How long does this go on for?" asked Kett.

"What?"

"This." He gestured at the screen.

"Oh, about ten minutes," said Old Bob.

"Can you fast-forward it?"

He could, and he did, scrubbing the footage to 12:27. He stopped it just as a long, black hearse pulled into the forecourt. It did a neat three-point turn, then reversed towards the camera. There were no plates on the front or the back. Kett looked over the top of the monitor into the smaller room.

"That roller door was open this morning?" he asked.

Old Bob shrugged.

"Weren't here," he said, tapping his finger on the mouse. "Must've been, though."

He was right, the hearse backed all the way inside the building, leaving the forecourt empty again.

"You recognise it?" asked Kett, straightening up to relieve his aching back.

"The hearse? No. Never seen it. Got to be a Ford, though. Granada, probably. Classic, whatever it is."

"Rare?"

He nodded, flashing his secret chin beard again.

"Something like that, I reckon there's fewer than ten in the country. Granadas were common enough in the eighties and nineties, but this one's got a wanky bonnet and a bigger back end. Looks almost like a Capri up front. Somebody's chopped it up and remade it. If it's still going, they did a mint job."

"Good to know," said Kett.

They waited again, Kett's body knotted with impatience. Another five minutes, and he was about to ask Old Bob how long it was going to take for something else to happen when the hearse pulled out again. It turned onto the street and accelerated out of sight.

"Where's the feed from inside?" Kett asked.

Old Bob used his filthy fingers to fiddle with the filthy mouse and the filthier keyboard. A new window popped up on the screen, this one showing the smaller room and the open roller doors. The hearse was right there, reversing slowly until it filled the space. From this angle, Kett couldn't see anything past its big back end.

"What's he doing?" said Porter, leaning in so close their

shoulders touched. The smell of his aftershave managed to overpower the meaty scent of Old Bob.

The hearse answered with a blast of its horn, one that punched out of the speakers so loud Kett almost screamed.

"This camera has sound," said Bob.

"Thanks for the warning," he muttered.

The hearse sat there, clouds of exhaust filling the air. The horn blasted again, but Kett was ready for it this time. It seemed to go on forever, surely loud enough for the whole street to hear.

It took thirty seconds for somebody to show up. A teenage boy walked through the door, the resolution clear enough for Kett to see the anger on his face. He was dressed in baggy overalls, his head shaved almost to the scalp. He approached the hearse like it was a bomb.

"Hello?" he said.

"That's Dennis," said Bob. "Or *Denise*, as the lads call him."

"Why Denise?" said Kett.

"Because they're little twats. He can handle it, though. He won't let them give them any shit. Always going on about how much of an alpha he is, whatever that means."

Dennis walked to the driver's door of the hearse, cupping a hand to the glass and peering inside. He tried the handle, but it was locked.

"Where's the driver?" said Kett.

He obviously wasn't behind the wheel, because Dennis walked around the front of the hearse, poking his head outside for a second before checking the passenger door.

"Hello?" he called out. "Kyle? That you? I'm not falling for it."

It's not Kyle, Kett thought, wanting to shout the words back through time, wanting to tell Dennis to run.

The boy walked to the rear of the hearse, the angle of the camera meaning Kett could only see the top of his head. Even though his hair was cropped short, it was clear he had a pretty impressive bald spot. The coffin doors were shut tight, a set of curtains pulled across the window.

"Lad's mad," said Old Bob, clearing his throat. "Don't understand why he didn't scarper."

Dennis pulled the handle of the back door and it opened. Nobody breathed as he leaned into the darkness, his head vanishing, then his shoulders.

"Hello?"

Something wrenched the boy inside, hard enough to pull his feet off the ground. His scream rattled the computer's old speakers as he tried to resist, but it was like he'd been connected to a winch. He slid through the open door, his legs kicking, the hearse rocking. Another scream ripped through the quiet of the garage, this one heavy with words.

"Stop! I don't want this! I don't want this!"

"Christ," said Porter, one hand to his mouth.

The kid screamed a little more before something muffled his voice. There were a few dull thumps as he was hauled all the way inside, then silence.

Or was it silence?

"Hang on," said Kett. "You hear that?"

He thought he could make out words from inside the hearse, a voice made of smoke and gravel. He couldn't make any sense of it.

"That go any louder?" he asked.

"No," said Bob.

Kett leaned in a little more, locking his breath inside his throat. The voice came again, just a whisper, barely louder than the rumble of the engine.

"Empty boys don't talk."

The hearse wobbled again, and somebody climbed out of it. It was a man, but from this angle all Kett could see was long, matted hair over a bright red face. He was holding something in his gloved hand, and when he turned back to the hearse Kett saw that it was a knife. He jabbed the blade into the vehicle, then pulled it free with a spray of blood. Dennis screamed again, but it was weaker now.

"Empty boys don't bleed," said the man.

He ducked out of sight, revealing the open door of the hearse and Dennis' legs. They kicked feebly, one shoe off, a white sock covered in blood. He was trying to escape, but something was stopping him. The man was still out of shot.

"He's drawing the pentagram," said Kett. "The skull."

It didn't take long. After forty seconds or so, he stood up.

"Empty boys don't see," he grunted.

He climbed back into the hearse, clambering over Dennis' body. He turned back when he was inside, and as he reached for the open door he looked up.

He was wearing a mask, a demonic, blood-coloured face with painted teeth and short horns. The eyes were black holes that stared at the camera. Five seconds. Ten seconds—his gaze so intense that Kett had to resist the urge to look away.

"Empty boys don't breathe," said the masked man, as if he was speaking directly to them.

Then he pulled the door closed.

The hearse rocked as he made his way back to the driver's seat. Then it pulled out of the garage in a flare of crimson light.

"Shit," said Porter. "You think he killed him?"

"I don't know," Kett replied. "Is there anything else?"

"Just Kyle and the others coming back," said Old Bob. "About an hour and a bit after this."

"They always take that long to eat lunch?"

The man shrugged his enormous shoulders, releasing a fresh waft of BO.

"Gregg's," he offered as an explanation. "They called me when they saw the blood. I called you."

Kett walked away, calling Spalding as he went.

"What, sir?" she said when she answered, even grumpier than usual.

"Can you do me a favour, Alison? Kidnap victim was taken away in a hearse. It's a Ford Granada, but it might have a Capri bonnet. Eighties or Nineties, no side windows, no plates. Probably quite rare."

"I'll check it out," she said. "Anything else?"

"Oh, yeah, big rear end, Spalding," he said, remembering.

"*What*?" she said, no small amount of fury in her voice. "Is that a joke?"

"No," he replied, frowning. "Obviously not. Thanks."

He hung up, heading outside. Porter was already there, chewing on a pen like he was trying to transfigure it into a cigarette. Kett stood beside him, both of them shivering—and only partly because of the wind. He stared back through the roller doors, seeing the pentagram, that bone-white skull in the middle of it.

"Empty boys?" he said. "What does that mean?"

Porter shrugged.

"Dead?" he said after a moment. "He proper went for Dennis with that knife. Feels more like a murder than a kidnapping."

Kett wasn't willing to think that. Not yet. Not until they knew for sure.

"He knew about the camera," he said. "The masked man. He knew we'd see it. He's not afraid of us. Can you check with the Uniforms, Pete, see if they've canvassed the street? Must be some more CCTV. If we're going to get Dennis back, we need to work out where he went."

"Will do, sir. Where are you going?"

"To talk to Dennis Lynn's parents," he said, heading for the road. "Somebody had better tell them their son's missing."

CHAPTER EIGHT

It wasn't hard to find the Lynn house.

For a start, it was the biggest property on the street, a Victorian gothic red brick almost-mansion that sat right at the end of a cul-de-sac full of kowtowing bungalows. The gardens were so well tended they looked boastful, pockets of colour defying the November gloom.

The other reason Kett spotted it was because the words LYNN HOUSE were wrought in iron on the main gate, each letter a foot high.

There was an intercom, but it didn't seem to be working, so he gave one side of the gate a shunt and it wobbled open. He followed a sweeping, leaf-strewn driveway to the house, skeletal trees craning their bare arms over his head as if to welcome him. To ensure there was no confusion, there was a second sign by the front door, this one carved in stone. The door itself was twice as wide as it needed to be, painted navy blue with a window of stained glass. The brass knocker was shaped like a cannon, and the sound of it was like artillery going off, echoing down the street.

Kett took a few steps back, peering through the nearest

window to see a large living room. He thought something was moving inside, dancing, then he realised it was the reflection of the agitated trees in the dark glass.

He went to knock again, only to see a shape in the patterned glass. A lock turned and the big door swung open soundlessly, revealing a tall, thin woman in a long floral dress and a brown buttoned cardigan. She must have been somewhere in her forties, but she looked older because her hair was thin, patches missing, her scalp red raw in places. She lifted a hand and scratched at it as she studied Kett with watery eyes.

"Good afternoon," he said, pulling out his warrant card. "My name is DCI Robert Kett, of Norfolk Constabulary. Are you Mrs Lynn?"

She continued to scratch her scalp, her fingertips bloody. She didn't look away, the intensity of her gaze making Kett feel so uncomfortable he stepped back. He closed the warrant card but held onto it.

"Uh, is there anyone else I can speak with?" he said. "Is your husband at home?"

The answer was yes, because more footsteps echoed down the hallway. Kett looked past the woman to see a man jogging up, flustered. He was a little older, pushing fifty, wearing brown cords and a cream shirt, his tie flapping.

"Sorry," he said. "Sorry."

He reached his wife, one hand resting gently on her arm, as if not to scare her. He gave Kett an uncertain look until Kett lifted the warrant card again.

"DCI Kett," he said. "Police. You're Mr Lynn?"

"Victor," said the man. He had an accent. Newcastle, maybe. "Vic. Sorry, Diane's not well. She gets confused."

He pulled her back from the door, his fingers digging into the flesh of her arm. She winced, still scratching at her scalp, still staring at Kett. Then, as if somebody had clicked their fingers and woken her from a trance, she snapped her head around to her husband.

"I told you, I can't handle this," she said, ripping her arm free. Her accent was a softer version of his. "Just sort it!"

She walked off, her bare feet slapping on the tiled floor. Victor watched her climb the enormous stairs, then he turned back to Kett.

"Sorry," he said again, scratching his head in the same way his wife had done. "She's—"

He was cut off by a door slamming upstairs.

"Why are you here?" he said.

"Can I come in?" Kett asked. "It's about Dennis."

"No, it's not," the man said, as if that might decide the matter.

"I'm afraid it is. May I come in, Mr Lynn? It's important."

Victor huffed out a sigh, checking his arm even though he wasn't wearing a watch.

"Dennis is fine," he said. "He's at work. Not that it's actual work. He's training at this godawful place. *Cars*."

He spat the last word out like it had tasted bad.

"I'm afraid he's not at work," said Kett. "A little over two hours ago, somebody took your son."

"Took him where?" said Victor.

He didn't want to use the word, but he did.

"We think he was kidnapped."

Victor's lip curled into an unpleasant sneer and he extended a long finger. He was a good few inches taller than Kett, and he was lean rather than skinny. Kett wished he'd brought a PC with him—it wasn't like there hadn't been any to spare at the garage.

"That cretin Bob put you up to this?" Victor said.

"No. This is real. I can show you my ID again, if you need to see it. Or I can get some uniformed constables on site. Your son was forcibly taken from his place of work this morning. He was loaded into the back of a hearse and driven away. He was hurt. I don't know how I can make it any clearer than that."

The sneer fell away, and Victor seemed to shrink. He shook his head.

"That's impossible," he said. "Who would do that? *Why* would they do that? You know where he is, though, don't you?"

"No," Kett told him. "That's why I need to speak with you. Has Dennis mentioned anyone threatening him lately? Any arguments? Any new people in his life?"

"No," said Victor.

"Has he had money problems? Is he in debt?"

The man lifted his hands as if showing off his house.

"He doesn't need money. He doesn't even need a job. He certainly doesn't need to be getting his hands dirty for a disgusting specimen like Robert McGarvey."

"Bob told me you were friends."

"Bob's white matter is so full of margarine he doesn't remember how to wipe his own arse," Victor spat. "I use his garage for my MOT, it doesn't make us friends. When Dennis told us he wanted to train as a mechanic, I asked Bob if he'd take him on. In all honesty, I hoped spending time with that corpulent freak might put him off."

"*You* haven't done anything else to put him off?" Kett said.

"You're saying I'm responsible for whatever's happened to Dennis?"

"I'm just asking a question, Mr Lynn. Did you have anything to do with it?"

The man looked like he wanted to start shouting, but he swallowed down his rage, his Adam's apple so big it looked like it was going to push through his throat.

"No."

"Your wife?"

"Diane is sick," he said. "Early onset dementia. She doesn't have anything to do with this."

"I'm sorry," said Kett. "But I need you to think. Whoever took Dennis knew what they were doing. They knew he was alone, and they used violence to get him inside their vehicle. Has he mentioned anything that might help us understand why he was targeted?"

"No," said Victor. "He's a normal young man. Kind. Takes after his mother, before she started to turn like... like rotting fruit. I hate that he wants to work with somebody like McGarvey, fiddling about with shitty little cars. I wanted him to be a military man, like I was, like his older brothers are. Told him he'd be better learning the trade in the army, be a mechanic there. But he's too soft for it. That's his mother's fault too, him being the youngest child."

He paused, putting his hand in what was left of his hair, shaking his head. Kett could see it finally sinking in, the awful truth. When Victor spoke again, his voice started breaking.

"He's a good boy. Why would somebody do this to him?"

"Did your son ever mention a place called Cold Iron Paintball?" said Kett. "Or a man by the name of Joseph Maynard?"

"No," he replied. "Never. Who is that?"

"Hollenbeck?" asked Kett.

"No."

"Do you mind if I come in?" said Kett.

He still didn't look sure.

"You were a military man?"

Victor nodded.

"Then you know that when somebody's taken captive, you only have a short window in which to find them. You have to move fast. Right now, somebody has your son, and he's badly injured. Our best shot at getting him back is figuring out who he's been in contact with. I need to look inside your house, I need to check his room. I can do that in twelve hours or so when we come back with a warrant, or you can let me through the door now."

Victor lifted his hands in surrender, retreating into the hall.

"He's got a phone?"

"Never off it," said Victor. "Takes it with him every day, though God only knows how he gets any work done when he's glued to bloody YouTube. His bedroom's the second on the right. Please don't go into the front bedroom. It's Diane's now, and she's disturbed enough already. She can't help you, Detective."

Kett nodded, heading for the stairs.

"Do you need me?" Victor called after him.

"I'll be fine," Kett said, grabbing the banister and hauling himself up.

"Good. Because I have some calls to make."

The staircase was enormous, a stained-glass window halfway up where the stairs folded back on themselves. Oil paintings hung on the panelled walls, along with a coat of arms and a dozen framed photographs of Victor Lynn and his family. Kett paused at one of what had to be a teenage Dennis, standing next to two much older brothers. He was dressed in a tennis outfit and holding a racquet, bright eyes and a huge smile. It was the first time Kett had seen his face, and the images flooded his head: the terror as he was taken, the anger as he pummelled the sides of the hearse, the panic as he screamed to be freed, and the pain of the knife wound.

He used his phone to take a photo of it, his hand trembling.

There were more photos at the top of the stairs, Victor and Diane standing in front of various buildings, straight-faced, looking like they were having a terrible time. They reminded him of the couple in the famous American painting of the husband and wife, him holding a pitchfork, both dour. *American Gothic* was the name of it, but he couldn't for the life of him remember who the artist was.

He stopped again outside the door to the front bedroom, hearing somebody inside. He locked the breath in his lungs, leaning in. It was Diane Lynn's voice, and she sounded like she was talking to herself—endless chatter that didn't make any sense. It broke off, then turned into a hysterical laugh that made him start moving again.

The first door on the right was a bathroom. The second door led into a large bedroom at the back of the house. The curtains were drawn, so Kett switched on the light, seeing a double bed, a desk, and a wardrobe that looked big enough to take him to Narnia—all made from walnut. The bed was made, and what little clutter there was seemed to be tucked out of the way. The walls were panelled and papered, making it look like a hotel room. There were no posters, just a large mirror hanging by the window and a smaller one over the desk.

Kett checked the wardrobe and the desk drawers, groaning onto his hands and knees to look beneath the bed. It took less than five minutes to search the entire room, because there was nothing to find.

Cursing beneath his breath, he turned to leave only to

see Diane Lynn standing right behind him. It was like he'd stood on a live cable, the shock of it almost folding him in half.

"Bloody hell," he said, his heartbeat thrashing in his throat.

"Who are you?" the woman asked, scratching at the infernal mess of her scalp.

"Police," said Kett. He didn't bother to show her his warrant card this time. "I'm looking for your son."

"My son?" she said.

"Dennis. He's been... He's missing."

Her gaze drifted sideways, her expression so full of sudden alarm that Kett glanced around, half expecting to see something behind him. When he turned back, she'd taken a silent step towards him, close enough to touch. He jumped again, his skin tingling.

"Okay," he said, drawing the word out. He stepped around her, escaping onto the wide landing. "Can you think of anyone who'd want to hurt him, Diane? Any enemies? Any friendships that have ended recently? Relationships? Anything at all?"

Her head rotated like an owl's so that she could keep her eyes on him, almost too far to be possible.

"He's not okay," she said. "I know you think he's a good boy, but he's not."

"What makes you say that?" asked Kett. Something about her voice was familiar, the accent, but he couldn't put his finger on it.

"Diane?" came a voice from downstairs. Kett heard the creak of the stairs as Victor began to climb.

"He's not a good boy," Diane said again, using both hands now to scratch at her scalp. "You only have to see the things he watches to know he's not good."

"Watches? On TV?"

Victor reached the top of the stairs, glaring at Kett.

"I asked you not to disturb her," he said.

"I didn't," Kett told him. "She came to me."

"Bad boy," said Diane. "Bad boy."

"You got what you needed?" said Victor, and his meaning was clear.

"Thank you," Kett said, walking to the stairs. Victor didn't make way, forcing him to sidestep between the man and a bureau. "If you think of anything else, let us know. I don't have to tell you how important this is."

"You do your thing, I'll do mine," said Victor. "We'll get him back."

He looked deadly serious, and Kett remembered his talk of being a military man.

"Best you leave it to us, Mr Lynn," he said.

The sneer was back on Victor's face, and Kett turned to leave. Diane sang him out, her hoarse voice filling the stairwell like startled birds.

"He's a bad boy, he's a bad boy, he's the Devil's child!"

CHAPTER NINE

"Well, if it isn't my favourite detective!"

Emily Franklin welcomed Savage with a wave as she crossed the car park of Cold Iron Paintball. The young pathologist was wearing her trademark dungarees and a new, bubblegum-pink puffer jacket, and there was a pair of bright purple clogs on her feet. She was struggling to pull her bag out of the back seat of her blue TVR, and Savage gave her a hand. It pinged free with such force that they both almost went flying, one of Franklin's shoes slipping off.

"You've popped your clogs," said Savage.

"Bloody things," Franklin said, working her foot back into it. "Bugger to drive in, and walking's not much easier."

"Begs the question, why would you wear them?"

"Because they make me feel like a sexy Dutch princess," she said, waddling towards the building in a distinctly unsexy manner. "Where do I start?"

"Actually, can you start here?" said Savage, looking back to see Duke jogging towards them from the car. He was holding the box she'd found in Ian Hipkin's bedroom, its contents rattling about inside. "Don't worry, mate," Savage said as she took it from him. "It's only vital evidence made of fragile glass."

"Huh?" he replied.

"Like asking a donkey to carry a glass of wine," said Franklin.

"Huh?" he said again.

Savage opened the box, tilting it so that Franklin could look inside. Thankfully, the little glass jar was unbroken, but its contents had been rattled into a crimson froth.

"Is that real blood?" she asked.

"Hard to tell, it's been shaken so hard," Franklin replied.

She dropped her bag, working on a pair of forensic gloves before picking up the jar. She squinted into it before giving it a little shake.

"How come she gets to shake it and I don't?" Duke protested.

"Definitely real," said Franklin. "It's started to separate, but it's not entirely congealed. I'd put it at about three to four days. Where'd you find it?"

"Teenage boy's bedroom," said Savage.

"Crikey. In my day they just had nudey mags. You want it back?"

"Hang onto it," said Savage, closing the box. "Can you let me know if it's human?"

"Or sheep," said Duke.

"Sheep?" asked Franklin.

"You'll see," Savage told her. "You've got a whole smorgasbord of delights in there."

"Goodie!" said Franklin, practically skipping through the door.

Savage followed her in, navigating through the crowded corridors until she spotted Superintendent Clare. He was standing at one of the arcade machines, and as she closed in she saw that he was *playing* it. He was using both hands to attack the joysticks and buttons, spittle flying from his mouth with such force it decorated the screen.

"Sir?" she said, walking up behind him.

Clare slammed a fist down on a button so hard the screen went dark for a second. When it came back to life, the words 'YOU DIED' flashed on and off.

"You're going to die, you jug of monkey toss!" he said, diving into the gap between the machines with enough force to make them both rock. He ripped the plug from the wall and the music conked out with a sad whine. Clare swung back upright, turning his red, swollen eyes to Savage.

"You, Detective, just stopped me winning a final boss battle against a rabid, psychotic gorilla. Do you have any idea how that makes me feel?"

Clare looked a little like a rabid, psychotic gorilla about to engage her in battle, but she didn't comment.

"I spoke to Ian Hipkin's mother," she said. "I don't get the feeling she knew much about what her son was doing. He had a box of stuff in his bedroom, including a jar of blood. Franklin's checking it now to see where it came from. There's a notepad, too, a few scribbles that look like the same stuff we found here. Pentagrams, runes, the works."

She opened the box for him to take a look.

"I called the hospital on the way over. Ian's still out of it. But this looks like Maynard's influence, sir. The skull ring, the knife, the blood. I think Maynard might have been training him."

"Training him to do what?" said Clare.

Savage shrugged.

"Kill?" she said. "That's what Maynard does. It's what Hollenbeck did. They turn people into murderers, twist their minds, give them everything they need. It's a sport for them."

"Figures. Kett thinks they were using the dead sheep as practice. Maynard's the teacher?"

"Either him, or this other man Ian was talking about. The master."

"Master-bator, more like," grumbled Clare.

He wiped his sweaty face, pushing the heels of his hands into his eyes. When he pulled them away, his eyes were redder than ever, like he'd been pepper sprayed.

"You alright, sir?" Savage asked.

"No," he spat. "I've had a rigid cystoscopy without anaesthetic that was less awful than this. You heard about the kidnapped lad? Dennis Lynn?"

She nodded.

"Kett checked in on his parents. Says they're weird, but he doesn't think they have anything to do with it. But the mum mentioned something about the lad being a Devil child, whatever that means."

"Maynard," said Savage, closing the box and handing it back to Duke. "Again."

"Maybe," said Clare. "He's still unconscious, thanks to Gorski. But what does Maynard have to gain from kidnapping a seventeen-year-old boy? And why Dennis? He had a whole warehouse full of young men who were willing to die for him. Why not take one of them?"

"He didn't need to, sir," she said. "Those men were here by choice. Do we know anything else about the shooters?"

"We've identified two of them," said Clare. "Local men, in their early twenties. They've both been inside on drug charges. No idea about the third. Spalding's on it. Speaking of which, do you have any idea why she's in such a foul mood?"

"No, sir," said Savage. "She did seem a little frosty earlier."

"Did you find any evidence that Ian Hipkin was into drugs? Is he known to us?"

"No, sir," said Savage. "I don't think so. He came here for the paintball. His mum had no idea it was closed. She mentioned he saw a friend here, but I don't know if that's one of our dead men. Name's Liam."

"Might be our third shooter," said Clare. "Maynard was obviously recruiting them for something. Keep working on Ian. As soon as he wakes up, I want you there. He might be able to shed some light on this place."

Clare looked at Duke.

"What's wrong with you, Constable? Your batteries run out?"

"Huh?" said Duke, holding onto the box.

"You forgotten how to speak?"

"No, sir. Just thinking about... sheep."

Clare shot him a look of disgust before spinning around, the tails of his furry jacket sweeping up like a magician's. Savage followed the Super down the corridor and into the enormous space that made up the back of the building. She spotted Franklin next to a wooden shed on the other side of the room. She was holding a glass jar in her gloved hands, studying it in the artificial light. She glanced over at the sound of the Superintendent's angry footsteps, calling out.

"You want the good news or the bad news?"

"I want to go home for a tossing break," said Clare, causing a ripple of disgust to cross the room. "What have you got?"

"Five jars," she said. "The bad news is the blood's real. I won't be able to tell you if it's human or animal until I run some spectroscopic tests."

"Sheep," said Duke.

"And there's good news?" said Clare.

Franklin grinned, looking positively ghoulish. She placed the jar down on the floor and unscrewed it, using a pair of tongs to pull out a shrivelled, prawn-like object from inside.

"Please tell me that's not the dick jar," said Duke.

"It's the dick jar," Franklin replied, giving the withered member a gentle shake. Blood dripped from it, plopping back into the jar. "But this is not a dick."

Everybody crowded in, Savage doing her best to ignore the smell of old blood.

"It really does look like a severed... *you know*," she said.

"A sergeant gobbler," said Clare.

"*What*?"

"A French cheese baguette, a yabadabadingdong."

"Sir?"

"*Penis*," he elaborated. "You're sure it's not real?"

"I'm sure," Franklin said, twisting the object around so they could see the place where it had been cut from the body.

"Sheep?" said Duke.

"My guess is it's some kind of polyurethane foam," she said, ignoring him. "The kind fidget toys are made of."

She looked at Duke.

"And no, Aaron, by *fidget toy* I don't mean your genitals."

"Huh?" he replied.

"It's one hundred per cent fake, and so are the other items in the jars. A fake finger, a fake eye, a fake ear, a fake tongue, and this."

"A fake fleshy bishop," said Clare. "Why?"

"No idea," she said. "But they're all foam."

"Foam replicas, but real blood," said Savage. "That doesn't make any sense."

"Nothing here makes any sense," said Clare. "Our priority is finding out what kind of blood that is."

"Sheep," said Duke.

"And can somebody do something about Duke's bloody ovine Tourette's?" Clare added, marching off. "Before his woolly Johnson ends up in a jar on my desk?"

Duke covered his crotch with Ian Hipkin's box.

"You need anything else, Emily?" asked Savage.

"I'm good," she replied, heading back into the shed.

Savage's phone rang, and she pulled it out of her pocket, seeing an unknown mobile number. She headed for the exit as she answered it.

"Hello?"

"Is this the detective?" said a voice, and there was anger in it. "The one who came to see me this morning?"

"Mrs Hipkin?" she asked. "Yes, this is DC Savage. How's Ian?"

"I'm with him now," said the woman. "He's in a bad way. You lot mashed up his fucking face. He can't barely speak he's so swollen up."

"I'm sorry," said Savage, walking outside. "Is he okay, though? Apart from that?"

The woman's sigh rattled the phone.

"He's scared," she said. "He's not making any sense. He thinks somebody's coming after him."

"There are police with you, aren't there?" said Savage. "In the hospital?"

"Yeah, but he says they can't do nothing. He says somebody's coming for him."

"Helen, the man who did this to Ian is in custody. He can't hurt anyone else."

It wasn't strictly true, of course. Nobody knew how extensive Maynard's network was, how many of Hollenbeck's ghosts were at his beck and call. He could have people in the hospital right now.

He could have people *here*.

Savage scanned the crowd of coppers, realising how few she recognised. She turned to the wall of the building, speaking quietly.

"Ian is safe."

"He's not worried about the old man," said Hipkin. "He won't say who's scaring him."

"Is he okay to talk, do you think? We really need to speak with him. I can come myself, I can—"

"No," said the woman. "He's not ready. They've given him something to help him sleep. But he asked me to call you."

"He did?"

"Yeah. He wanted me to tell you something. I didn't make much sense of it, but I said I'd pass it on. He said he weren't alone at the paintball place this morning. He said there were four other guys with him."

"We know," said Savage. "Three young men, and an older one."

"Nah, that ain't right. He said there were four other kids like him, all of them working for the older bloke."

"Hang on, so there were six of them here this morning?"

"Maybe. I don't know. I don't know *anything*. He just asked me to ask you if you'd found his mate."

"Liam?"

"Yeah. Said he was in the hellcat."

"Hellcat?"

"That's all he'd tell me. When he's sorted himself out,

I'll let you know and you can ask him yourself. But he's been through enough. You leave him alone, yeah?"

"Look, if there's somebody else here, I need to know... Helen?"

She'd gone, the line dead.

Savage swore, heading back into the building and almost colliding with Duke. He dropped the box, scattering its contents over the sawdust floor.

"Whoops," he said, bending down to collect them.

"There's somebody else," she said, heading across the room. "There were five lads, not four. Ian mentioned Liam again. He might still be here."

She spotted Hay, and called over to her.

"Have you searched the whole building, Cara?"

"As well as we can," she said. "But we found one secret room and a bloody great tunnel, so who's to say there's not more?"

Savage scanned the warehouse, her brain on overdrive.

"Hellcat," she said.

"Huh?" asked Duke.

"Ian said Liam was inside the hellcat. Mean anything to you?"

Duke stared at the ceiling, his brow furrowing.

"Do *not* say sheep, Aaron."

"I wasn't going to say sheep," he protested.

"Hellcats are cars, aren't they?" said Savage, jogging down the short corridor towards the outside door. "Dodges. I'm sure of it."

"Haven't seen any," said Duke. "But the hellcat was a plane, too. An American one."

They stepped outside, the overgrown paintball yard stretching all the way to the distant fence. There were a dozen buildings out here of various shapes and sizes, plus countless barricades and shelters—all drenched in colourful paint. On the far left of the field was an army truck, the canvas stripped from its back to expose its skeletal, empty frame.

On the far right, hidden from the sky by sheets of camouflaged netting, and barricaded by a maze of boxes, was a—

"Tank," said Duke, seeing it too. "There was a tank called the Hellcat in World War Two."

Savage leaned back through the door. Hay had vanished, but the room was still full of coppers.

"Anyone check the tank?" she shouted.

"Bolted shut," one yelled back. "Nobody's been in there for a long time."

She turned back, only for Duke to thrust his phone in her face. On the screen was a photo of a tank.

"That's it, the Hellcat. Looks exactly the same."

She set off, wading through the overgrown meadow, tripping on loose bricks and slipping on old paint. The tank was smaller than it looked from the other side of the field, short enough that she could see the hatch on the turret if she stretched up on her tiptoes. Just like the PC had said, it was sealed—ten enormous bolts rusted with age and glued with paint.

She rapped her hand on the body of the tank, hearing the echo reverberate inside like a drum.

"Anyone there? It's the police."

Nothing.

"Definitely a Hellcat," said Duke as he caught up. He had the box under one arm and was staring at his phone. "Did you know these things could hit fifty-five miles per hour? That's insane."

She made her way around the tank. Her foot snagged on

a tuft of long grass and she slipped, catching the back of her hand on a corner. The pain was unreasonably bad, and she put her bloodied knuckle to her mouth.

"You alright?" asked Duke.

She ignored the question, ducking beneath the enormous turret gun and using her other hand to knock again.

"Police," she said. "Anyone there?"

She was answered by a thump of metal, loud enough that she almost vomited out her heart.

"Anyone inside?" Duke shouted, and she realised *he'd* made the noise, kicking the tank with his shoe.

"That's really not helpful," she told him.

She stretched up to check the bolts again, but there was no way they could be opened—a glue of rust and paint that looked decades old. She ducked down to look underneath the vehicle, finding only weeds and old drink bottles between the broken tracks.

"What else could it mean?" she said, walking back the way they'd come. "Hellcat?"

Something knocked weakly against the tank again, a metallic whisper.

"I said that isn't helpful, Aaron."

But when she turned to Duke, she saw that he was right behind her.

She stopped, willing her heart to quieten. Duke froze too, his face serious. She counted to ten, wondering if it had been her imagination, and she was just about to say it when the knock came again.

There was no denying it this time, it had come from inside the tank.

"Shit," she said, running back. "Hello? This is the police. If you're in there, knock again."

Ten more beats of silence, then a soft *clank*.

"Give me a hand, will you?" she said.

Duke dropped the box on the ground, cradling his hands and letting her step into them. He lifted her with such strength she almost flew over the top of the turret, and she had to grab a metal strut to steady herself.

"Go get help," she said to Duke. "Find an angle grinder or something."

He scarpered, lumbering over the field. Savage turned her attention to the hatch, grabbing one of the enormous bolts and trying to twist it. It didn't budge, but when she adjusted her position, she heard the entire roof of the tank rattle.

She scooted back, finding a ridge of metal next to the circular hatch. When she dug her fingers beneath it and tugged, the panel wobbled. She got into a squat and tried again, managing to lift the heavy iron lid a few inches before it slipped out of her grip and clanged down again. Somebody had sheared off the entire roof, she realised, hatch and all.

"Hang on," she said. "We're coming."

She jumped down, searching the tangled grass and the scenery until she found a flag jutting out of the ground. It took most of her strength to pull the iron pole free, and she hurled it onto the top of the tank, planting a foot on the caterpillar tracks and hauling herself back up. Her hand was bleeding badly now, leaving crimson smears everywhere. She'd jarred her knee, too, when she'd jumped.

It didn't matter. She jammed the spiked root of the flagpole beneath the panel and shunted hard. It lifted an inch or so and she kept pushing, driving her shoulder into the pole. The panel—including the bolted hatch—rose another few inches before slipping free, sliding off the edge of the turret.

Savage tried to stop herself from falling, but the sudden movement of the panel had thrown her. She dropped into the tank, cracking her elbow on the edge as she fell, landing on something soft. It was pitch black inside, even with the roof open, and the stench was unreal—like an open sewer. Gagging hard, she pushed herself to her feet, clicking on her torch, seeing the mechanical interior of the tank, seeing the walls smeared with faeces and blood and God only knew what else.

Seeing the body wrapped in black bin bags at her feet.

It was practically mummified, its legs bound together, its hands wrapped against its sides, its head completely covered except for the mouth and the nose—both crusted with vomit. Savage couldn't tell if it was a man or a woman, but they were alive, breathing weakly.

"You're okay," said Savage, dropping back down. She rested her free hand on the person's plastic-wrapped cheek. "You're going to be alright. Give me a second."

She planted her torch on the ground and tried to prise the plastic away from the person's face. It was wrapped too tight, she couldn't get her fingers beneath it. They were struggling now, writhing from side to side, uttering a series of wet gasps and half-spoken words. The voice seemed too deep to belong to a woman.

"Easy," she said. "You're okay."

Savage took the man's head, trying to lift him up. He jerked back, a whispered word.

"Don't..."

"We have to get you out," said Savage.

She pulled again, wondering where the hell Duke had got to. The mummified guy still resisted, like he wanted to lie down again.

"Don't," he said again. "He'll kill us both, he'll kill us both, he'll—"

"He's gone," she said. "Maynard's been arrested."

"No," he said. "Leave me. Please. Please. Please. Please."

"Not going to happen."

She grabbed the man again, using all of her strength to haul him into a sitting position. Past the thrashing beat of her pulse she heard footsteps, Duke calling her name.

"I'm inside," she said, her shout echoing. "Hurry!"

A clatter of feet on the outside of the tank, then Duke appeared above the hatch—just a silhouette against the netting overhead, blotting out the light.

"Shit," he said. "What is that?"

"Not what, *who*," said Savage. "Help me get him up."

"You want to cut him out of that stuff first?"

She would have, but it was so cramped inside the tank, and so dark, that she was more likely to hurt him than free him.

"Just get him out," she said.

There was no room for Duke to climb in, so he reached down, his fingers wiggling. Savage managed to grab the mummified man around the waist, heaving him up like a caber ready to be tossed. He was surprisingly light, but he was struggling so much Savage almost dropped him. Duke took hold of the man and hauled him up through the hatch.

There was a string attached to the guy's feet, Savage noticed. No, a *wire*, one that grew taut.

And suddenly went slack.

Something small and metallic hit the floor of the tank. Savage didn't have her torch in her hand, but there was enough light to see the circular pin lying in the filth-encrusted interior.

And there, right next to it, a grenade.

Fuck.

She grabbed the lip of the turret and hauled herself up, seeing Duke and the plastic-wrapped man waiting for her on the roof. There was no time to speak. She planted two hands on Duke and pushed him off the turret, watching him fall, squawking, into a sea of waiting constables. She grabbed the man and rolled both of them off the roof.

They hit the ground together, hard, her on top.

"What the—" said Duke.

Inside the tank, the grenade exploded—the loudest sound Savage had ever heard. The concussive force of the blast knocked all of the light from the day, strong enough to turn her brain to jelly. A whine broke out inside her ears like somebody was using a dentist drill inside her skull, and she clamped her hands to her head, burying her face in the wet ground.

She felt hands on her back, on her arms. Then Duke lifted her like she was a child, cradling her to his chest, carrying her away from the smoke and the fire and the screams.

CHAPTER TEN

"A *WHAT*?" SAID KETT.

He was riding in the passenger seat of Porter's Mondeo, the world a grey blur through the rain-lashed windows. The wipers were going ten to the dozen, a frenzied heartbeat that echoed his own.

"A grenade," said Clare, his voice crackling.

Kett switched it to speaker so that Porter could hear.

"Everyone alright, sir?" Porter said, slowing the car down to a crawl before pulling into a lay-by.

"Barely," Clare said. "Maynard rigged some sort of trap inside the tank. He'd wrapped a young lad in bin bags and duct tape and left him there, in the dark. We don't know how long, he's not talking. Kid was covered in his own shit and piss and vomit. There was a wire connected to his ankle, rigged to pull the pin on a grenade if he tried to leave."

"Or if somebody tried to rescue him," said Kett.

"Right. Savage found him, she pulled him out."

The warmth drained from Kett's body, the car icy cold.

"She's okay?"

"She's okay," said Clare. "She got out, but only just. A few cuts and bruises. She's riding to hospital now with the kid."

"Duke?"

"No. I mean yes, he's there too, but the kid she rescued... Paramedics tried to cut him out of the plastic sheeting but... they think it's glued to his skin."

"Christ," said Kett. "We know who he is?"

"Savage thinks his name might be Liam. Ian Hipkin, the paintball kid, was the one who told her about him. They were friends. Spalding's trying to find an ID."

A lorry blasted past on the road, rocking the car and spraying rain over the windows. Kett had to swallow his heart back down before speaking.

"This is insane, sir," he said. "That's two kidnapped boys. Three, if you count Ian."

"Ian was there because he wanted to be," said Porter. "I don't think he's a victim. Not in the same way."

"Two, then," said Kett. "One stuffed in a tank and rigged to a grenade. The other loaded into a hearse and stabbed. What's Maynard getting from this? What's his end game?"

"Whatever it is, we're going to stop him," said Clare. "He's in custody. He can't control anything. Forget Maynard. The person we want is the man who was driving the hearse. He's the one we focus on. Hipkin told Savage that he went by the master, whatever that means. Anything else on him?"

"No, sir," said Kett. "We found a few cameras, followed his progress to the A1065 then we lost him. He was heading south. There's a full alert. Everyone is looking for him."

"Can we see his face on any of the footage?"

"No, sir. He's wearing a mask, maybe a wig too."

"Of course he bloody is," said Clare. "Keep looking."

"You want us back there, sir?"

"Christ, no."

And he hung up.

"Bit rude," said Porter, drumming a tune on the wheel. "You believe that? A grenade?"

Kett could believe it. He'd seen it before, the weapons these people had access to, the damage they could do.

"What now, sir?" said Porter. "I could murder a burger. Maccy D's not too far from here."

"Sure," said Kett, feeling his stomach twist with hunger.

Before Porter could even put the car in gear, though, Kett's phone rang again. It was Spalding, and he reluctantly answered it.

"Alison, how's it going?"

"I'm not sitting down, sir, if that's what you're asking," came the reply. She sounded out of breath.

"That's not what—"

"There's nobody called Liam on the missing person register," she went on, still huffing. "But, like always, I dug a bit deeper. Social services did a welfare check on a group home in Horsford at the weekend. Three kids, two of them brothers. They filed a complaint because the place was filthy and the woman running it wasn't there."

"They got the kids out?"

"No. They deemed it wasn't bad enough for an intervention, just a warning. Anyway, they did a follow-up check yesterday. Place was empty, no sign of anyone."

"They called us?"

"They did, but nobody's been out yet. One of the brothers is called Liam Uysal. Brother is Emil. They're twins, seventeen years old."

"Can you send me the address?" he asked.

"I wasn't planning on keeping it to myself, sir," she shot back. "Unlikely it's the kid you're looking for, *but* there's always a chance."

"Big but, Alison," he said.

"What?" she shouted back, loud enough to rattle the speakers.

Kett hung up, frowning.

"Does she seem extra angry to you today?" he asked Porter.

"Just the usual level of angry," he replied, shrugging. "Where are we going?"

The answer arrived as a text, an address spelled out in angry capital letters. Kett held it up and Porter pouted.

"Maccy's is the other way," he said.

"Then it will have to wait."

THE HOUSE WAS a red-brick ex-council place on the northern edge of Horsford, separated from its neighbours by high hedges and knackered fences. The overgrown garden was a museum of forgotten furniture: rattan sofas that were rotted away, a shattered glass table, and a parasol that lay on the grass like a defeated king at the end of a chess game. A cat was licking its arse on the cracked path that led to the front door, and it didn't move even when they stepped over it.

"Don't mind us," Kett said, knocking on the front door. "Check the back, Pete."

Porter sloped off, swearing at the monstrous hedge as he pushed past it and down the side of the house. Kett knocked again, then opened the letterbox and stared into the dark interior. There was no sign of anyone, and the air was still.

"Hello?" he called out. "It's the police, can you open up?"

"It's useless," came a high-pitched reply. "It won't work."

"What won't work?" he said. "Who's in there?"

"I'm not in there."

"What?" Kett said, squinting into the dark.

"You ought to get your bloody hearing checked," the voice said. "I'm over here."

Kett straightened up, looking behind him to see nobody on the street. The garden was deserted too, and when he took a few steps back there wasn't anyone in any of the upstairs windows.

"Where?"

"Here!" said the voice.

Kett turned to the enormous hedge that stood between this house and the next one along. It had to be ten feet high, and it waved in the wind like a madman.

"That's it," said the squeaky voice. "Here."

"You're in the hedge?" said Kett, half expecting to find some kind of leprechaun peering through the branches.

"I'm not in the hedge," said the person, and as if to disprove its own words, a hand emerged from the branches, waving.

Kett walked over, angling his head until he could see through the foliage to the garden on the other side. Somebody stood there, a woman with a round face and small glasses. She was short enough that Kett had to duck down to see her. She really did look like some kind of hedge fairy.

"You the social?" the woman asked. "Knew you'd be back."

"We're police," Kett told her.

"Knew you'd be here n'all," she said. "For them boys."

"You've seen them recently?" said Kett, pulling at a branch to get a better look at who he was talking to.

"Oh, sure," she said. "Arseholes."

"The boys?"

"No, not them. They're good as gold. Two of them are brothers, you know? They always tell me their names and I always forget. Turkish, they are. Got no mum or dad, and they ended up here. Arseholes."

"Sorry, who are the arseholes?"

"Maggie, twat who runs the place," said the woman. "And her boyfriend, Doug, whenever he shows up. You know, they used to run a dog place here, look after your dogs and cats or whatever. Then they got in trouble because they weren't treating them right. So what did they do? Set up a bloody group home instead. For kids. How were they allowed to do that? I seen how they treat those boys. They were kinder to the dogs."

"When was the last time you saw them?"

"The arseholes or the kids?"

"Any of them."

"Haven't seen Maggie since the weekend, and haven't smelled her cigarettes either. Saw the boys yesterday morning, gave me a wave as they headed up the street."

"What time was that?"

"School time," she said. "They get the bus into the town. Good boys, like I said."

"They didn't come home?"

"No idea."

"You mentioned they're brothers. You know the other kid who lives here?"

"No," she said. "He's not so friendly. Comes and goes. He's a little older. Haven't seen him for..." She clucked her tongue. "No idea, to be honest."

"We'll take a look," said Kett. "If you think of anything else, let us know."

"Will do," said the hedge fairy. "Key's under the cup by the front door if you need it."

He looked back, seeing an upturned mug by the step. When he turned back to thank her, though, she'd completely vanished.

"Weird," he said, heading for the house.

He lifted the mug, and sure enough there was a Yale key there. He picked it up just as Porter was returning. The DI kicked and beat his way through the groping branches of the hedge like he was having a karate fight.

"What's up with you?" Kett asked him as he stomped over.

"They've got a bloody pond," he said. "But it was so full of green shit I didn't see it."

The laugh was out of Kett before he could stop it.

"To be fair, your sock was already wet," he said.

"That was the other one! Now I've got two!"

Kett slid the key into the door, still chuckling.

"Where'd you get that from?" asked Porter.

"Magical hedge fairy," he replied.

He pushed the door open and stepped inside, smelling something unpleasant.

"You getting that?" he said.

Porter inhaled through his nose, then nodded.

"Food?"

"Maybe."

The house was freezing, the way old council places always were. Kett had a flashback to visiting his gran as a kid, an ex-council home in Bowthorpe that was always colder than the day outside, no matter what time of year it was. The decoration wasn't far off, either, floral wallpaper that was peeling in the corners, knock-off G-Plan furniture that was covered with so many chips and scratches it might have been rescued from a skip.

A photo of two boys hung over the sideboard by the front door, and Kett popped his glasses on so he could see it. They sat on a wall, one lad's arm around his brother, a football on his lap. Both squinted into the sun, but neither smiled. They were clearly brothers, although far from identical.

"Did Spalding say they were twins?" Kett said.

Porter nodded, heading into the living room.

"What a shithole," he said.

He wasn't wrong. There were two chairs in the room, and a TV that looked like it was older than Kett was. Half of the carpet had been rolled up, the wooden boards beneath heavily stained. In the corner was a basket of toys that looked better suited to a toddler—a plastic garage with no cars, eyeless teddies with their stuffing hanging out. Next to that was a football that had been deflated. The smell wasn't so bad here.

"How do people get away with this?" Porter went on, walking to the window.

"Too many kids, not enough homes," said Kett. "Gives people plenty of opportunity to be arseholes. I'll take upstairs."

He hauled himself up the creaking staircase to the landing, hitting a wall of odour that made him stop dead. He put a hand to his face, his skin crawling as he followed the stench to the bedroom at the back of the house. It was pitch black inside, the curtains closed.

Reaching in, he switched on the light.

"Christ," he said.

In the middle of the room was a bed, and lying on the

bed was a dead woman. Her enormous fluffy dressing gown had fallen away, revealing blue pyjama trousers, an Oasis T-shirt, and the handle of a kitchen knife jutting from her chest. There was a smaller wound on one leg, like somebody had cut away a piece of skin. Her face was covered with a towel, which Kett was immensely grateful for.

On the wall above her, four feet wide and painted in blood, was an upside-down pentagram—two points aimed at the ceiling like horns. A skull had been drawn in the middle of it, one eye hollow, one red.

"Christ," he said again.

He retreated onto the landing, heading into the room next door and using his elbow to click on the light.

"Pete," he yelled as he went. "Gonna need you up here, mate."

The second bedroom was perfectly normal, if a little like a prison cell. A set of bunk beds took up almost all the space, a lopsided poster of a football team pinned to the wardrobe. A chest of drawers with no drawers held a pile of clothes.

"Pete!" he yelled.

He was answered by a shout.

"Oi!"

Porter's voice from downstairs, raised in anger.

"Stop!"

A clatter of feet, a door crunching open at the back of the house. Kett ran for the landing then changed his mind, doubling back and ripping open the heavy curtains of the back bedroom—just in time to see a man dressed in black legging it across the small garden. He vaulted the fence at the back, vanishing into the neighbour's bushes seconds before Porter appeared. The DI stopped halfway across the grass, unsure.

Kett wrenched open the window, yelling down.

"That way! He jumped the fence."

Porter took off, making it three steps before plunging into an invisible, algae-covered pond.

"Aargh!" he screamed, up to his thighs in stagnant water.

"Seriously?" Kett shouted.

He turned, racing for the landing, pulling his phone out as he went.

"Christ!"

CHAPTER ELEVEN

PORTER WADED THROUGH THE BASTARD POND, everything from his toes to his arsehole absolutely drenched in freezing sludge. He grabbed the thick grass, hauling himself out an inch at a time, breathless by the time he was back on solid ground.

Gasping, he glanced back at the house—no sign of Kett, thank God—then turned to the fence. There was no sign of the man, either, but he couldn't have got far.

He moved as fast as his sodden trousers would let him, water spraying from his Cleverleys. The stench of the pond clung to his clothes and his skin, bad enough that he still couldn't get a breath.

"Oi!" he said, hoping the guy was close enough to hear him. "Stop!"

The man had been hiding in the pantry, and he'd scared the shit out of Porter when he'd opened the door—enough that he'd actually fallen on his arse. Thankfully nobody had seen it, the guy bolting through the back door before Porter had even found his feet. He hadn't got a good look at him—partly because the man was wearing a hood, and partly because Porter had been on the floor. He'd looked young, though.

The fence was six feet tall and reinforced with ivy, but it was rotten enough that Porter charged right through it. Past that was a wall of bushes, and he punched and kicked his way through them, driven by fury.

"Out of the way, you leafy bastards!"

He exploded from the border into a long, narrow garden, the back of the neighbouring house twenty yards away. There was a woman in the window, washing up, and she gestured frantically to her right.

Porter followed her finger to another fence, this one shorter but much sturdier. He peered over it, seeing nothing in the garden next door. He started to climb, but stopped when he heard a noise behind him—a crash that came from the *other side* of the garden he was in.

He doubled back, glaring at the woman in the window, who flashed her middle finger at him. There was a hedge on this side of the garden, but the place where it met the garage was sparse enough for him to squeeze through, branches scratching at his face and neck, a twig ramming itself so far up his nose he thought he'd been lobotomised.

"Bloody twig!" he roared at it, falling out of the hedge.

He pinched his aching nose, scanning the garden through watering eyes. His legs and his feet and his crotch were itching something rotten, and he wondered how many pond creatures he'd picked up.

"Where are you, you prick?" he called out. "Get back here!"

His phone was ringing and he answered it as he crossed the grass, the wet screen barely working.

"Pete, you okay?" said Kett.

"No, I'm not okay," he said.

"You got him?"

"I've got pond herpes," he said, scratching his thigh. "No, I don't have him."

He sped up as he ran to the next fence, his shoes squelching.

"Where are you? I'm going to find you, you little turd."

"Be careful," said Kett. "There's a dead woman in the house. She's been stabbed."

Porter slowed down.

"Shit, really?"

"Yeah. Bloody great pentagram on the wall, too. *Literally* bloody. You see who it was?"

"No," he said. "Black tracksuit, hood. Definitely male. Probably young, he took off quick enough."

Porter reached the fence, peering over it to see another garden. There was no sign of the kid. He set off towards the house, making his way down the passage and out onto the street.

There, twenty yards ahead, a figure in black.

"I've found him, sir, he's heading for the main road."

Porter took off again, his legs freezing cold as he blasted down the street. He lowered the phone, yelling.

"I am in no mood for this! Stop running!"

The man didn't hear him, or didn't care. He reached the end of the road and swung right, almost slipping over. It took an age for Porter to catch up, and he cut across a small green to save time—planting his foot in a pile of dog shit the size of an actual dog. He screamed again, missing his step and sprawling onto his hands and knees.

"Bastard dog shit!" he shouted, picking himself up.

He rounded the corner, limping, reeking of shit and pond water, only to see that reinforcements had arrived. Two members of the tactical unit, Chester Andilet and Joe

Carmichael, stood on the street, both aiming their rifles at the kid who had run from the house. He had curled himself into a ball, which wasn't surprising. Kett was jogging up behind them.

"Where did you two come from?" Porter asked.

"The Super sent us, sir," said Carmichael. "To keep you out of the shit."

He wrinkled his nose as the DI ran up.

"See it's too late for you, though."

Kett looked Porter up and down.

"What the hell, Pete?" he said. "Where have you been? The zoo?"

"No," he spluttered, pulling leaves from his hair. "That scrote led me through the bloody gardens. Ponds. Hedges. There was a..." He pointed back. "Big shit."

He planted his hands on his soggy hips.

"Can you cuff him, Joe?" said Kett.

Carmichael stowed his weapon, pulling out a plastic zip tie. The kid didn't resist, he just lay there, his face pressed to the ground. He seemed to be sobbing beneath his hood. Kett pulled it away from his face, revealing a teenage boy—dark hair, red eyes, a fuzz of hair on his top lip and plenty of spots. His tracksuit was a Nike one, as were his trainers, and he had an expensive-looking watch on his right wrist. It looked like an Omega, and a nicer model than Porter's one. His phone lay on the pavement a few feet away, along with a bunch of keys.

The kid craned his head around to look at Kett, nothing but fear in his expression.

"Don't kill me," he said.

"Kill you?" Kett replied. "We're not going to kill you. We're police."

"I might," Porter grumbled beneath his breath.

The boy didn't seem to relax, turning to the two tactical officers, then to Porter. His face screwed up, his breathing shallow.

"To be fair, that smell could kill anyone," Kett said. "Back off a bit, will you, Pete?"

Porter retreated a few steps, giving the kid evils.

"I wouldn't smell like this if you hadn't bloody run," he said. "What were you thinking?"

"I thought you were going to hurt me," the kid said. "I thought you were going to do me like you did Miss Poovey. I got scared, I ran. Shrek followed me."

"Shrek?" said Porter.

"You are a bit green, mate," said Kett. "We said we were police."

"Yeah, but then he screamed at me and I panicked."

"You screamed?" said Carmichael, looking at Porter.

"He jumped out at me!"

"Then you fell on your arse," said the kid. "And I didn't think police did that."

"You fell on your arse?" said Andilet, deeply unimpressed.

"I did *not* fall on my arse. It was an evasive manoeuvre. And yeah, police *do* do that when somebody jumps out of a pantry."

"What's your name?" said Kett.

The kid sniffed, resting his cheek on the cold pavement. Porter could hear sirens floating on the wind, and he wondered how he was ever going to explain the wet trousers and shit-caked shoe. He already knew the tactical team would be gossiping about it for the rest of the week.

"Jon," he said. "Heath."

"And Miss Poovey, that's Maggie, right?"

He nodded as well as the pavement would let him.

"You live in the house, with the Uysal brothers, Liam and Emil?"

Another nod.

"I didn't kill her, though. I swear."

There wasn't any hint of a lie in his voice, and Kett helped him into a sitting position. The kid shuffled back until he was leaning against a wall, his face a solid block of misery. People were out of their houses now, watching from the doorsteps and gates. They didn't look friendly.

"We're police," said Porter, holding up his warrant card.

"*You* don't look like police," one woman called back.

"Because I fell in a pond," he said. He gestured at the two tactical officers. "Police, obviously."

"Can you tell us what happened, Jon?" Kett asked, ignoring the crowd.

"I don't know," he said, squinting into the sun. "I just came home, found Miss Poovey like that. Dead. I didn't think it was real except for the... for the smell. Proper rancid. *Is* it real?"

"Yeah," said Kett. "It's real."

The sirens were closer now, and an IRV pulled around the corner, its lights on. It revved up the road, stopping beside them. A single constable got out, adjusting his hat. He looked at Porter with a bemused expression.

"I fell in a pond," Porter yelled before the man could say anything. "And stood in a big shit."

"You want to sit in the car, Jon?" asked Kett. "Get off the cold ground?"

The kid shook his head, curling his knees up to his chest.

"When did you get here?" asked Kett.

"Just before you," he said. "I swear. I came home, got a drink, went upstairs to my room and... and *she* was in it."

"That's your bedroom?" said Kett.

He nodded again, sniffing.

"I ran back down. Thought the person who did it might still be there. Was gonna leave, then I saw you in the front garden, so I hid."

"Hid from the police," said Porter.

"I didn't know you were police, I swear," he said. "You could have been the ones who did it. It's only when I saw these two with... with *guns* that I knew."

"Where were you this morning?" Kett asked him.

He looked up, his face wrinkling.

"What?"

"Where were you, before you were here?"

"Dad's," he said. "Stay there some nights, when he's about. Been there since Monday. Don't spend more time here than I have to. All the shouting."

"Who does the shouting?"

Another IRV rolled into the street, stopping a little way off.

"Liam and Emil," he said. "Always arguing, fighting. Seen them knock ten shades of shit out of each other sometimes."

"Today?"

He shook his head.

"Haven't seen them since Monday morning. They were leaving the house."

"For school?"

He laughed, his next words dripping with sarcasm.

"Yeah. School."

"They don't go to school?"

He didn't answer.

"When was the last time you saw Maggie?"

He glanced up like it was a trick question.

"Last time you saw her *alive*?"

He shrugged his bony shoulders, sniffing.

"She fucked off after the social came. Stays with her other half."

"Doug?"

"Yeah. Proper cunt. I hate him. Seen him beat ten shades of shit out of Liam, too."

Kett met Porter's eye, the same rage passing between them.

"You haven't seen her since the weekend?" said Kett.

He shook his head.

"Liam and Emil have been here alone, then?"

He didn't know, it was written all over his face.

"How old are you, Jon?" said Kett.

"Eighteen," he said. "Only for another couple of weeks, though."

"You got a job?"

He didn't reply, staring at his knees.

"Because that's a nice watch," said Porter. "Omega?"

"Fake, innit," he said.

"Nah," Porter went on, looking at his own Omega, which had set him back nearly eight grand on his fortieth birthday. "I know a real one when I see it. I've got expensive taste."

"No you don't," said the kid. "You're wearing *shit* shoes. Literally."

Carmichael barked out a laugh, then stifled it behind his hand.

"Where did the money come from?" asked Kett.

"Nowhere," he said.

"Jon, I'm not messing around here, mate. We just found you inside a house with a dead woman, an abusive guardian you had a pretty decent reason to kill."

"I didn't!" he said, trying to get up.

Kett put a hand on his shoulder, gentle but firm. He leaned in.

"I believe you, but you have to give me something. Where did the money come from?"

"There wasn't no money," he said, agitated now. "It was a gift."

"The watch?"

"The watch, the clothes, some other stuff too."

"The phone?" said Kett, picking it up. "This one? Looks brand new."

The kid swallowed hard, his face gurning.

"Not mine," he said.

"What's the code?"

"Don't know, because it's not fucking mine."

Kett gave him a look that was so stern even Porter felt his bollocks crawl up into his pelvis.

"I'm going to say it again, one last time," the DCI said. "Dead body. Motive. You ran from the police. What's the code?"

"All sixes," said Jon after a moment.

Kett typed it in and nodded.

"Who gave you this stuff?"

The boy licked his lips, desperate.

"I can't tell you, he'll kill me."

"Who?" said Kett.

"You don't understand. He's not like us, he's... You can't keep me safe from him. Nobody can. I can't say."

"You just did," said Kett. "His name's Joseph Maynard, right?"

It was like he'd slapped Jon across the face. He rocked back so hard his head connected with the wall.

"How..."

The boy looked from Kett to Porter to the tactical officers.

"He sent you, didn't he? He's testing me. I won't tell you nothing."

He threw his head back again, deliberately this time, the crack of it hitting the brick echoing down the street.

"Oi!" yelled Andilet, moving in.

"Fucking kill myself before I talk."

The kid tried to crack his head against the wall again, but Porter managed to get a hand between the back of the kid's head and the bricks. The pain throbbed through his knuckles, making him cry out.

"Enough," said Kett, grabbing Jon under the arms and hauling him up. Carmichael helped, bracing the back of his head. The kid struggled, but he didn't have much left in him.

Porter nursed his aching hand, seeing an ambulance turn into the road. It picked up speed as the driver spotted them.

"Enough, Jon," Kett said again. "Maynard's in custody, we arrested him this morning. He can't hurt you."

Jon shook his head, scattering tears like raindrops.

"He can," he said. "You don't understand. He can still get to me, he can still see me. His red eye sees everything. He's still out there."

"He's not. He's done. He's finished. He gave you the watch, right? What did he ask for, Jon?"

The boy was sobbing, his shoulders lurching up and down with the force of it.

"Nothing," he said. "He didn't ask for nothing."

"Liam and Emil, he gave them stuff too?"

Jon nodded, scattering tears like raindrops.

"What did he ask from them?"

"Nothing," he pleaded. "Just..."

They waited for him to find the answer.

"Just ink," he said. "That's all."

"Ink?" said Porter. "A contract?"

"No, *ink*," he said. "A tattoo."

"Where?" said Kett.

"On my stomach," he said.

Porter lifted Jon's tracksuit top and the T-shirt beneath. He didn't resist, he just howled his grief at the grey sky.

Sure enough, there was a tattoo on the washboard of the boy's stomach—a black pentagram, in the middle of which was a red-eyed skull.

"Maynard made you get this?" said Kett.

"He did it," said the boy. "Said if I agreed to it, he'd give me anything I wanted. If I agreed to it, it would keep me safe. We all did it."

"Liam and Emil?"

"Yeah, I think so. I never saw. But there were others. Fucking loads of us. He was..."

He groaned, his eyes like blood-flecked blisters in his face.

"He wanted an army. That's what he told us. He said if we followed him, if we marked ourselves, we'd have anything we ever wanted."

"Like an Omega," said Porter.

"And a dead guardian," added Kett.

"I didn't do it," he said. "I didn't kill her. I... He knows I said something. I can feel it. He's here, he's here."

He was growing more agitated, tugging at his cuffs. Carmichael held onto him, the sheer size of the man dwarfing the kid.

"He's coming for me."

"Maynard's in a cell," said Kett. "He's—"

"Not him! I'm not talking about him!"

Jon screamed, the sound sending a chill down Porter's spine. Then he wrenched himself violently out of Carmichael's grip, ploughing into Andilet and spinning off him. Andilet tried to grab him as he ran, almost snatching the back of his hoodie.

"Shit!" he yelled.

"No!" Porter cried out.

Jon fell into the road and the ambulance crunched into him, knocking him back. It wasn't going fast, probably not more than fifteen miles an hour, but Jon had angled his head to connect with the bumper. He lay on the street, crimson foam exploding from his lips as he let loose another, weaker scream.

Kett ran over, Porter with him, the paramedics scrambling out of the ambulance.

"Shit," Carmichael said again. "He got free. I couldn't stop him."

"He ran right into us," said the driver, dropping onto her knees beside the kid. "What's his name?"

"Jon," said Kett, his hands in his hair.

"Jon, can you hear me?" said the paramedic.

The kid broke into a fit, spasming on the ground. His eyes were two blood-filled blisters, wide open, seeing nothing.

And that infernal tattoo peeked out from beneath his clothes—the single red eye glaring as if Maynard himself was watching them.

CHAPTER TWELVE

THE AMBULANCE PULLED AWAY, ITS SIREN TEARING A hole in the quiet street. Andilet was in the back—the least he could do, he said, after letting the kid get hurt. The tactical van followed, Carmichael at the wheel.

"What a cock-up," Kett said, speaking to himself.

Only when both vehicles had turned the corner and gunned out of sight did Kett put on his glasses and look at the phone he still held. It was an iPhone, one of the newer models, and the image on the screen was completely black. He typed 6-6-6-6 and it unlocked, a handful of apps against a dark background. It was hard to make them out in the brightening day.

He smelled Porter walking over before he heard him.

"Unbelievable," said the DI. "Who runs into an ambulance?"

"Somebody who's terrified," said Kett, struggling to make sense of the screen. "Somebody who thinks there are worse things than death."

"There are," grumbled Porter. "Wet socks."

Kett made his way back to the house, where a couple of constables guarded the door. It was darker in the front hall, although the creeping stench of death from upstairs was infinitely worse than Porter's aroma. Luckily, the DI had decided to wait outside.

Kett opened Jon's text messages. There weren't many, most from the other lads who lived in the house, or Maggie, a few from work and plenty of marketing texts from places like Dominos and Netflix. Nothing from anyone who looked like a parent. His WhatsApp didn't reveal much more, mostly spam messages from buxom women in very few clothes that he'd eagerly replied to. It looked like he'd sent money to at least two of them.

"Idiot," said Kett, opening the photos instead.

"Can anyone else smell that?" asked one of the constables by the door. "It's like somebody's shit themselves."

Porter glared at the man. Kett ignored them, cycling through the images. Most were selfies of Jon in various places, a few where he was shirtless in front of a mirror, making gang signs. The tattoo must have been fairly new, because it hadn't been there before the summer. He flicked through the deleted photos album as well, finding a few shots that he couldn't make much sense of until he realised Jon had been trying to photograph something—or someone—through the crack in the bathroom door. Fortunately, he hadn't been successful.

"I can bloody *taste* it," the constable went on. "It's right in the back of my throat."

"I'm going to search the garden," said Porter, moping off.

"Wait, Pete, can you call the schools, find out where Liam and Emil go and whether they've been in this week?"

"Sure," he said.

"And don't fall in the pond!"

Kett opened the emails, finding nothing but spam and receipts until he spotted something unusual. The sender was a random string of numbers attached to a Gmail address, and there was no subject line. Clicking on it took him to a single link, and another string of random digits. He'd had emails like this before, and he had no doubt at all that the link would take him to a website that would try to steal his money.

Good job it's not my phone, he thought, thumbing the screen.

To his surprise, YouTube opened. It was a video titled *Actuate Your Core Principles and Attain the Five Steps: Part Two*, by a user with the name 4522912—the same numbers that had been in the email address. There was a password. Kett copied the digits from the email and pasted them in.

The video began to play, darkness peeling open to reveal somebody sitting at a desk in a red-walled room. They were wearing a mask, and it would have been impossible to tell if it was a man or a woman if it wasn't the same mask that Joseph Maynard had been wearing when they'd struck Cold Iron that morning, a crown of thorns pointing to the ceiling.

And if there had been any doubt at all, it was gone as soon as he started speaking.

"The lesson continues. We work our way deeper into the wound."

It was Maynard's voice, speaking in a low, predatory growl. He sat straight, his gloved hands steepled in front of him, his body hidden by black and gold robes.

"Have you noticed changes yet? Have you seen things that you did not before? Have things started to turn in your favour? We adjust our focus. We activate our deeper senses. We actuate our core principles. One."

He lifted a hand, pointing a finger to his eye.

"Divination. In order to see what cannot be seen, you have to peel back the skin of your vision, you have to replace the eye which shows you only the base untruths of the world."

He lifted his finger.

"Two: Exsanguination. We drain the blood and the life of our enemies, we feed on their suffering, we watch gleefully as they become less than human. To cut the flesh, we must use our hands."

He pointed to his ear.

"Three: Veneration. We listen to the voice in the dark, the quiet man, the master. We hear his command: reject all that is good, all that is saintly, all that is kind. We worship these words."

The smell of death from upstairs, mixed with Maynard's voice, was too much. Kett stepped back outside, pushing past the two constables and heading into the shade of the enormous hedge. Maynard was still talking, pointing the same finger to his mouth.

"Four: Invocation. We do not sleep until we see demons in the day. Only when your mind is at breaking point can you invoke his spirit. Only then can you summon him through unholy speech."

"The hell are you on about?" Kett asked.

Maynard answered by pointing beneath the desk.

"Five: Limination. Know you are more than a man. See how you are different to everyone else. See how you are better. Only when you witness people for what they are—scum, filth, empty flesh—can you cross the liminal. Only then can you fuck your way to eternity. Only then will your procreation and rebirth be permitted."

Kett heard a roar from the back garden, loud enough to make him flinch. He peered down the side of the house to see Porter walking back this way, furious.

"What?" Kett called out.

"There was another pond!" Porter roared. "I am *done*."

"Only a select few of you will make it to the final stage," Maynard said. "Only one in ten thousand will transform. But the rest of you still play a part. No matter which level you reach on your journey, you are a cog in the machine that will pull this world apart. You are a pillar on which the true master will mount his throne. You are—"

"Who's that?" said Porter, walking up.

Kett held up the phone so the DI could see.

"Oh," he said. "What's he saying?"

"If you stop talking, I can tell you."

Porter huffed into silence, both of them watching the screen as Maynard rattled on.

"... this secret is not yours to share, even with another disciple. Silence is paramount. You must endure every stage of the process without help from me, or from others. I will know if you do not follow the rules."

On-screen, Maynard leaned forward, the eyeholes of his mask utterly black.

"The punishment for breaching the code is death. And it is not a death you will welcome. It is a death that will be long, and painful, and even while you scream for mercy, your flesh will be fed to those who are more deserving."

"Cheery," said Porter.

Maynard let his words settle before sitting back, almost like a teacher in front of a class.

"Now then, let us move on to the next part of the

course. Exsanguination. What does it mean? What will it bring you? What does it have to do with a gouged eye? In Latin terms, the word…"

Kett stopped the video, clicking on Maynard's username to load up his profile. It had no photos, no descriptions, and no public videos.

"That number mean anything to you?" Kett asked. "4522912."

"Phone number?" said Porter, who was scraping his shoe on the grass.

"Seven digits," Kett said.

"Oh, right. No, then."

"Useful. You get anywhere with the schools before you went swimming?"

"Yeah. Liam and Emil are enrolled at Neatherd, but they're not there very often. Secretary says they've been absent since the middle of last week. No contact with them or with a parent or guardian."

"So where have they been going, then?" Kett asked.

He navigated back to Jon's YouTube history, looking at the other videos he'd watched. They were all mostly video game tutorials and music videos until maybe three months ago, when more sinister influencers began to pop up.

"I recognise some of them," said Porter, leaning in. "That floppy bollock is the kickboxer obsessed with giving bad sex advice to young boys. Pervert. Can't seem to get rid of him."

"Jon seemed to like him," said Kett.

"Yeah, he targets disenfranchised kids like him, makes them think they can get what they want by being a talentless, abusive, violent prick like he is. Beating up girlfriends, destroying friendships, boasting about being alphas. Never met a more zeta looking arsehole in my life than that guy, but it's the power of the Tube, isn't it?"

"YouTube," said Kett. "Not the first time I've heard it mentioned. Old Bob said Dennis was always on his phone, and so did his parents. He was watching this sort of stuff. Didn't Savage say Ian was as well?"

"Yeah, they want to be part of something," said Porter. "Easy to feel isolated when you're a kid. Makes them good prey."

"So Jon finds all these influencers while he's on YouTube," said Kett. "Then he finds Maynard."

"Or Maynard finds him," said Porter.

"Right. That's what Jon said. Maynard's building an army of angry teenage boys, making them mutilate themselves with his tattoo, making them do whatever he's talking about in these videos. Isolating themselves, hurting themselves, maybe. But he's not an influencer, he's not doing it for the money, or because he wants to feel like less of a loser. He's got something else in mind."

"Maybe he's just a pervert too," said Porter.

Kett didn't answer, switching the phone off and pocketing it.

"I'll get this to tech, see if we can find some answers. You can—"

"If it's all the same to you, sir," said Porter, "can I go home and get changed? I feel like a frog's undercarriage."

Kett laughed.

"Sure. I'll wait here until forensics arrive."

"It'll be a while," said Porter. "They're already split between Cold Iron and the garage."

"I've got plenty of videos to pass the time," said Kett, patting the phone in his pocket. "When you're done, get back to HQ and get some of this on the wall."

"Sir," said Porter, walking off.

Kett's phone buzzed in his other pocket and he pulled it out, seeing a text from Savage. He felt his stomach twist as he read it, and he had to read it again just to make sure.

He called out to Porter just as the DI reached the street.

"Hold up, Pete, change of plans."

"Sir?" said Porter, frowning.

"Yeah, we're going to the hospital. Maynard's awake."

CHAPTER THIRTEEN

THE HOSPITAL WAS MOBBED, THE CORRIDOR LEADING TO Maynard's room a throng of police officers who parted to let Kett pass. Most were in uniform, the tactical unit amongst them. Chris Sutagon nodded to Kett as he walked past.

"Your tank lad's alive," she said. "Just."

There were detectives here too, even some coppers Kett hadn't seen in years. It was an impressive and intimidating show of force in the wake of Ben Milford's death.

Clare stood at the head of the group, and he welcomed Kett with a glare, baring his teeth like an angry camel. Savage and Duke stood next to him, their clothes streaked with dirt, their hair a mess. There was a nasty bruise on Savage's face, her eye swollen. One of her hands had been bandaged.

"You okay?" Kett asked her as he walked up.

She shook her head, and he thought she was answering until she pointed to her ear.

"Can't hear a thing past the ringing, sir, sorry."

"What?" said Duke, a finger in his own ear.

"The grenade?" said Kett.

"Lemonade?" said the PC.

"What?" said Savage.

"Ignore them," said Clare, snapping his fingers in Kett's face. "Where's Porter?"

"Parking the car, sir," Kett told him. He looked past the Super to the closed door of a hospital room. "Maynard's in there?"

Clare glanced back, as if to check, then nodded.

"With his brief. Doctors say he's fractured his cheekbone and orbital socket, and he's lost a few teeth. They didn't want him to talk, but I told them about the police officer he killed, and *how* he killed him, and now they couldn't give a toss what we do to him. I want you in with me, Kett."

"I thought you didn't want me anywhere near this?"

"I didn't. Then I realised I couldn't get rid of you even if I tried. Like an antibiotic-resistant strain of gonorrhoea. You know Hollenbeck better than anyone. You know Maynard. But I take the lead. You hear me? I'm tossing first."

"Not going to get in the way of *that*, sir," said Kett, pulling a face.

"What's the latest? You get anything from the Uysal's place?"

Kett nodded, taking a breath.

"Liam and Emil are missing, last seen by a neighbour yesterday morning heading for school. But they haven't been to school since last week. I think they're working with Maynard. There's another young man in the house, Jon Heath. He's eighteen. He told us Maynard was collecting disenfranchised kids, making an army. He gets them to prove their allegiance to him by getting a tattoo on their stomach. Upturned pentagram with a skull, same one we've seen. In return, he buys them stuff, does things for them.

Their carer, Maggie, is dead in the house, pentagram on the wall drawn in blood. Looks like it happened in the last twenty-four hours."

"Christ."

"I found a video on Jon's phone. It's Maynard, talking about, uh, five pillars of consciousness, or some demonic shit. Looks like a series of them. It's a process he's putting them through. Isolating them, turning them into... I don't even know. But I think he's brainwashing them into something."

"Jon's willing to testify to this?"

"Jon tried to headbutt a moving ambulance, sir," said Kett. "He's alive. How's the kid from the tank doing?"

Everyone turned to Savage, and she stared at them.

"What?"

"He's in surgery," Clare answered for her. "He was superglued into a roll of bin bags, left there for at least twelve hours. They don't know if he'll make it. No name. He can barely talk."

"This guy," said Kett, the anger blazing so bright that he started to sweat. He looked back, searching the crowd. "You hear about Milford and Gorski? They were together."

"I did," Clare said. "Julia's well away from this, for her own sake. I'm amazed she didn't put a bullet through his head, all things considered."

He wiped his face, his red eyes blinking.

"I think I would have," he added.

"There's still time," Kett told him, speaking quietly. "Let's do this."

Clare opened the door, walking into the room. Kett followed, nodding to the watching audience before closing it behind him. It was bright in here—brighter than it should have been, given the grey day—the light streaming through the window like a spotlight, illuminating the single bed and its occupant.

Maynard looked older than ever, shrunk into his blankets, his head propped on several pillows. His face had puffed up like a Halloween mask, bright purple and streaked with bandages. One eye was so puffy that it was sealed shut, the other a milky white orb that watched them enter. He smiled, revealing the stubs of his broken teeth. Gorski must have kicked him like she was going for a field goal. Both his hands were cuffed to the bars on the side of the bed, his wrists red raw.

Another man sat on a chair by the bed, somewhere in his thirties, although there was more grey in his hair than there should have been at that age. He wore a dark suit, a blood-coloured tie, and a pair of expensive shoes. He stood up as Kett closed the door, moving protectively in front of Maynard.

"We explicitly asked for another police contact," he said, his voice an octave lower than Kett had been expecting. "My client was attacked and horrifically injured under your watch, Superintendent Clare. I don't trust you not to assault him again."

Clare walked up to him, close enough that the other man had to lean back.

"I'll tell you what, Mr Berrycloth. I'll open the door right now and tell that lot to come in, shall I? At the last count, there were thirty police officers out there. You can pick a new contact. You've seen them? You know why they're here? You don't know anger until you've seen a group of coppers mourning one of their own."

The solicitor stood firm for all of three seconds, then he moved back. Maynard watched it all with his one good eye, the pupil dilated. He must have been on some serious painkillers, which was a good thing. If he was doped up, he might talk.

"So, Mr Maynard," said Clare. "I trust you're comfortable?"

He adjusted the pillows, jiggling Maynard's head with some violence.

"Hey!" said Berrycloth. "Get off him."

"Just trying to make sure he's okay," said Clare, giving Maynard a couple of not-so-gentle slaps on the cheek.

Maynard groaned, trying to lift his hands only for the cuffs to snap tight. Clare backed off, his rage radiating from him like he was a blast furnace. Kett couldn't remember a time he'd ever seen the Super so angry.

"You're enjoying this, Joseph, aren't you?" Clare asked.

Maynard tried to smile, but it was obviously hard, his cheek trembling. He let his hands drop, adjusting his body as best he could beneath the thin blanket. He stared at Clare for a moment, then let his eye drift to where Kett was standing. He may have been old, and broken, but that look still made goosebumps break out on Kett's arms.

"It's started," Maynard said, lisping past his broken teeth.

"What has?" said Clare.

Kett walked to the end of the bed.

"The game," he said. "Right?"

Clare shot Kett a look, but Maynard was laughing.

"Dennis Lynn," said Kett. "Where is he?"

"Is that his name?" asked Maynard, licking his dry lips. "Dennis Lynn."

He rolled it around his ruined mouth a couple more times before carrying on.

"Wrong question, I think."

"Who took him?" asked Kett.

"That's better," said Maynard. "And I have no answer for you. I don't know his name. I don't know anything about him, other than his destiny."

"His destiny?" Kett scoffed. "Right, his journey through the five pillars of consciousness. That it?"

This caught Maynard by surprise, Kett could see the ripple of confusion that crossed his face.

"Which stage is he at? Exsanguination? No, let me guess, he's right at the end. Limination."

Clare didn't have a clue, but Maynard looked decidedly uncomfortable. He tried to push himself up the bed, but the cuffs wouldn't let him. The solicitor stepped forward to lend him a hand, but Kett shot him a look.

"Sit down," he said. "You can help him when we're done."

"I won't let you bully my—"

"Let me guess," said Kett. "You've got a tattoo as well. On your stomach."

Berrycloth looked like he'd been thumped. He put his hands to his gut like he was cradling a pregnant belly.

"Because this little cabal you've created, Joseph, isn't as tight as you'd like it to be," Kett went on, glaring at Maynard. "That's the trouble when you prey on teenage boys, when you're into that kind of thing."

"I'm not into that kind of—"

"Sooner or later, they all realise you're full of shit, that your gifts, your watches and your phones and your shoes, are payment for something they don't want to give you any more. Nobody likes an old pervert, Joseph."

"It's not like—"

"Especially one who mutilates young boys, who brutalises them, who coerces them into doing terrible things. They're all going to talk to us, sooner or later, and this murder charge that you think you might be able to weasel out of is going to become something so immense that it buries you alive. Forever. So I'm going to ask you again, who took Dennis Lynn? And where is he?"

Maynard licked his lips again, his one eye blinking. The anger was there, but he was doing his best to control it. Kett could see that in the way he clenched and unclenched his fists, in the way he slowed his breathing.

"You think you know what's happening," he said. "But you don't. This is beyond anything you're willing or able to comprehend. You'll find out, though."

"Sir," said Berrycloth, a word of warning. Maynard ignored him.

"You think you've seen this before. Hollenbeck, the Pig Man. Remember him, Kett? Does *Billie* remember him? I'd wager she does."

Kett didn't give him the satisfaction of an answer, but the temperature in the room seemed to rise even further. He felt a bead of sweat roll between his shoulder blades.

"It's what we did, for so many years. We found a champion, we trained them in the art of death, we financed their hatred, we encouraged their violence, we nurtured their sick and twisted desires until they became the very best version of themselves."

"Then you pitted them against each other like greyhounds," said Kett. "Who could get the most kills. Who could do the most damage."

"Fun," said Maynard. "But this is different. You see, I've devoted decades to the arcane laws, to researching the occult. I've spent my entire life searching for evidence of evil—pure evil, Robert—beyond any true rationale of mankind. Like the tip of a knife slowly pushed into flesh, all it takes is enough force to puncture the skin. Pop. I've been trying to find that forever."

"What?" said Kett.

Maynard's ruined face peeled open into a smile.

"And now I have. Because what's out there is not a man. Not for much longer, anyway. He has pushed the limits of humanity for so long that he has grown into something else. This is his final test. After tomorrow, he will be so much more. Unstoppable. Untraceable. He will be a thing that spirits itself inside your home, that suffocates your wife, that burns your children."

The fury raged, but Kett clamped his jaw around it.

"He will be madness incarnate. What time is it, Mr Berrycloth?"

The solicitor checked his watch, his hand trembling.

"Almost four, sir."

"Then it is done."

"What's done?" said Kett.

"On the hour, you will know," Maynard told them. "On the hour, the bells will toll for another soul."

"Another kidnapping?" said Kett. He met Clare's eye, just for a second, before turning back. "Who?"

"You think I would allow myself to know?" said Maynard. "You think I would consider myself worthy?"

He made a noise that sounded like a groan, but which Kett quickly realised was a laugh. He was enjoying it, *revelling* in it. Madness incarnate was right, but Maynard would have been better off using it to describe himself.

Kett checked his watch, seeing that there were only seconds until it turned four. He counted them down until the hand ticked well past the hour, feeling a rush of relief that Maynard might be bluffing.

"I think you're full of shit," he told the old man. "I think you assumed you were too clever to ever be caught. I think this is some half-arsed plan that you've rushed into motion because we found you."

"You know what I think, Robert?" said Maynard. "I think your watch runs a little fast."

Superintendent Clare's phone rang, deafening in the small room. He didn't look like he wanted to answer it, but he pulled it from his pocket and held it to his ear. Kett heard a voice on the other end, speaking quickly. After a minute or so, Clare hung up without saying a word. Maynard watched him gleefully.

"Sir?" asked Kett.

Clare swallowed noisily, then jutted a long finger towards Maynard.

"There is a special place in hell for men like you," he said.

Maynard seemed to shiver with delight.

"Oh, I'm counting on it."

Clare retreated across the room, barking Kett's name as he opened the door. Kett hesitated, studying Maynard in his bed.

"What's in this for you?" he asked, the noise from the corridor filtering in. "You're finished. You're going to be behind bars for the rest of your life. Why do this now?"

The man in the bed seemed to seriously consider the question, his tongue flicking over his chapped lips. Berrycloth sat in wide-eyed silence, like a kid in church.

"Because I have to know," Maynard said. "You think I'm a bad man, but I'm not. I'm merely a curious one. Somebody who wasn't afraid to see behind the veil of civilised thought. I have been accused of being a devil by many people, including by you, my friend."

"We are not friends," growled Kett.

"Kinsmen, then," said Maynard. "United by bad people. I have been called a devil, but I am not one. I am a man, and will never be anything more, no matter how much I might wish it. And you're right. I'm finished. This is the end for me, although not in the way you think. But in the time I have left as a free man, I want to see it with my own eyes. I want to see *him*."

"Him?" said Kett.

Maynard nodded as much as the pillows would allow him, his mouth peeling open into a grotesque, toothless smile.

"I want to see the Devil before I go."

CHAPTER FOURTEEN

"He's off his head," said Kett once he'd closed the door of Maynard's room.

The swell of noise in the corridor had dulled, everyone watching, waiting to find out what had happened. Clare grabbed Kett's arm, pulling him through the crowd like an angry dad with an unruly child. They turned into the next corridor, and when Clare couldn't find an empty room for them to talk in, he opened a toilet door and shoved Kett inside.

"What's going on, sir?" said Kett.

Clare started to close the door, but Savage appeared, stopping it with her foot.

"What are you doing in there?"

"Get in!"

"What?" said Savage.

Clare gestured frantically, and Savage stepped inside, followed by Duke.

"Lock it!" Clare barked.

"What, sir?"

"That lot out there are riled up enough as it is! I don't

want them getting any angrier."

Savage closed the door, only to hear a yelp from outside. It was Porter, nursing his fingers as he walked in.

"Bloody charming, that is," he said. "Slamming the door in my face."

"What?" said Savage, wiggling a finger in her ear.

"I'm going to slam your face in the bog if you don't shut up, Pete," said Clare as Savage turned the handle to lock it. "That phone call was from... Jesus, has somebody hoofed out a shit in here?"

"Yes," said Porter, glancing at his shoe. "That's exactly what it is. The toilet. It's not me."

"I didn't say it was you, you puckered baboon rectum. That phone call was from Spalding. Around twenty minutes ago, a young man was attacked and snatched from outside the village hall in Marham."

"Another one?" said Savage, who had leaned in to hear better.

"His name's Vincent Kinghorn, he's sixteen."

"He's definitely been taken, sir?" said Kett. "He didn't just wander off?"

"According to the witness, he was stabbed and bundled into the back of a hearse by a man in a mask."

"Oh."

"In the middle of the day, sir?" said Savage, who was struggling to hear. "It's one thing to take somebody from inside a building, but on the street? With witnesses? It's rash. Why would he risk it?"

"Because it's a game," said Kett. "I don't know what, yet, I don't know the rules. But Maynard's waiting for something to happen, and he thinks he doesn't have long left to see it. Whatever he's set in motion, it's moving fast."

"Two kidnapped lads," said Porter.

"Three," said Kett. "If we're counting the one in the tank."

"Maybe more, if Liam and Emil are involved in this," said Clare.

"I don't know, sir," said Kett. "Kate, the kid in the tank, did you see his stomach? Was there a tattoo?"

"Sorry?" said Savage.

"What?" asked Duke.

"He was mummified in tape," Clare answered for them. "Nobody's seen him since he went into surgery. Why?"

"Maynard made his followers tattoo themselves, a pentagram with a skull. Jon Heath was one of them, and he said Liam and Emil might have been too. He didn't know for sure. Did anyone check Ian? And the other shooters?"

"No," said Clare. "But they're all here."

"We can do that, sir," said Savage, leaning in.

"Huh?" said Duke.

"Why does it matter?" asked Clare.

"I'm not sure," said Kett. "But if Maynard's gathering an army, it doesn't make sense that he'd kidnap his own soldiers. He's training these guys up to work for him. I think the kidnap victims are different, they're outsiders."

"Right," said Porter, nodding. "But why these guys? Why Dennis Lynn and..."

He frowned, trying to remember.

"Vincent Kinghorn," said Kett. "I don't know why, but that's what we need to find out. There must be a link between the missing men. Maybe something to do with what they've been watching on YouTube. We find that, we find them."

He didn't think it would be so easy, not with Maynard, but they had to hope.

"If there's no pattern, we're tossed," said Clare. "You think he's done at three?"

"Three victims?" said Kett, shaking his head. "No. I don't. But I have no idea what his game plan is, or where he'll stop. We need to keep pressing him, we need to be relentless. If we can grind Maynard down, we can break him."

"Leave that to me," said Clare. "If anyone can toss that piece of shit into releasing his inner essence, it's me."

Everyone grimaced.

"Kett, Porter, you're on the second missing boy," Clare went on, oblivious. He'd started jiggling, his words urgent. "Savage, Duke, you're technically still patients, so stay in the hospital, find out about the tattoos, get as much information from Ian Hipkin and the tank lad as you can."

"Yes, sir," said Savage.

"As insane as Maynard is, he must have an escape plan. He's not going to risk a lifetime in prison. Find out what his get-out-of-jail-free card is."

To Kett's horror, the Superintendent began to undo his belt.

"What are you doing, sir?" he said.

"Pavlov," he barked, unbuttoning his trousers. "I'm in a toilet, I need to go. So if you lot don't mind, kindly toss off."

Savage unlocked the door, everyone tumbling into the corridor so fast they almost tripped over each other. Clare turned the lock, and a handful of seconds later it sounded like somebody had smuggled a brass band inside.

"The spirit of Louis Armstrong is very much still with us," said Porter. "Right, you want to call Spalding for an address?"

"I'd rather not," said Kett. "She just about bit my head off this morning. Besides, I need to check something."

He moved away from the toilet, nodding to some of the constables who had spread out into the surrounding corridors. It took him a moment to find a nurse, and she was in such a hurry she almost didn't stop.

"I just need to ask something," he said. "Sorry. It's about the man we brought in. Joseph Maynard. You scanned his head, right? For the broken cheekbone."

"And the eye socket, yeah," she said, not entirely friendly. "Did he deserve it?"

"You have no idea," Kett told her. Then he shook his head. "But no, not like that. Did anything else show up on the scan?"

"In terms of how much you broke him?" the young woman replied. "No. But you know about the tumour, don't you?"

"What?" he said. "A tumour?"

"Glioblastoma in his brain stem. Been there a while. All his records are private, but it's not hard to miss."

"Shit," said Kett. "How long's he got?"

The nurse shrugged.

"Not long."

She walked away before Kett could ask another question. He headed back the way he'd come, finding the others waiting for him outside the toilet.

"What's wrong, sir?" asked Savage, seeing the look on his face.

"I'll tell you in a second," he said. "Clare needs to hear this."

"I can hear you just fine," said the Super from inside. "Go ahead."

"It can wait, sir."

"It can't. Don't make me open this door."

Kett took a breath.

"When we spoke to Maynard just now, he told us he was finished. I assumed he meant he knew he was going to prison. Turns out he meant he was dying. He's got brain cancer. Not much time left. This isn't just a game to him, it's his final chapter."

"Shit," said Porter. "That explains the rush."

"He's set something in motion," Kett went on. "Some*body*. This person has gone through Maynard's training, he's proven himself. Maynard thinks he's the Devil, or maybe about to be. I don't know. He's actually lost his marbles, I think. But there still has to be some logic there. A plan."

"A deadline," said Savage, and Kett nodded.

"He mentioned tomorrow."

"All the more reason we get a move on," bellowed Clare from the toilet. "So *move*!"

THEY DROVE through the pitch-black evening, Porter behind the wheel, Kett engrossed in Jon Heath's phone. There had only been time to watch one of Maynard's videos on the drive over to Marham, but one was enough. It was textbook emotional manipulation, designed to make the viewer feel as if the world was against them, gaslighting them into turning away from their friends and family, into skipping classes at school, into picking fights with the people they loved. It was the same set of procedures used to pull people into cults, and it was incredibly persuasive.

Maynard made his points clearly and powerfully. Even his voice seemed designed to pull you in, a low, monotonous drone that peeled back the skin of Kett's scalp and needled into his brain. By the time Porter pulled the car up behind a sea of rolling blue lights, Kett felt like *he* was ready to join Maynard's cause.

"Brainwashing bastard," said Porter, cutting the engine. "As if these kids don't have enough to worry about."

Kett stopped the video, swallowing down a throatful of acid. He felt sick, and he wasn't sure if it was because of the journey, or because of what he'd been watching. The fact he hadn't eaten all day didn't help either.

"Where are we?" he asked. "Marham, right?"

Porter nodded, watching the uniformed police through the windscreen.

"Why here?" said Kett. "Maynard was in Thetford. Dennis Lynn was taken in Fakenham. If the Uysal brothers have been kidnapped, it was from Horsford. This guy is all over the place."

Porter shrugged.

"Harder for us if we don't know where he's going to strike next," he said. "Especially if it's random."

"It can't be random," said Kett. "He can't just be driving around kidnapping anyone he sees walking down the street. He must have known Dennis Lynn was working in the garage, and that he was alone. He's done his research. There's a pattern, we're just not seeing it."

He opened the door, cold air flooding into Porter's Mondeo along with a handful of sleet.

"I hate this weather," he said as he got out. "They must have crimes in Spain, right? Italy? Greece? The Bahamas? Why aren't we working over there?"

"That is a very good question, sir," answered Porter.

The street was a narrow one, houses crowded together on one side and an impressive church-like building on the other. Three IRVs sat in the car park, their lights making it look like there was a disco taking place in the village hall.

A square of tape marked off a section of the asphalt, enough light from the cars to reveal a pattern of blood. A PC stood there with an umbrella, trying to keep the rain off it—presumably waiting for a forensic tent to arrive.

Kett didn't have to get any closer to see that it was another pentagram.

One of the constables jogged over to meet them as they made their way towards the open front door. She took off her hat like she meant to doff it, then held it awkwardly as she spoke.

"No sign of him yet, sirs."

"The missing kid?" asked Porter.

"Yeah," she said. "The man who reported it is inside. He runs an after-school club of some kind. I'll take you in."

She led the way through the door and into the large room beyond. It could have been any village hall anywhere in the country: scuffed floorboards, enormous cast iron radiators, a small kitchen and dozens of tables laden with boxes. A couple more constables waited there alongside a man in his sixties who looked like he could easily have auditioned for the role of Santa Claus, if Santa enjoyed wearing cargo shorts and Hawaiian shirts and walked around in bare feet. He glanced up from his chair, scratching his rosy cheeks through the white curls of his beard.

"This is Gilbert Rogers," said the constable who'd brought them in. "He's the man who made the call."

"Hi," said Kett, walking over. He'd been hoping for a little heat in here, but the hall felt colder than the world outside. He didn't know how Gilbert wasn't freezing to death in his shorts. "I'm DCI Kett, and this is DI Porter. Can you tell us what happened?"

Gilbert nodded, leaning forward in his chair and

exposing a flabby chest covered in silver hair. When he spoke, it was in a broad Welsh accent.

"It's like I told the police, we were just about to start."

"Start what?"

"The club," said Gilbert. "It's nothing much, just a place to go if you don't have anyone at home. There's a handful of kids live in these parts who are a little short of... I don't know what you want to call it. Love?"

"Love?" said Kett.

"Right," said the man. "They don't get much love at home, is what I'm saying. So they come here."

"For some love?" said Kett.

The man smiled, nodding.

"Lots of love. We have fun, plenty of games, cuddles. There's only five of them."

"Boys and girls?"

"Only one girl. Keighley. Four boys."

"Including Vincent Kinghorn?" said Kett. "He's the one who went missing. Can you tell me about him?"

"Vin," said Gilbert. "Like the actor. He's a solid kid. Quiet. Struggles at school. Home life sucks, as you can tell."

Kett waited for the man to explain, and Gilbert gestured to the empty room.

"Been an hour now, and no sign of his father."

Kett turned to the constable.

"You've informed the parents?"

"Just the dad," she replied. "He's at home. He was drunk, as far as I know. He told us to let him know when we found Vincent."

"Seriously?" said Kett.

"Like I said," Gilbert went on. "No love. That's why I'm here. Got enough love for everyone."

"So Vincent was here," said Kett. "What happened?"

"We were just setting up," said Gilbert, leaning back and scratching a hairy nipple through his open shirt. "Vin's always the first one here, because he's not always at school, you know? He was helping me with the tables. I went into the kitchen to grab something, and when I came out, he'd gone."

"What time was this?" asked Kett.

"Shortly before four," said Gilbert, nodding to the front of the room. "I went to the window there, just to see if he'd left. He does that sometimes, if he's not feeling it."

"Feeling the love?"

"Right. I don't pressure him. Nothing worse than an old man forcing his love on you."

Kett glanced at Porter, who mirrored his expression with a solitary raised eyebrow.

"And he was on the other side of the car park, by the road," Gilbert went on. "There was a car there, a hearse. I think it was a hearse. I don't know. Long, black. Yeah, it must have been a hearse. You hardly ever see them these days, do you? I couldn't spot the driver because Vin was leaning over, talking to him. I figured they must have been asking for directions or something, didn't put much stock into it. Left them to it while I fetched the toys."

"Toys?" said Kett.

"Yes, the toys," said Gilbert. "I've got plenty of things for them to play with. They love all that stuff. Dangly bits to prod and twist, sausages to swing about, big balls to squeeze. All sorts."

Kett rubbed his face.

"Right, so, uh..."

He'd lost his train of thought, but Porter stepped in.

"The hearse," he said. "You saw Vincent getting pulled inside?"

"Right!" exclaimed Gilbert. "I heard a noise from outside, a shout. It's nothing new. These kids always yell at each other, all in good sport. But it happened again, and something about it..."

He hesitated, rubbing his hands up and down his thighs.

"I walked back to the window, and I saw... I'm not sure, to be honest, it happened so quickly, and it was growing dark. The back door of the hearse was open, and somebody was... It looked like they were pushing Vin inside. But it might not have been him, because he wasn't struggling."

"Who wasn't struggling?" asked Kett.

"The thing getting stuffed in the back. I thought the driver might have been trying to push a bag or something into the hearse. They were giving it a right good heave-ho, and it wasn't moving, wasn't fighting back. It looked like a..."

He paused, licking his lips as he relived it.

"Like a dead weight. I thought it was a bag until I saw a leg, saw Vin's shoe. His trainers. It was *him*. And the other man had a knife. I think it was a knife. He stabbed it into him, right in his leg. Twice. Vin was screaming. It was awful. Awful."

"Can you describe the driver?" asked Kett.

"No," said Gilbert. "He had something on his face, a mask. Red, it was. With these kind of yellow marks on it. I couldn't really make it out. But he looked at me."

The man seemed to shrivel up, drawing his legs under the chair and folding himself as tightly as his belly would allow.

"He looked at me through the holes in his mask and for a moment..."

He didn't seem to want to continue, and Kett waited.

"He wasn't afraid," he went on. "He looked at me while he closed the back of the hearse, and he started... he started walking towards me, like he was going to put *me* in there too."

Gilbert sucked in a sudden breath through his nose, snorting so loud that it made Kett jump.

"I'm so ashamed," he said, hunkered over. He looked up like a turtle from its shell. "I should have gone to help him, help Vin. But I... I just left him there. I closed the door. I locked the door and just left him out there."

He snorted in another breath, releasing it as a sob.

"I locked the door and ran to the window and he wasn't coming after me. Thank God." He crossed his fingers over his chest. "He drew something on the car park, you've seen it? He did that, and I watched him climb into his hearse and drive away. Vin in the back. But I called you straightaway. I did that much. That was enough, wasn't it?"

He looked like he wanted forgiveness, but Kett didn't offer it.

"You didn't see his face, but what else can you tell me about him? Tall, short, fat, skinny, broad shoulders, skin colour, hair colour? What was he wearing? What did the mask look like?"

"Uh..." the man's eyes scrolled back and forth. "Tall, I think. Not as tall as you, but it was hard to tell."

"Because you were hiding behind the door?" said Porter.

"Right. Yes. He was all in black, with gloves. Long hair, hung over his face, down to his shoulders. I saw his neck, if that helps? I can describe that?"

"You can describe his neck?" asked Kett. Gilbert nodded.

"It was a normal neck," he said. "But I could tell he was white."

"You're sure?"

"Yes," the man said, although he was shaking his head.

"That's all?"

Gilbert licked his lips again.

"He was fearless," he said after a moment. "You know how you get cats that aren't afraid of people? I love cats, but sometimes you'll meet one and it will... it will look you in the eye and you can see the lion there. You get that fear in *you*, something right in your spine. You know this thing won't run if you try to scare it off, it will claw your eyes out, it will clamp its teeth into your throat. You know?"

"I've met a cat like that before," said Porter. "The one I was telling you about, sir, from the cult. Right evil bastard."

"Wasn't a cult," said Kett. "What are you saying, Gilbert?"

"I'm saying that's what he looked like, this man. He looked like he would have murdered me on the spot, would have ended my life and never thought about it again, like it was nothing. Like *I* was nothing. If I hadn't locked that door, I'd have died, I'm sure of it. If I'd gone out there to help, I'd be dead."

Kett puffed out a breath, wanting to tell the man it didn't matter if he'd been afraid, wanting to tell him that he should have done the right thing and tried to help.

"I'll need the names and addresses of Vin and everyone else who comes to your group," he said instead.

"We've got everyone's details," said the PC, her hat still in her hands. "We're rounding them up as we speak."

"These kids, they're vulnerable, right?"

Gilbert nodded, wiping away a tear before it could bury itself in his beard.

"Very," he said.

"You ever heard any of them talk about videos on YouTube? A course, of sorts, about... I don't really know what it's about. Becoming a devil. The five pillars of consciousness. It's by a man called Joseph Maynard, but he doesn't call himself that. He goes by a number: 4522912."

Gilbert shook his head.

"They're on their phones all the time. I don't know what they watch. I don't want to know. Nothing good on there, is there?"

"Vincent never spoke about somebody new in his life?" said Kett. "A new group of people, maybe? He hasn't had new clothes? Watches?"

"No," said Gilbert. "Kid has nobody, other than me. Dirt poor. He's been coming here half his life, you know. I do love him. I love all of them." He looked up through his tears. "Please find him."

"We're doing everything we can," he said. "Thank you."

Kett walked away, heading for the open door, stopping before he reached it.

"You're right," he said, turning back, feeling a sudden wave of pity for the old man, for his church hall and his little box of fidget toys and his endless love. "If you'd gone out there, he'd have killed you. You locked the door. It was the only thing you could do."

Gilbert nodded a quiet thanks, but the guilt was still there. It would always be there.

Kett knew that because it was always there in *him*, too. All the times he hadn't done the right thing. All the times he'd locked the door.

With a sigh that filled the hall, he walked out into the cold.

CHAPTER FIFTEEN

Savage sat in the waiting area of one of the Norfolk and Norwich's surgical theatres, listening to her ears wailing a tune. The tinnitus was the worst she'd ever known it, an unbroken, high-pitched whine. Every sound was muffled like she was underwater, and the panic of it, the thought that it might be like this forever, made her feel like she was drowning.

Still, better deaf than *dead*. The grenade in that tank could easily have killed her. And the doctor who'd taken a look said her eardrums hadn't burst.

Something nudged her arm, and she turned to see Duke. He was talking, she realised, although she couldn't make out a word he was saying.

"Huh?" she said.

"Poke?" he said.

"Poke?"

"Yeah?" Duke frowned. "See?"

"What?"

"See this," he said.

Savage swallowed, the tinnitus fading for a second

before coming back with a vengeance. Duke was nodding like a dog in a car. He got up, adjusting his equipment belt as he headed out of the room.

"Huh?" Savage said again, this time to herself.

She was thinking about following him, in case it was something important, when the door to surgery swung open and a nurse appeared, holding it for a hospital bed being pushed by an orderly. A small team of doctors and nurses followed, all looking like they'd just run a marathon.

Lying in the bed was the kid she'd last seen inside the tank. The plastic around his face had been replaced by bandages, his hair shaved. His eyes were closed.

She walked over, cranking her jaw to try to get the ringing to stop.

"Hey," she said, her voice sounding like it was coming from another room.

The convoy paused as she reached them. Savage took a moment to study the boy's bandaged face, the tube that disappeared into his nose, the weeping wounds on his skin where the plastic bin bags had been surgically removed. His shallow breaths were the only thing that let her know he was still alive—he looked like a mummy that had been removed from its tomb.

The doctor was speaking, and she held up a hand, pointing a finger at her ear.

"I'm really sorry, you'll have to shout," she said. "Explosion knocked out my hearing."

"You were there?" the doctor asked, walking closer.

Savage nodded.

"He going to be okay?"

"Yeah," the doctor said, spraying spittle in her ear as he leaned in. "He's lost quite a bit of his epidermis, but we got most of the plastic off with a solution. He's severely malnourished and dehydrated, and there's quite a bit of infection. He was in the tank for a long time."

"You know how long?" Savage asked.

The doctor shook his head.

"Hours," he said. "He's lucky you found him, but he's lucky he's strong, too. He'll make it."

Another breath, the relief growing.

"Did you get a good look at him?" she asked. "Enough to make a description?"

The doctor thought about it for a second.

"Dark hair, curly. Darker skin, Mediterranean, maybe."

Savage pulled out her phone, finding the photograph of the Uysal brothers that Kett had sent her.

"Could it have been one of these men?"

He took his time.

"I can't be sure, but yes, maybe."

"I need to ask you something else," Savage said. "Does he have a tattoo on his stomach? A pentagram with an eye in the middle?"

The doctor nodded.

"You need to see it?" he asked.

"No, let him rest," Savage said. "Any other tattoos?"

"No," said the doctor. "He's young. I wouldn't put him past eighteen. Did the guy who wrapped him up give him the tattoo as well?"

"Yeah," said Savage.

"You caught him?"

"Yeah," she said. "I think so. One of them, anyway. He's here."

The doctor's face grew taut, his jaw set.

"Maybe I'll pay him a visit, then," he said.

"You'll have to get in line," she told him. "Thank you."

She stood to the side to let the orderly wheel the bed

past, watching them file out of the door. When they'd gone, she texted Kett.

Tank boy alive. Maybe Liam Uysal, can't be sure. He's got the tattoo.

Duke reappeared as she was sending the message, a cup in one hand and a bottle of Diet Coke in the other. She reached for the Coke, but he pulled it away.

"Fine," he said, or something like it.

"What? Aaron, you can't mumble, you need to shout."

"I said it's mine!" he yelled, offering the cup. "You said you wanted tea."

"I never said I wanted anything," she said. "Oh, wait. *Poke*."

"No, *Coke*," he told her.

"Don't mind if I do," she said, and she snatched the bottle from him. "Thank you, Aaron."

He pouted, glaring at the cup of tea like this was all its fault. Savage opened the bottle, taking a long, deep swig that fizzed all the way to her stomach. She took a few more, then handed it back to Duke.

"Kid from the tank had a tattoo," she said, heading out of the room.

"Bless you," he said.

"A *tattoo*!" she just about screamed.

"Really?" said Duke, leaving the cuppa on a chair as he followed. "The pentagram? I thought that was just for Maynard's followers."

Savage nodded, heading for the wards. She'd texted Emily Franklin from the surgery waiting room, asking her if any of the dead men at Cold Iron had the tattoo. It turns out they had.

Big old angry pentagram on the belly of all three soldiers, she'd written back. *Skull in the middle. Well, a skull on two of them, anyway, last one looks like a doughnut. Is that relevant? Why would somebody tattoo a doughnut in a pentagram? Is that how you spell doughnut? My phone's telling me it's wrong.*

The only person they hadn't checked was Ian Hipkin.

She reached the lift, pressing the button to head up. Duke swigged most of the Coke in one go, unleashing a belch she could hear past the tinnitus.

"Sorry," he said, offering her the bottle. There was about half an inch of backwash left.

"No thanks," she told him as the lift doors opened.

He polished it off himself, following her inside. The doors were sliding shut when somebody else joined them, a teenage boy skidding through the gap at the last second, only just making it. He moved to the corner, scratching his neck and staring up at Duke as if wondering how he'd ended up sharing a lift with King Kong. Savage nodded at him, but he didn't even acknowledge her. He was wearing a tracksuit that looked like it hadn't been washed in weeks, and the smell of him seemed to fill the lift like dirty water.

They began to rise. Savage didn't take her eye off the boy, and he finally turned to her.

"You okay?" she asked him.

He sniffed, then grinned. There was something in the smile that made her instantly tense up, and she elbowed Duke.

"What?" he asked, oblivious.

The lift reached the next floor, the doors opening. The kid escaped first, shooting her another wide-eyed look before scuttling off. Savage walked out in time to see him disappear around the corner.

"Nothing," she said. "Just jumpy."

They set off the other way, the corridors here less busy

than the ones they'd just left. It took her a moment to find the ward she wanted, waiting for a nurse to buzz her through. She approached the desk, touching the bruise on her face and wincing.

"You guys on the job or checking into a room?" said the nurse. "Because you look like shit."

"Thanks," said Savage. "On the job, sadly. Ian Hipkin?"

"Still in there," said the nurse, nodding to the first room. "He's fine. We're about to discharge him. His mum's just stepped out."

Savage nodded her thanks before walking to the open door. Ian sat on the edge of the bed in a fresh pair of pyjamas, his legs swinging beneath him. His face was badly bruised, his nose covered with a bandage, but his hair had been brushed and he looked brighter. PC Felicity Niven stood next to him, laughing about something as Savage knocked on the door.

"Oh, hi, Kate," said Niven. "Are you okay? I heard what happened."

"I'm alright," she said. "Deaf as a post, though. You doing okay, Ian?"

The kid nodded, giving Savage a nervous smile, revealing his chipped tooth. The smile fled his face as soon as Duke loomed through the door.

"We're literally going to be here for two minutes," she told him. "Then we're gone. You heading home?"

Ian nodded, his legs still swinging like a much younger child's.

"Your mum here?" Savage asked.

"She's gone to get sweeties," he said.

"Sounds good," said Savage. "Look, Ian, I hate to ask you this, but it's important. We know you were hanging around at Cold Iron, we know you love the paintball, but it was more than that. Right?"

"It wasn't," he said. "It was just the paintball, I swear."

"Then you don't have a tattoo?" Savage asked. "On your stomach?"

"A tattoo?" he said, horrified. "No, of course not."

"You mind if we have a look?"

Ian's legs stopped swinging.

"At my *tummy*?" he said.

"One quick peek, then we're gone."

Ian glanced at PC Niven, as if she might be able to save him.

"You can wait until your mum's back," said Savage. "There's no hurry."

He nodded, his legs started to pendulum back and forth again, like a dog's tail.

"If it helps," said Niven, "I've been here for a while, and I haven't seen any evidence of a tattoo."

"I don't have a tattoo," said Ian, laughing like it was the craziest thing in the world.

"That's good," said Savage. "That's great, Ian."

She wondered whether to press him, and decided she might not get another chance.

"You had a box of stuff in your room. On top of your wardrobe. You remember?"

Ian's legs stopped moving again.

"No," he said, although Savage wasn't sure if he was denying it, or just horrified that she'd found it.

"The box for the paintball gun. Only there was no gun, there was a ring, and a knife, and a glass jar full of blood."

"No," he said again, putting his hands to his ears. His pyjama top lifted as he did so, revealing his stomach—no sign of ink.

"You're not in any trouble," Savage told him.

"It's not mine," he told her.

"The box? Or what's in it?"

"None of it," he said, dropping his hands and looking at Niven again. "None of it."

"I believe you," said Savage. "Who gave it to you, Ian? If it's not yours, who gave you all that stuff?"

The boy's mouth opened, but nothing came out.

"You're really not in any trouble," Savage said again. "You've done nothing wrong. We just need to know whose stuff that is. And, more importantly, whose blood is in the jar."

"I don't know," he said, looking at her, then at Duke, then past them both. "I promise. Mr M just gave it to me, told me to look after it for him."

"Mr M?" said Savage, wondering if she'd heard him right. "Maynard? Joseph Maynard, the old man at Cold Iron?"

Ian nodded.

"So he gave you the box and told you to keep it. You haven't touched it?"

The kid squirmed, looking at Niven for a third time.

"It's okay," the PC told him. "Kate's one of the good guys, she wants to help."

He didn't seem sure.

"And Aaron's a teddy bear," Niven added. "Right?"

"Huh?" said Duke from the door.

Ian looked down at his knees, his legs starting to swing again.

"He just gave it to me," he said. "With all the stuff, said it was mine to keep, said it would help."

"Help with what?" asked Savage.

"The dreams," he said. "Told me all the silver would keep the nightmares away."

"And it worked?"

He shook his head.

"What about the container? Maynard gave it to you like that? With the blood already in it?"

"No," said Ian. "It's my blood."

"Your blood?" she said. "You cut yourself?"

"Just a little bit," he said. "It wasn't bad, and it wasn't all at once."

Savage waited, shaking her head.

"Like, I'd cut myself a bit, and a trickle would come out, but it just filled it up. I added water too."

"Over days?" she asked. "Weeks?"

"Yeah. And it didn't hurt, not really."

"This was for the nightmares, too?"

"Yeah."

"But it didn't work?"

Ian shrugged.

"Maynard, Mr M, he told you to do this? To cut yourself and collect the blood?"

The kid's face crumpled.

"I want my mum," he said.

"I'm really sorry," Savage told him. "Just one more question. Did he ask you to do anything else? Anything that might keep the bad dreams away? Did he ever tell you to have a tattoo? Or show you some of his videos on YouTube?"

Nothing.

"We found Liam," Savage said. "At Cold Iron. You were right, he was in the tank."

"He's always in the tank," said Ian with a faint smile.

"You know who put him in there?"

Ian didn't answer.

"Did you ever hang out with some other boys there? Liam's brother Emil? Or a kid named Dennis? One called Vincent?"

"No," he said, frowning.

"And the man you mentioned before, the master, can you tell me anything—"

"Oi, you, clear off!"

The shout rang out before Savage could finish the question. It was a woman's voice, and she turned, expecting to see Ian's mother. The apology was already on her lips, but it died there, because it wasn't Mrs Hipkin at all. It was the nurse, yelling over her desk at somebody out of sight.

"Go on, get out of here. I won't tell you again."

"Hang on," Savage said to Ian. "Don't go anywhere."

She pushed past Duke into the ward's reception, rounding the corner and spotting a young man standing at the entrance, holding the doors open. At first, she thought it was the same one from the elevator, but when she took another couple of steps she realised it wasn't. This guy was older, and he was dressed in jeans and a charcoal-coloured hoodie rather than a tracksuit. His trainers were bright red.

The weird smile on his face was the same, though. The men could have been twins.

"Hi," he said to Savage.

"Who are you, then?" she asked him.

"He's been hovering about here all evening," said the nurse, walking to Savage's side. "He slipped in just now when the door was open." She raised her voice again. "Leave, or I'm calling security."

"No need," said Duke, who had joined them. "Last chance, mate, off you trot."

The man lifted the front of his jumper, revealing his slim stomach.

And the pentagram tattoo that had been inked across his ribs.

"Shit," said Savage.

She started running, but the kid was as fast as a whippet, whirling on his heels and bolting through the open door. By the time she'd reached it the lock had clicked shut again, and she hammered her fist against the release button.

"Come on!" she said when it wouldn't engage. Through the windows she saw the guy reach the end of the corridor and swing right, vanishing.

She whacked the button again, heard the click. She wrenched the door open and Duke bounded through it, barrelling ahead of her.

"Careful, Aaron," she yelled, pulling her phone from her pocket. She had to slow down to find Clare's number, breaking into a run again as it rang.

Duke was out of sight, his footsteps echoing like gunshots. Savage reached the junction and swung right, colliding with a nurse who was doing her best to stay out of the way. The curved corridor angled to the left, nobody in sight.

"Shit," she said, sprinting.

"What is?" came the Superintendent's voice in her ear. "The case? The job? Life in general?"

"We've got one of Maynard's tattooed followers in the hospital," she said. "He was hanging around Ian Hipkin's room. Saw us and started running."

"Shit," said Clare. "Where are you now?"

"Third floor," she said. "I can't see him, Duke's in pursuit."

"We're on our way."

"He's in his twenties, sir, jeans and a black jumper. Red shoes. He's... hang on."

Twenty yards away, a door was swinging slowly shut.

"He's going for the stairs," she said into her phone, then she slid it into her pocket to free up her hands.

She ran to the door, shouldering through it into the freezing stairwell. Duke's shouts echoed up from below, along with a thunder of footsteps, and when she leaned over the handrail she saw two figures racing to the level below.

"Aaron?"

She set off down the steps, taking them three at a time. She was swinging around the bend when she heard a shout of pain from below, but she couldn't tell who it was.

"Aaron?" she cried out.

She grabbed the handrail and spun around the next turn to see Duke at the bottom of the steps, both hands to his face. He was backing away from something, falling against the dark window. The man with the red shoes was walking towards him, a plastic water bottle clenched in both hands.

"Hey!" Savage yelled. "Get away from him!"

Duke was screaming, the worst sound she'd ever heard. He dropped onto his backside, curling his legs up to protect himself.

The man holding the bottle laughed, turning to Savage, wearing that same awful, dead-eyed grin. She stopped a few steps from the bottom, seeing the younger kid standing by the fire escape door. Duke was still crying out, his hands covering his face.

"Stop," she said, her voice a whisper.

"Or what?" said the guy with the bottle, turning it towards her. "Melt your fucking face, too?"

The younger boy laughed like a hyena, opening the fire escape. Almost immediately, an alarm began to sound. He walked through it like he didn't have a care in the world, still laughing. The other guy backed slowly after him, jerking the bottle towards Savage. The fluid inside sloshed, leaking from the cap and pattering to the floor.

"Acid, bitch," he said. "You should try it, not like you can get any uglier."

And with that, he bolted.

Savage crashed down the last few steps, crouching next to Duke and grabbing his hands. He resisted, holding them to his face. His skin was red and wet, and there was an acrid, chemical smell in the air that made her want to throw up.

"Aaron?" she sobbed. "It's okay, let me have a look, let me look."

She pulled harder, bracing herself for the worst as his big hands came away.

"How bad is it?" he said. "I can't see."

Savage rocked back, releasing another sob—this one of relief.

"You're alright," she said, taking his hands again and holding onto them. "It's okay, Aaron. It's not acid."

His skin looked sore, but it wasn't burning. There were flecks of red and black stuck to his cheeks, his forehead, his eyelids, and when she leaned closer she realised what it was.

"It's not acid," she said again. "Looks like chillies and pepper. Homemade mace."

"I'm not melting?" said Duke, sniffing. He sneezed violently.

"Don't open your eyes," she said. "I'm going to find some milk."

"I'm not thirsty, Kate."

"For your face, mate."

She stood up, checking the fire door to make sure it was

closed—at least the men wouldn't be able to get back in. Duke sneezed again, then twice more, groaning.

"Can you wait here?" she said.

He didn't look like he wanted to, but he nodded. Savage ran up the steps and through the door onto the first level.

"Help!" she shouted into the deserted corridor. "I need help!"

It was lucky she was in a hospital, because within five seconds half a dozen nurses had stuck their heads out of various doors.

"I've got an injured officer at the bottom of the stairs," she said. "He's been pepper sprayed."

The nurses moved quickly, following Savage into the stairwell where they were almost bowled over by two constables tearing down the stairs.

"Duke's at the bottom," Savage told them. "Two men ran out the fire door, they've got some kind of homemade mace, so watch your eyes."

She didn't wait for a reply, heading up again, every muscle in her body burning like she had chilli water for blood. As she pushed through the door of the third floor, she remembered her phone, pulling it out of her pocket. The call was still live.

"Sir," she said.

No answer, but she could hear Clare yelling at the top of his voice. She lowered the phone and realised she could still hear it, and when she rounded the corner she spotted the Superintendent up ahead, flanked by four constables.

"What's going on?" he roared.

"Duke," she said, sucking in a breath. "We followed the guy, but it was an ambush. They sprayed him with something. He's okay."

She doubled up, her hands on her knees.

"They got out the fire door, sir. I'm sorry."

"What the hell are they playing at?" said Clare. "This entire place is mobbed with police."

"Wait," said Savage, suddenly understanding.

As hard as it was, she broke into a run again, heading past Clare to the entrance of the ward. The door wouldn't open, and when she looked through the window, she couldn't see the nurse. She pounded on it.

"What's going on?" Clare asked, right behind her.

"It was a distraction, sir," she said. "They wanted us to follow them, they wanted us out of the ward."

"Stand back," the Super said. "Sully, get through there."

Savage backed off as one of the constables charged the door, shouldering it hard enough to disengage the magnetic lock. It swung open, thumping into the wall, the PC crashing to his hands and knees. Savage ran through, heading for the ward.

Stopping when she saw the leg that jutted out from behind the desk.

She moved around, seeing the nurse. She was on the floor, a halo of blood around her head.

"Sir! Get some help!"

She moved to the open door of Ian Hipkin's room, knowing before she got there that they were too late. PC Niven lay crumpled against the wall like a ragdoll, her face swollen.

Ian was gone.

CHAPTER SIXTEEN

"SAY THAT AGAIN, SIR?"

Kett had to press the phone hard against his ear to hear the Superintendent, because the signal out here was so bad. He was standing on a country lane in the middle of the Norfolk wilderness, but he might as well have been in space, the world swallowed by night. The cold wind cut through his coat and his jacket, creeping down his collar and up his sleeves. Twenty yards ahead, Porter's torch picked apart the dark.

"Because for a second, I thought you said somebody attacked you at the hospital."

"It's because that's exactly what I said, you tossbodger," Clare barked. "A bunch of Maynard's men. Or *boys*. They maced Duke and knocked Niven into the middle of next week. Tried to kill a nurse, too."

"They're okay?" asked Kett.

"They'll live. But it could have been worse. And Ian Hipkin has gone."

"Shit," said Kett, moving the phone to his other ear.

"Gone as in he went willingly, or gone as in he's been taken?"

"How the toss should I know?" Clare said. "I'm about to check the security feed. But they played us, Kett. They were organised. They knew what they were doing. There are, at my last count, forty police officers in the hospital. Maynard's creeps waltzed through all of us and took a child from under our noses."

"They've got form for this, sir," said Kett. "They destroyed half of HQ in order to get hold of those two kids in the Clegg case, and that was on Maynard's orders too. We should have been better prepared."

"Well thank you for those words of wisdom," said Clare. "I don't know what I'd do without you. What are you doing, anyway? Fiddling with your floppy friend?"

"*What*?" said Kett.

"I mean Porter, you pervert."

"Oh, right. No, sir. I mean, he's here, but we're not... fiddling. We've got a lead on the hearse, camera saw it turning off the A47 just east of Dereham. There's not a lot up here, so we might get lucky."

"You're there now?"

"Yeah."

Clare took a breath, sighing down the line.

"Be careful, Kett."

He hung up.

Kett kept his phone out, switching on the torch and sweeping the light over the potholed road, into the thick hedges. The wind did its best to bully him, but he pushed through it, following Porter into the wilderness.

"Anything?" he called out.

"Yeah, plenty," the DI shouted back. "Of absolutely nothing. What are we even looking for?"

A hearse. A kidnapper. A murderer, thought Kett. *Hopefully just hanging out, willing to turn himself in.*

"I have no idea," he said, shivering. "Honestly, when this case is done, I'm booking a holiday. Abroad. Beaches. Kids' clubs."

"Kids' clubs for who? Duke?"

Kett laughed quietly, switching his torch to the other side of the road. Another few minutes and he'd be ready to pack it in, because this was the most pointless exercise in the history of policing. Google Maps showed that the lane cut up from the dual carriageway to the next main road, so the driver of the hearse was probably just using it as a shortcut. He could be miles away from here by now.

But it wasn't *that* much of a shortcut. Maybe there was another reason he'd come this way.

Kett checked the time on his phone, then used it to call DS Spalding.

"Hey, Alison," he said when he heard the call connect. "How's it going?"

"Fine," she snapped back. "What do you need?"

"Can you just check some property records for me? Station Road, just north of Middleton, before it hits the main road. Is there anyone here on the system?"

"That's it?" said Spalding. "No snide remarks? No casual insults?"

"Uh... No?"

She waited a little longer.

"Unless you want them?" he said, confused.

Spalding hung up.

"What has got into her?" he asked, shining the torch up the street to where Porter was. Or where he *had* been, because he seemed to have disappeared. "Pete?" he called out. "Where are you?"

"In here, sir," Porter called back.

"Where?"

"The hedge."

Kett jogged up the road, the cold making his bones ache. He couldn't see the DI anywhere.

"Pete?"

"You've gone past me," said Porter.

Kett swung around, aiming the phone at the hedge on his left in time to see Porter's pasty face push out of it.

"Fire, sir," he said, vanishing again. "Can't you smell it?"

"I can't smell anything past... well, *you*."

But he sniffed anyway, the tang of smoke clawing its way into his sinuses.

"Fire," he said, following Porter into the hedge.

It was thicker than it looked, the heavy branches molesting him, digging into his face and his armpits and his crotch. The light from his torch was doing nothing, and he pushed blindly forward until the hedge regurgitated him on the other side.

"Argh," he grunted, spitting leaves.

Past Porter's broad shoulders was a narrow, barren field, a collection of brick outbuildings on the far side. Somewhere behind them was a faint orange glow, tongues of flame reaching up over the low barn.

"Shit," said Kett, moving forward, almost turning his ankle on the furrowed ground. "Call it in, Pete."

"It's a nightmare out there, sir," said Porter. "Muddy as anything. Might want to go around."

"No time," said Kett, immediately planting his shoe in a puddle of wet dirt so deep he almost couldn't pull it out again.

"There's a path right here," said Porter.

Kett ignored him, pressing on. The field was a bastard,

the ridges hard but the valleys so soft it was like trying to run through a swamp. There were tangles of vegetation, too, which did their best to trip him up. It seemed to take all night to cross it, and by the time he'd stepped onto solid ground on the far side, he was so breathless there was a firework display going off overhead.

Porter had taken the long way around, and was waiting for him.

"You should have—"

"Don't say it," wheezed Kett.

They were right behind the brick barn, the air full of smoke, the quiet night broken by the roar and crack of fire. Kett rounded the building, his boots like lead weights because of the mud. Ahead was a courtyard, a burning car in the middle of it.

Not a car. A *hearse.*

The cabin was lost to the inferno, the windscreen shattered, flames blazing from the doors like gas burners. The back of the vehicle hadn't caught yet, but it wouldn't take long.

Kett moved towards it, the heat impossible, singeing his eyebrows from a dozen yards away. He held his hands in front of his face as he skirted around the hearse, heading for the coffin doors.

"Sir, what are you doing?" Porter yelled.

"There might be somebody in there," he called back, thinking of the kid who'd been taken from the church hall—thinking of the driver, too. "Just watch out, he could still be here."

"Sir, it's gonna blow," Porter replied. "It's not worth it."

It *was* worth it.

Kett reached the back, the thunder of the flames dulling every other sound. The world shimmered and trembled and shook beneath the force of the fire. He touched a finger to the handle and drew it back immediately. He tried again, the metal hot but not boiling. He yanked the coffin doors open and a tsunami of smoke rolled out, drowning him.

He reeled back, hacking up his lungs, a high-pitched explosion erupting inside his skull. He was blind, deaf, the heat stripping him of any sense of which way he was facing.

Then he felt Porter's hands on his back, grabbing a fistful of his coat and pulling him away.

"Easy, sir," he said. "There's nobody in there."

Porter kept pulling, and Kett let himself be steered across the courtyard until he felt like he could breathe again. He blinked the tears from his eyes, leaning against the wall of the barn until he felt like he wasn't about to keel over. From here, he could see inside the hearse, the interior lit up by the fire.

Empty.

"You alright?" said Porter.

Kett nodded, then doubled over and threw up on the DI's shoe—nothing but bile.

"Sorry," he said as Porter danced back.

"No!" said Porter.

"Sorry," Kett said again, wiping his mouth and straightening up. "It's the smoke."

"Don't worry about it, sir," Porter said mournfully. "They were going in the bin anyway."

"You see anything else?" asked Kett, smudging the tears from his eyes.

"Yeah," said Porter, suddenly tensing. "People."

"People?" said Kett, still coughing.

Porter didn't reply, heading around the burning hearse and giving it plenty of space. There were buildings on all sides of the courtyard, the barn behind them, a stable block, and three smaller structures, all brick with tiled roofs and open doorways. Kett stared into the darkness of the building that Porter was walking towards, seeing a tall shadow, a blank face picked out by the firelight.

"Oi!" Porter yelled. "Police! Get out here."

"Careful, Pete," said Kett.

He followed the DI, checking the next building as he went.

A second man stood there in the dark, perfectly motionless.

"We've got another one," he called out. "To your right."

His phone was ringing, and he pulled it out to see Spalding's name on the screen. He answered it, talking over her as she started to speak.

"Alison, we're at a farm just off Church Road. We've found the hearse, it's on fire. Got hostiles, two of them."

"Three," yelled Porter, who was on the far side of the burning vehicle.

"Three," said Kett. "We're going to need people out here right now. Tactical, if you can. Air support, in case they bolt. And quick."

"Got it, sir," said Spalding, her snarkiness replaced by concern. "Hang back until they get there."

"Too late."

He hung up, skirting the fire. Porter was at the door of the first building, firelight dancing on his back as he leaned inside.

"Get on the floor!" he shouted. "Right now!"

None of the men were moving, all of them standing stock still. Kett jogged to Porter's side, sweating in the unbearable heat. The man waited for them, his face hidden by a crimson mask covered with ornate gold symbols, a hood pulled over the top. His arms rested by his sides, hands covered by the long sleeves of his robes.

"On the floor," Kett shouted, making Porter jump.

The man still didn't move.

"Your funeral," said Kett.

They ran forward together, Porter grabbing the man's arm and swinging him around. The figure toppled, Porter falling on top of it with a squawk. The mask pinged off, skittering across the floor and revealing the featureless white face of a mannequin.

"Well," said Kett. "You got him."

He offered Porter a hand, pulling him up. The DI dusted himself off, using his boot to open the black and gold robes to reveal the rest of the dummy.

"The hell?" he said.

Kett walked out of the door, shielding his face with his hand as he walked to the next building along—a shed of some kind, most of the roof missing. He didn't even bother to shout, he just gave the figure that stood there a hefty kick that sent it sprawling to the floor. The robes parted, revealing the plastic torso beneath. The mask stayed on this time, dead eyes pointed at the night sky through the holes in the ceiling. It was different to the last one, the eyes narrower, the brow bigger, two short horns curling up from the forehead.

"Dummy here too," Porter shouted.

Kett walked into the courtyard, the inferno too bright to look at. Porter was to his left, emerging from another shed. A third mannequin lay on the floor behind him.

"What's going on?" he said.

"Can you see any more?" Kett asked him.

Porter angled his head to the left, nodding.

"Got another one over there, sir," he said.

He waited for Kett to catch up, and they approached a small stable block together. The fourth figure stood just like the rest, arms at its sides, its body covered with black robes. Beneath the hood its mask was larger, the horns longer, black pits for eyes.

They rounded the hearse and Kett checked the final building—the barn they'd walked past to get to the courtyard. A fifth figure waited there for them, motionless.

"Which one do you want?" Porter asked.

"Honestly? Neither."

Porter laughed, making his way cautiously to the stables. Kett angled towards the barn.

"You think one of these guys is going to be alive?" he asked.

"He'd have to be crazy," Porter replied. "Just standing here waiting to be caught."

"Right," said Kett. "But just so we're on the same page, this guy *is* crazy."

Porter had vanished through the stable door, and Kett heard a clatter as he knocked the mannequin to the floor.

"Dummy," he called back.

Kett walked into the barn, hearing the warble of the pigeons on the rafters. It was completely empty in here, half of the space drowning in darkness, the other half squirming in flickering light. The figure watched him, its sleeves hanging limply, its robes so long they touched the floor. Its mask was crimson, like the others, but this one was featureless other than the eye holes.

"Don't move," Kett told it.

The figure moved, cocking its head.

Kett choked on his own scream, staggering back. The figure took a step towards him, its head still tilted at an unnatural angle. It lifted its arms, gloved hands flexing.

"Pete!" Kett shouted, still retreating.

A whistle from the courtyard, too loud and too long to be human. It sounded like a falling bomb, and it was followed almost immediately by an explosion as the hearse's fuel tank finally blew.

The world burned white, the concussive force blasting into the barn hard enough to knock Kett off his feet. He sprawled, hearing a second explosion—even louder than the first.

He looked up, waiting for the figure to attack him, waiting for the flash of a blade or the bark of a gun.

There was no sign of the masked man.

"Pete!" he shouted again, heaving himself to his feet.

"Sir?"

Porter ran into the barn, his coat over his face. Behind him, the hearse was a pyre, churning smoke into the night.

"You alright?"

"He's here," said Kett, turning back. "He's..."

There was a mannequin on the floor of the barn, covered in flowing robes. To the side, lying face down, was a mask. The blaze was bright enough now to light up the whole barn, and it was clear there was nobody else here.

"What the..."

Kett used a muddy boot to kick the clothes away from the mannequin. Like the others, it was made of plastic, the face blank, the limbs skinny. A metal pole emerged from its backside, connected to a stand.

"You sure you're okay, sir?" asked Porter, by his side.

"Yeah, I... This thing was moving, I'm sure of it."

"Knocked over by the explosion?"

"No, before then. It walked towards me, it held its hands out."

He could still see it, the way it had twisted its neck like

it was trying to work out who he was. He could see those gloved fingers flexing.

"It was coming right for me," he said.

"Pretty hard to believe, sir," said Porter, leaning over the mannequin. "With the rod up its arse. *And* the fact it's made of plastic."

Kett crossed the barn, heading for the far wall. There were alcoves here, pockets of shadow that the firelight couldn't reach. The first was empty, but when he stepped into the next, he saw a wooden door in the wall. When he put his shoulder to it, it creaked open. Beyond was the field they'd crossed to get here, as black as pitch to his light-blinded eyes.

He walked into the fresh night air, scanning the dark, trying to hear anything past the roar of blood in his ears.

"Police!" he yelled, just because he couldn't think of anything else to do.

Nothing.

He turned back, entering the barn to see Porter collecting the robes and the mask from the floor.

"Fire's spreading," the DI explained before Kett could tell him to leave them alone. "Whole place is going to go up."

Kett nodded, walking outside and making his way to the stable next door. He paused before he went in, the fire almost pleasant now as it kept the chill of the evening at bay. Past the farm, the world might as well not have existed, like it had been erased.

All the same, he couldn't shake the feeling that something was staring right back at him.

CHAPTER SEVENTEEN

Porter was right. The whole place went up, and *fast*.

The flames were ravenous as they chewed through the old buildings, swallowing the smaller sheds whole before starting on the barn and the stable block. One by one, the old structures sacrificed themselves to the pyre, burning so brightly that Kett couldn't stare straight at it. The sound was like artillery fire: beams cracking, tiles exploding, loud enough to drown out the arrival of a tactical van twenty minutes after they'd called for backup.

Chester Andilet clambered out, checking his rifle before walking over.

"You guys called?" he said.

Kett nodded a greeting.

"That was quick," he said. "I don't think we need you. If our guy was here, he's long gone."

"Well, I can hang about," said Andilet. "Just in case."

"You on your own?" asked Kett, staring past him at the empty van.

"Superintendent wants to keep an armed presence at

the hospital," he replied. "And at HQ. But they can spare me for an hour or two. Just yell if you want me."

He headed back, lit by the lights of the fire engine as it trundled down the road, a couple of IRVs in tow. It parked behind the van, the driver leaning out of the window.

"Anyone in there?"

"No," said Kett.

And if there was, it was too late to save them.

Clare's Mercedes was the last to arrive, the Superintendent an angry smudge in the windscreen.

"Probably gonna let it burn out," said the fireman. "Ground's wet, and there's nothing out here. You know how it started?"

"Arson," Kett told him. "Somebody set fire to a car. Blew up."

"You alright?"

"Somehow, yeah," said Kett.

But the truth was, he *wasn't* alright. The explosion had rocked him, but the memory of that figure shambling towards him had done far more damage. He'd imagined it, obviously, and it wasn't hard to understand why: the stench of the fire was toxic, choked with smoke and fumes. Even now, with the cold biting through his coat and a fine rain falling, he felt as high as a kite. The air had been alive, too, a mirage from the fire. It had only *appeared* as though the man was moving—or maybe the mannequin had simply toppled over towards him in a gust of wind. The explosion had knocked him over before he saw the truth.

Right?

"Right," he told himself, watching Clare finally get out of the car. The Super stretched his arms up, arching his back and groaning like a mournful walrus lost at sea.

He plodded down the street and past the fire engine, shooting daggers at the firefighters who were lounging inside.

"Oh look," he said when he spotted Kett. "It's you. Why aren't I surprised?"

Kett didn't know what to say.

"You know, you can fight crime without blowing stuff up," Clare went on. "It's not compulsory to just explode the toss out of everything."

"I didn't—"

"First it's Savage with a tank, and now you with a... What was it? The hearse?"

Kett nodded.

"Was alight when we got here, sir."

"Intentional?"

"Yeah, sir," said Kett. "I mean, I don't know for sure, but the cabin was engulfed. You don't see that unless it's deliberate."

They stood on the edge of the field for a moment, watching the blazing barn a hundred yards away. The light picked out the ridges of the field, making it look like they were standing on the edge of an ocean of fire. Porter had retreated down the road a little. He noticed Kett watching and offered a sad little wave.

"Anyone here?" Clare asked. "Other than that soggy wank biscuit?"

"No," said Kett. "I mean, I don't think so."

The Super eyeballed him.

"We thought there was," Kett went on, stumbling over the words. "There were five mannequins in the courtyard where the hearse was, all wearing robes and masks, all standing inside a building and watching the fire. I thought..."

He shrugged, seeing it again—the flash of life through the eyeholes in the mask, the way it had lifted its hands.

"I thought one of the figures was real, sir. I thought I saw it move."

"But you didn't?"

"No, sir. I didn't. I don't know what it was. Fumes, probably."

He could smell them from here, and so could Clare, sucking in a breath through his hairy nostrils and shivering like he was getting off on it.

"We got the masks out before the farm went up," Kett went on. "A set of robes, too. But if there was anything else here, it's long gone. And the hearse is history."

"Do we know anything about this place?" asked Clare. "It's a farm?"

"Kind of," said Kett. "There's no farmhouse, just a load of outbuildings spaced around a courtyard. Spalding was looking into it."

He remembered that she'd called him before the explosion, and he pulled out his phone to see two more missed calls from her. He thumbed her name, shuddering in another blast of frozen wind.

"Hey," he said when she answered.

"You're alive then, sir?" she asked.

"As alive as I ever am these days. Did you find anything?"

"Found some larger trousers, sir, you'll be pleased to know," came her enigmatic reply.

"That's, uh... nice?"

"Put her on speaker," barked Clare. "I can't hear her."

Kett did as he was told.

"Super's here," he warned her, out of courtesy.

"Land's owned by a woman called Martha Weiner,"

Spalding said. "She's in her eighties, inherited it from her late husband who farmed the area. She wasn't interested in carrying it on, sold most of the fields and moved to Cornwall. Kept the buildings at the front of the farm in case her kids ever wanted to develop them, and a few fields out the back end, almost fifty acres. Kids are all retired and living out of the county. Grandkids have long gone. Not a sniff of a criminal record anywhere."

"And?" asked Clare when she didn't continue.

"And what, sir? That's all I've got. Weiner hasn't been there in years, and she doesn't know anyone else who would use it."

"So it's derelict?" asked Kett. "Disused?"

"I'm guessing so, sir."

"Then it could have been anyone," Kett said, kicking a clod of dirt with his filthy boot. "Can you keep digging, Alison? We've had a good look at the smaller end of the farm, but if you can do a search on that big back side, we'd be grateful."

"What?" said Spalding, choking on the word.

He hung up, pocketing his phone.

"She really does seem angry today, sir," he said. "Maybe you should speak with her, see if she's okay?"

"No," grunted Clare. "I like my bollocks untossed, thank you very much."

"Not sure what that has to do with anything," Kett replied. He shivered, wondering whether he should move closer to the fire before he came down with hypothermia. "You need me for anything here?"

Clare spluttered out a sigh.

"No. I want you back at HQ. It's been a day from hell, and we need to start getting stuff on the board if we're ever going to make any sense of it. Take Porter, and get those masks and robes or whatever you found to forensics. I'll deal with this mess."

He stomped over to the fire engine and gave the bumper a solid kick.

"If you hadn't bloody noticed," he roared at the firefighters inside, "there's a fire over there. So why don't you pull out your big tossing hoses and start spraying!"

He set off without waiting for a reply, heading into the fire-lit field and leaving a truckful of confused faces behind him.

"Uh, sir," Kett said. "There's a path around the outside, it's a little boggy in there."

"You're a little boggy!" Clare bellowed back. "Toss off!"

The Super seemed to be stuck, doing his best to yank his foot out of the mud.

"Toss off!" he yelled again, although it wasn't clear who he was talking to.

Kett left him to it, walking up to Porter.

"Toss off!" Clare roared again, this time faceplanting in the mud.

"Tossing off is good advice," said Porter, watching the Super as he tried to get back to his feet. "We've almost died in one explosion today, and it looks like there's going to be another one any second now."

"Agreed," said Kett. "Let's go."

IT WAS ONLY when Kett walked into the bright reception of Norfolk Constabulary HQ that he realised how knackered he and Porter looked. They were both caked in mud from the crotch down, their coats covered with burrs and leaves. Porter had about half a hedge in his hair, and he still stank of stagnant water and dog shit. Their faces were smeared with smoke, their eyes red.

"Bloody hell," said Kett, looking Porter up and down.

"Yeah," said Porter, who was holding the collection of masks and the robe they'd taken from the burning building—secured in a clear plastic bag. "I am more than happy to forget today ever happened."

"It's not over yet," Kett told him.

Two members of the tactical team were standing guard in reception, and Kett nodded to them as he passed. It seemed like overkill, but it wasn't. Maynard's men had attacked the police station once already, less than two months ago. He had people everywhere.

Kett trod to the bullpen, giving Spalding a nod as he cut through to the kitchen—one that she didn't return. He was absolutely famished, but the fridge was empty, not even any milk to make tea. He groaned his way back through to see that Spalding had opened a packet of crisps, and he walked to her desk, practically salivating.

"You haven't got any more of those, have you, Alison?"

"Why?" she shot back, spitting crumbs. "Afraid they'll go right to my arse, sir?"

Kett opened his mouth, but he didn't know what to say. Thankfully Porter saved him, opening the door and calling out.

"Hay's here, she's checking out the masks. You coming?"

Kett took one last look at the crisps before following Porter into the corridor. They trudged in silence to the other side of the building, too exhausted to talk. The door to Cara Hay's room was open, loud voices bubbling out, and when Kett looked inside he saw Emily Franklin standing alongside the forensic technician. She was midway through a story.

"All of them, at once, right in the Superintendent's office!"

"Evening," said Kett.

"Oh, hi," said Franklin, waving.

Kett entered the room, Porter right behind him, both yawning in tandem. Hay had laid out all five masks on her desk, along with the single set of robes that Porter had managed to carry with him. It was a terrifying ensemble.

"I was just telling Cara," Franklin said, looking at the masks, "I've had dreams like this."

"You mean nightmares?" said Kett, studying the five crimson faces.

"Uh... sure," said Franklin. "Nightmares. *Definitely* not sex dreams."

She stared at her fingertips.

"Right," said Kett. "So, um, yeah. This is what we recovered from the farm. The masks were mounted on mannequins, the bodies covered with robes."

"Where are the rest of the robes?" asked Hay.

"At the farm," Porter told her. "The fire got most of them, they were too heavy to carry. I figured the masks were more important."

"You touched them all?" she asked.

"I mean, it was hard not to," Porter said. "They'd have gone up, otherwise."

"I'll dust for prints anyway. You never know. I've had a quick look. There are no hairs, there don't seem to be any blood or skin samples. The masks themselves are impressive."

Hay picked one up in her gloved hands, turning it.

"They're wooden frames covered with leather. Very soft, I'm not sure what animal it's from."

"Please don't say human," said Kett.

"No, it's not human. I'm guessing lamb. It's been dyed red. These symbols are gold thread, stitched with a great deal of care."

She put the mask down and lifted another, this one more demonic.

"The horns here are glued on. They're actual horns, I think, from a goat, perhaps, or a sheep. They're professionally made props. I'd guess they were produced by some kind of carnival costume company, but it's more likely the suspect made them himself."

"We've seen them before," said Kett. He reached out to pick up a mask, then stopped—partly because he wasn't wearing gloves, and partly because he realised he didn't *want* to touch it. "Agnes Clegg and her father had masks like this when they were trying to sacrifice the kids to bring back Aggie's mother. You remember, Pete?"

"I mean, it's pretty hard to forget," Porter replied, "given I was strung upside down, ready to be bled out, then stabbed in the shoulder."

He rubbed the wound through his jacket.

"But yeah, sir, the masks they wore were very similar to these."

"And the couple I met in the woods last week, in the Red Room, they had masks on too. They were ribbons, wound around their heads, but they were red. Too much of a coincidence not to be connected. This is Maynard's trademark. He loves the drama of it, the show."

"The couple in the woods weren't necessarily linked to Maynard, though," said Porter. "Right? They were the ones who told you where he was. They told you about Cold Iron Paintball."

"Yeah, but why would they tell me, unless he wanted them to?" Kett said. "I've been thinking about this, a lot.

Maynard was ready for us; he wanted us to find him. He's dying, he hasn't got long left. He's got this... this disciple, or whatever, who he thinks is going to become the Devil. But it's still a game to him, and to make it a game, he needs us to be involved. So he uses them to point us towards him."

It didn't sound massively convincing, and he rubbed his face to try to wake himself up a little.

"I don't know," he said. "Keep working on it, will you, Cara?"

Hay nodded, giving Kett a sympathetic smile. He rapped his knuckles on the desk then headed out of the room, Porter yawning his way after him.

CHAPTER EIGHTEEN

As soon as Kett entered the bullpen again, he smelled food.

"What is that?" he asked, his nostrils flaring.

"I'm not sure," Porter replied. "But it smells amazing."

Kett followed his nose through the desks, sniffing like a bloodhound. He followed the scent into the corridor on the other side of the office, and from there through the open door of the Incident Room.

Here, he almost started crying.

There was a stack of McDonald's burgers on one of the tables, along with a mountain of fries and chicken nuggets. Savage stood next to them, still unloading food from a carrier bag.

"I didn't know what to get, sir," she said. "So I got everything."

"Kate, I could kiss you," he said, picking up a box of chicken nuggets, then a Big Mac, then dropping them both in favour of a Quarter Pounder. "But instead, I'm going to kiss this."

He unwrapped it, taking a bite that was so big he almost

choked. He didn't care, it would be a good death. He wolfed down the entire burger in three mouthfuls then picked up another one, peeling off the wrapper as Spalding walked into the room.

"Dig in, Alison, there's loads," he said through a mouthful.

"Oh, you'd love that, sir, wouldn't you?"

She glared at him with such ferocity that he had to turn away.

"You doing okay?" he asked Savage. "How's Aaron?"

"He's still at the hospital, sir," she replied, wiping her lips with a napkin. "He was sprayed in the face with chilli water. I thought it was... God, the men who attacked us, they said it was acid. I thought he was going to be scarred. *Blind*."

She shook her head.

"You should have seen the look on their faces. They were enjoying it, enjoying the violence. If they'd had acid, they would have used it, I don't doubt that for a second. I think they would have happily killed us, if that's what they'd been told to do. They're brainwashed, sir. They've found a... a leader in Maynard, somebody they're happy to follow, no matter what."

"That's what he does," said Kett. "You've watched any of his videos?"

She nodded.

"He's giving their lives meaning," Kett went on. "They're disenfranchised, forgotten, neglected, and he's giving them a reason to be alive. A cause, based on cruelty and intimidation and violence. We don't know how bad it is."

"And we don't know how many of them there are," said Porter, a Big Mac in each hand. He alternated between them, one bite at a time. "Could be hundreds of followers out there."

"Right," Kett said. "Maynard's not exactly going to tell us, is he? You saw two of them at the hospital?"

"Yes, sir," said Savage. "But there had to have been more, because those two were only a distraction. We don't know who took Ian yet. Superintendent Clare has seen the footage, but I haven't heard from him. He left when you called from the farm."

She nibbled a chicken nugget.

"I'm compiling a list of vulnerable kids who fit Maynard's profile, but there are hundreds of them. Thousands. It'll be like finding a needle in a haystack."

Kett took another Quarter Pounder, heading across the room. Somebody had made a good job of tacking the case notes and photographs to the wall. Maynard sat at the top: the single, blurry image they'd started with. Beneath him, on the left side of the wall, were the young men who had been kidnapped. Dennis Lynn glared out of a passport photo, but both Vincent Kinghorn and Ian Hipkin's pictures had been taken at school. They looked ridiculously young in their uniforms.

A big question mark had been drawn beside Ian, because they didn't know for sure yet if he was a victim or a follower.

On the right were the five other men they'd met so far, the ones who'd proven their allegiance to Maynard by inking his symbol onto their stomachs: Jon Heath, the three soldiers that Gorski's team had eliminated at Cold Iron, and the kid from the tank, who might have been Liam Uysal. There was no sign of his brother, Emil.

"You found the hearse then, sir?" asked Savage.

"Yeah, it nearly barbecued us," he replied. "It was set

alight deliberately, and it can't have happened long before we got there."

"Why would the kidnapper set it on fire?"

"To get rid of any evidence," Kett said, turning to look at her. "That's obvious, right?"

"Yes, sir, but he didn't get rid of all of the evidence, did he? He left the masks, and the robes, probably some other stuff. If he was that worried about us finding something, why not put it all in the car?"

"He probably knew it would be destroyed," said Porter. "The whole farm burned down. He just didn't count on us finding him, I guess."

"Bit of a gamble, sir," said Savage. "Fire like that, in the dark, it would have been visible for miles. Somebody would have called the smokies sooner or later."

"What are you saying, Kate?" Kett asked, polishing off the last of the burger. It sat in his stomach like a greasy brick, and he belched into his hand.

"I don't know, sir. It's like... maybe he wanted us to find the hearse?"

"Why?"

Savage thought about it for a moment, staring at a chicken nugget like it might be able to offer her answers.

"The masks and the robes were on mannequins, right?"

Kett nodded.

"Five of them?"

"Yeah."

"We've seen this guy wearing the masks," Savage went on. "The video from the garage, right? We saw him wearing the mask with the horns when he took Dennis."

"Right," said Kett. "But the old guy from the village hall in Marham said the mask was plain. No horns, I mean. Yellow symbols."

"What if he wore a different mask for each victim?" said Savage.

"There are only three victims," said Porter.

"That we know of. We don't know for sure that Liam was the kid in the tank, and if we include him and assume Emil has been taken too, and we count Ian as a victim, then that's five. Five masks, five robes. He collected them all in the hearse, but he wore a different mask each time."

"Or there are five different kidnappers," said Kett. "Not impossible, if Maynard's building an army."

"I don't know," said Savage. "Maynard made it seem like he was training one man. The master. He wants to see the Devil, singular. His videos, they're like a course, a test. You follow the plan, you become something else. Something more than human. You..."

"Evolve," said Kett, nodding. "So one guy, five masks. Why?"

Nobody replied, the only sound in the room the rustle of paper as Porter unwrapped a third Big Mac.

"Maynard's videos are all about the five pillars," said Savage. "Five stages you go through to become this thing."

"Right," said Kett. "Good. Five pillars, five stages. Uh..."

He walked to the whiteboard, grabbing a pen from the tray. He wracked his brain, trying to remember.

"Divination, sir," said Savage.

"Oh, yeah."

He wrote it down, hesitating again. Savage took pity on him, walking up to the board and pulling the pen from his hand. She marked up the four other stages in her immaculate handwriting.

"Exsanguination, Veneration, Invocation, Limination," he read out. "Anyone any closer to working out what they mean?"

"Devil," said Spalding.

"Huh?" Kett asked, turning back to see her munching on a packet of fries. He wondered if she was slinging another insult at him, but she jutted a chip at the board.

"They spell Devil," she said. "The five words."

Everyone looked.

"Oh yeah," said Kett. "Good spot."

"Wait a minute," said Savage. "Devil."

She returned to the board, writing the names of the kidnapped men.

"Dennis Lynn, Vincent Kinghorn, Ian Hipkin," she said. "We know they've been taken. D, V, I. Liam and Emil give us the rest. DEVIL."

"Holy shit," said Kett. "You're right. That's it, then. Surely. The Uysals are victims too, and Ian. Five boys, five kidnappings, five masks, five pillars of bullshit. That's the plan. But why five?"

"The five-pointed star," said Savage. "The pentagram. We've seen it a few times already, in the garage where Dennis was taken."

"And in the house where the Uysal brothers live," said Kett. "Painted in blood over the body of the woman who was looking after them."

"And in the car park at Marham," said Porter.

"It's ancient," said Savage. "The symbol. We looked into it during the Clegg case, when Aggie was trying to bring her mother back from the dead. Uh..."

She closed her eyes, concentrating.

"It represents the elements, doesn't it? Earth, air, water, fire and spirit."

"But turned upside down, it represents the horned head of the devil," said Kett, remembering. "Wasn't there something about the blending of human and spirit realms, too?"

"That fits," said Porter. "According to Maynard, this guy, whoever he is, he's trying to become the devil. Blending the realms, opening the door, making the impossible possible. Whatever."

He shrugged, a dollop of ketchup squirting from his burger and landing on his shoe—invisible amidst the mud, grass, vomit and everything else.

"I loved these shoes," he said.

"Okay," said Kett. "So the number five is important. This guy loves the symbolism, it's real to him. He's taken five young men. Why?"

The answer hung in the air like a neon sign, as obvious to him as anyone else.

"He's going to kill them," said Savage, the only person brave enough to speak it aloud. "When Angie and her dad kidnapped the kids—"

"And me," said Porter.

"And you, sir, yeah. She wanted to use them as sacrifices. She thought that by killing them, she'd open up a... a gateway, or something, that would let her bring her mum back from the dead. It was the same thing, thinning the barrier between this world and the other side, letting something come through."

"Yeah," said Kett. "And Maynard was the man who was helping her do it. He's the one who told her it would work."

"He believes it," said Porter. "It's insane."

"It's only insane if you *don't* believe it," said Kett. "To Maynard, this is as real as it's possible to be, as sane as anything. But I think you're right, Kate. He's going to kill them. Except he can't kill them all, because we rescued Liam from the tank. He's alive."

"He can still kill the others," said Savage. "Or maybe the

guy in the tank is a red herring. Maybe he's not one of the five."

"So we're looking for *another* victim?" said Kett, shaking his head. "I hope not."

"It makes sense, sir. The kid in the tank had a tattoo. I think we're missing someone."

Nobody argued with her.

"So if you were a man who thought he was going to become the Devil, how would you do it?" Kett asked.

Savage sat up straight in her chair, looking at the collection of photos on the wall.

"The sheep," she said.

"The sheep?" Kett echoed, turning to see the photograph of the butchered animal that had been hanging from the ceiling in the secret room at Cold Iron. "You'd kill them with a sheep?"

"No, sir, obviously not. We thought the sheep might be somebody practising, right? The cuts, the wounds. It wasn't butchery, it was surgery. And we found the jars, five of them, with fake body parts and real blood. A finger, an eye, an ear, a tongue, and... the *other* thing."

"The rib tickler," said a voice from the door.

Superintendent Clare marched in, reeking of smoke, smudges of soot on his face and clothes. His shoes were as filthy as Porter's. Everyone watched as he marched to the table.

"The Dirk Diggler, the Bavarian pickle dip, the custard chucker, the monkey mangler—"

"Stop, sir!" Kett yelled.

"Why are you lot yammering on about genitals?" said Clare, picking up a packet of fries.

"We're talking about the kidnapper, sir," said Savage. "Five victims, but we think he might have been—"

"Genitals," said Clare, cutting Savage off. "Genitals. *Gen. It. Als.*"

"Sir?" she said, horrified.

"Good word," said Clare. "Rolls off the tongue."

"Genitals roll off your tongue?" said Kett, wondering if it was possible to bleach the inside of his skull.

"Genitals," said Clare. "Tell me why you're all so obsessed with them."

He unhinged his mouth like a python, tipping half the fries inside.

"Uh..." said Savage, struggling. "The jars, I think our suspect was training. They were practising whatever they were going to do to their victims. Five jars. The blood was real, but the body parts weren't."

"What are you saying, Kate?" said Kett, the burgers sitting unhappily in a stew of stomach acid.

"I don't know, sir," she said. "I'm just thinking aloud. But what if that's the plan? A ceremony? Five victims, all sacrificed for a piece of their body. He's going to fill the jars with blood and body parts, but this time it's all going to be real."

"Why?" said Clare, spraying chunks of food.

"It's part of his transformation," said Savage. "The kidnapper. By doing this, he becomes the Devil."

She paused for a second.

"In his head, not the real one."

It would have been unthinkable, *impossible,* except the horror of it was all too plausible.

This was Maynard, after all.

"Ian Hipkin was taken from the hospital by two people," said Clare. "While you and Duke were tossing about on the stairs, two young men walked into the ward, cold-cocked the nurse with a hammer, then did the same thing to PC Niven. Security footage shows the three of them walking out the front door."

"Ian went willingly?" said Kett.

"He wasn't being dragged, if that's what you mean," Clare told him. He upended the packet of fries into his mouth, then spoke through them—nothing but noise.

"But he didn't look happy?" said Savage, trying to translate.

Clare nodded.

"He doesn't have a tattoo," said Savage. "Ian's one of the victims, he has to be. But I don't think Liam is. I think we're missing somebody. I think someone else has been taken."

"No," barked Clare, with no further explanation.

"If they're willing to march into a hospital and steal a kid, it means they're working to a deadline," said Kett. "They're running out of time."

He leaned against a table, staring at the wall, trying to fathom Savage's theory. The room stank of smoke from his and Porter's clothes, and it brought him right back to the hearse, to the fire at the farm.

"I still don't get why the kidnapper burned everything," he said. "If he's going to do this, then why get rid of the car? Why destroy the masks?"

"Because he doesn't need them any more," said Savage.

Everyone turned to her.

"What if he's already finished?" she said. "What if he burned everything because his ceremony is over? Because he's sacrificed his victims."

A chill passed through the room, lifting the goosebumps on Kett's arms.

"Shit," he said. "You don't think..."

Savage shrugged, her face lined with sadness.

"What if we're too late?"

CHAPTER NINETEEN

THEY WORKED FOR A WHILE IN SILENCE, BECAUSE nobody had the energy to talk.

Kett sat at his desk, tasting smoke every time he swallowed, smelling it every time he breathed. A sheaf of paperwork sat in front of him, but he could barely read a line without his tired, fire-ravaged eyes filling with tears. He had to keep smudging them away with the back of his hands.

Everything ached, his back full of broken glass, his head thumping. More than once, he sat back in his chair and coughed out a startled grunt as his exhausted muscles began to cramp. It had taken so much from him, the job, and he knew it wouldn't stop. He'd seen it so many times before. It took, and it took, and it took, until there was nothing left to give.

You have to destroy a little piece of yourself in order to save everyone else, Savage had said, a lifetime ago. *You have to give that sacrifice, or it won't be enough.*

It would eat him down to the bone, if he didn't get out.

"So go," he told himself. "Just go."

Then he lifted a sheet of paper and saw a photograph of

Vincent Kinghorn underneath—the kid smiling next to some school friends, oblivious to the horror of what lay ahead—and he remembered that leaving wasn't an option.

It was *never* an option.

"Sir," said Porter from his desk behind Kett's. He was rocking his chair back on two legs, chewing on a pen. It was coming up for nine but the bullpen was busier than he'd ever seen it, coppers from all divisions crammed into the MIT offices as they hunted for the missing boys.

"What, Pete?" said Kett when the DI didn't continue.

"Come and look at this."

"I will, as soon as you bring it to me," said Kett.

Porter grumbled his way over. He'd kicked off his shoes and left them out in the corridor, but he still stank of pond water. He laid a photograph on Kett's desk. It was an aerial shot of the farm where the kidnapper had burned the hearse, and Porter had used a sharpie to mark the outbuildings.

"The mannequins were here, right?" he said, using the pen to mark five dots—one in each of the three sheds, one in the stable and one in the barn.

"Roughly, yeah," said Kett. "Why?"

Porter used the sharpie to draw lines between the dots. After three, Kett realised what he was doing.

"Pentagram," said Porter, demonstrating his work with a big grin. "They're almost perfectly spaced, the hearse in the middle."

Kett nodded.

"And?" he said, when Porter didn't continue. "We already know he's obsessed with them."

Porter took his photo back, his face falling

"Not sure, sir," he said. "Just thought it was interesting."

"It's great, Pete," Kett said, taking pity on him. "Keep going."

Kett's back was killing him, and he gently stood up, trying to crack his spine and only succeeding in making things worse. He walked the discomfort off as best he could, his hands braced against his lower back, fully aware that he looked like a man twice his age.

"You shat yourself, Kett?" asked Clare from the open door of his office.

He was tempted to say yes, just so he'd be sent home.

"Just achy, sir," he said.

The Super walked out, holding a document.

"Report just came back from forensics on the device used to kill Ben Milford," he said, slapping it down on Kett's desk. Porter walked over, Savage too, all of them leaning in —then immediately recoiling as Clare turned the page to reveal a photograph. It was a close-up of Milford's neck, or what had been left of it.

"God," said Savage, her hand to her mouth. "Poor Ben."

"It's atrocious," said Clare, turning the page again to show them a photograph of the device after it had been freed and cleaned. "There's a battery-powered motor inside the casing, connected to a length of wire. The motor turns, the wire tightens. The batteries are welded in, and there's just a button, no off switch. Once it's going, there's literally no way of shutting it off until the wire's pulled all the way in."

"Christ," said Kett. "Can't cut the cable?"

"It's steel," said Clare. "Maybe if you had some mechanical bolt cutters. Regular ones probably wouldn't do it. Besides, it's fast. Less than thirty seconds from start to finish. Once it's cut into the skin, you wouldn't even be able to get the bolt cutters to the wire without inflicting even more damage."

"Maynard say anything about it, sir?" asked Porter.

"Of course not. He didn't say a damned thing. The report says every component can be bought at a hardware or hobby shop, there's nothing here that can identify the person who made it."

"We've seen these before," said Kett. "Or something like it. Back on the Sweet Briar Rose case. Bert had a whole bunch of machinery like this when we found him, traps and weapons and all sorts. Hollenbeck's toys."

Clare nodded.

"Why did he do it?" asked Savage. "Why kill Milford like this? What's he trying to prove?"

"He's not proving anything," said Kett. "He did it because he could."

"We don't know if the kidnapper has access to these machines," said Clare. "But I'm assuming he does. In the event that we ever find this tosser, do not go anywhere near him. You hear? If he gets one of these on you, it's thirty seconds of agony followed by certain death."

"Do you think this is how he's planning to kill his victims, sir?" asked Savage.

"I bloody hope not," Clare replied. "But all the more reason to find them, and quickly. Any leads?"

"I can't find any connection between the victims, other than the brothers," said Savage. "They lived in completely different parts of the county, they were in different school years in different schools or workplaces, they had different friendship groups, no link between the parents at all. It looked like they were picked at random, although they can't have been, because of their names, the way they spell devil."

"Maybe they spell something else," said Porter. He counted the letters out on his fingers. "L. I. V. E. D. Lived?"

"Yes, that must be it," said Clare, disgusted. "Lived. He wants them all to live, which is why he's bloody kidnapped them and stabbed them. You're a genius, Pete, take the rest of the day off."

Porter looked like he'd been stung by a bee.

"We haven't managed to find any of their phones," said Kett. "We're assuming they had them on their persons when they were taken, right?"

Nobody said otherwise.

"Because that's one thing they *do* have in common," he went on. "They were always watching stuff on their phones. Ian's mum said it, the Santa guy from the village hall said it, Dennis' parents said it. That's what connects them. Somehow, they all found Maynard's videos, they all watched them, they all signed up for whatever he was selling, even if they didn't know it."

"So what makes the victims different to the followers?" said Savage. "If the Uysals were getting gifts from Maynard, they were in on it, right? Liam had the tattoo, maybe Emil too. So why did he take them?"

"Maybe they failed?" said Porter.

"Right," said Kett. "They were followers but they messed up. Maynard said in one of his videos that the price of failure was serious. They failed, and they were taken as punishment."

He shook his head, doubting himself.

"But that doesn't work, because then how would the names of the victims spell devil?"

"Maybe something else is going on," said Porter. "Something—"

"Do not say supernatural, Pete," said Kett.

Porter's words dried out, and he fell silent.

"Well if nobody's got anything better than this toss, why are you wasting my time?" Clare roared. "Bugger off, all of you."

"It's, uh... It's my desk, sir," said Kett.

Clare snorted like a bull, then thumped his way back to his office, slamming the door so hard the entire building seemed to tremble.

Kett pulled out his chair, but his back locked up before he could sit down.

"Ow," he said, bracing both hands on the desk.

"You okay, sir?" asked Savage from her desk. "Why don't you head off for a bit? I'll call you if we catch a break."

It was a good idea, but he didn't want to leave them.

He didn't want to go home, either. Billie had texted after school to say she was taking the girls to his mum's for the night, as she'd promised. But he hated the house when it was empty. It made him think about what his life would be like if the Pig Man had won. If Hollenbeck had beaten him.

If his wife and children had died.

"I'm fine," he said. "Just need to stretch it out. I'll be back in five."

He limped through the door, heading for reception. There were still two members of the tactical team on duty, both bored out of their minds as they watched the trickle of people waiting in the lobby. By the time he'd walked outside he felt a little looser, the agony in his back dulled to the normal throb. It was freezing out here, though, a mist of rain falling, soaking through his jacket in seconds. His teeth chattered as he took in a couple of long breaths.

"Nope," he said, ready to head back inside.

He stopped when he heard the bark of a horn from somewhere in the car park. Turning, he scanned the mob of vehicles until he saw a flash of headlights. He glanced back to make sure the tactical officers were still there, just in case something was about to kick off, then started walking. It was a truck, he saw, and the window wound down as he closed in.

"Julia?" he said, when he recognised the driver.

"Kett," said Gorski, her face carved from granite. She was wearing civilian clothes, a black hoodie and jeans.

He leaned against the truck, spotting Joe Carmichael in the passenger seat, still in uniform.

"Joe," he said. "You guys okay?"

"You found him yet?" said Gorski.

"No. And you being here isn't going to make it happen any quicker, Julia. Go home, we'll keep you updated."

"Go home," she said, fixing her dark eyes on him. "That's what you'd do?"

Kett breathed a laugh through his nose.

"Fair enough," he said. "Look, I know about you and Ben. I know about the..."

He glanced at her belly, and she moved her hands across it protectively.

"How?" she asked, shooting a look at Carmichael.

"Wasn't me," he said.

"The boss know?" Gorski asked.

"He doesn't care," said Kett. "All he wants is to find this guy. Put him and Maynard behind bars."

Gorski scoffed.

"Yeah, he doesn't deserve prison," said Kett. "I know."

"He deserves a hammer in the head," said Gorski, and Kett didn't like the look she gave him—like she was asking *him* to hold the hammer.

"We need Maynard alive," Kett told her. "He's the only

one who knows who this guy is, the only one who can get these kids back. But he's dying, Julia."

Gorski frowned.

"Brain tumour. He won't last long. Weeks, at most. Take that as a victory."

"A victory?" she spat. "Let him go out on his own terms? Fuck that."

"Jules," said Carmichael. He put a hand on her arm and she batted it away.

"He doesn't get to do that," she said. "He doesn't get to kill Ben and then just fucking float away. He doesn't get to win."

"Julia, he only wins if you do what you're thinking about doing."

He glanced back to make sure nobody was watching, and even though the car park was clear he still leaned through the window, keeping his voice low.

"If you take out Maynard, your kid won't have a dad or a mum. You'll be locked away for years, till she's out of nappies and out of school. A long, long time. Stay out of it, Julia. Let us find the kidnapper. Let us handle Maynard."

"Only if you promise to *handle* him," she said. "No ifs, no buts."

"Julia," said Kett at the exact same time Carmichael said it.

"No. You did it before, for your family," she told him. "Somebody has to do it for mine."

The doors to reception opened, a handful of uniformed officers walking out into the night. Their laughter carried through the dark, as alien a sound as Kett had ever heard.

"Do it," said Gorski. "After all these years, you owe me."

Kett didn't answer, standing straight. The rain tickled

his face, running down his collar. He couldn't think of many times in his life when he'd felt more miserable than this.

"Go home," he told her.

She nodded at him like he'd given her a secret signal, starting the engine. Carmichael said something to her that Kett couldn't catch, and then he climbed out. They both watched as Gorski pulled out of the space, the truck roaring onto the street, fading slowly.

"She going to be okay?" Kett asked.

Carmichael shrugged.

"Would you be?"

There was only one answer Kett could give, but he chose not to. He wiped the rain from his face.

"You any closer to finding this guy?" asked Carmichael, one hand on his sidearm.

"So you can take him out for Gorski?" he asked.

"No, sir. Much as I'd like to. I just want him behind bars before *she* messes up, you know? Never seen her like this before."

Kett nodded.

"We'll get him," he said, without much conviction. "You guys doing okay?"

Carmichael considered the question, blowing out a breath that looked like cigarette smoke.

"We will be, sir," he said. "They're keeping us busy here and at the hospital. We're ready to roll, too, when you catch his scent."

Kett nodded, starting back towards HQ.

"Sir," Carmichael called out behind him. "Meant to ask, you seen Chester anywhere?"

"Andilet?" said Kett, spinning back around. "Yeah, he was at the farm where we found the hearse. Said he was sent out there just in case the kidnapper showed up."

"Oh, right," said Carmichael, frowning.

"Said you were stretched a little thin," Kett added.

"Well, he's not wrong," said the tactical officer. "Cheers, sir."

Kett jogged back as fast as his broken body would allow, pushing through reception into the meagre warmth of HQ. As he was approaching the bullpen, Savage came crashing out of the doors—fast enough that he had to step back to stop her from hitting him.

"Whoa!" he said. "Easy, Kate. The place on fire?"

He regretted his choice of words immediately. Savage didn't even seem to have heard him.

"Breakthrough, sir," she said, holding the door open and letting him through. "I was just coming to get you."

A cluster of people had gathered around Porter's desk, and Kett pushed through them to see the DI leaning over a map of the county. He'd marked it with black dots the same way he had the aerial photograph of the farm. Everyone else —Clare, Spalding, and a few other detectives—seemed to be taking turns to yell at him.

"What's going on?" Kett asked.

"It was the mannequins," said Porter, placing the ruler on the map. "The way they were spaced, it got me thinking about pentagrams."

He drew a long line between two of the dots on the map.

"That isn't straight, you fanny," said Clare. "Pay attention."

"Sorry, sir," Porter went on, trying again. "We talked about it earlier. How we didn't think the kidnappings were connected because they were so far away. But they're connected by something else. Look, there's Thetford. Cold Iron is there, and Ian Hipkin's house."

He pointed to the map, then ran his finger up the line he'd drawn.

"Fakenham, where Dennis Lynn was taken."

He pointed to a third black dot.

"Marham. And Victor Kinghorn."

"Holy shit," said Kett, seeing it.

There was a fourth dot just north of Horsford, and Porter drew a line between them.

"That's where the Uysal brothers live," said Kett.

Porter drew another line from there back to Thetford.

"That's all we've got," he said. "Four points."

"Then it's not a pentagram," said Clare, who looked disappointed. "It's just you spaffing toss all over my map."

"It's not a pentagram *yet*," said Kett, tapping the map somewhere to the southwest of Norwich. "It needs one more point. Here."

He looked up at Porter.

"Smart," he told him.

"No, it's not," said Clare. "Because we've already got five kidnappings. Dennis, Emil, Vincent, Ian and Liam. Pete can dirty my atlas all he likes, but it doesn't mean we have to listen to him."

"Unless it wasn't both brothers who were taken," said Kett. "Unless Kate was right, and it was only one of them. Liam was in the tank, with his tattoo. But we have no idea where Emil is."

Clare opened his mouth to argue, then closed it again.

"Jon, the kid who lived with the brothers, said they were always arguing," Kett went on. "He said he thought they were both involved in Maynard's shit, but what if it wasn't both of them? What if it was only one?"

"That might have been what they were arguing about?" said Porter.

"Right. Liam falls for Maynard's lies, he sides with Jon. Emil doesn't fall for it, so he becomes a victim instead."

"You think Maynard's that persuasive, sir?" said Savage. "That he could turn somebody against their own brother? Their own *twin*?"

"Yeah, I do," said Kett, tapping the map. "Have we had any reports in today from this neck of the woods? Uh, where is that? Long Stratton?"

Porter lined up his ruler, drawing the last couple of lines. The pentagram looked a little wonky, but there was no doubt it was pointing to that area.

"Tibenham, sir?" said Savage.

"Nothing on the system," said Spalding, who had returned to her desk.

"Then maybe he's not finished," Kett said.

He grabbed his coat, running for the door.

"Maybe there's still time."

CHAPTER TWENTY

"You have any idea what we're supposed to be looking for?" asked Porter.

He was driving, the Mondeo cruising along the country roads to the west of the village of Long Stratton. Smooth jazz vomited from the speakers, thankfully quiet enough that Kett could ignore it. It was so dark and so wet outside that they may as well have been in a submarine, the wipers beating hard and filling the car with their frenzied pulse. All Kett could see through the passenger side window was his own faint reflection, and it wasn't much to look at.

"Anything odd," he answered. "Anything that doesn't belong."

"I can see one thing that doesn't belong," Porter said, looking in the rear-view mirror.

Duke sat in the back, next to Savage, sniffing the way he had done every three seconds since they'd picked him up on the way out of Norwich. He looked like he'd been crying for a week solid, his eyes swollen, his nose leaking, but he'd insisted on coming.

Unfortunately, Kett had agreed.

"Huh?" said the PC, sniffing again.

He was still as deaf as a post, too.

"I said I see something that doesn't belong!" Porter yelled.

"The pong?" said Duke. "I have no idea, but it isn't me. Smells like somebody stepped in dog shit."

It really did, even though Porter had cleaned his shoe a dozen times.

"How can you smell anything?" said Porter. "Your nose looks like a baked potato."

"Can the pair of you stop bickering?" said Savage, her face glued to the window. "Some of us are trying to concentrate."

Kett checked his watch, seeing that it was after ten. All he could think about was his bed, the soft pillows, the warm duvet. It felt like he had sash weights tied to his eyelids, and with the warm air blowing and Kenny G playing his saxophone, it was a miracle he was still awake.

"Sir?" said Savage, and he realised she'd asked a question. "Is that your phone?"

He sat up straight, wondering if he *had* actually dozed off. His phone was ringing, and he pulled it out of his pocket to see Spalding's name. He answered, putting it on speaker.

"You've got all of us," he said, the end of the sentence becoming a yawn.

"Lucky me," said Spalding. "Okay, I've tidied up Porter's map, using the real-world locations. We've got two options: where the victim was taken from, and where they live. In some cases, they're the same."

"Okay," said Kett. "Go for it."

"If we're going by where they were taken from, we've got the garage in Fakenham for Dennis, and Marham Village Hall for Vincent. We don't know about the Uysal brothers, but it's likely to be Horsford. Ian's tricky because he wasn't really taken from anywhere except the hospital."

"That was a blip," said Kett. "I think we assume he was taken from Cold Iron or his house. Even if he went to Cold Iron willingly, he's still a victim."

"Okay. I can't find a way of getting a pentagram to fit. The garage throws it out, and so does the village hall."

"What about if we go by their addresses?" Kett asked.

"That works better, for sure. If you lay a perfect pentagram on top of their actual addresses, then it fits. Kind of. Kinghorn lives three miles away from Marham, which helps. If we do it this way, the fifth point is aimed right at a village called Gissing."

"Pissing?" said Duke, one finger in his ear.

Porter slowed down, fiddling with the satnav screen.

"We close?" asked Kett.

"We're pretty much there," he replied. "It's right up ahead."

He picked up speed.

"You can't pin it down any tighter?" asked Kett.

"I'm not even sure about what I've just told you," Spalding said. "The points are so far away from each other that it'll be near enough impossible to pin down the fifth location."

"Keep trying," Kett told her. "If anyone can make a big old shape like this sit straight, it's you."

"What?" said Spalding.

"And see if you can find anyone in Gissing who matches the age range of our victims."

"And whose name starts with an L," said Savage from the back. "Because if Liam isn't a victim, then we've lost one of our letters."

"Right," said Kett. "Thanks, Alison."

He hung up.

"Good call, Kate," said Kett. "This guy is obsessive. He's set himself rules on who he can take, and where he can take them from. The locations have to be the tips of a pentagram, the names have to spell DEVIL. The amount of work needed for that..."

He shook his head.

"It's insane," he finished.

"It's only insane if you don't believe it," Porter said, throwing his own words back at him. "If he really believes this will make him a devil, it's worth the work."

"Huh?" said Duke from the back.

Porter made his way around a bend, a couple of houses appearing on the left. A handful of seconds later they were inside the village, although there was barely enough here to justify it being called that. Kett spotted a bus shelter lurking in the dark, a village hall, and then nothing but bungalows all the way out the other side.

"Well, that was useful," said Porter, slowing to a halt.

"Turn around, try again," Kett told him.

Porter did as he was told, just about taking off both bumpers as he did a nine-point turn in the narrow lane. He drove them back the way they'd just come, Kett searching the properties for any sign of life. A few had lights on in their windows, the curtains drawn, but most were so dark it looked like they were trying to hide in the night. There wasn't a single other car on the road, or any pedestrians. Gissing, it seemed, was a village that liked to turn in early.

"This is bloody pointless," said Porter. "It could be any of these houses."

"Or none of them," said Savage, her nose practically pressed against the window. "Hang on, you just passed a turn."

Porter slammed on the brakes, although they were barely doing ten miles an hour.

"Right there," said Savage, pointing. "Can you see it?"

Kett could, but he would have missed it if he'd blinked. Porter reversed until he'd passed the little junction, then made the turn. It was tight, and the lane they found themselves on was so narrow that the bushes threatened to take off the paint on both sides of the car. More bungalows cowered behind the hedges, gradually giving way to a field on the right and houses on the left.

"This is bloody pointless," Porter said again. "There's fu... ck!"

He rounded a corner and hit the brakes again, Duke's head connecting with the back of Kett's seat.

"Ow!" said the PC. "What did you do that for?"

The answer was clear enough. Right in front of them was a car, parked half in and half out of a passing place. Its engine was on, its rear lights so bright that Kett couldn't see what make and model it was.

"The hell?" said Porter, squinting through the windscreen.

The Mondeo crawled down the road, everyone craning forward to see if they could make out a driver through the dark windows. The other car's engine rumbled, exhaust pouring from the back and filling the dark street like dry ice.

"Let them know who we are, Pete," said Kett.

Porter rolled down his window, leaning out.

"Police," he shouted, his voice swallowed by the night. "Turn off your engine."

He kept the Mondeo moving, almost level with the other car now. They were too close for Kett to make out what model it was, but it was big. The interior was dark, but he could just about see the outline of the driver.

"I said switch it off," yelled Porter, reaching out and hammering on their passenger side window. "Now!"

Kett heard the clunk of gears.

"They're going to—"

He didn't have time to finish as the other car took off, spraying mud from its back wheels as it launched itself from the passing place. It slammed into the front of Porter's Mondeo as it cut into the road, then it was off, accelerating down the lane.

"Go!" said Kett.

Porter hit the gas, the Ford speeding up—*slowly*. The other car had already made it around a bend, only the fiery echo of its taillights remaining.

"I said go, Pete!" Kett yelled. "As in speed up!"

They trundled around the corner, the other car up ahead, fifty yards away now. Porter had both hands on the wheel, his knuckles white as he tried to keep them in the middle of the lane. It seemed to be getting narrower, the verges scraping the sides of the car, the hedges battering the windscreen.

"Christ, Pete, we're going to lose them," said Kett. "Can you go a little faster?"

"It's dark, sir," he replied. "If I go any faster, I'll crash."

"If you go any slower, we'll bloody rust," said Kett.

"I can drive, sir," Savage said, unbuckling her belt and leaning between the seats. "Swap over."

"No!" Porter told her.

He sped up a little on the straight, the other car already invisible past the next bend.

"Just switch, sir," said Savage. "I'll squeeze in."

"You don't need to bloody squeeze in!" Porter told her. "I'm going to catch him."

He sped up a little more, the dial reading fifty—then slowing immediately to thirty as he reached the bend.

"It's so bloody dark," he said, his chest almost touching the wheel as he took the corner.

Savage reached over and flicked on the high beams for him, the world suddenly blazing. On the other side of the bend was a longer stretch, the car almost at the end of it. Porter sped up again, the world zipping past the window.

"He's going right," said Savage, leaning between the front seats. "There *is* no right."

She pointed to the satnav, and sure enough the road went on for another mile without a single junction.

"Must be a four-wheel drive," said Kett. "This is your last chance, Pete. Floor it."

Porter did as he was told, the Mondeo roaring down the lane. The other car had slowed in order to bump up the verge, passing through a gap in the hedge before heading into the field. Its headlights revealed nothing but mud all the way to a distant woodland.

They slowed down as they reached the same point, and Porter made the turn. The other car was struggling, spinning out as the tyres fought for traction.

"Go!" Kett said as the other car stopped.

Porter hit the accelerator again, but the Mondeo's wheels slipped on the wet ground. In front of them, the door of the other car was opening, and a figure lurched out. They were perfectly lit by their own headlights as they ran across the field—short, wide, dressed almost entirely in white.

"Second gear!" yelled Savage. "Go easy."

Porter wrestled with the gear stick, something crunching as he put his foot on the gas. The Mondeo crawled forwards, painfully slowly, then found purchase, speeding up, bouncing over the ridges of the field. They skirted around the other car, catching up to the driver in seconds. He was struggling, his feet sticking in the mud.

"Oi!" Porter yelled out of the window. "Pack it in, you muppet."

The man dropped onto all fours, lifting his head and lowing mournfully at the sky. His bald spot glowed ferociously in the Mondeo's high beams.

"Is he pretending to be a cow?" asked Porter, bringing the car to a stop.

Nobody opened their door, all of them watching as the man tried to crawl through the quagmire of the field. He was still making a noise like a lost calf trying to find its mother.

"Bagsy not getting out," said Kett.

"Bagsy," said Porter.

"Bagsy," said Savage.

"Huh?" said Duke.

"Go get him, Aaron," said Kett. "And wind your window up, will you, Pete? It's bloody freezing."

Duke got out, squelching to where the man was still trying to crawl to freedom. The PC leaned over him, speaking quietly, then he turned back to the car with a shrug. Porter wound his window down a crack.

"This is the bit where you cuff him!" he shouted. "With your handcuffs. They're the dangly things on your belt."

He closed the window again.

The man seemed to have given up, planting his face in the mud. Duke left him there, walking back to the car and standing by Porter's window until the DI rolled it down again.

"What?" Porter said. "Have you forgotten how to do it?"

"It's not that, sir," said Duke, leaning in, water bouncing

off his hat onto Porter's lap. "He says we don't have to arrest him."

Porter shot Kett a look of disbelief before returning his attention to Duke.

"Oh, he said that? That's fine, then. Let's leave him to it. Doesn't matter that he could be our kidnapper. If he says we don't have to arrest him, let's not bother!"

"No, he says we know him," Duke went on. He ducked lower so he could talk to Kett. "He says you and him are best mates, sir."

Kett leaned back, laughing quietly.

"His name doesn't happen to be Norman, does it?"

"Yeah," said Duke, turning to look at the guy—who had managed to roll onto his back. "Hard to tell with all the mud, but I think it's Norman Balls."

CHAPTER TWENTY-ONE

"Of all the things I didn't expect to find on this case," said Kett. "Balls was right at the top of my list."

He sat in the back of the Mondeo, Norman Balls shivering in the seat next to him. The strange little conspiracy theorist, owner of the *Balls Knows It Alls* website, was coated head to toe in mud, looking like a prehistoric fish that had crawled onto land for the first time and had no idea what to do with itself there. What made it worse was that he was dressed all in white: white chinos, white shoes and a white woollen cricket jumper that barely stretched over his bulging stomach.

But true to form, he was as defiant as always.

"Balls should be at the top of your list for everything," he said, his teeth chattering.

"It's true," said Porter from the front. "You do love Balls."

Kett ignored the DI, staring through the windscreen for a second to where Savage and Duke stood by Balls' Rover, the doors open. It was such a distinctive car that Kett was surprised he hadn't recognised it.

"But you seem to have forgotten that we're best friends," Balls went on, his giant bottom lip pouting. "You missed my birthday, for one. And our anniversary. Did *I* miss them?"

Kett opened his mouth to reply, but Balls didn't give him the chance.

"No, because I sent you cards. And presents."

"I must not have got—"

"I *know* you got them," said Balls.

"What? *How*?"

"Because Balls knows it alls," said Balls. "Where are my cards now? Where is the mug I sent you? The one with my face on it? What do you have to say for yourself, Robert?"

"Yeah, sir," said Porter, who was clearly enjoying himself. "That's a terrible way to treat your best friend."

"We're not best friends," said Kett.

"Well here, at last, we find something to agree upon," said Balls. "You lost your best friend badge a long time ago. Literally. Because I sent you a badge."

Porter rubbed his eyes like a sad clown, and Kett glared at him until he stopped. He turned the glare to Balls.

"What are you doing here, Norman?"

"I'd like to ask you the same thing."

Kett's glare intensified, and Balls threw his filthy hands up in surrender.

"Fine! If you must know, I got kicked out of my house. I had nowhere else to go."

"Your mum finally kicked you out?" said Kett. "At the grand old age of... How old are you now?"

Balls quivered in his seat.

"One: age has nothing to do with it. Two, Mother didn't throw me out. It was Ron. Her stupid husband thinks he has more of a claim to my own mother, my own house, my own property, than I do. The buffoon."

"So where are you living?" said Porter.

"In my HQ," said Balls. "The garage."

"The garage, as in the garage that's part of your house?" Kett said.

"Yes! That garage."

"So she *hasn't* kicked you out?"

"Dear God," said Balls, slapping a hand to his muddy forehead. "It's like talking to a wall."

"You're going to be talking to a wall very soon," Kett said, looking through the window to see if he could find one. "I'm going to ask you again, Norman. What are you doing here?"

Balls spluttered out a long breath.

"Fine," he said again. "I heard about the kidnapped boys on the news. Figured I could be of some help to you. I tried calling and asking for you, but nobody would pass on my messages."

That was probably true. After several cases where Balls' involvement had almost scuppered them—not least the Jack Valentine case back in February—Norfolk Constabulary's official policy was no more Balls. It was a shame, because past the blustering exterior, and the desperate, cloying need for a best friend, Norman was a pretty good detective.

Not that Kett would ever tell him that.

"Must be something wrong with the phones," said Kett.

"Well, yes," said Balls, clearly mollified. "I did point that out to them when I called, but it doesn't explain why nobody could get you when I showed up in person."

"I must have been—"

"Four times," said Balls.

"It's been a busy day," said Kett, rubbing his face. "What made you think you could help us with this particular case?"

"Because of the locations," said Balls, wiggling his eyebrows at Kett. "Thetford, Fakenham, Marham, Horsford."

"Wait, how did you find out about that?" Kett asked.

"Wouldn't you like to know?"

"Yes, that's why I asked," said Kett.

"Oh, right. Well, you know me, I have my methods."

Savage climbed into the driver's seat, closing the door before too much of the warm air could escape.

"He's still got his scanner, sir," she said.

"I thought we told you to get rid of that, mate," said Kett.

Balls shuffled uncomfortably.

"As an official deputy of Norfolk Police—"

"You're not official, you're not a deputy, you're not police," Kett told him.

Balls waved his words away.

"You have no authority here," said the little man.

Duke had wandered over, and he opened the back door, trying to slide in next to Balls.

"No," Kett told him.

"But it's cold out here, sir."

"There's no room," Kett said. "Just suck it up."

"By myself?"

"Go!" Kett barked.

Duke closed the door, folding his arms over his chest and huffing like a teenager.

"Like I was saying," Balls went on, "I heard about the missing boys, figured out the pattern in the crime scenes. A pentagram. It didn't take much to work out that the final point was somewhere around here."

"Right," said Kett, a little defensively. "That didn't take much brainpower at all. We worked it out literally..." He checked his watch, realising it hadn't even been an hour. "*So* long ago. You really shouldn't know any of this, Norman."

"Well, I do," said Balls. "If you want to keep secrets, do a better job of looking after them."

Kett heard Porter laughing quietly in the front.

"If you know about this place," Balls went on. "Then you'll know who Maynard has been targeting, and why. I won't bother going into details."

"Wait," said Kett. "You know who Maynard was after? His fifth victim?"

"Of course," said Balls. "It was painfully easy to figure it out. Are you telling me you haven't?"

"We have," said Kett, trying not to let the lie show on his tired face. "I just need to know if you came to the same conclusion."

"Then tell me who *you* think it is," said Balls.

"No, you go first. I can't just go spilling restricted information to a civilian."

"*Deputy*," said Balls. "Okay, just because it's you, and we're best friends..."

He left the statement hanging until it became a question.

"Best friends," said Kett, nodding. "Right."

"You know about Maynard's videos?" said Balls. "There are some on YouTube, the beginner ones. Maynard *lite*. But he's got more on a private server hosted out of the country, and they're all password-protected. You can only access them if Maynard sends you a link. I stumbled onto them a while ago, while I was designing my own influencer course."

Kett knew he shouldn't ask, but he did anyway.

"Your influencer course?"

"Yeah, I'm sure you've seen it. Balls *teaches* alls. It's all about finding your inner confidence in order to land your dream job, woo your dream partner, get your dream body, that kind of stuff."

"And you film these at home, in your mum's garage, where you live alone and unemployed and overweight?" said Kett, feeling a little mean as soon as the words had left his mouth.

Balls didn't even seem to register them.

"Yes," he said. "They're quite popular. I watched a lot of influencers while I was making them, and stumbled onto Maynard's stuff a couple of months ago, completely by accident. I didn't realise it was him, of course, not until today."

"How did you manage to watch them?" asked Kett. "I thought he had to send you the password?"

"I simply masqueraded as a teenage boy," said Balls. "It was easier than you might think. I was sent the link to the first video and told to watch it. It's faux-mystical bullplop of the highest order, I've seen it a hundred times before. Arcane nonsense. Thinning the veil between this world and the next, allowing demons to cross, providing safe vessels for evil. All quite boring. But what was interesting was what he was asking his followers to do. You've seen the videos?"

"No," said Kett. "Well, a few, not all of them."

"Let me paraphrase them for you. There are nineteen videos in total, the first five easy enough to access if you know what you're doing. The rest are better protected. Essentially, Maynard was attempting to convince his followers to commit an increasingly serious sequence of criminal acts."

Balls leaned in, barely able to contain his excitement.

"They start small, little more than petty meannesses. Be unkind to a friend for no reason, let the air out of somebody's tyres, cut down some flowers in your neighbour's garden."

"Why would he ask them to do that?" said Savage.

"Next," Balls went on, ignoring her, "steal a few things, stuff that nobody will really notice. Spread lies, slander random strangers, undermine a friend's relationship with another friend. It's all low-level stuff at this stage, but it gets worse."

He took a breath, wiping mud from his wet lips as he carried on.

"It's in the sixth video that Maynard encourages his followers to hurt themselves. Not a mortal wound, but not a scratch, either. In the eighth, he tells them to hurt an animal. Again, nothing big, just an insect to start with. Then a bird, or a mouse. By the tenth video, he's goading them into hurting a pet. In the next..."

"A person," Kett finished for him.

"Right," said Balls, nodding. "The tenth is as far as I got. Anything past that was too well hidden, and there are certain things you have to do before you can get them."

"Like get a tattoo?" said Kett.

"Yes. And I don't defile the temple of my body for any reason. But the sequence is only heading in one direction. It's incredibly subtle. Maynard works his way into their minds, insidious, relentless. By that point, he's encouraging them to meet each other in chat rooms, to plan their next crimes. He pushes the boulder, but once it starts rolling it's going all by itself."

"You went to the chat rooms?" said Kett.

"Absolutely not," said Balls. "I don't want to be anywhere near those kinds of people. Even with my expertise at hiding my identity, I wouldn't want to pop up on their radar. Understand, ninety-nine percent of people watching Maynard's stuff won't do anything about it, they'll get bored and move on to the next thing. They'll never get to the final sequence. It's that last one in a hundred you have to watch out for. The ones who believe it."

"Like the kidnapper?" said Kett.

"Right. Maynard mentions him at various points during the videos. Not by name or anything, but he refers to a man who will give birth to the beast. A man who has elevated himself to the pinnacle of his process. He talks about a knight of hell, a warrior king who will reign over the world. He calls him the master."

He stopped, staring out of the window for a moment.

"I think only the most devoted people reach the end of the course. The ones who really want it. I think they have to prove themselves in other ways before Maynard lets them progress. I got as far as I did out of morbid curiosity, but even I lost my stomach. It takes a certain type of person to get to the end."

"What happens in the videos?" asked Kett.

"Not what you're thinking," Balls replied. "They're not snuff films. But Maynard definitely goes into intimate details about what he'd like his followers to do. And *why*. He calls it his five pillars of consciousness. Five pillars that, when knocked down, collapse the boundaries between worlds."

Outside, Duke's radio bleeped. Kett almost leapt out of his seat.

"He wants them to become something else, doesn't he?" said Kett. "His followers. He wants them to turn into devils."

"Literally," added Savage.

"Not all of them, just one," Balls replied. "This *master*. Maynard seems to believe that only one person has what it takes to finish the course. Only one candidate has the strength to make it through all nineteen videos and follow the instructions perfectly. This person will become something more than human. The thing is, the instructions aren't really instructions. They're clues. Maynard doesn't make it easy. But it's all there, if you look hard enough."

"You figured it out?" said Kett.

Balls shook his head.

"Not all of it. Like I said, I didn't have the constitution for it. But it's there if you allow yourself to see it. Five pillars. Divination. In order to see what cannot be seen, you require an eye. Exsanguination. The draining of the blood, the cutting of the flesh, for which you need a finger. Veneration. To revere, or adore. In order to believe, you must listen. The ear. Invocation, the act of summoning a divine entity through speech. The tongue. And finally Limination. The boundary, the threshold which must be crossed. For some reason, that's a..."

He hesitated.

"King ding dong," he finished with a shrug.

"King ding dong?" said Kett.

"Yes! You know, a knobgoblin, a kitty Longfellow, a Mr Happy. Ron's dirty mushroom. A *willy*. Those are the five pillars, those are the requirements of the ceremony."

"Hang on," said Kett. "We already know that our kidnapper is going to sacrifice his victims. He's going to take each of these parts, one from each victim. An eye, a tongue, an ear, a finger, and a... the other thing. Do the videos say anything about where it will happen? Or when? Anything that can actually help us?"

"I don't know," said Balls. "All I managed to glean from what I watched is that after the end of the final video, you prepare a gift."

Kett rubbed his temples to try to mute the pain in his head.

"A gift?" he said after a moment.

"An offering," said Savage. "That's why he needs the body parts, the blood, the jars. He prepares his victims, he offers them as a sacrifice, and in return he... he becomes a devil."

Balls nodded.

"*The* Devil, I think. And on the surface, all the evidence points to it being real. Five victims, their names spelling devil, perfectly positioned on the points of a pentagram."

"Right," said Kett. "It's impossible. The odds are—"

"Astronomical," said Balls. "Yes. And yet here we are."

"Right," said Kett. "Here we are, in a village in the middle of nowhere, in the middle of the night. Why?"

"A simple process of deduction," said Balls. "We're looking for a teenage boy or a young man who lives in or close to Gissing, and whose name starts with either an E or an L. Because I don't think both Uysal brothers are involved."

"You really should not know about that," said Kett.

Balls leaned in again, grinning.

"I ran the calculations. It's like you said, the odds are fairly low. But not that low. There are about two hundred and fifty people in this village, and a quick search tells me only twenty-eight of them have a first name that begins with an E or an L. Of those, only three are teenagers. And only one is male. Ethan Mortimer. He lives here."

"In the village?" said Kett.

"On this street," Balls replied, wiggling his eyebrows again. "I was right outside his house when you lot arrived. Been there all evening."

"Bloody hell, Norman" said Kett. "You could have bloody led with that. Let's move!"

CHAPTER TWENTY-TWO

WITH SAVAGE BEHIND THE WHEEL, IT TOOK LESS THAN a minute to drive back the way they'd come. Duke had crammed his immense frame into the back seat beside Balls, and both of them did nothing but moan about how cramped they were until Savage brought them to a halt.

"Stay in the car," Kett said as he got out, jabbing a finger at Balls.

They were right next to the passing place where they'd first found the Rover. Directly across from it, hunkered low beneath the night sky and barely visible past a hedge, was a run-down cottage. Balls had already confirmed that this was the Mortimer place, although he hadn't been inside.

"I mean it," Kett told him. "You leave the car, I cuff you to a tree. Forever."

He slammed the door, pulling the collar of his coat tight to his neck. There was a driveway to the right, almost hidden by the overgrown hedge, and he crossed the road to get to it. Savage had left the Mondeo's engine on, but the lights didn't seem to want to reach this far. Past the driveway, the small front garden was pitch black.

"Take the back, Kate," he said, clicking on his torch. "Aaron, you too. Yell if you see anything at all."

He walked to the front door, Porter right behind him. Together, they aimed their torches at the lock, seeing the splintered wood where somebody had wedged a crowbar into the frame.

"Shit," said Kett. He shouted out. "We've got a break-in. Be careful."

He used his boot to nudge the door open, the creak of the hinges the loudest thing in the quiet night.

"Police," he said, his voice echoing into nothing. "If you're in there, yada yada yada."

He tailed off, because nothing about the house suggested there was anyone inside. The air was perfectly still, utterly dead.

He ran his hand over the wall until he found a switch, clicking it on. The bulb took a moment to wake up, blinking sleepily, revealing a narrow hall—fragments of wood on the tiled floor from where the door had been forced. Photos hung from the papered wall, a man, a woman and two children in various stages of their lives. The older kid was a girl, the other a boy.

"That must be him, sir," said Porter.

It was roasting in here. Kett put his hand to a cast-iron radiator and immediately pulled it off again because he thought he could hear his skin sizzle.

"You could cook an egg on that," he said.

There was a crunch from the back of the house, then Savage's voice.

"Police! Is anyone in here?"

"Just us, Kate," Kett called back.

"You sure?" bellowed Duke. "Have you been upstairs?"

He charged into the corridor like an angry silverback, his baton out.

"No," Kett told him. "Knock yourself out, mate."

The PC bounded up the narrow stairs so energetically that the entire house seemed to shift, the overhead light swaying. Kett half expected him to fall through the ceiling as he stomped from room to room, dust raining.

"Clear," he yelled after a minute.

Kett walked into the minuscule living room, seeing more photos on the wall arranged around the TV. He rummaged in the sideboard, flicking through paperwork to confirm Ethan's name. There were plenty of letters to his mother, Ruth Mortimer, and a few for his sister—the university address letting Kett know she lived away. There was nothing for the father, though.

The house trembled again as Duke clattered down the stairs.

"I'll check the garden," he yelled, his voice deafening.

"I'm literally standing right next to you," Kett said, watching him go.

"Got another pentagram, sir," said Savage, poking her head around the door.

"Shit"

Kett followed her through to the cramped kitchen. The table was set out for a light supper, a basket of bread between two plates, a butter dish that had been left open, its contents misshapen from the heat. Two bowls of tomato soup sat untouched. A legion of ants were making the most of a pot of jam, filing back and forth over the stained oak. An apple had been cut up, the segments brown and shrivelled. There was a packet of medicine, too, Circadin. A glass of milk sat next to one plate, slightly curdled. Another lay beside a chair, shattered.

There was blood on the floor, smudged into a pentagram maybe two feet in diameter. It wasn't a careful job, the sides uneven, the blood mixed with milk and dirt and countless dead ants.

"I'll let Clare know, sir," said Porter, leaving the room.

Kett blew out a long breath as he took in the kitchen, shaking his head.

"You think this happened last night?" he asked Savage.

She nodded.

"Milk's started to turn," she said. "But only just. Could be breakfast, I guess? But no coffee, and Circadin is melatonin. It helps you sleep."

"Yeah, we give it to Moira sometimes," said Kett. "So they're sitting having supper and somebody forces the door. Which is weird, right?"

"Sir?" said Savage. "Oh, you mean why didn't they knock?"

"Right."

She thought about it for a moment.

"We're quite isolated here, away from the village. If it was late, maybe they didn't want to spook them, give them a chance to call the police."

Kett opened a couple of cupboards, finding nothing out of the ordinary.

"So the kidnapper cracks the door and runs in. Then what?"

They both looked at the blood, a bigger streak beneath the table that he hadn't seen before.

"Two plates," said Savage. "Ethan and his mum?"

"Dad's not on any of the paperwork I found," said Kett. "Divorced, maybe, or passed."

"So the kidnapper attacks the mum," said Savage, acting it out. "Then he grabs the kid. He's stabbed two victims that we know of, Dennis and Vincent. It's part of his MO. He wants to hurt them, but he doesn't want to kill them, not yet. But if he only wants the kid..."

She stopped, cocking her head.

"Where's the mother?" finished Kett.

"Maybe he took them both?" said Savage. "Maybe he wasn't on his own?"

A shape loomed up in the doorway, Duke's face appearing like an ogre.

"I think I found something," he said. "Outside."

"We'll be there in a bit," said Kett.

"I think you might want to come now, sir. Whatever it is, it's making a lot of noise."

The PC led them out of the kitchen. They were on the far side of the house, at the foot of an immense garden that stretched into the infinite dark. Duke had his torch on, the beam falling short of whatever lay at the far end. He ran the light over an empty chicken coop, a huddle of wheelbarrows, a lopsided trampoline, then left it on what looked like a coal bunker.

"It's coming from there, sir," he said.

Kett could hear it in between breaths—a dull, hollow thump. He started to run, then stopped when it felt like his vertebrae were going to detach. Duke was already ahead of him, his equipment rattling as he sprinted. Savage was close behind the PC. He caught up to them eventually, bracing his hands on the small of his back. Porter was wandering over, still on the phone.

The bunker was maybe five foot cubed, made of breeze blocks that had been cemented in place. There was a hatch at the front that looked like it had been rusted shut, and the hinged metal roof was secured with a chain.

There was definitely a thumping sound coming from inside.

"Hello?" Kett called out. "Is somebody in there? It's the police."

The noise grew in volume and speed, a drumming of feet or hands. Kett grabbed the chain, giving it a shake.

"Somebody find a way of getting this off," he said.

Savage bolted back towards the house. Kett kneeled beside the hatch, working at it with his fingers and losing some skin to the corroded metal. It obviously hadn't been opened in months, maybe years.

"A crowbar or something," he said, looking back to see that Duke was still there. "Move, Aaron! And call for an ambulance."

Duke moved away, shining his torch across the garden. Kett had to pull out his own as darkness flooded in.

"We're trying to find a way in," he said. "Try to stay calm."

Duke returned a few seconds later, armed with a hammer that looked rustier than the hatch. Kett was about to swing it at the bunker when Savage called to him from the back door.

"Maybe don't, sir. Until we figure out if it's rigged like the tank."

He held onto the hammer for a moment more, then dropped it, taking a few steps back.

"Good point, Kate."

"Ambulance is on the way," Duke said. "Clare's going to send out the bomb squad too."

Kett nodded, retreating even further, calling out as he went.

"Try to stay calm. It won't be long."

THAT WAS A LIE.

By the time the bomb squad rolled in, midnight had come and gone. They turned up in an army truck, four camouflaged soldiers and a technician in full protective gear. It took them all of twenty minutes to check the panel at the top, then another five to sever the steel chain with a set of pneumatic bolt cutters. The lid lifted like a coffin, everyone flinching as it crashed down on the other side.

The bomb technician examined the inside of the bunker with her torch, reaching deep inside. Kett felt like he didn't take a single breath until she began to walk back.

"It's clear," she said. "No explosive devices. But you've got a body in there."

"Body?" Kett said.

He moved in, Savage and Porter beside him as he leaned over the top of the coal bunker and aimed his torch inside. There was a pile of rags at the bottom, as black as the coal they lay on. The person had fallen completely still, looking like a long-dead thing.

"Hey," he said. "Hold this."

He passed his torch to Savage and climbed inside the bunker, careful not to stand on the body that lay there. There was barely space to duck down, his back resting against the concrete blocks. He pulled at the rags until he found a face, working his fingers down to the neck, searching for a pulse.

"Hey," he said again. "Ruth? Can you hear me?"

The figure groaned, the noise becoming a scream as she woke. Her eyes opened, impossibly bright against her coal-stained skin, her mouth gaping as she screamed again.

Fingers scratched at Kett's arms, his face, the woman shifting and bucking beneath him.

"Calm down!" he yelled. "We're police!"

He stood up before she could hurt him, throwing himself out of the bunker. Only Porter's hands on his arms stopped him from falling.

"Get the paramedics!" he yelled.

The woman had managed to lift herself into a sitting position, the rags falling away to reveal her face. It was the same woman from the photos inside the house, Kett saw, only ravaged by filth and by fear. She bared black teeth at Kett, her eyes as bright as moons, full of insanity.

"You're going to be okay, Ruth," Kett told her. A paramedic appeared, almost barging him out of the way. "I promise. We're here to help you."

The woman was trying to push herself up, but she didn't have the strength. She grunted, the deep guttural sound of a snared animal—sounds that gradually became words.

"Where is he? Where's Ethan? Where's my son?"

CHAPTER TWENTY-THREE

Thursday

Kett watched the ambulance pull away from where he sat in the passenger seat of the Mondeo, the door open. His body was numb from the cold, but he didn't care any more, because his mind felt numb too.

They hadn't got much out of Ruth Mortimer, the woman they'd pulled from the coal bunker. Ravaged by fear and dehydration and hypothermia, she'd uttered a handful of words before collapsing into a state that was almost catatonic—her eyes open, but her gaze utterly blank. She'd scratched at her own legs with such ferocity that the paramedics had been forced to sedate her before she took off her own skin.

Somewhere in her garbled speech, though, they worked out what had happened to her. A man had burst into their house late on Tuesday evening while she and Ethan were having supper, his face hidden by a crimson, horned mask. He'd driven his knife into the teenage boy without the slightest hesitation. Then he'd turned on her, knocking her out. She'd woken up inside the coal bunker.

She'd spent the next twenty-four hours there, in the cramped dark. Not knowing if anyone was coming, not knowing if her son was alive.

Kett couldn't even imagine it.

"She's lucky she made it," said Savage, walking over from where the ambulance had been parked. "If we hadn't been here..."

It didn't bear thinking about. There were no neighbours within earshot, no sign of friends or family coming to call. It would have been a slow, lonely, awful death.

"Say what you like about Norman," Savage went on, "he's saved one life."

"Just don't tell him," said Kett. "He'll be insufferable. Where is he, anyway?"

"Up by his car, sir," she said. "He managed to convince the bomb squad to pull it out of the mud with their truck."

Despite everything, Kett laughed.

"Only he could talk the Explosive Ordnance Disposal Team into becoming roadside recovery."

His smile fell away.

"Ethan's our E," he said. "In devil. So Liam *was* kidnaped and left in the tank. Right?"

"I'm not sure," said Savage, turning her head to the night sky. "The brothers were twins. Not identical, but similar. We thought it was Liam in the tank because Ian told us he was at Cold Iron. But what if it was his brother we found there? What if Emil was in the tank, being punished for something? It's impossible to be certain because of the injuries to his face."

"Then Liam's our fifth victim," said Kett. "It fits. Did you find anything inside the house?"

"Not much in the building itself," Savage told him, leaning on the Mondeo. "Usual teenage boy stuff. He had a YouTube channel. Video game stuff. Kept it updated for a few years but hasn't uploaded anything for a while. Big following, for a kid."

"Made him easy to find," said Kett. "But still, the chances of him being here, at this exact point on the map..."

"Yeah, I was wondering about that," Savage said. "It doesn't make sense, unless it does."

"What?" said Kett, wondering if the exhaustion was making him miss her point.

"I found some financial statements inside," she said. "Ruth's. She was a teacher, back in the day, but she's been off work for a couple of years now."

She shivered.

"Get in the car, Kate," Kett told her.

"I'm okay, I'll fall asleep if I sit down. So yeah, Ruth's unemployed, she's got no discernible income other than PIP. Certainly not enough to pay rent on a place like this, right?"

"Right," said Kett. "That's a few acres of land back there, not cheap. How does she do it?"

"I don't know," said Savage. "There are no rent payments on her statements, no mortgage payments, either. Nothing, going back years."

"Weird," said Kett. "How many years?"

"Three. It looks like they moved out here in 2020, from King's Lynn. And they've lived here ever since without paying a penny to anyone."

"So who owns it?"

"That's the question, sir," said Savage. "Land registry lists the owner as a limited company, and that's owned by another company, and so on. It'll need some work to get to the bottom of it. But it goes back to what we were saying. What are the chances of Maynard's victims living exactly where he wanted them to?"

"Holy shit," said Kett, finally understanding what she was saying. "You think Maynard owns this place?"

"Makes sense. He's loaded. We know he has property everywhere. We know he plans everything meticulously, and that he's been obsessed with the demon stuff for years. Decades, probably."

"So he buys a bunch of houses in exactly the right place to form a pentagram on the map, and over the years he fills them with his victims, so they're ready whenever he needs them. That's..."

He didn't have a word for it.

"That's Maynard," Savage said.

"But why? Why go to so much trouble?"

Savage shivered again, and this time she walked around the car, climbing into the driver's seat. She closed her door and Kett closed his, trapping them in the quiet dark.

"You remember a few years ago we had the Six Days case?" she said. "Back when I was a PC."

"I remember," said Kett. "The guy who thought he was a demon, terrorised that poor family."

"Yeah, that's the one. He was convinced he was Satan. He believed it."

"You think Maynard was involved in that?"

"I'm not sure," said Savage. "Maybe. That guy had people working with him too, disenfranchised kids. It's similar. But this is what Maynard's trying to do, isn't it? The videos and everything, he's trying to convince his followers that they can become something more than human, they can become *super*human, if they follow his instructions. He's picking some pretty low hanging fruit, these impressionable young men who desperately want to belong to something. But still, he has to make them believe it. If they don't truly believe, then it doesn't work."

"Right," said Kett, nodding. "So Maynard's working behind the scenes, pulling strings to make it appear like something *else* is at play here, something inexplicable."

"Like putting five kids whose names spell Devil at five addresses that mark out a pentagram on the map. If you're one of his followers, that must feel like proof."

"That's really clever, Kate," said Kett. "He lays the groundwork so that whoever this person is, the kidnapper, they look at the evidence and assume Maynard's right, the Devil is real. They believe they can *become* the Devil."

"If they believe it, then they're capable of anything," Savage said. "And if Ethan was taken last night, then we're even further away from finding them. That's well over twenty-four hours. We could still be too late. And that's if they're still alive. That's a lot of blood for a kid to lose. Dennis was stabbed too, and Vincent. He may not even be trying to take them alive."

"No," said Kett, although he didn't say it because he believed it, but because he couldn't bear to think otherwise. "No, he wouldn't go to all that trouble to take a corpse. They're alive, but they won't survive forever, not with those wounds. I need you to find out who owns the other houses, see if you're right."

"Yes, sir."

"Did Porter ride with Ethan's mother?"

Savage covered a yawn with the back of her hand, nodding.

"Then he won't mind if I borrow his car."

"Where are you going, sir?" she asked.

Kett checked his watch, the hour hand hovering around the one. He was so tired he could barely keep his eyes open.

"I'm going to speak to Maynard."

HE ARRIVED at the hospital forty minutes later, pulling Porter's Mondeo into the deserted car park. When he cut the engine, the silence was so deep and so glorious that he almost lost himself to it.

"Nope," he said, giving himself a gentle slap on the cheek. "You can do it."

He counted to three before opening the door, exiting into the freezing drizzle. Back in the day, he'd have handled an all-nighter like this with a couple of Red Bulls, a ten-pack of Marlboro and a smile on his face—and he'd have carried on through the next day with no bother. He'd once stayed up for seventy-four hours straight while working on the Otley brothers case for the Met. Now, though, just the thought of not getting to bed at ten after a cup of tea and an episode of *Grand Designs* and he felt like he'd been kept awake for a week as part of a sadistic sleep deprivation experiment. Caffeine only made it worse, turning his mood so fast that he made Clare look like a happy fairy.

Still, it was the job. He might have changed, but policing was the same inconsiderate bastard.

He thumped through the doors into reception, grumbling his way past the front desk and flashing his warrant card as he went. There was a smattering of people here, a few staff, a young mother in a wheelchair with a baby, a man with his arm in a sling. He pressed the button for the lift, riding up with his forehead pressed against the wall because his head felt too heavy to hold upright. When it dinged, he almost shed his skin—halfway into a dream.

"Wake up," he told himself, yawning into the corridor.

There were still a few coppers in the waiting area down from Maynard's ward, two constables who looked like they were on duty, and a couple more dozing on the uncomfortable chairs. A single member of the tactical unit stood sentry at the end of the corridor, one that Kett didn't recognise, but who must have known him because he nodded a welcome. Two MIT detectives kept the vigil, waving to him as he walked up. They both stared at his suit, and when he looked down he saw that he was caked in grime, a layer of velvety coal dust over the day's accumulation of mud, vomit and dust.

"Sleeping in a skip, sir?' said one.

"Yeah," he said. "You got anything else out of him?"

"Not a peep," said the same guy. "His weird brief's been in and out all day."

"He in there now?"

The man nodded, and Kett glanced at his watch again.

"He *sleeping* in there?"

Both detectives shrugged, and Kett moved past them, heading up the corridor to Maynard's room. He put his ear to the wood, hearing a rasping snore from inside.

Then he turned the handle and opened the door.

The room was dark, the only light creeping in from the corridor, angled like a blade across the single bed. Maynard lay beneath his covers. The swelling in his face had gone down a little, but with his gaping, toothless mouth, he looked a hundred years old.

Kett opened the door a little further, seeing the solicitor in the chair. He was awake, keeping watch with eyes that looked almost silver in the gloom. It may have been Kett's imagination, fuelled by exhaustion, but he looked like he was grinning. Kett couldn't remember his name, but it was something unusual.

He reached for the light.

"I wouldn't do that, if I were you," said the man in the chair.

Kett ignored him, finding the switch and clicking it on. In the sudden blaze, the solicitor looked normal again, his face creased into an expression of tired displeasure. He squinted at Kett, then at Maynard, who continued to sleep.

Kett pushed the door closed.

"I need to speak to him," he said, walking up to the bed and giving it a solid kick. "Hey, Maynard, wake up."

"Don't," said the solicitor, standing.

Berrycloth, Kett remembered. Stupid name for a stupid man.

"He needs his rest. He needs to recover."

"He needs to answer some more questions," Kett said, giving the bed another kick. This time Maynard snorted, frowning in his sleep.

"He's been sedated," said Berrycloth, walking up to Kett. "For the pain. He wouldn't be able to talk to you even if he was awake. Leave him alone."

"Maybe it's you I need to be talking to, then?" Kett said, turning on the man. Berrycloth was a good few inches shorter than Kett, and as wiry as a greyhound, but he stood his ground. "You're Maynard's brief. You deal with his everyday stuff, or just the crime?"

Berrycloth didn't answer, studying Kett like he was a specimen in a petri dish. His mouth was a straight line, but there was a smile in his eyes—one that Kett would happily have gouged out with a spoon.

"We found his fifth victim," Kett said. "Ethan Mortimer."

"I don't know what you're talking about," said Berrycloth. "My client has been here all day, thanks to you."

"Mortimer was taken on Tuesday night," Kett said. "Late."

Berrycloth shrugged, the corner of his mouth twitching like it wanted to peel open into a rancid smile, like he was in on some terrible joke.

"As my client already pointed out, this has nothing to do with him."

"It has everything to do with him," said Kett. "We've watched his videos, we've seen the way he manipulates people. This kidnapper is working for Maynard, which makes your client responsible for anything that happens to those boys."

Berrycloth breathed a laugh through his nose, his eyes boring into Kett with no sign of fear.

"We know Maynard owns the Mortimer house," Kett went on.

He'd chanced it, but it was true: the glint in Berrycloth's eye dying in a moment of shock.

"We know he owns all of them, that he's been putting pieces into place for a long time. Why? To convince somebody there's something supernatural going on. To make him think Maynard's bullshit is true."

In the bed, the old man snorted, dribbling from the ruin of his mouth.

"It has always been him, pulling the strings, playing his game. But it stops now. You're going to write down the details of every property he owns, the names of everyone who's working with him."

Berrycloth continued to stare at Kett. He'd barely

blinked, and with his wide eyes and his tentative smile, he looked like he was high on something.

"That's where you're wrong, Robbie," he said, and he took a step towards Kett, close enough to touch, close enough to push Kett onto his back foot. "You won't stop it, because it never ends."

"Back off," said Kett, but he was the one who stepped away.

Berrycloth closed the gap almost instantly, his thin lips twisted into a shark's grin.

"It's astonishing, really, how far people will go to deny the inevitable. Men like you, who dedicate their lives to searching for the truth, only to do everything in their power to look away when it finally appears."

Kett retreated, the solicitor following him step for step.

"Back the fuck off," Kett growled.

"After everything you've seen, after all the evil you've encountered, is there not even a small part of you that wonders? Aren't you the slightest bit curious whether Maynard is actually right?

"No," said Kett.

"Because if there's any proof of the Devil, it's right here," Berrycloth went on. He'd slipped a hand into his pocket, taking another step towards Kett. "Not in him, but in *you*. How many times have you heard him whisper in your ear? How many times have you felt his hand on your shoulder, pushing you where he wants you to go? You know him better than anyone, Robbie, because he has always worked through you. You are his puppet. You think you have free will, but you don't. He owns you, he can pluck any string he likes. If he wants you to become a Devil, all he has to do is say the word."

Kett backed into the wall hard enough to wind himself. Berrycloth closed in, relentless.

"How is Billie these days? How are the girls? I doubt they remember much about the Pig Man, but there's always time to introduce them to somebody new, somebody worse."

His eyes flashed with deranged glee.

"Easy enough to do, when their father isn't around any more."

He pulled his hand free, a flash of steel, a slim blade.

Kett punched him, his fist connecting with Berrycloth's face like a sledgehammer hitting a steak. The solicitor reeled back, spraying blood, and Kett hit him again, sending him crashing into the bedside table.

"Knife!" he shouted over the clatter of plastic crockery.

Berrycloth sprawled across the floor, spitting more blood. His shirt had tugged up, the pentagram tattoo visible on his stomach as he tried to crawl away from Kett—the red-eyed skull winking.

"Help," he said, his voice feeble.

The door crashed open, Chester Andilet running in, his Taser in his hands as he moved towards the squirming solicitor. The other tactical officer was right behind him.

"Stay down!" Andilet screamed.

Maynard was awake, his rheumy eyes revolving in their sockets as he tried to make sense of what was going on. Berrycloth had grabbed the chair in an attempt to get back to his feet. He looked like he'd been hit by a car, his teeth bloody.

"You okay, sir?" Andilet asked Kett, never taking his eyes off the solicitor.

"Yeah, he's got a knife," said Kett, scanning the floor to try to find it. He rubbed his wrist as the pain burned through it. "He's armed."

"I'm not!" gargled Berrycloth. "He attacked me!"

Andilet planted a knee on Berrycloth's back, pinning him to the floor. Two of the constables had flooded the small room, and one of them cuffed the solicitor. He'd given up struggling, his body curling into itself like a hair in a fire.

There was no sign of the knife.

"He must have put it back in his pocket," said Kett.

The PC patted him down, then shook his head.

"This it?" said Andilet, who had holstered the Taser. He was looking under Maynard's bed, and when Kett followed his gaze he saw a silver ballpoint pen lying on the floor.

"He told me to write down some names for him," Berrycloth said, sobbing. "I was just doing as he asked, but he said I wasn't going quick enough, said..."

He groaned like he was going to be sick.

"That's not true," said Kett. "I..."

"I'm going to sue you for this," said Berrycloth. "You won't get away with it."

"He's lying," Kett said.

"No, he's not," said Maynard, trying to push himself up in bed. "I heard it all, he threatened us both."

"You piece of shit." Kett took a step towards the old man, only for Andilet to block his path. He planted one hand on Kett's chest, firmly, the other resting on his pistol.

"Maybe you should step out for a moment, sir," he said. "Give us some space."

Kett started to argue, then held his tongue. Everyone was watching him, the tension in the room making it hard to breathe. After a second or two he nodded, backing towards the door. From this angle, he could see the solicitor's face, and the bastard was smiling again. Once more, his eyes looked silver—a trick of the light, but one that made the goosebumps raise their heads on Kett's arm.

Nobody else saw it, of course. All eyes were on Kett as he stumbled into the corridor.

Berrycloth's lips moved, a single, silent word.

Devil.

Then Andilet pushed the door shut.

CHAPTER TWENTY-FOUR

Kett didn't say a word to anyone as he left the hospital, ignoring the shouts of the constables who watched him leave. He was seething, his entire body vibrating with the force of his anger—so much so that by the time he got back to Porter's car, he almost couldn't open the door.

He dropped into his seat, slamming the door shut, managing four seconds of silence before letting a shout of fury and frustration rip its way out of him. He punched the wheel, then again, then again, this time loosing a deafening blast of the horn across the empty car park. Then he stopped, his knuckles red raw, his wrist throbbing.

"Prick," he growled, aiming the word at Maynard, at Berrycloth, at the kidnapper, at every single one of them.

At the pain, too.

And the job.

He searched his pockets for Porter's keys, starting the car. When he pulled out of the space he saw a PC standing in the open door of the hospital, speaking into his phone as he watched Kett go. It was all he could do not to give him the finger. He knew that sometime in the next five minutes or so he'd be getting a call from Clare.

Or, worse, the Chief Constable.

He was too angry to care.

"Prick," he said again as he reached the main road.

This one was aimed at himself. He'd been an idiot, he'd let Berrycloth play him like a fiddle. The solicitor had even told him what he was doing.

If he wants you to become a Devil, all he has to do is say the word.

He'd said the word. He'd pulled the string, and Kett had given him exactly what he wanted. There had been no knife, there had been no threat.

He thumped the wheel again, but there was no force behind it.

Sure enough, as he accelerated back towards the city, his phone began to ring. He pulled it from his pocket, seeing Clare's name on the screen. His first thought was to open the window and hurl it out into the night, but he managed to restrain himself. He answered it, putting it on speaker and throwing it onto the passenger seat.

"You don't have to say it, sir," he said before Clare had a chance to speak. "I'm an idiot."

"You know, Kett," said the Super, his voice heavy with sleep. "I was dreaming about you, before my phone woke me up. That's how awful it is. You're there all the time, in my tossing dreams. The two of us, tossing about. You know how awful that is?"

"I can imagine," he said, although he was trying not to. "Look—"

"No, Kett, *you* look," said Clare. The Super took a long breath. "I could go on all night about what I want to do to you for messing up like this. I could do a TED talk on all the ways I'm going to rearrange your jumbly bits. I could find a job as a lecturer, and spend the rest of my life detailing exactly how many knots I can tie in your ballywacker. But would it change anything?"

Kett realised it wasn't a rhetorical question.

"No, sir."

"No, it wouldn't. Tell me what happened."

"I messed—"

"Tell me what happened," Clare said again.

"Berrycloth threatened me, sir," said Kett. "My wife, my girls. He said I was a dead man, and he pulled a... I thought it was a knife."

"Then that's all I need to know tonight. The prick threatened you, he pulled a knife, you subdued him. I can rest easy and go back to sleep."

"Right, sir," said Kett. "Except it wasn't a knife, it was a p—"

"Knife."

"No, a pe—"

"It was a tossing knife, Kett!"

"Okay, sir, it was a knife," he said, giving up. "Did Savage get in touch? We think Maynard owns the houses the kidnapped boys were taken from. Their homes. He's been planning this for years."

"Tell it to the night shift," said Clare, slurring his words. "And go home, Kett. It's three in the bloody morning, and we're reconvening in four hours."

"Those boys are still out there, sir."

"And you're not going to find them by punching solicitors. Go home."

Kett nodded, the tiredness like a bag over his head.

"Yes, sir."

"And stay the hell out of my dreams, you pervert."

Clare hung up. Kett kept driving, heading home for as long as it took him to remember that nobody was there. He turned off, making his way through the deserted city streets and pulling onto the road where his mum lived. He drove the entire length of it, checking every parked car in case somebody was waiting inside. Then he doubled back, parking just up from the little terraced place his mum rented.

It was the middle of the night, but the lights were on, the way they always were in any house Billie stayed in—an unwanted gift from her time with the Pig Man. But the house was quiet, peaceful. It was safe.

He closed his eyes, sleep ready to ambush him. He surrendered himself to it, if only to escape the horrors of the day. Five kidnapped boys, one insane man who believed he was turning into the Devil.

And looming over it all, Joseph Maynard.

He fell into dreams of dead men, of women trapped in coal bunkers, of pentagrams scribed onto the walls in blood —only for what felt like seconds, though, before the cannon blast of a horn shook him awake.

Daylight streamed into the car, blinding him. The horn blasted again, longer this time, loud enough to crack his skull. Somebody was hitting him on the arm, then the face, and he blurted out a sound that wasn't quite a word.

"Dadda!" said a little voice. "Wake up!"

"Urgh," he said.

He scrubbed his eyes, turning to see Evie and Moira right next to him on the Mondeo's passenger seat. They were both in their school uniforms, Moira thankfully out of her toga phase. They took one look at his face, bleary-eyed and coated with drool, and screamed in mock horror.

"Who are you and where's Dad?" said Evie. "Why do you look like a zombie? Why is your hand bleeding?"

He looked at his knuckles to see they were swollen, the middle one crusted with dried blood.

"Must have caught it," he said.

"Why are your clothes so gross?" said Moira. "You smell like Gran's bin."

She planted both hands on the steering wheel again, detonating the horn.

"No!" said Kett, pulling her away. "Don't do that."

His brain was still telling him it was the middle of the night, despite the fact the sun was up. Through the car's filthy windscreen he saw Billie walking out of his mum's house, pulling Alice behind her. She offered an apologetic wave as she walked up the little path.

"Beep beep!" Moira said, pushing at the wheel again but thankfully not managing to sound the horn. "Dadda, why are you even out here?"

"They're getting a divorce," said Evie, matter-of-factly. She opened the glove box, then closed it again. "That's why we're staying at Gran's, that's why he's sleeping in the car."

"We're not getting a—"

"Does that mean we get two houses?" said Moira. "And two bedrooms? And two lots of Christmas presents, and two dogs, and two cats, and two cars?"

They looked at each other with excitement.

"Yay!" they yelled. "Divorce!"

He honestly couldn't tell if he was dreaming, the exhaustion as profound as it had been when he'd closed his eyes. He did his best to ignore the celebrations, rolling down the window as Billie reached the car.

"Sorry," she said. "They spotted you from the house, I said they could come over. I didn't realise you were asleep."

"It's okay," he said. "I wasn't asleep."

"Then you should probably see a doctor, because that's a lot of drool for somebody who's been awake."

He wiped his face. She looked at his clothes in disbelief.

"It's a long story," he said before she could ask.

Moira was kneeling on the seat, jiggling with excitement.

"We're all getting divorced and I can have an electric car," she said.

"Divorced?" Billie asked.

"I want to live with you, Mumma," their littlest went on.

"Me too," said Evie.

"Hey!" Kett said. "We're not getting divorced! And why does nobody want to live with me?"

He looked past Billie to where Alice stood.

"Will you live with me?" he said.

"In that old car?" said Alice. "With you and your smelly clothes? No thanks. I'm staying with Mum."

"We're not getting divorced!" Billie protested. "What are you doing out here? Have you been home?"

He picked sleep from his eyes with filthy fingers, flicking it away.

"No," he told her, not wanting to go into details in front of the girls. "It was a late one. I thought I'd check in on you before I went to the house. I must have dozed off."

Billie nodded, her expression unreadable, her eyes dark. The question on her face was obvious, and he answered it.

"It's fine, it's safe," he said, and he wasn't sure if it was a lie or not. He turned to the girls before Billie could grill him further. "You guys ready for school?"

"No," said Moira.

"No," said Evie.

"We don't need to go to school," said Moira. "Marnie's

mum and dad got divorced and she was off for a whole week."

"I don't think I can ever go back," said Evie, her hand to her forehead. "I'm too sad."

She didn't look it. She was positively revelling in the idea.

"We're not getting—" Kett started, but Evie leaned over her sister and planted two sweaty hands over his lips. She tasted of jam.

"Sorry, Dadda," she said. "We have made our decision. Two houses, two bedrooms, lots of presents."

"An electric car," said Moira.

She leaned on the horn again, and he almost threw her out the window.

"No, Moo-moo!"

"Can I have another horse?" said Alice, finally getting into the spirit of it. "That would make me feel better about the divorce."

"Dad will buy you one, so he gets in our good books," said Evie. "We'll say we're going to live with him and he'll buy three horses, one each. And an electric car for Moo-moo, and a Jelly Cat for me. But then we still won't live with him. Sorry, Dad, you're just too smelly."

"Girls!" said Billie, laughing.

"Who votes for it," said Evie, her hand almost hitting the ceiling.

Moira's followed, then Alice's.

"I guess that's settled then," said Billie. "You win."

There was another round of cheers. Even Alice was grinning.

"Now how about we put that community spirit together and actually get going," said Billie. "We're going to be late."

"Hop in," Kett told her. "I'll drive you. I've got to be at HQ, anyway."

He checked his watch, his stomach contracting when he realised how late it was. It made him realise how desperately he needed the toilet, his bladder close to exploding.

"Well, I had to be there an hour and a half ago," he said. "Anyone seen my phone?"

"It's dead," said Moira, holding it up. "And filthy."

"Right, anyone seen the car key?"

"It's up my bum," said Evie, and she started cackling.

"Maybe it *would* be better if you walked," he told them. "I really do need to go."

"We can walk," said Billie. "It's ten minutes. You're not going to say hi to your mum?"

"I'll never get to work if I do," he said.

"Good point. She baked croissants, though."

It was insanely tempting, as was the proximity of her downstairs loo, but he shook his head.

"Come on, girls," said Billie. "Let's go."

"Yeah, move, or your mum and I will get married again," he told them.

"No!" yelled Evie, horrified.

She escaped onto the pavement. Moira followed, blowing him a kiss before slamming the door shut.

"Love you, Dadda."

"Yeah? Not enough to pick me over Mum, though?"

She didn't hear him, chasing Evie around the side of the car. She must have thumped into her sister because they started yelling at each other.

Billie sighed through the open window.

"Swap?" she said. "I'll chase criminals, you chase these guys?"

"No thanks," he said. "I've got the easy job."

Evie and Moira's argument seemed to have escalated, the pair of them screaming at each other. Evie was slapping her little sister's shoulder, and Billie turned to them.

"That's enough, girls! What's wrong?"

"*She's* wrong!" yelled Moira, and she planted both hands on Evie's chest and shoved her off the pavement.

Evie staggered into the road behind the car, sprawling out of sight. At the same time, a white van tore past, the sudden roar of noise and rush of adrenaline almost taking Kett's head off.

"Shit!" he said, opening his door and almost falling out. "Evie? Evie!"

She lay in a heap behind the Mondeo, too shocked to cry. He scooped her up, struggling with the weight of her as he hefted her off the road. Moira was screaming her way down the pavement, her hands over her head.

"Jesus," said Kett, feeling like his heart was on its last legs. "Are you okay? Did it hit you?"

"She pushed me!" Evie replied, the tears finally starting. "My leg hurts."

Billie had opened the passenger door, and he dropped Evie gently onto the seat, giving her a quick once over and finding nothing except a scratch on one knee.

"Mummy will check it," he said, giving way to Billie. "I'll get the other one."

He jogged after Moira, who had stopped a little way ahead. She was sobbing, her hands still covering her head. When she saw him coming, it looked like she was going to start running again.

"Hey," he said, slowing down so as not to scare her off. "Just wait, listen to me."

"You're going to tell me off!" she wailed. "I didn't push her! She fell!"

"Hey," he said again, creeping closer. He ducked down onto one knee like he was about to propose, wondering if he'd ever be able to get up again. "Moo-moo, listen to me."

"No!" she said. "I didn't do anything."

"Yeah, you did," he said. "And it was a bad thing."

She started running again, shaking her head, her blonde hair falling over her face, sticking to her rosy cheeks.

"I didn't!"

"But it's okay," he called out after her. "I know you didn't want to hurt her."

Moira stopped, her little shoulders rising and falling with each breath.

"We all do bad things sometimes, mate," he said. "Everyone in the world does. *I* do."

He glanced at his swollen knuckles.

"But nothing is *that* bad. You can always turn around, you can always find your way back. Yeah? I'm always on your side."

She huffed, the sobs dying out.

"Turn around, Moo-moo. Come back."

It took another few seconds, but eventually she did, slouching towards him. Her face was flushed, her eyes red raw.

"I'm sorry," she said.

Kett opened his arms and she stepped into them, a sweaty mess that he gathered in a hug. She smelled of his mum's perfume.

"Maybe I'm not the one you should be saying sorry to."

He let go of her, watching as she trudged back to the car. She hugged Evie, and just like that they were laughing again. Moira helped her sister out of the seat, and they walked past him like nothing had happened.

"Bye, Dad!"

"Bye!"

Billie closed the car door and walked over.

"If that's what a night at Mum's does to them, then you're better off at home," he told her.

She laughed, pressing her lips to his. She tasted of butter and jam and coffee. The taste of what his life would be without the job.

"Be safe, Robbie," she said when she pulled away.

She ran off after the little ones, Alice loitering for long enough to ask:

"Can I really get a new horse?"

"No!" he told her.

She walked off, and he watched them go, his heart only just starting to find its normal rhythm again. They looked so small, his girls, so fragile. And yet at the end of the road Evie and Moira laughed again, and it felt loud enough to wake up the entire world.

"Love you," he told them, just a whisper.

He dropped into the car, rummaging on the seat, then on the floor, before finally finding the car key in the ashtray. One of the girls had stuck a sticker to it, a grumpy little frog, and he smiled.

It didn't last.

"Right," he said, thinking of the case, of those five missing boys, of his bladder, which was about to rupture. "Let's do this."

CHAPTER TWENTY-FIVE

He had to swing by the house first, because he looked like he'd been rolling around with Stig of the Dump. He plugged in his phone then jumped into the shower, the water freezing cold. Slinging on a new suit, he collected his phone on the way out the door to see a dozen missed calls from practically everyone on the team.

Only Clare had left a text message, and he couldn't face reading it.

He put the phone on speaker as he drove to HQ, listening to a couple of voicemails from Savage. Fortunately, it didn't sound like he'd missed much. When he jogged into the bullpen twenty minutes later, he found everyone sitting at their desks, the usual buzz of urgency tempered by a fug of exhaustion and frustration.

Every single person looked up as he walked through the door. He tucked his injured hand behind him, self-consciously, but there was nothing he could do about his roaring cheeks.

"For what it's worth, sir," Porter called out from the other side of the open plan office. "He deserved it."

The DI started clapping, and a few other people joined in, but the applause fell silent when Superintendent Clare's door crashed open.

"Oh look! He's finally decided to join us. Out all night whacking off lawyers."

"That doesn't mean what you—"

"Tossing over suspects," Clare went on, oblivious. "Jerking me to the point of no return."

"Oh God no," said Kett. "Sir, I—"

"It doesn't matter," said Clare. "You're lucky. Berrycloth says he doesn't want to press charges. He said he *did* pull a silver pen from his pocket, and in the heat of the moment, after everything that had happened yesterday, he understands why you might have thought it was something else. He'll want an apology, of course, which I know you'll give freely and willingly—"

"Sir," said Kett, but Clare was still going.

"Because if you don't, I'm going to use your danger noodle to make myself a swimming cap."

"*What*?"

"You heard," barked Clare. "Porter will catch you up on what you missed this morning. Which isn't much."

"We haven't found the boys?" Kett asked.

"Yes, of course we have," said Clare, aghast. "The case is solved, they're all back home, everything's fine and dandy, Kett, that's why I look so happy."

He grinned like a possessed gargoyle carved by a deranged sculptor.

"And yes, you twat, I did dream about you again. So thanks for that."

Clare returned to his office and slammed the door.

"Wow," said Kett, walking to his desk.

"That was pretty bad, sir," said Savage, looking up from

a pile of paperwork. "Even for Clare. You okay?" She nodded to his fist. "You must have hit him hard."

He glanced at his hand, gingerly opening and closing it.

"I can't believe I did it," he said, perching on the edge of her desk. Porter walked over, dressed in a fresh suit and, thankfully, a different pair of shoes. "How are you, Kate? How are the ears?"

"Better, sir," she said. "A little sleep sorted them out. What happened last night?"

Kett shook his head.

"Honestly, I was so tired. I never should have gone. Berrycloth knew what he was doing, he wound me up, told me they were going to go after the girls, that they'd be easy prey without me around. Then he pulled out that pen and he wanted me to think it was a knife. He knew what I'd do. You should have seen the look on his face when I hit him. Hhe was enjoying it."

"Like I said, sir," said Porter, resting a comforting hand on Kett's shoulder. "He had it coming."

"He believes it," said Kett, remembering the fervour in the man's face as he spoke about the Devil. "He's fallen for Maynard's cult hook, line and sinker."

"Did you get anything out of Maynard?" Savage asked.

"No, he was asleep. But I mentioned the fact that Maynard owned the Mortimer place and Berrycloth looked like he was about to shit himself. That's confirmation if ever I saw it. That was a great piece of detective work, Kate."

"We confirmed it here too, sir," she said. "Or Spalding did, anyway."

They all turned to where Spalding was sitting, at Kett's old desk by the radiator. She must have sensed it, because she glanced up.

"What?" she barked.

"Properties," said Kett.

It took her a moment, as if she'd been expecting something else. She typed something into her computer.

"Well I'm not coming to you," she said.

They filed over, crowding around her as she brought up a document on the screen. Kett pulled out his glasses and turned the blurs into words.

"Three of of our five properties belong to limited companies," Spalding said. "They're all different, but they can all be tied back to a business running out of the Isle of Man. This, in turn, leads offshore, but I managed to match it to one of the companies we were investigating when you were abducted. There's a link to Hollenbeck, sir."

"Which three?" Kett asked.

"Mortimer, as you know. The Hipkin place and the Kinghorn one. The Uysals were in a group home but it's a private one, I'm trying to track down the details. The Lynns own their house outright. The family has been there for generations."

"Yeah, I visited," said Kett, remembering the carved stone that read Lynn House by the door. "But that's weird, isn't it? Why would Maynard try to control every point on the pentagram but leave that one to chance?"

"I was wondering the same thing," said Spalding. "Maybe he started there and worked outwards?"

"Which implies some kind of link between the Lynns and Maynard," said Porter.

"Not necessarily," said Savage. "I mean, I'm not saying there isn't, but Maynard was targeting kids with certain names, and names starting with D are pretty common. David, Daniel."

"Darren," said Porter.

"Right, so there's a good chance that—"

"Duncan."

"Yeah, so there's a good chance—"

"Derek," Porter went on. "I've got an uncle called Derek."

"So do I," said Spalding, and they both nodded in mutual appreciation.

"So there's a chance that..." Savage scratched her head. "I've lost what I was saying, sir, but I think maybe it didn't matter so much about this one."

"I don't know," said Kett. "Maynard doesn't leave a lot to chance."

"Well, we can ask the Lynns in a bit," said Porter, looking at the clock on the wall. "Clare's arranged a press conference for later this morning, the parents are coming. Well, the ones who are able."

"Or who care," said Spalding. "Paul Kinghorn still hasn't bothered showing up to look for his son."

"Really?" said Kett. "Anyone like him for the kidnapper?"

"He's got one leg," she said. "Diabetes."

"Oh," said Kett. "Alison, can you dig into the Lynns a bit, see if you can find a link to Maynard?"

She nodded, shooing them away with both hands.

"Have you worked up any other leads?" Kett asked as he walked Savage back to her desk.

"Not really," she said, taking her seat. "But I got in early and scrubbed through the phone of the kid who headbutted the ambulance. Jon Heath. I found links to a couple more videos. Maynard was clever. He used specific passwords for each of his followers, presumably so he could track who was actually watching them. The videos were hosted on rotating servers, so they didn't stay up in the same place for long, and it looks like as soon as somebody watched one, he'd either delete it or move it. It makes them hard to find, but not impossible."

Kett perched on the desk as Savage opened a video. Maynard was there in his red-walled room, sitting at the same table as before, wearing the same mask and robes. His hands were stretched out before him, his fingers steepled. The title of the video was '*Pillar 3, the Tangental Nature of Evil.*'

"Isn't that spelled wrong?" said Kett.

"Yeah," said Savage. "Sloppy. The video's not much better. It's an hour long, and trust me, it feels longer. Maynard drones on for most of it about how evil isn't what we think it is, how it starts small and grows, how the Devil doesn't win you over with a grand gesture but with countless acts of cruelty. Honestly, it almost put me to sleep. The last ten minutes is where he starts offering actual suggestions on how to hurt people."

"Hurt people?"

"Not physically, just emotionally. It's pretty awful stuff. Oh, and I figured out his username. 4522912. It's alphanumeric. 4 is a D, 5 is an E, V is 22. And so on. Devil. He's nothing if not predictable."

"To the point of being boring," said Kett. "For a serial killer, this guy has zero imagination."

"I can play the video, if you like?"

"No," he replied, not wanting to hear Maynard's voice again. "Just give me the CliffsNotes."

"I don't need to," said Savage. "Jon did it for us."

She lifted a stack of papers from the far side of her desk, handing them to Kett. They were printouts from an app on an iPhone, and when Kett scanned through them he realised they were annotations written while somebody was watching one of Maynard's videos.

"He took notes," said Savage. "Extensive ones. It's all there, everything from the first eighteen videos."

"What about the last one?" said Kett. "There are nineteen, right?"

"He didn't watch it. At least, there's no mention of it here. I can't find it anywhere. But..."

She returned to her computer, loading up an email.

"I also found this on Jon's phone."

There was a single line of text: *The test for Limination will take place independently. We will be in touch about your final viewing.*

"That's it," said Savage.

"What does that mean?" said Kett. "Independently?"

Savage shrugged.

"Don't suppose Jon's awake?" he asked.

"Not a chance," said Porter. "They don't even know if he'll make it."

"Can you get anything from the place the videos were hosted?"

"It's all out of the country," said Savage. "Even if we had warrants, it would take weeks."

"Did we manage to get hold of any other phones? Computers? Anything from anyone who might have been following Maynard?"

"A couple of laptops from Cold Iron," said Savage. "We think they belonged to the shooters. But they did a better job of scrubbing their history. The phones of the victims were taken, and Emil didn't have his in the tank. If it *is* Emil. He's still out of it, too. Heath's the only one we know for sure was watching Maynard's videos."

"Keep looking," said Kett. "It all goes back to this, to Maynard trying to convince his followers they're evil, trying to make them commit a crime. If we can find out where they had to go to watch the last video, then we might be able to work forward from there."

He shook his head.

"This can't be all we have to go on. There's nothing else at the paintball place?"

"No, sir."

"We've checked Maynard's information for anywhere else he might be working from?"

"We have."

"Nobody's found any link between the victims? Anything at all, other than the fact their names start with a certain letter, and they live at the points of a pentagram?"

"Nothing, sir," said Porter.

"What about Balls?" he asked, a last resort. "Did he have anything else to offer?"

"Actually, he did," said Porter. "He told us to tell you he'd like you to take him out for dinner, to make up for being such a bad best friend."

"He gave us a list of acceptable places," added Savage. "They were all service stations."

"The hearse, then?" said Kett. "We must have dug something up. Who was it registered to?"

"Nobody," said Savage. "Plates were fake, the VIN belongs to an entirely different vehicle that's been off the road since the nineties. We've contacted every single person we can find online who's ever owned one, and nobody can tell us where this thing came from."

"A magic hearse?" said Kett, close to screaming.

"We did spot it on another couple of traffic cams," said Porter. "But the driver's wearing a mask in every one. A different mask for each victim, as we thought."

"So we can't even be sure it's one man," said Kett. "With everything going on, it could be five kidnappers, one for each kid. It's Stillwater, Percival and Figg all over again."

"Which ties in with the videos," said Savage. "Maybe the final test in the nineteenth video, the last act of cruelty, is to kidnap a child."

Nobody argued.

"You know what else it reminds me of, sir?" said Savage. "Whip crack, the Elsham case. We thought those kids had been kidnapped, but they were just playing around."

"Yeah," said Kett. "I thought about that too."

It was impossible to be involved with any kidnapping case now without remembering Ocean Everett and the other teenagers—a twisted game that had led to more than one death.

"But these kids are injured," he said. "The kidnapper stabbed at least three of them. It's different."

He picked up an enormous map of Norfolk from Savage's desk, looking at the pentagram she'd drawn between the homes of the five victims. It swallowed an enormous chunk of the county, a brutal, five-lined scar.

But something about it seemed wrong, something he couldn't put his finger on.

"Come on," he said, throwing it down again. "What about that arsehole Berrycloth? We've had a look at his office?"

"He doesn't have one," said Savage. "No listed place of work, although he's registered with the SLA. We've swung by his address, but unless we can prove he's in on this with Maynard, we can't get inside."

"He's in on it," said Kett. "Last night, when I hit him, when he fell, I saw his stomach. He's got the same tattoo Jon Heath has, and those lads from the paintball place. What's his address?"

Savage and Porter shared a look.

"Clare specifically told us not to go there," she said.

"He told you, not me," said Kett. "The address."

He gave her a look that meant she could only answer one way.

"I'll get it, sir. But really, this is a bad idea."

"Well I'm all out of good ones," said Kett, heading for the door. "You can drive."

CHAPTER TWENTY-SIX

It wasn't an office, it was a house—a semi-detached new build a few miles northwest of Wymondham. It was entirely unremarkable in every way, as bland as they made them and instantly forgettable.

"This is his work address?" Kett asked when Savage had parked her Audi outside. The engine ticked like a bomb as it started to cool, the only sound in the entire street.

"Yes, sir. Only one we have on file. He practices privately, probably works from home."

Kett surrendered the pleasant warmth of the car for the bitter chill. The day was bright, but it was an illusion, the temperature hovering in the low single digits. If this was hell, then it was close to freezing over.

He heard the growl of an engine and turned to see an IRV driving down the street. It parked behind Savage's car, two tactical officers climbing out in full gear. The first was Joe Carmichael. The second, to Kett's surprise, was Julia Gorski.

"Hey," said Kett. "You back on duty?"

"Yeah," she replied, stone-faced as she checked her rifle.

Kett locked eyes with Carmichael, who gave an almost imperceptible shrug.

"You think you're the only one allowed to get stuck in?" Gorski said. "We heard what happened last night."

"From Andilet?" asked Kett. "Did he say what happened in the room after I left?"

"Chester was there?" said Gorski, frowning. "You're sure?"

"Yeah. Good job, too, or I might have finished the job. Why?"

"Wasn't his shift," said Gorski. "But I don't think anyone knows what's going on at the moment. Unit's in chaos after what happened to Ben. *We're* not supposed to be here, but..."

"But fuck it," said Carmichael. "These arseholes don't follow the rules. Why should we?"

There were too many answers to that question to even begin, but there was no time. Besides, having two armed coppers with them as they made their way to the house wasn't exactly a bad thing. Kett walked to the front door, which was set back from the pavement by all of two feet's worth of path, opening the letter box and peering into the gloom. His sinuses were assaulted by a chemical reek, one that gave him an instant headache.

"You in there, Berrycloth?" he yelled. "It's the police. *Armed* police."

No reply. The man was probably still at the hospital at Maynard's bedside—or maybe lying in a bed of his own, if the pain in Kett's hand was any indication of how hard he'd hit him. He felt bad for the three seconds it took him to remember the tattoo on Berrycloth's stomach, that masochistic smile on his bloodied face.

And the words he'd spoken.

Easy enough to do, when their father isn't around any more.

"Well, we're coming in," he shouted. "Fair warning."

He tried the door, but it was locked.

"That smell like anything to you?" he asked Savage, holding open the letter box.

"You want me to smell it?" she said, her nose wrinkling. "Do I have to?"

"Yeah," he said.

She leaned in, sniffing cautiously.

"Smoke?" she said, more of a question than an answer.

"Let me have a sniff," said Carmichael, pushing through and inhaling deeply. "Definitely smoke. Somebody's had a fire in there."

Kett walked around the side of the building and down a narrow driveway. The garage was barely big enough for a toy car, let alone a real one, and it was separated from the house by a wooden gate that looked like it could have been blown in by an asthmatic wolf. Kett kicked it open, walking into a microscopic garden with a square of plastic grass that had, inexplicably, turned brown.

"How bad at gardening do you have to be to let fake grass die?" asked Savage as she followed him in. The two tactical officers were right behind, tight-lipped, hawk-eyed.

The kitchen had a set of French doors, and Kett tried the handle. The relief he felt when they opened was quickly swallowed by doubt, and he looked back to see it written on Savage's face as well.

"Too easy," she said, shaking her head.

"Move, sir," said Gorski.

Kett happily stepped aside, letting her through.

"Just watch out, Sarge," said Savage. "These guys like their explosives."

"Armed police!" Gorski called out. "And not in the mood to piss about."

She moved into the kitchen, sweeping her rifle from left to right. Carmichael was right behind her, moving in sync. They vanished into the hallway, yelling loud enough to shake the little house to its foundations. Kett glanced into the upstairs window of the house next door to see two moon-eyed children pressed against the glass. He waved, but they ignored him.

"You ever fancied that job?" he asked.

"Tactical?" Savage shook her head. "Not a chance. Aaron always talks about going for it, though."

"Aaron, as in the guy who can't walk down a street without tripping over something?"

"Yes."

"Aaron, as in the guy who once accidentally shot a man in the bollocks with his Taser?"

Savage laughed.

"Yes, that's the one."

"Good luck to him," said Kett.

Gorski opened the upstairs window, leaning out.

"Empty," she said. "And not just of people. Your fire was in the living room."

Kett made his way inside, seeing a kitchen that had been almost completely stripped. There was a fridge, which wasn't plugged in, but no washing machine, no table or chairs, and nothing in any of the cupboards.

The only thing here, in fact, lying on top of a folded sheet of paper on the spotless counter, was a slim, silver pen —identical to the one that Berrycloth had pulled out of his pocket at the hospital.

Kett waited for Savage to walk into the hallway, then he flicked the pen away and unfolded the paper. Drawn there, little more than a scribble, was a puppet hanging from four strings—one each on its arms and legs.

A fifth was tied around its neck, knotted like a noose.

"What's that?" asked Savage, reappearing.

"A message," said Kett, letting her see.

He turned the folded paper onto its back, seeing another doodle. This one was easier to understand, because they'd seen it so many times already.

A pentagram, a skull in the middle of it, its right eye painted red with a smudge of what might have been blood.

"Berrycloth knew we'd come here, knew we'd take a look inside," he said.

"Probably why he cleaned it out," said Savage.

She walked off, and Kett followed her through the hallway into the lounge. There was nothing in here except for a blackened mound in the middle of the room, a twisted shape the size of a footstool that gave off such a powerful chemical smell Kett thought he was going to be sick.

"The hell is that?" he asked.

It had been burned out of all recognition, taking most of the carpet with it and leaving a crater in the fake wooden floor beneath. The magnolia walls were black with smoke. The fire alarm in the ceiling had been opened, the battery removed. The windows were shut tight.

Savage leaned in next to it, sipping air through tight lips. After a second or two, she stood up, shaking her head.

"Nope," she said. "No idea. It reeks."

"Nothing upstairs," said Gorski as she peeked through the door. "No furniture, no clothes, no belongings. Nobody lives here. You worked out what that is?"

"No," said Kett. "Any ideas?"

"Nope," she said. "Joe?"

"I'm not getting anywhere near it," he said. "Stinks of poop."

It *did* stink of poop, now that Carmichael had mentioned it.

"Is that what this is?" Kett said. "A bag of poop?"

"A bag of poop?" said Carmichael. "Why?"

"Who sets fire to a bag of poop, sir?" asked Savage.

"People used to do it when they were pissed off at dogs," said Gorski. "Fill a bag with poop, put it on a doorstep, set fire to it, then whoever lived there would have to stamp it out. Typical bag of poop trick."

"But this bag of poop is inside," said Kett.

"It might not actually be a bag of poop, sir," said Savage.

"That's one hundred per cent a bag of poop," said Carmichael. "Look, you can see the plastic from the bags. And the poop, from the poop."

"Bag of poop," Kett said, incredulous.

They all stared at it for a moment, then the smell got to be too much. Kett fled the room, picking up the notepaper as he walked back through the French doors. He took a big breath of cold air as he watched the others emerge. The frustration gnawed at him like a carnivore, teeth scraping bone.

"I am lost," he said. "I can't figure this out at all."

"That makes two of us," said Savage.

Her phone pinged, and she read a message.

"It's Aaron," she said. "Press conference is starting. You want to go back for it?"

"No," said Kett.

He stood in the little back garden of Berrycloth's house, staring at the bright sky. It hurt to look at it, like he'd just walked out of a cave, but he didn't blink. Better to burn his eyes out, he thought, than have to keep working this case.

Savage's phone bleeped again.

"Aaron says only the Lynns showed up," she said. "Ian Hipkin's mum and Vincent Kinghorn's dad both sacked it off."

"The Lynns are at HQ?" Kett said, blinking spots of light. "Both of them?"

"Looks like it, sir," said Savage.

"Then maybe it's time we had another look at their place."

THEY WATCHED the press conference as they drove. Kett held Savage's phone, Facetiming Duke, who had a front-row seat at HQ. Clare was a pale-faced gargoyle behind the conference table, and he downed almost a full glass of water before tapping his microphone.

Next to him were Dennis Lynn's mum and dad, looking older and more exhausted in the unforgiving light of the room. Victor was wearing a black suit and tie that would have been better suited to a funeral. Diane was all in black, too, looking like a ghost in the shadow of her husband. She was holding a little brown teddy bear to her chest.

"Hello, and welcome," said Clare, clearing his throat. "As you're all aware, this is an ongoing case, so don't ask me questions I can't answer. I'm not here to be tossed off."

"Now *that* would make the news," said Kett.

"What?" asked Clare. "Who said that?"

The screen wobbled, Duke's face appearing.

"Forgot to mute you, sir, hang on."

"Idiot," Kett muttered as the scene returned.

Clare stood up, giving a summary of the case. He skipped most of the details except for the kidnapped boys' names, ages, and the locations where they were taken. He read these in a sombrous voice as if he knew, deep down, they were already dead.

He spoke briefly about the hearse, and the masks, and Cold Iron Paintball, asking people to call in if they knew anything at all about them. He mentioned the videos, too, although he was so vague about those that it was absolutely useless.

"I repeat," Clare said, ten minutes or so into the conference, "if anyone has seen any dodgy videos at all on the internet, please get in touch."

Kett almost laughed.

"The phones will be ringing off the hook," he said.

They were driving into Fakenham when Clare stood down and offered the microphones to the Lynns. Diane was sobbing into the little bear as she stood up.

"I'm surprised they've let her speak," Kett said. "She's got dementia, according to her husband. She seemed pretty confused when I visited them."

Victor Lynn stooped towards the microphone, his face taut.

"Hello," he said. "Dennis, this is your father. I want you to know that your mother and I love you very much."

His voice was deep, the northern accent more pronounced. Diane sobbed even harder, the teddy bear pushed against her face like she was trying to smother herself.

"We are looking for you, son," Victor went on. "We won't stop until we find you. If you have any means at all of letting us know where you are, please do. Only if it's safe."

Clare nodded. He'd probably told them exactly what to say—or at least Kett assumed so, until the man carried on.

"And you, the man who has taken my son. You listen to me."

He jabbed a long finger against the table.

"I'll find you, and when I do, there will be hell to pay. You hear me, you Devil? There will be hell to pay."

Clare was on his feet, muscling past Victor to get to the microphone.

"Thank you very much, Mr Lynn. Now, questions."

Kett lowered the phone to his lap. He couldn't shake the feeling that the man's voice was familiar, and not just because he'd met them yesterday.

"That was weird," he said. "Right?"

"Calling him the Devil?" said Savage. "Yeah, definitely. I mean, he's obviously angry, but that's way too much of a coincidence. Unless Clare filled them in on Maynard's plans?"

Kett shook his head.

"Diane mentioned the Devil too, when I went to their house," he said. "She told me Dennis was the Devil's child. I assumed it was because of the dementia. You think she was talking about his father? Victor?"

Savage didn't reply straightaway, concentrating on the road as they skirted through the town.

"That's not all that's odd," she said. "What are his parents' names? Diane and Victor? D and V?"

Kett nodded, wondering why he hadn't spotted it himself.

"This is weird," said Savage. "I don't like it."

He didn't either, and he turned in his seat to make sure Gorski's car was still behind them. She was there, Carmichael too, both of them silhouettes in the dark windscreen.

They drove in silence, making their way up the road to

Lynn House. The ornate iron gates were closed, the building sulking behind its wild hedges. Savage cut the engine, and they sat there for a moment. Kett's heart was thrashing, and he didn't know why—some unspoken instinct that was screaming at him to turn around, to go home.

"Come on," he said, before he lost the will to fight it. He opened his door, offering himself once again to the cold. "We don't have long."

CHAPTER TWENTY-SEVEN

"So that's two illegal break-ins in two hours, right, sir?"

Gorski asked the question as they walked up the driveway to the Lynns' imposing house, her rifle slung, her hand resting on her pistol. Her eyes were narrowed into slits against the sun as she took in every square inch of the building, every dark window, every bush that might serve as a hiding place. Carmichael walked behind and to the side, equally alert.

"It's not a break-in," said Kett, approaching the front door. "They've already let me inside."

"You're not a vampire," Gorski commented. "You have to ask for permission each time. Why are we even here, if you've spoken to them?"

"Just a hunch," said Kett. "A vibe, when I was here yesterday. There was something odd about them. Can't put my finger on it."

He could still feel it now, that gut punch instinct that he'd met them before, that he'd heard their voices.

He let Savage go ahead, and she rapped on the solid

door with her usual strength. It echoed inside, almost like footsteps, and when it faded away she tried again.

"Doesn't seem to be anyone here, sir," she said after a handful of seconds had ticked by.

Kett tried the handle, but the door was locked. He set off around the side of the house instead, battling overzealous shrubbery as he entered the back garden. It was immense, a good acre of grass surrounded by old-growth trees. A double garage sat on the far side of the house, the side door open, the interior dark.

"Nice," said Carmichael as he gazed over the garden. "How the other half live, right?"

Kett hammered his fist on the back door, his injured wrist aching. He turned the handle, and to his surprise it opened into a shadowy hallway. To his right was a room, and on the left was a rickety staircase.

"Anyone here?" he yelled. "It's the police."

He stood back to let Gorski through, watching her and Carmichael storm into the house. When he glanced over his shoulder, he saw that Savage had reached the garage. She leaned through the open door, then recoiled, her hand to her face.

"What?" Kett asked, walking over.

"That smell like anything to you?" Savage asked, gesturing at the door.

"You want me to smell it?" he said, his nose wrinkling. "Do I have to?"

"Yeah," she said.

He gave her a wry look as he leaned in. The smell was a slap to the face, instantly recognisable.

Death.

Kett covered his mouth with his sleeve, following Savage into the garage. The space was drenched in inky darkness. The windows at the front had been papered over, the only light trickling through the door they'd just used, revealing two cars parked side by side. Savage cupped her hand to the window of the first, an old Morris Minor.

"Careful," Kett told her.

She pulled out her torch, trying to angle it through the glass. Then she aimed it at the windscreen.

Smudged on the glass was a bloody pentagram.

"Could have seen that coming," said Savage.

Kett headed for the second car, which was a much newer Volvo. He clicked on his torch, finding another pentagram on this windscreen, drawn in blood. There was a shape behind the wheel, and it looked like a person.

"Kate," he said. "Got somebody here."

"And here," she replied.

"Police," said Kett, trying to make sense of the shadows. "Put your hands where we can see them."

"Bit optimistic, sir," said Savage.

She was right. Living things didn't give off a smell like this.

Kett didn't want to risk opening the driver's door, so he made his way to the passenger side of the Volvo. He tugged the handle, a current of white-hot adrenaline fizzing through him as it opened. A wash of stench rolled out, and he gagged, his eyes watering so much that it took him a moment to realise the thing that sat behind the wheel was a woman.

She was dead, that much was obvious in the way her glassy eyes stared out of the windscreen at the closed garage door. Her hands gripped the wheel like she was planning to drive away, her bony joints locked tight with rigor mortis.

Somebody had taken a knife to her throat, the wound as perfectly formed as a mouth. Her white blouse was drenched in blood, and it had pooled in her lap, too. It looked dry.

"Christ," he said, retreating from the car so fast he cracked his head on the top of the door. "Body."

"Make that two," said Savage, leaning on the top of the Morris. "Man, in his forties. Throat cut."

"Kett?" came Gorski's shout from the garden.

"In the garage!" Kett replied.

Gorski and Carmichael appeared a few seconds later.

"Bodies?" said Carmichael, his nose wrinkling.

"Yeah," said Kett. "Two, a man and a woman, one in each car. Both have their throats cut. Can one of you call it in?"

"I will," said Gorski, heading back outside, her hand on her radio.

"Fresh?" asked Carmichael.

"Blood's dry," Kett replied. "Looks tacky, though. Probably a day or two."

"That can't be right," said Savage. "That would be before Dennis Lynn was taken, yesterday morning. You were here after that."

Kett nodded, walking to the Morris Minor and peering through the passenger door. The man at the wheel looked in a worse state than the woman, his throat practically sawn away. He had a couple of puncture wounds there too, where the blade had been driven into his flesh. His face was marked with slashes and lacerations, one particularly nasty one across the bridge of his nose and into his eye. Whereas the woman's passing had looked relatively peaceful, his had been brutal.

His hands rested on the wheel too, and when Kett shone his torch onto them he saw that they had been secured with parcel tape.

"You think he's got ID?" Kett asked.

"I think there's a good chance, sir," said Savage.

"In his pocket, maybe," Kett went on.

"Almost certainly a wallet."

They looked at each other.

"Can I bagsy not doing it?" said Savage.

"I mean, you can bagsy all you like. But you're still doing it."

Savage swallowed noisily as she pulled on some gloves. The corpse was resting slightly against the driver's door, so she slid into the passenger seat as carefully as she could, groaning as she worked a hand into the man's pocket. There was a distinctive squelching sound.

"Ugh," she said, swallowing again. "So much blood."

She slid out again, holding up her trophy—a little square wallet.

"You want me to do the honours?" she asked.

Kett nodded, and she opened the wallet up, pulling out a driving licence. Despite the injuries to the man's face, he was quite obviously the same guy as the one in the photograph. Kett glanced at the name, and he felt like the ground had opened beneath him.

"Victor Lynn," he said.

He ran around to the Volvo on legs made of cardboard, looking at the dead woman. There was no sign of a purse or a bag.

"If that's Victor Lynn, this could be Diane."

"Sir?" said Savage.

"And if these are the Lynns, then who did I talk to yesterday?"

"And who was doing the press conference at HQ?" said Savage.

Kett ran for the garage door, pulling out his phone as he

went and dropping the bloody thing on the grass. He scooped it up, feeling his back twang as he straightened. He limped as fast as he could towards the house. Gorski stood by the back door, speaking into her radio, but she stopped when she saw him coming.

"You alright, sir?" she said.

He ignored her, calling Clare as he entered the house. He pushed through the first door he came to, seeing a larder. The next one was the kitchen, and he ran through it, scanning the walls, looking for the photos he'd seen yesterday.

"Speak!" boomed Clare as Kett walked into the wide, airy front hall.

"We've found two bodies at the Lynn house, sir," he said, checking a framed photograph by the front door. It was the one he'd seen already, Victor and Diane Lynn with their son, Dennis. He pulled it off the wall so hard the nail came with it, clattering to the tiles.

Up close, it was painfully obvious that somebody had cut out a photograph of Dennis and glued it to the image behind.

"The Lynn house? What are you doing there?"

"Fuck!" Kett said.

"Fuck what?" said Clare.

He dropped the photo on a sideboard, heading for the stairs. There were no more photographs of the Lynns with their son, just pictures of Dennis at various stages of his life, and photos of his parents together in various locations, still looking like the stern couple from that painting.

"If you don't tell me who or what we're fucking, Kett, I'm going to hang up."

"The dead man's ID said he was Victor Lynn," he replied. "Dennis' dad."

"Well you can't have had your glasses on, because I've

just had Dennis' dad here at my tossing press conference. And his mum. I know that, because they sat there and told the whole world what happened to their son."

"I know, sir, I was watching."

Kett reached the top of the stairs, his back on fire. On the right was the first bedroom, the one he'd been told not to enter when he'd visited. The door was closed, and it was with a profound terror in his heart that he pushed down the handle.

The door clicked open, the horror movie creak of it deafening. The smell that crept out of the dark room wasn't anywhere near as bad as the one in the garage, but it wasn't far off—the copper tang of blood making his stomach contract.

"Kett?" said Clare.

"Hang on," he croaked, running his hand along the wall until he found a switch.

The bulb blinked on, revealing a butchery. The large room was drenched in blood, a puddle of it on the sheepskin rug, more dripping through the ancient floorboards. There were splashes up the walls, and some had even made it onto the high ceiling.

On the wall opposite, five letters had been painted in blood. He'd seen them before, of course, but not in this order.

"D, V, L, I, E," he read aloud.

"What?" said Clare.

"D and V lie?" he said. "Diane and Victor. They weren't who they said they were."

"Dennis' parents?"

"Are they still there, sir?" said Kett. "Don't let them leave."

"They've gone," said the Super. "Hang on, I'll send somebody after them."

Kett skirted around the edge of the room. There were three boxes on the bed and he peered into the first to find a stack of framed photographs. He could only see the top one. In it, Dennis stood between his parents—his *real* parents, who were in the garage—on a beach somewhere. He was maybe four or five here, his mum smiling, his dad sour-faced, both much younger.

He left the room, his skin prickling with adrenaline, almost painful.

"Kett?"

He lifted the phone back to his ear like it weighed a tonne.

"They've left," said Clare. "Drove away ten minutes ago. We're chasing the reg, but be careful, they might be on their way back to you."

"They're not," said Kett. "They're long gone."

"How do you know?"

Kett wasn't sure, not yet.

But still, that gut instinct nagged at him.

The feeling he'd met them before.

He looked at the wall again, the letters. Then he turned to the room, soaked in blood.

The *red* room.

It rushed back like a passing train, stripping the air from his lungs. He *had* met them before, just a week ago in the woods outside of the rave. Only back then, their faces had been hidden by red ribbons, and they'd spoken in riddles.

What is your wish?

"Kett? Stop tossing about and talk to me!" bellowed Clare.

"It's them," he said, practically falling through the door

onto the landing. He leaned against the opposite wall. Savage was coming up the stairs, her face creased with concern. "When I was in the woods, when I found the Red Room. There was a man and a woman there, their faces were hidden. They're the ones who told me where to find Maynard. They escaped. I never saw their faces. But those voices. Those *accents*."

He cracked the back of his head against the wall in frustration.

"I should have realised, I should have figured it out."

"What, sir?" said Savage.

Kett put the call on speaker.

"Kate's here, sir," he said. "I don't know what's going on. But these two must be working for Maynard. They gave us the information we needed to find him, but he *wanted* us to find him, he wanted us to raid his place at Cold Iron in order to set this stupid game in motion. He uses the couple as bait, in the red room in the woods. Then he sends them here to kill Dennis Lynn's parents after he's been kidnapped."

"That doesn't make any sense," said Clare. "Why kill the parents? Dennis wasn't even taken from his house, he was snatched from his work. Why go to the trouble of taking somebody only to go back to their house and kill their parents?"

"It *doesn't* make any sense," said Kett. "Unless... Maybe they came here first, looking for Dennis. He wasn't here, so they killed the parents and then went to the garage?"

"Then came back to speak to you?" said Clare. "Why?"

"Because they could," said Savage. "Because this is a game to them as well. They're all playing along with Maynard, and that's the problem, isn't it?"

Kett waited while Savage gathered her thoughts.

"We assume Maynard's playing a game with rules. But what if he isn't? What if he's making it up as he goes? What if making us run around in circles trying to find meaning to all this *is* the game?"

Kett rested his head against the wall, closing his eyes for a moment. All he could see there was Maynard, that old grin, those dead eyes.

"No," he said. "That can't be it, Kate. Maynard's obsessed with the Devil, we know that. All of this, the letters, the pentagrams, the names, the locations, it all fits his plan. There are rules, we just don't know them yet."

When he opened his eyes and looked at her, she didn't seem certain.

"There have to be rules," he said. "Because if there aren't, if this is just some madman's joke, then we're screwed. It's game over."

He pushed himself off the wall, heading for the stairs.

"And those boys are all going to die."

CHAPTER TWENTY-EIGHT

There wasn't much point in hanging about for the forensic team.

Kett left Gorski and Carmichael on site to secure it, making his way back to the car with Savage. His head was ringing like a struck bell, and when they climbed into the Audi, it was all he could do to keep the emotion from spilling over. Savage must have noticed, because she gave his arm a squeeze.

"When is enough enough, Kate?" he asked her. "Where do we draw the line? Because if I carry on like this for much longer..."

He shrugged, looking out of the window at the Lynn House, thinking of the secrets it contained, thinking of the horrors he had missed. That same prickle of electric adrenaline flowed through him, twisting his stomach into knots, making his heart rev like an old engine. He couldn't switch it off.

"I *can't* go on like this for much longer," he said. "It's going to kill me."

"Then don't, sir," said Savage. "It's not worth it. Nothing's worth this. You've done so much good. You brought down Hollenbeck, you took out the Pig Man, you found Maynard. Let us do the rest."

He nodded.

"I know you think this is personal, sir," she went on. "But it doesn't have to be. Maynard's probably mad at you for Hollenbeck. He's mad because you got involved in the Aggie Clegg case, too. You're a thorn in his side."

"That sounds pretty personal, Kate."

She laughed.

"I mean, just because it's personal for him doesn't mean it has to be personal to you. This is his world. You're free to leave anytime you like. You could literally go home, grab Billie and the girls, and get on a plane. You'd be in Greece for a late lunch."

The thought of it made the world feel a little brighter.

"You realise Clare would be on the next plane, though," he said. "Ready to twist my jiffy stick into a pretzel."

Savage laughed so hard she snorted, covering it with her hand.

"True," she said.

They both fell quiet again, the street impossibly peaceful.

"Where now?" Kett asked after a moment. "We've got five missing boys, all violently kidnapped. You think the fake Lynns are the ones driving the hearse?"

"Maybe," said Savage, chewing her lip as she thought about her answer. "Easier to do this if there are two of you. Kidnap five people, that is. But I think it's worse than that, sir. I think these two are part of something bigger. I think they're helping Maynard with whatever he's trying to put together. I think they're working with the kidnapper. You said Maynard wanted to see the Devil?"

Kett nodded, and she carried on, speaking breathlessly.

"If he's dying, if this really is his last shot, then he's going to put everything he has into it. He's going to recruit as many people as he can. That's a lifetime's worth of contacts and experience, funded by a lot of money. Honestly? I think the fake Lynns are a red herring. I think they're meant to distract us, keep us busy. Think about it, there's no reason they needed to do the police conference. It's insanely risky. All it would have taken is for us to check their house twenty minutes sooner, or somebody who knew the Lynns to call in and say that it wasn't Victor and Diane. They were right in the middle of the police station, easy pickings for us."

"Maynard wants us chasing them," said Kett. "To take our attention away from the boys."

"To give him time to do what he needs to do," said Savage.

"Him, or the person he's training up."

"Right, sir. The master."

"So we ignore the bait," said Kett, nodding. "Where do we go next?"

Savage lightly drummed the wheel.

"I keep coming back to the pentagram, sir," she said. "It's everywhere in this case. Game or not, it means something to the kidnapper, because Maynard told him it was important."

"You think he believes it has power?"

"I don't know. Possibly. If he's bought into Maynard's bullplop, then yeah, the pentagram is part of his demonic tool kit. It's serving him, somehow. He's not the first. Richard Ramirez was famous for drawing pentagrams on his victims' walls."

"The Night Stalker?" said Kett.

"Yeah. He was obsessed with Satanism, occult stuff. So was the Son of Sam. He told police that legions of demons made him kill. But neither of them believed it. It was an excuse, a distraction. Killers who claim to be murdering in the name of Satan are rare. People who do it because they *actually* believe they're the Devil, or the Devil told them to, are rarer still."

She paused to take a breath.

"But it doesn't mean they don't exist. This case follows a pattern, right? The kidnapper takes his victims while wearing a mask. He inflicts an injury on them, he spills their blood to draw a pentagram at the place where they're taken. He uses a hearse to transport them, as if they're already dead. These things mean something to him, because once he's taken all of his victims, he burns the hearse and the masks."

"Or tries to, anyway," said Kett.

"Yeah. But it's a ritual to him. People who follow rituals like this, they're often under the influence of somebody smarter, somebody influential. In this case, Maynard. He's charismatic, powerful, rich. He knows how to manipulate people. He's a Charles Manson, essentially. He convinces the kidnapper that if they follow the rules, if they use the pentagrams and the masks and everything, then whatever he's trying to do will work."

"So the pentagram is important," said Kett. "How does that help us?"

"Five lines, five points," said Savage. "We know the points are the homes of the victims. Maynard planned it that way, he's been putting the pieces into place for years now. But maybe the points aren't the only part of the shape we need to be looking at."

"Good thinking," said Kett.

Kett pulled the map of Norfolk from the back seat, unfolding it as carefully as the car would allow. It was big, covering most of the dashboard as well as his lap. He ran his hand over it to get rid of the creases, only succeeding in making it more crumpled. He started at the top, the street where they were sitting right now.

"Fakenham," he said. "The Lynn house."

He trailed the straight line of the pentagram down towards Thetford, and Ian Hipkin's home, stopping when he reached the intersection with the line that ran from Marham to Horsford. They crossed just south of the village of Fransham, close to the A47.

"Shit," he said. "That's where the hearse was burned, isn't it?"

"Yeah," said Savage. "Close. Maybe a mile north of that?"

"How the hell did we not spot that before?"

He ran his finger over to the next intersection, this one close to the A47 as well.

"Anything here look familiar?" he asked.

"No, sir. But that one there..."

She pointed to the next intersection of lines.

"We've literally just been there. It's Berrycloth's house."

The line wasn't perfect, maybe a mile or so out.

Close enough.

"There was a fire there too, sir," said Savage.

"The bag of poop?"

"Smaller, but still, that can't be a coincidence."

Kett grabbed his phone, calling Clare and putting it on speaker. The Super answered after four rings, speaking through a mouthful of food.

"Don't you dare ruin my breakfast, Kett," he said.

"I'll try not to, sir. Kate found a pattern on the map. We

were focussing on the points of the pentagram, but the intersections mean something too. One's the place the hearse was burned, one's Berrycloth's house. We don't know about the others."

"But there was a fire at the hearse, and a fire at Berrycloth's," said Savage. "Might be worth checking in with the smokies."

"I will," said Clare. "Good find."

"Thanks, sir," said Kett.

"I was talking to Kate, you buffoon."

The Super hung up.

"We going to check them out, sir?" asked Savage, starting the car. "The other intersections."

"Be rude not to," he told her.

THEY DROVE south until they hit the A47, then east. Kett traced their path along the map, realising how closely it followed the line of the pentagram. The road carved through the Norfolk countryside like a scar, like the wounds that had been cut into the face of Dennis Lynn's father.

He wondered what kind of person held such hate in them, such violence, that they could do that to another human being.

Kett's phone rang as they were nearing their destination, Clare mid-sentence before Kett had even answered.

"... trying to put it out all morning."

"Put what out, sir?"

"The fire, you tossbunkle. Are you going to make me repeat myself?"

"I hadn't answered the phone? How was I supposed to—"

"A fire on a farm just off the A140, near Long Stratton. Started sometime this morning, the fire service is still trying to put it out. It's not quite at the intersection on the map, but it's close. Where are you?"

"Nearly there, sir. We've just passed Dereham, won't be... Sir?"

Clare had hung up.

"You're the bloody tossbunkle," said Kett to the dead line, dropping his phone into his lap. "Fire at the third intersection, Long Stratton. He doesn't know any more about it."

"Can't see any smoke from here," she replied as she pulled them off the A47.

Neither could Kett, the big sky perfectly clear. He studied the map, finding the road they were on, and the intersection of lines they were heading towards.

"Another mile or so," he said.

There was nothing but fields and high hedgerows, the occasional line of oaks watching the world go by like old-timers gossiping quietly in the wind. There was no other traffic, so Savage slowed to a crawl, quiet as she searched the sides of the road.

After five minutes or so, they spotted the rear end of a car poking from a hedge. The sun reflected so brightly from its back bumper that they were almost on it by the time they realised it was an IRV.

"The hell?" said Kett.

Savage parked her Audi next to it and they both got out. There was a conversation going on behind the tall hedge, two voices. Both were easily recognisable, and when Kett scraped past the IRV he spotted Duke and Norman Balls sitting in the open boot of the same giant Rover they'd chased down last night. They were each holding a dainty China teacup, and Duke had an iced bun in his other hand.

"What on Earth is going on?" said Kett as he popped out the other side of the hedge.

Balls burst into laughter like he'd just heard the funniest joke ever told. He slapped Duke on the arm hard enough to make the big PC spill his tea over his lap.

"Brilliant, Aaron," said the little man. "Hilarious! You tell the best jokes."

Duke brushed tea from his trousers, managing to smear icing on them as well.

"Aaron, what are you two up to?" said Savage as she emerged.

"I texted you," Duke said. "Norman called me half an hour ago, told me to meet him here."

"Oh," she said, pulling out her phone. "So you did. I was driving."

"Why did you ask him to meet you?" asked Kett.

"Because he's my *best friend*," Balls replied, giving Kett a look. "I've never had a better friend than him."

"Look," said Duke, pointing to his uniform.

Kett had to walk a little closer to see the badge pinned beneath his name tag.

"BFF?" he said, reading the giant yellow letters.

"As in brilliant, fabulous friend," said Balls, giving Duke another clap on the arm that sent more tea sloshing out of the cup.

"Doesn't mean that," said Savage.

"Jealous, are we?" said Balls, still talking to Kett. "Aaron actually answers my calls."

"I didn't know it was him, to be fair," said Duke, munching the iced bun.

"And he came straight out when I asked him," Balls went on. "None of this '*I don't have time, Norman. I have a family, Norman. I'm in the shower, Norman. I'm at work, Norman.'*"

Balls picked up a thermos, refilling his own cup and then Duke's. The smell of fresh tea was heavenly, and Kett had licked his lips before he could stop himself.

"Oh, *now* you want to be my friend, don't you, Robbie?" said Balls, loving it. He capped the Thermos and tucked it behind his back, before picking up his cup again. "Now you want to be Norman Balls' beautiful, fantastic friend."

"Doesn't mean that either," said Savage, leaning on the bonnet of the IRV.

"What a shame," said Balls. "I only have two cups. One for me, one for my best buddy here."

Balls took a sip of his tea, instantly spitting it back out again.

"That's so hot," he wheezed.

"As entertaining as this is," said Kett, "I could really do with knowing why you're here, Norman."

"Well, you must have figured it out," said Balls, "otherwise why are *you* here?"

"The intersections on the map," said Kett.

"Right," said Balls. "Five lines, five places where they cross. Did you know, in arcane theology, it's the lines of intersection that carry a lot of the power? They symbolise the merging of worlds, the place where the planes pierce one another, the opening of doors."

"We really could have done with knowing that last night," said Kett.

"I did tell you last night," Balls said. "I was literally sitting there saying, 'Robbie, did you know that in arcane theology, it's the lines of intersection that carry a lot of the power? They symbolise the merging of worlds, the place where the planes pierce one another, the opening of doors.' But then I turned around and *you weren't there,* because you're not my best friend. So whose fault is it that you don't know? Mine or yours?"

Kett blew out a long breath, the same one he often found himself exhaling when he was arguing with his children.

"Yours," he said. "And I just want to point out that withholding vital information is classed as obstructing an investigation."

"Obstruct *this* investigation," said Balls, glugging his tea.

Once again, it came straight out.

"How is that still so hot?" he asked, wiping his mouth.

"Did you find anything here?" Kett asked Duke. "Other than a new best friend?"

"Found breakfast pudding," Duke replied, lifting what was left of his bun. "Oh, and there's a body hanging from a tree over there."

"What?" said Savage. "Why didn't you call it in?"

"I did," he protested, spraying crumbs. "And it's not a real one. At least, not a real human. I'll show you."

He hopped down from the boot, rocking the car.

"Hold up," said Balls, beckoning Duke towards him. He took a napkin and gave the PC's BFF badge a polish, all the while eyeballing Kett. "We want this to stay nice and shiny, don't we? My buxom, full-figured friend."

"That one's just weird," said Savage.

Duke set off across the field, Kett and Savage following. It was a narrow strip of land, maybe a hundred metres from one side to the other, and within a few minutes they'd reached the woodland on the far side. The trees were old, their trunks substantial, their branches knitted into a leafless canopy. They shifted in the breeze, the play of light and shadow so disorienting that even when Duke pointed ahead, it took Kett a moment to see it.

It could have been a body. The likeness was so convincing that his heart jolted in shock. It hung by its neck from the branch of a monstrous yew tree, its feet dangling inches from the ground. The effigy had been wrapped in bin bags and set alight, scraps of burned plastic coating the scorched undergrowth. The smell of it still hung in the air, overpowering the mulch and the rot.

A pentagram had been carved into the bark of the old tree, a crude skull in the centre of it.

"Sheep," said Duke.

"Oh God, not this again," Kett told him.

"No, it's a sheep," Duke replied, walking up to it. "Not a whole one, just a lot of wool. I checked, just in case it was still alive."

"It's burned to a crisp," said Savage.

"There might be other stuff, but I could definitely see wool," said Duke. "Wrapped in loads of bags. It's held up by wire. I didn't want to touch it too much, in case I got stuff on it."

"Icing," said Kett, seeing a smudge of it on the body.

"Yeah," said Duke, oblivious. "Fire was out when I got here."

The hanged body swung in the breeze, the branch creaking. Its head was covered with the same plastic bags, no sign of the contours of a face in the creases and folds.

"Why would somebody make a fake body out of sheep wool and plastic bags and set fire to it?" Kett asked.

"Fire!" came a booming answer, one that made them all just about leap out of their skins. Balls was striding into the woods, his face plastered with icing. "Fire," he said again, doing a good David Attenborough impression. "Man's oldest and purest invention."

"We all know a woman invented fire," said Savage.

"Fire!" said Balls.

"That's right," said Kett, massaging his stuttering heart. "Fire."

"Yes, fire!"

"Oh, for the love of..." Kett rubbed his face. "*Why* fire, Norman? I sense you're dying to tell me."

"No, I'm dying to tell Aaron," Balls said, walking to Duke and adjusting the PC's badge like a best man adjusting the groom's tie. "Ask yourself, why would you want to set a man on fire?"

"I can think of a few good reasons right now," said Kett, glaring at Balls.

"Specifically," the little man continued, ignoring him, "why would a man like our kidnapper, who believes in the power of the pentagram, set a man on fire?"

"It's symbolic," said Savage, staring at the swaying body. "You said the intersections on a pentagram are powerful because they are the places where the dimensions or whatever—"

"The planes," said Balls.

"Where these planes meet. Where the lines cross is where *you* can cross, if you believe in it all. Or where you can pull something through from the other side."

"You're getting there," said Balls, infuriatingly smug. "But why fire?"

"Can you not just bloody tell us?" snapped Kett. "We've got five kids who are counting on us, Norman, and we might already be too late."

Balls didn't rise to the bait, watching Savage as she worked her way to the answer.

"But these places where you can cross, they're still whole," she said. "They're still closed doors, however weak they are. The kidnapper has to punch through them, he has to open the door."

"Or burn it down," said Duke.

"Bingo," said Balls, grinning. "In arcane lore, unholy fire can be used to burn a hole between worlds, to open that door."

"We saw it in the Aggie Clegg case," said Kett. "Porter almost died in that bunker. But this isn't the same. We've got five fires, each one at an intersection, and each one different. This one's a fake corpse strung up to a tree, one was a burning vehicle, one was a field, one was a bag of poop."

"A bag of poop?" said Duke.

"Yeah, a bag of poop."

"Dog poop?" asked the PC.

"I didn't stop to check. The fires are all different. Why?"

"They all represent something," said Savage, glancing at the fake body. "Something important to the suspect. This one's death. Burning a field might be an offering of some kind. Maybe the hearse was him burning the bridge. He's reached the point of no return."

"And the bag of poop?" said Kett.

Savage shrugged.

"I have no idea about that one."

"Demonology is full of excrement," said Balls. "They can't get enough of it."

"The demons?" asked Duke.

Everyone looked at him.

"Oh, right," he said. "No such thing."

"It doesn't matter what the fires mean," said Kett. "It's a pattern, it's another part of his ritual. He takes the..."

He glanced at Balls, wondering whether he should ask

him to leave before realising the little man probably knew more about the case than he did.

"He picks his victims based on their names, and where they live. He creates the pentagram on the map, then in the places where the lines meet he sets a fire to weaken the door or plane or whatever."

Kett walked to the tree, giving the burnt not-corpse a wide berth. The pentagram and the skull had been carved into the trunk with some fury, chunks of bark ripped away, sap collecting in the damaged wood like blood. He put a finger to the topmost point and it came away sticky.

"The points are where it starts, each victim's home."

He moved to an intersection.

"Here he weakens the door, thinning the divide, getting ready to break through."

He paused for a moment, then moved his finger to the skull in the centre. It had been drawn so crudely that if he didn't already know what it was, he would have struggled to figure it out.

"He's closing in," he said, tapping it. "That has to be it. He starts at the points and works his way in towards the centre. He's literally drawn us a map. The skull, that's where he's keeping his victims."

He turned to the others.

"We just have to figure out exactly where it is."

CHAPTER TWENTY-NINE

THEY REACHED HQ HALF AN HOUR LATER, THE morning mostly spent. The bullpen was heaving with detectives from practically every division, the entire Force working as one to find the missing boys. Clare, Porter and Spalding had escaped to the Incident Room, the Super front and centre. He was holding his Big Tossing Mug to his bosom like it was a baby.

"... which is why I never believe it," Clare was saying as Kett walked through the door. "And what do you have to say to that, Robert?"

"Uh, what, sir?" said Kett.

"Pay attention!" Clare roared. "I don't expect to have to repeat myself."

"Literally wasn't even in the room," he muttered to Savage as he sat down at an empty desk.

"The fire at the fifth intersection was inside a lock-up," Clare said, pointing to the wall. Somebody had fixed an even bigger Ordnance Survey map there and drawn the lines of the pentagram on it, marking the homes of the victims and the intersections. "A cardboard box that contained what appears to be entrails and internal organs."

"That's offal," said Duke from where he perched on a desk.

Everybody looked at him, wondering if he'd cracked a joke or stated a fact. His blank expression didn't give much away.

"Offal, yes," said Clare. "From an animal."

"Sheep," said the PC, nodding sagely.

"That makes five fires, all different," said Kett. "When we found the hearse yesterday, we thought we might be too late, that the suspect was burning it because he was finished with his victims. But it was just another part of the ritual. Five kidnappings, followed by five fires. He's working his way inwards."

"To the centre," said Clare, nodding. "I got your message, Kett. It makes sense. We've found a skull in the centre of every pentagram on the case. We see the same ones tattooed onto the stomachs of Maynard's followers. The trouble is, the skull is huge in relation to the pentagram. It takes up the entire middle of the shape. Plotted on the map, that's approximately twenty square miles of territory."

"Maynard's precise, sir," said Savage, walking to the wall. "He's been planning this for years. If we're right, then we need to find the exact centre of the shape."

She drew five lines with her finger from each outward point to its opposite inward angle, then tapped the very centre where they all conjoined.

"Somewhere around these villages," she said. "Cranworth, Southburgh, Woodrising."

"We figured the same," said Spalding from where she sat. "There's not much there. A lot of fields, farms, trees."

"Ugh, trees," said Porter, shuddering.

"I've already dispatched every available unit to scour the area," said Clare. "If the boys are there, we'll find them. But this only works if the pentagram is the key. The truth is, our kidnapper could have taken his victims anywhere."

"Any luck with the fake Lynns?" asked Kett.

"No," said Clare. "They left on foot. Cameras caught them walking past Waitrose five minutes or so later, then they vanished. Who are they?"

"I'm certain it's the two people I spoke to last week," said Kett. "The ones in the Red Room, the ones who told us where to find Maynard. I knew their voices, I just didn't place it until it was too late."

"They're working with Maynard?"

"They have to be," said Kett. "Unless they're just along for the ride. One thing I'm sure of is they have no intention of helping us. They almost certainly killed the real Lynns, or knew that our kidnapper had done it. They posed as them after Dennis had been taken, spoke to me like he was their son. And they were good at it, too."

He shook his head.

"They were the ones who told me Dennis was the Devil's child. Why do that?"

"To distract us," said Clare. "To throw us off."

"That's what I think," Savage said. "That's why they showed up here, to put us off the scent long enough for the suspect to finish whatever he started."

"And we still don't know what that is," said Clare, leaning against a desk. He looked ashen.

"Maynard knows," said Kett. "Any word from him, or Berrycloth?"

"Plenty," said Clare. "But nothing useful."

"Let me have another crack at him, sir," said Kett. "At Berrycloth."

Clare opened his mouth to argue, but Kett lifted his hand.

"Maynard is never going to talk. He's been planning this for too long. In his head, there's too much at stake. But Berrycloth is a follower, he's one of Maynard's minions. We can break him."

"Like you almost broke him last night?" said Clare. "When you punched him in the face? If I let you talk to him again, we all lose our jobs."

"Then maybe we lose our jobs, sir," said Kett, looking at the wall where the five teenage boys watched from their photographs. "Honestly, at this point, I couldn't care less. We talk about this guy's ritual, the rules, but these guys aren't playing by any rules. They don't have to. That's why he's going to win."

He jabbed a finger at the wall.

"And why they're all going to die."

"Kett," said Clare, but once again Kett rode over him.

"For decades, that prick has trained his killers and set them loose. How many people are dead because of him, because of Hollenbeck? And now he's doing it again, knowing he's going to die, knowing it doesn't matter because we can't get him. He thinks he's invincible because *we* have to follow the rules, and he's clever enough to use that against us."

The room had fallen deathly quiet, every pair of eyes on Kett. The emotion made his voice quiver. It was all he could do to hold it back.

"Sometimes I feel like the only damn bit of good I've done in this job is taking out Angus Schofield. *He* thought I was going to follow the rules, but I didn't. I put a..."

He had to swallow a mouthful of bile.

"I put a fucking hammer through his head, and if I

hadn't done that, my girls would be dead, and who knows how many more. I broke the rules for him, and I'm glad I did. We have to do it again, sir. Because if we don't, those boys are never coming home. They're going to end up cut to pieces, burned, buried in shallow graves. The kidnapper wins. Maynard wins."

He leaned over the desk.

"Not this time."

For what seemed like forever, Clare studied him.

"Okay," he said eventually. "Talk to Maynard and his lawyer. Show him we're not playing his game."

Kett nodded, pushing himself up and heading for the door, hearing Clare call out behind him.

"But no bloody hammers!"

HE TOOK the entire Extreme Crime Task Force with him —not as a show of strength, but because he didn't trust himself to be alone in a room with Maynard and Berrycloth.

Not after what had happened last time.

Porter drove them in the Mondeo, meaning they arrived at the hospital twenty minutes later than they would have done if anyone else had been driving—with a headache to boot, from the soft jazz that leaked from the speakers. He parked on the kerb, because there were no free spaces, the security guard making a beeline for them before he spotted Duke unfolding himself from the back.

"How are we going to play this, sir?" asked Savage as they walked through the main doors.

"I don't know," he replied. "But it's not going to be pleasant for anyone."

He reached the elevator, pressing the button.

"You don't have to be in the room, Kate," he said. "You don't have to be a part of it. Just stay by the door, make sure nobody comes in. You too, Aaron."

Savage looked deeply uncomfortable as they filed into the lift, but she didn't say anything.

"What about me, sir?" asked Porter, jabbing the button for the top floor.

"Need you in there, mate."

"Like the good old days," said Porter, steeling himself. "Got it."

The lift slowed, the doors opening. Most of the coppers who'd been part of the vigil outside Maynard's room were gone, but a few remained on duty. One constable sat in the waiting area, and she waved them through into the corridor, where two more waited.

"Alright, lads?" said Duke as they walked past. "Anything happening?"

"Nope," said one.

Kett was surprised to see Chester Andilet sitting outside the closed door of Maynard's room, in full tactical gear. He looked exhausted.

"You still here?" Kett asked as they made their way over.

"Yeah," he grunted, cracking his neck. "Somebody's got to be, make sure nothing else happens."

"Gorski know you're here?" Kett said.

Andilet stared at him for a moment, licking his lips.

"You going in, sir?" he asked, instead of answering the question.

"Yeah," said Kett. "Berrycloth in there too?"

"Always," said Andilet. "Though you left him in a pretty bad state last night. I'm not sure if going back in there is a good idea."

"Good job it's not up to you, then," said Kett.

He walked to the door, surprised when Andilet stood up and blocked his path. He had one hand on his pistol, the other resting lightly against Kett's chest. He was built like a brick shithouse, and Kett knew he was ex-army.

"This won't end well," Andilet said, his voice low, his eyes locked on Kett's.

"This is the *only* way it ends," Kett replied, pushing himself towards the man even though his fingers felt like steel rods. "We've got five boys out there, Chester, and they're as good as dead unless I get inside that room."

"Let me call the boss first," said Andilet. "Make sure he knows."

"He knows," said Kett, pushing harder. "Move."

Andilet stood firm for a second more, then backed away so suddenly he hit the door behind him. He opened it, stepping into the room. The curtains were still closed, the lights dimmed. It took Kett a moment to make out the hunched figure in the bed, and the smaller man who sat in the chair next to him.

"What the hell is he doing here?" said Berrycloth, shooting up like he'd been launched from a catapult. In the dark, Kett could barely see the bruise on his face, but he spoke like he'd been chewing a wad of toffee.

"I'm staying," said Andilet, walking to the bed. "It's not going to happen again, not on my shift."

"Far as I'm aware, Chester, this isn't your shift," said Kett, entering the room. Porter walked with him, Savage and Duke waiting by the door. "Get out."

"Don't leave us with him," screeched Berrycloth.

Andilet was about to answer, but a groan from the bed stopped him in his tracks. Maynard was struggling to sit up. He wasn't cuffed any more, but he was weak, his body trembling with the effort.

"Leave," he said, coughing the word out with a wad of phlegm.

Kett thought he was talking to him, but he stared at Andilet and spoke again.

"Leave, I want to talk to Kett alone."

Andilet chewed on it before crossing the room.

"Big mistake," he said.

Kett waited for him to go, giving Savage a nod of reassurance before he closed the door. He could barely see anything in the twilight dim, so he flicked all the switches and then tugged the curtains open so hard he almost ripped them off the rail. Light flooded in, overwhelmingly bright. In the bed, Maynard lifted his hands to his face like a vampire, and Kett thought about how much easier this would be if he would just explode into flames.

"I won't stand for this," said Berrycloth. His face was inked with bruises, his lip swollen. "I'll have your job."

"You're welcome to it," said Kett, walking to the bed.

Berrycloth tried to block his path, but Porter intercepted, giving the man such a firm shove that he dropped back into his chair.

"Hey!" said the wiry solicitor. He tried to get up again, but Porter planted a hand on his shoulder. He knew the playbook. They'd worked like this before, back in the Met. The good old days, as Porter had called them, when the rules were a little greyer.

They were never good, that was for sure.

Kett turned to Maynard, who still had his eyes closed against the rush of light.

"Game's over, Joseph. I'm done playing."

The old man looked half dead, his face still swollen, his gums bleeding. One of his eyes was so red it might have been filled with blood. He was still trying to sit up, but his body had rebelled against him. One arm slipped, and he crashed back into his pillows. He gave up, deflating beneath his blankets.

"You know what I think, Joseph?" said Kett, sitting on the end of the bed. "I think you're full of shit. All this talk of the devil, all this talk of evil and demons, you don't believe it."

Maynard blinked at him, the loathing in his eyes so potent it felt poisonous.

"Because for a while there, I believed you," Kett went on. "Not that *it* was real, but that *you* thought it was real. Everything you did to help Aggie Clegg bring her mother back from the dead. All this stuff with the kidnapped boys. I thought maybe you were insane enough to believe in something beyond our understanding, something..." He threw his hands into the air as he searched for the word. "Impossible."

Maynard was making a noise like laughter, but there was something else in his face, something Kett couldn't identify.

"But you don't, do you?" Kett said. "It literally is just a game."

"He believes," spat Berrycloth from his chair. He reached into the pocket of his suit and Porter loomed over him, but when his hand reappeared there was a handkerchief in it. He dabbed at his bleeding lip. "We all believe. There's nothing you can do to stop it, Robert. Not now."

"You believe it?" said Kett, talking to the solicitor.

"I've seen it," said Berrycloth, his face twisted with glee. "I've seen how the parts have arranged themselves, how the patterns form. This is meant to be."

Kett laughed, patting Maynard on the leg hard enough to make him grunt in pain.

"You did a good job with this one," he said.

A frown landed on Berrycloth's forehead, but only for a second, before that smug grin returned.

"Is this what it's come to?" he said. "Good cop, bad cop? You think that will scare us, after what we've seen? After what we've done?"

"It's bad cop, bad cop," said Porter. "Make no mistake."

"He'll swallow you whole," said Berrycloth, savouring every word. "When the master is born, he'll devour you and everyone you love."

"I hope he's hungry, then," said Kett. "Because that's a lot of people. But let me ask you this, Mr Berrycloth. You think this is real because of the pattern of the kidnappings? The pentagram? The names of the kids?"

"That and so much more," said Berrycloth, resting his handkerchief in his lap. "You only see the patterns when *he* chooses to let you see them. By his red right eye, we witness the birth of the new world."

"Bullshit," said Kett. "Because *we* saw the patterns. We figured it out. It's right there on the map. A pentagram. Five points, five intersected lines, and a big juicy X in the middle."

Berrycloth's frown appeared again, and this time the solicitor glanced at Maynard. The old man in the bed was still staring at Kett like he could blow a hole in the back of his head with the sheer power of thought.

"And that's really something," Kett went on. "Five boys, their first names spelling out devil, living exactly where the points of the pentagram lie. Five victims. Five, what? Sacrifices? That aligns with the five pillars of consciousness. A man with five faces who drives his prey to the middle of the pentagram and offers them up so that he can become something bigger."

"Something so much bigger," said Berrycloth.

"But here's the problem," said Kett. "We found your property records, Joseph. We've traced all five of the kidnapped boys' houses back to you."

They hadn't, of course, not entirely, but the bluff was working. Maynard blinked hard, his tongue rolling back and forth over his swollen lip.

"You did it carefully, you hid it well, but you bought those houses and offered them to parents of young boys. Specifically, young boys with certain names."

Berrycloth's head was swaying back and forth between Kett and Maynard, his expression unsure.

"It's a remarkable feat of organisation. Audacious, possibly. Insane, absolutely. How long have you been planning it for?"

Maynard didn't reply. His body writhed beneath the blankets as if the bed was full of snakes.

"How long was it, Pete?" Kett said.

"Ten years or so, at least," Porter replied. "Judging by the records we found."

"All leading up to this," said Kett. "And the question I have is, why? If you have to manipulate the rules, then you can't believe it's real. And if you don't believe it's real, why bother? You must have better ways to get your kicks."

"You're lying," said Berrycloth. "This is bullshit."

"You're a solicitor," said Kett. "Look it up. If you're going to follow some old fart into his plan to bring the dark lord back to planet Earth, then do some due diligence."

Berrycloth tried to get up again, but Porter pushed him down.

"Stay there," he said.

"You didn't know, did you?" Kett asked the solicitor. "You looked shocked when I mentioned the property thing last night, and I assumed it was because you didn't think we'd find out. But you actually didn't know."

Kett gave Maynard's leg another painful pat through the thin blanket.

"You know what I think, Joseph?" said Kett. "I don't think this has anything to do with the devil, or demonology, or any of that. I think this is all about your legacy. You were part of Hollenbeck when it started. A founding member, along with Grant Schofield and all those other pieces of shit. You bred your little psychopaths because you were rich and bored, you competed with your serial killers for fun, because why not? Boring people have to fill their lives with something."

Maynard's one good eye blazed with fury, but his body was too weak to do anything but squirm. Kett actually laughed at how pathetic he was.

"You think you're a legend in the underworld. Joseph Maynard, master of them all. But that's not enough. You're a dead man. A handful of weeks left and they'll all be spent here or in prison. You want to be remembered for something more. Something that will fill the front pages for years to come. This isn't about creating a demon, it's about making sure you're remembered as the one true *human* devil. Am I close?"

"No," said Berrycloth, weakly. "You're wrong."

"I'm here to tell you that you've failed. We know where the boys are, somewhere in the middle of that pentagram. We've got every single copper on the Force scouring the area right now. And when we find them, alive, when we take down your deluded minion, you know what you'll be remembered for?"

Maynard didn't answer—or maybe he *couldn't,* there was white foam bubbling out of his mouth.

"Nothing," Kett said. "Nobody will remember you. You'll be a footnote in the Hollenbeck case, buried inside a police file in a drawer somewhere. And you."

He looked at Berrycloth.

"You and all those other little boys with your tattooed stomachs. You'll be the punchline to this stupid joke."

"Fuck you," growled Berrycloth, flapping his handkerchief like it was a weapon. "You're wrong, you'll see. When the sacrifice happens, when the new dawn begins, you'll pay for this."

He turned to Maynard.

"Right? Tell him."

"The game's over, Joseph," said Kett. "The only way it ends is this. Tell me where you're keeping them. Tell me where it's going to happen. Tell me who's doing this. You do that, then maybe your legacy won't be *this*."

He gestured to Maynard.

"This sad little sack of shit falling apart in a hospital bed," he said. "Tell me what I want to know, and we'll make sure you're comfortable for however long you've got left."

Maynard stopped squirming, his lizard's tongue darting across his lip again. He'd barely blinked since Kett came in, his good eye almost as bloodshot as the other one.

"That's your best offer?" he said, his voice a witch's croak.

"I'll dismantle every single thing you've ever done," said Kett. "I'll make sure nobody ever speaks your name again."

"They're lying," said Berrycloth, but he didn't seem certain. "Tell them the truth, sir. Tell them about what is coming. Tell them about the master."

"Just piss off, Gerry," said Maynard. "Don't be so fucking naïve."

It was like he'd physically struck the other man, Berrycloth rocking back in his chair.

"No," the solicitor said. "Tell them. You told me, you promised me. Our father, who dwells in hell."

He tugged his shirt out of his belt, revealing that awful tattoo splayed over his scrawny abdomen. It hadn't been done with any care, the lines of the pentagram wonky, the skull more like a potato.

"It's real, it has to be real. He's coming, and the only ones he'll spare are—"

"You see how easy it is?" said Maynard. "How simple it is to take a mind and twist it? That's why we'll always win, Robert. Because men like me *are* devils."

"Tell me where the boys are," said Kett. "It's not too late."

"What time is it?" Maynard asked.

Kett checked his watch.

"Coming up for one," he said.

"Then maybe you do have time."

"Who is he?" said Kett. "We know about the couple from the Red Room, the ones posing as Dennis Lynn's parents. But who was driving the hearse? Who took the boys? What's his name?"

"I'll tell you, but I need a guarantee," said Maynard, struggling to catch his breath. "And there are certain... *comforts* I want, to ease my passing."

"Deal," said Kett. "Tell us where they are."

"What?" said Berrycloth. "No! Don't you dare! This is too important."

Maynard licked his lips again, considering it for a moment.

"Beat," he said. "They're in the—"

Berrycloth jumped up, giving Porter a shove that sent

the DI staggering across the room. The solicitor dug his hand into his pocket again, pulling out something long and thin, a flash of silver.

Just a pen, thought Kett.

But this time, it wasn't.

Berrycloth lunged at the bed, driving the tip of his blade into the wrinkled meat of Joseph Maynard's throat. It slid in without a sound, right to the hilt—Maynard's mouth forming a perfect O of surprise.

"No!" Kett roared.

He grabbed Berrycloth by the lapel of his suit and swung him across the room, hard enough to send him crashing through a rack of electronic equipment. The knife skittered across the floor, leaving a streak of blood behind it. Porter dropped onto the man, pinning him there.

The door opened, Savage running in, Duke right behind her.

Kett ignored them, clamping a hand to Maynard's throat where the blade had gone in. There was only a trickle of blood, but then the old man tried to speak and a crimson geyser erupted from his mouth, splashing over his face, into his eyes.

"Christ!" Kett said, almost a scream. "Get a doctor!"

It was pointless, he knew. Blood was filling Maynard's mouth faster than he could clear it, choking him. His eyes roved in their sockets, bulging so much they might have popped free and rolled over the floor like marbles. Kett pushed against the wound, Maynard's hands scratching at his own, his strength ebbing away.

"Where are they?" he said. "For Christ's sake, Joseph, just tell me."

Maynard's lunatic eyes met Kett's for a second, boiling with fury, with terror.

Then he arched his back—one final, failed attempt at a breath—and fell still. His eyes drifted up, finding a peace he didn't deserve.

"You prick!" Kett said, slamming a fist onto the man's chest hard enough to detonate another spray of blood from his mouth.

"Sir!" said Savage, taking his arm and pulling him away. "He's gone."

Kett turned, shouldering past Savage to get to Berrycloth. The solicitor lay on his back, his shirt rucked up, that obscene tattoo coated in a sheen of sweat. Porter had cuffed his hands in front of him.

"Where are they?" said Kett. "Or I swear to God you're going out the same way he did."

It was another bluff, of course, but he wasn't sure if even he believed this one.

Berrycloth didn't reply, his eyes lost in the middle distance.

"It's not real," said Kett. "It never was. Maynard lied. There is no Devil. Those kids are going to die for nothing. It's not too late to save them, to save *yourself*."

"It doesn't matter," said Berrycloth.

"It matters," said Kett, desperate now. "For fuck's sake, it matters. Tell me."

"No, it doesn't matter what you do to me," said Berrycloth. "Maynard never told me where it was going to happen. I don't know."

Kett put his hands in his hair, the smell of blood and the churn of adrenaline too much for him. The back of his throat itched, his stomach contracting like a fist. He ran for the sink, making it halfway before a jet of vomit exploded from his mouth.

"Sir?" said Savage, running to him. He braced his hands

on his knees, retching hard. Savage rubbed his back. "You're okay, take a breath."

There was a cry of alarm as a doctor ran into the room.

"What the hell is going on? What have you done to him?"

"Let's go," said Savage, pulling Kett towards the door. "We can't do anything else here."

Not here, not anywhere, Kett thought. He'd said it himself, when he'd walked into this room a million years ago.

The game was over.

And they'd lost.

CHAPTER THIRTY

Savage sat on the kerb of the hospital car park, watching Kett as he paced back and forth. He was on the phone, but he wasn't doing much talking. Even from here, twenty yards away, she could hear Superintendent Clare's voice on the other end. Kett's suit was ruffled, dark stains where Maynard had bled on him. There was blood on his fingers, too, and even in the grey of his hair. His face bore such a profound expression of misery that he looked like a painted marionette.

"You think he's okay?" asked Porter, who sat next to her.

"Kett?" she said. "No, sir. I don't."

And it was no wonder. Maynard was dead. Their best shot at getting the kidnapped boys back was on his way to the morgue.

Kett ended the call, pocketing his phone before pushing both hands to his face. He stood there for a moment, like he could hide from the world.

"What did he say?" asked Porter.

"You mean you didn't catch it?" said Kett, dropping his hands. "I think I could have heard him without the phone."

He managed a ghostly smile, but it vanished after a second or two.

"Berrycloth's in custody," he said, walking over. "Duke's with him. I'm pretty sure he's not going to give us anything. I'm an idiot. I should have seen that coming."

"Nobody saw that coming, sir," said Savage, pushing herself up from the kerb.

"They're as mad as each other," added Porter. He raised a hand and Savage took it, hauling him to his feet.

"That's just it, though," said Kett. "They're not mad. Maynard knew exactly what he was doing. He's a cult leader, manipulating and coercing his victims into believing his lies. But *he* doesn't believe them. He never did."

"So that's what we need to do," said Savage. "We need to go public with Maynard's deceptions. Get it on the news. If the kidnapper is caught up in the lie, then maybe he'll stop once he learns Maynard planned the whole thing, when he finds out none of it is real."

"That's a really good idea, Kate," said Kett. "But we're too late. Even if we get this on every channel, the chances of him seeing it before he kills the boys are too slim. Maynard said it was going to happen imminently. Today."

"Have they found anything on the map?" Savage asked. "In the middle of the pentagram?"

Kett shook his head, studying his bloody hands as if he had been the one to drive a knife into Maynard's throat.

"They're still going door to door, but the area's too big and we've got nothing to go on."

Kett's phone started ringing, and he lifted his head to the sky, groaning quietly. After a second or two, he pulled it out and answered it.

"Sir," he said, walking away. "Yeah, yeah, I know."

Savage walked the other way, heading for the car. Porter followed her, kicking stones.

"We must have something to go on," she said. "Maynard didn't say anything at all?"

"He didn't get a chance before Berrycloth killed him," Porter told her. "He admitted he was beat. That's what he said. Beat. And he was about to tell us where the boys are, I'm sure of it. It was literally going to be the next thing out of his mouth."

Savage opened the Mondeo's door, reaching in and grabbing the Ordnance Survey map from the back seat. She unfolded it over the bonnet. The wind licked at it, tugged it, trying to pull it free, and Porter planted his hands on two of the corners to keep it in place.

"What are you looking for?" he asked.

Savage didn't know. She smoothed the map down, running her hands along the five lines of the pentagram. There was no skull in this image, but she could see where it would go—the image of that grinning, red-eyed skeletal face burned into her mind.

"You got a pen, sir?" she asked.

Porter pulled a Parker ballpoint from his inside pocket. Savage took it, tapping the end against her lips as she studied the map.

"Ruler?" she asked.

"Sure, Kate. I've got a whole stationery shop in here. You need Tipp-Ex? Sticky tape? A protractor?"

She glanced up at him and he shrugged.

"Of course I don't have a bloody ruler."

Even without one, it was easy enough to see where the dead centre of the pentagram would be. Savage lightly sketched the shape of the skull onto the map, adding the eyes and the nose and the teeth. The nose was the most central point, and she jabbed the tip of the pen into it hard enough to clang the bonnet.

"Please don't put a dent in my car, Kate."

"Sorry, sir," she said. "So here, you think?"

"Maybe. But have you done that right?"

He took his hands off the map and she almost lost it in a sudden gust. They pinned it down together.

"The skull isn't that way round, is it?" he said. "With a single point above it."

"Oh, yeah," said Savage, wondering how she hadn't noticed before now. "The pentagram is upside down. Two points are turned upwards, like horns. You got that Tipp-Ex?"

Porter laughed as Savage began to draw again, angling the new skull so that the top of its head was facing northeast. The problem presented itself immediately.

"We don't know which way round it goes in the pentagram," she said. "We don't know which two points make up the top."

She leaned in, studying the map, drawing imaginary lines inwards from the tips of the pentagram, then again from the intersected points. Whichever way she did it, the skull's nose formed the perfect centre. She tried working outwards instead, running her finger away from the lines on the page—northwest to Holkham, northeast to Waxham, then southeast into Suffolk.

Nothing clicked until she drew a line from the tip in Marham to the opposite inner angle where Berrycloth's house had been, then kept going.

"Wait," she said, tapping the pen on the map. "If we do it this way, this line leads right to Hopton."

"Hopton?" said Porter. "You're sure?"

"No, not without a ruler. But it's close enough, it has to be. Hopton, where Agnes Clegg was going to conduct her ceremony, where those kids were going to be sacrificed to the Devil, where..."

She looked at Porter, whose face was pale.

"Well, you know, sir."

"I do," he said, rubbing his shoulder. "Kind of hard to forget being kidnapped and strung up and stabbed."

"But Agnes and her dad were following Maynard's plan," Savage went on. "He's the one who told them to do the ceremony there, right at the start of St Michael's ley line. It's a place of power. It's... it's their due north, it has to be. The crown. Budge up a sec."

Porter stood back, and she twisted the map so that Hopton was at the top. The pentagram was perfectly straight, its top two points stretching like horns towards the car's wing mirrors. She began to draw again, sketching the skull the way she'd seen it so many times.

"It's a little rough, sir," she said.

"You don't say," Porter replied, squinting. "Looks like a bowl of noodles."

"But this must be right. I'm sure of it. This is our skull. The nose is in the same place, obviously, but the position of the eyes is different, the middle of the forehead. These are the places we should be looking."

She tapped the pen against the skull's forehead.

"That's going to leave a mark," said Porter.

"Sorry," she said again. "If they're doing this in the middle of the forehead, then they're doing it in a field. Where else? The eyes?"

"Wait," said Porter. "Back at the hospital, Berrycloth

mentioned something about an eye. About *his* red right eye, as in the Devil's. I wasn't really listening."

"We've seen red eyes," said Savage. "Pretty much every skull we've found has had a red right eye. If we go by that, then it puts us here."

Savage moved the pen, driving it down again.

"Sorry," she said, before Porter could comment. "Yaxham, maybe? What's up there?"

"It's further east," said Porter. "Over Mattishall way."

"Mattishall," said Savage, moving the pen. She managed to restrain herself this time, tapping it gently. "What's in Mattishall? The church?"

Porter shrugged.

"That's it, from what I can remember. A hall. School. Same as anywhere."

Savage circled outwards, the map tugging ferociously like the wind was trying to stop her.

"Fields," she said. "More fields, woods, trees."

Porter shuddered.

She ran the tip of the pen up and down the spidery lines of the roads, imagining that she was driving, seeing the countryside roll past. Then she stopped, her heart giving a mighty kick inside her chest.

"Hang on," she said. "Hang on, this place."

She tapped the pen hard against the map, the Mondeo's bonnet ringing.

"Kate!"

"There's an old farm out there, I'm sure of it," she said. She looked up at Porter, blinded by the sun that hung over his head. "I've driven past it a million times. Huge place, big buildings, chimneys. I'm not sure if it's even used any more."

He wasn't listening. He was trying to lift the corner of

the map to see if she'd scratched the car. She slammed her hands on it to keep it where it was.

"Sir," she said. "A farm?"

"Maybe," he said. "But who knows, Kate? There are a million farms out there."

She heard footsteps, and glanced back to see Kett walking over. He looked even more drained than he had five minutes ago, Maynard's blood bright against his pale skin.

"It's hopeless," he said as he joined them by the car. "Clare's drafting in more officers, but we're never going to find this place in time. We're going to need a miracle."

He hung his head as he looked at the map.

"You found anything?"

Savage drummed the pen into the skull's eye again.

"For the love of God, Kate!" said Porter.

"We figured out the angle of the pentagram was wrong, sir," she said. "It goes this way round. The eye of the skull's here. The red right eye. You've been out there, there's a farm, a big one, just here. Remember?"

She lifted the pen to tap it down again, but Porter snatched it from her grip, sliding it into his pocket.

"Use your finger," he said.

She did just that, prodding the map.

"Massive place, just outside of Mattishall."

"But what makes that farm any different to any of the others?" said Porter. "It's still a massive leap."

"Because that's not a farm," said Kett, pushing in between them. "I know the exact one you mean, Kate. It's abandoned. We had squatters in there a couple of years ago, remember?"

"Right," said Savage, another kick to the heart. "It's not a farm, it's a factory. It's the old British Sugar plant."

"Beat," said Kett. "It's what Maynard was telling us in

the room. I thought he was talking about us beating him, but he was talking about—"

"*Beet*," said Savage. "Sugar beet."

They turned to the map together.

"That's it, it *has* to be," said Kett. "That's where he's got the boys."

CHAPTER THIRTY-ONE

THEY TOOK PORTER'S MONDEO, BUT SAVAGE DROVE.

She stopped at Kett's house on the way, mercifully. He dashed in for a change of clothes, scrubbing Maynard's blood from his hands and his face and his hair like it was poisonous. Then they tore west along the A47, carving a path through traffic.

Porter sat in the passenger seat, one eye on the road, the other on Savage as she overtook slower-moving cars, the big engine growling.

"Careful," he said, more than once. "Slow down, Kate!"

The DI kept planting a hand on the dash, but Kett couldn't work out if he was trying to brace himself in his seat or reassure his car—the same way you would a frightened pet.

Thankfully, Savage had turned the music off.

Kett sat in the back, studying his phone as the world passed by in a blur of green and brown. On the screen was a photo of the sugar factory where they were heading, a vast complex of warehouses and silos that had spread across the surrounding countryside like a cancer.

"Place looks bloody huge," he said, opening Google Maps and zooming in on a satellite photo of the site. "There's at least ten buildings, big ones. If this is where he's keeping the boys, we'll need the entire Force to find them."

"I think that's what we're getting, sir," said Savage, glancing into her mirror.

Kett looked over his shoulder to see an IRV on their tail, its siren on. Savage slowed down to let it pass, then rode in its wake. More followed, the fast lane a river of blue light that buoyed them down the dual carriageway.

He returned to his phone, scanning through a handful of articles.

"They shut this place down after a fire nearly fifteen years ago," he said.

"Yeah, I think British Sugar moved to a bigger site over in Wissington," said Savage. "There's a factory in Cantley, too. Big business round here."

They'd hit the outskirts of Dereham, filtering south on the Yaxham Road. It was a little too familiar for Kett's liking.

"We found Kieran Spicer's body up here," he said. "In the park."

"Feels like a million years ago," said Savage.

As if he'd conjured it from thin air, the little play area appeared on the right, still marked off by police tape. Only the crows enjoyed it now, and they exploded into the bright sky as the convoy of police thundered past.

"Another sign we're in the right place," he said.

The wrong place, he added silently. Because absolutely no part of him wanted to be here.

It wasn't long after the park that Kett spotted the first of the silos, monstrous metal structures that towered over the neighbouring trees like something from a sci-fi movie. Chimneys followed, a forest of brick and steel. Then Savage turned a corner, and the complex appeared at the end of the road, surely too big to be real, bigger than he had any memory of it being the last time he'd driven past.

"Holy shit," said Porter.

The closer they got, the bigger it grew—exponentially so, as if it was swelling up to scare them away. The rocket-like silos touched the sky, dwarfing the buildings at their feet. Kett counted six warehouses, all connected by an array of pipes and conduits and machinery that he couldn't make any sense of. Around them were enormous concrete yards and countless circular pools, like the ones you find in sewage facilities.

It wasn't a factory, it was a *city*.

They thumped over a railway track, the lead car pulling off to the side to let them pass. A handful of IRVs were already here, as well as the tactical van, and Savage parked the Mondeo next to them. They got out together, everyone pulling a face at the same time as the stench engulfed them. It was a mix of sickly sweet rot and toxic smoke, so bad that Kett's throat clamped shut.

"Well, if this guy thinks he's the Devil, he's in the right place," said Porter, his hand to his face. "Because it stinks like Satan's toilet."

"What does?" said a voice.

Clare stepped around the back of the tactical van, swallowed whole by his Big Tossing Jacket. It looked even worse than it had the last time Kett had seen it, the fabric so worn that there were holes in more than one place. The furry collar was pulled so tightly around his face that he looked like an ugly baby pushing its way out of its mother—an image that Kett instantly tried to exorcise from his mind.

The Superintendent held a phone in one hand and a folded map in the other. He sniffed the air.

"This place? Can't smell a thing."

"I mean, compared to that coat, everything must smell like roses," said Kett.

"What?" Clare barked.

"I said, have you seen anything, sir?"

Clare studied him for a moment, then looked back at the van. Gorski had appeared, Joe Carmichael by her side and a handful of other officers standing back, waiting for orders. Kett was relieved to see they were all in full armour, their weapons readied. The yard was gradually filling with uniformed constables as the IRVs emptied out. There had to be fifty coppers here already, and more were arriving. There was a chopper inbound, the sound of it like a distant storm.

The police were outnumbered only by the seagulls who perched on the roofs of the warehouses—hundreds of them, their cries deafening.

"Nothing," Clare said. "We've only just got here, but Gorski had to cut through the chain on the gate, and it was an old lock. Hasn't been used in years. You're sure about this?"

"No, sir," said Kett. "But Savage worked it out, and it's our best guess. When Maynard agreed to tell us where the boys were, he led with 'beet'. This place lies in the middle of the right eye of the skull when the pentagram is oriented to Hopton, and the ley line we found on the Aggie Clegg case. And the park where we found Kieran Spicer's body is literally up the road. This has to be it."

"You'd better hope so," said Clare. "Because I've pulled half our tossing search force to help out here. It's a massive gamble."

"Kate!"

Everyone turned to see Duke running over from a car, waving at Savage like he hadn't seen her in a month. For a second, it looked like he was going to leap into her arms, but he settled for a cuddle. She peeled away awkwardly, glancing at the smirking police officers.

The Super slammed his hand against the side of the tactical van until his audience fell quiet.

"There's a good chance we've got five teenage lads somewhere on site, all injured. At least one suspect, certainly armed. We have reason to believe he's going to kill the boys as part of a ritual sacrifice."

It hadn't exactly been a secret, but a ripple of shock still passed through his audience.

"We don't know when. We don't know where. We don't know who. Or why. Or what. The only thing I know for sure is I'm cold, tired, constipated, and I hate this gerbil toss of a job. Gorski!"

The hawk-eyed sergeant walked up to him, one hand on her rifle. Kett was surprised, again, to see her on duty. When a case was this personal, you didn't usually get an invitation.

Still, she was the very best at what she did.

"This place is stupidly big," Clare went on. "You're going to need to split your team. I want six two-person units, each breaching from a different entry point. You lot."

He pointed a long finger at the PCs.

"Split into six groups, one for each firearms squad. Tactical clears, you search. Understood?"

There was a low muttering of agreement.

"Christ, can we try that again?" said Clare, like an angry headmaster during an assembly. "Do you understand?"

"Yes sir," came the reply, without much more enthusiasm.

Clare glanced at the factory again, which seemed to

have grown even in the time they'd been standing here. The gulls screamed at them, warning them away.

"There's a good chance our man knows we've found him," said Clare. "If anything, it will push him to kill the kids faster. But this guy's a believer. He's conducting a ritual, which means he has to follow rules. If we're lucky, that will slow him down."

He paused for a moment, looking at each member of the team in turn.

"Go find this tosslord."

There was a rush of movement as the uniformed police stampeded past the van, their feet drumming on the cracked concrete. Kett walked to Gorski, who watched him with dark, unfriendly eyes.

"You alright to do this?" he asked her.

"I *have* to do this," she said, checking her weapon for a moment before looking up. "Maynard's dead."

It wasn't a question, but Kett nodded anyway.

"You were there?"

"Yeah," he said.

He looked at Clare, who nodded once, as if to give him permission.

"His solicitor knifed him in the throat, Julia," Kett said. "Maynard choked on his own blood, he died gasping. It wasn't quick, and it wasn't nice. I saw it in his face. I saw the terror, the panic. He felt every second of it."

The stone wall of Gorski's face cracked, but only for a second. She sniffed, nodded.

"Good," she said.

"It's not bloody good at all!" Clare protested, flapping his arms. "Maynard was the only one who could tell us for sure where the boys are being held, and who's holding them. It's the opposite of good. It's..."

"Bad?" suggested Kett when Clare seemed to run out of steam.

"Yes, *bad*, you useless bloody dictionary of a man. Now stop farting about and get in there."

Clare stomped off, his arms still flapping like he was trying to blend in with the seagulls. Gorski had returned to her team, shouting orders.

"We going together?" asked Duke. "The four of us?"

"No," said Kett. "We stand a better shot at finding them if we split up. Pete, you come with me. Aaron, you can stick with Kate."

"Yay," said the PC.

"Why this place?" said Kett, staring at the building. The seagulls had multiplied, crowding the rooftops like archers on the ramparts of a castle. The sound of them was almost overwhelming.

"It's the right place on the map," said Porter with a shrug. "Maynard planned this whole thing, he might have found the factory first and bought the properties in relation to it."

"He might own the factory," said Savage. "It would have been sold off pretty cheap after the fire."

"Yeah," said Kett, nodding. "Good point. But there's got to be something about this place. Maynard must have given the kidnapper a reason to conduct the ceremony here."

"Because it's a place of power," said Savage.

"Right. So if this is a place of power, which part is the most powerful?"

"The canteen?" said Duke.

"The canteen?" said Kett. "Why?"

"Because food is fuel," said the PC, frowning. "Because you can't make an engine work without it. Because..." He spluttered out a sigh. "Honestly, I'm just hungry."

"There's the water, sir," said Savage. "The lake, on the other side."

"Or the boiler room," said Porter. "Heart of the factory."

"Or all of them," said Kett, his heart sinking. "He might have set up another pentagram. Five victims, five rooms."

"Shit," said Porter.

Gorski had finished giving orders and was walking back over. Carmichael was next to her, watching her like a worried parent. He met Kett's eye, and it was like he'd broadcast a message into his head.

This is a bad idea.

Kett wasn't going to argue with that.

"We're ready, sir," said Gorski. "Joe and I will go with you, we'll breach the main building first. I've got Sutagon and Andilet free."

"Andilet?" said Kett, frowning.

"Yeah." She saw his expression. "Why?"

"Because he was in Maynard's room today," said Kett. "Again."

Gorski chewed on it for a moment, looking past the van. Kett followed her gaze, finding Andilet in the swarm of black-uniformed tactical officers. He was staring back, not an ounce of welcome in his dark eyes.

"Chester's okay," said Gorski.

"You're sure?" he asked, because she didn't seem it.

"I'm sure. But I'll bring him with me. Keep him close. Joe, you're with Sutagon."

She walked off, rejoining the crowd. Kett turned to Carmichael.

"Are *you* sure?"

"Got no reason to doubt him," Carmichael said. "He's been in the unit longer than I have. Goes above and beyond."

The tactical unit was splintering off, each pair leading a tail of uniformed officers towards the buildings. Shouts rang out from every direction, answered by the cry of the gulls and the roar of the helicopter as it closed in.

"Be safe," Kett told Savage as she made her way past the van. "Be careful."

"You too, sir," she said.

She jogged over to where Chris Sutagon was waiting, Duke and Carmichael right behind her.

"Don't worry about her," said Porter. "It's Kate. She can look after herself."

"I know, Pete."

"And if anyone attacks her, Duke will just eat them."

Kett was surprised at the laugh that spilled out of him. He clamped his lips shut as Chester Andilet walked over. He was still eyeballing Kett, his jaw flexing as he chewed a wad of gum. His rifle hung from his shoulder, his hand resting on his holstered sidearm.

"Have we got a problem?" Kett asked him.

Andilet didn't answer.

"Nobody's got a problem," said Gorski, looking between them. "That clear?"

Kett breathed out slowly, his stomach churning at the thought of what they were about to do. He looked past Andilet to the factory, wondering what horrors they'd find when they got inside.

Or what horrors they *wouldn't* find, if they'd got this wrong.

"You ready?" he asked.

Porter nodded, and so did Gorski. She checked her weapon one last time.

"Let's end this thing," she said.

CHAPTER THIRTY-TWO

THEY CROSSED THE COURTYARD LIKE THEY WERE IN A war zone, heading for the hulking factory. It was built like a fortress, with only a single door and no windows. Gulls screeched at them from the ridged roof high overhead. Anyone could have been watching from the endless rows of pipes that hung between the buildings like spiderwebs, from the shadowy spaces between the warehouses, from the tangled bushes that grew up next to the walls.

Gorski led the way, her rifle braced against her shoulder. Andilet followed, sweeping his own weapon along the face of the structure ahead, grunting hard with every step. Porter was next, two uniformed officers by his side. Kett followed as fast as he could, losing ground quickly. His back was killing him, and halfway across the yard he slowed to a fast walk, two hands braced against his lumbar region. By the time he'd reached the door, everyone was looking back at him.

"In your own time, sir," said Gorski, unimpressed.

"Sorry," he said, limping up to them. "You don't have to wait for me."

Gorski checked with Andilet, a silent communication between them. She took a moment to examine the door, and only when she was confident there was nothing rigged to it did she turn the handle and shoulder it open. Andilet moved in, his voice echoing back.

"Armed police! On the floor!"

Gorski ran after him, her own voice competing with his.

"Armed police!"

Their voices faded as they walked swiftly down a narrow corridor, their mounted torches lighting the way.

"You alright, sir?" asked Porter, watching Kett rub his lower back. "Need a poo?"

"*What*?"

"Understandable. My guts always loosen on a raid like this."

"No, Pete, it's my back."

He turned around to prove that he wasn't fondling his arse.

"My back," he said again.

"Oh, right," said Porter.

"Clear," came Gorski's voice. "Moving in."

Porter stepped into the corridor, clicking on his torch as he went. Kett waited for the constables to move in next before once again taking up the rear. The stench in here was even more unpleasant than outside, a concentrated aroma of burned plastic, rot and something worse. He rubbed his watering eyes, forcing his lungs to take in the fetid air even though they were resisting it. The walls and ceiling of the corridor were scorched, making it even darker than it first appeared. Kett could see graffiti, though, colourful tags competing with each other on the smoke-damaged plaster.

"Watch your feet," Porter called back. "Like a bloody minefield."

The floor was littered with debris, loose bricks and metal pipes and hundreds of sheets of paper that had been fused to the damp ground like a *papier-mâché* art project. Despite the warning, Kett stumbled three times as he fought his way through, once planting a hand on the officer in front to stop himself falling, and almost knocking her over instead.

They emerged into a larger space that had once been a lobby, a single desk in the middle of the room that had been obliterated by fire. Gorski and Andilet had cleared it already, and had moved through a door on the far side. They were still yelling, but it felt like they were shouting into a void. There was no sign of anyone here.

"Shit," said Porter.

"What's up?" Kett asked.

The DI pointed to the floor.

"Shit," he said again.

He was right. There was. And it was impressive.

"How the hell is there dog shit in here?" Porter asked. "The door was shut."

"Then it probably didn't come from a dog," Kett told him.

It was a sign of life, at least.

Kett made his way to the door, following the roar of the tactical officers into the body of the factory. Natural light fell reluctantly from green-tinged roof windows two storeys overhead, the colour of it making Kett feel like he was inside a giant aquarium. The room was filled with a chaos of machinery: tanks, pipes, control panels and vats, all burned by the fire and frozen by time.

Gorski and Andilet were deep inside the forest of equipment, fingers of torchlight poking through the gaps. Kett took in the rest of the giant space, seeing metal steps that headed up to a walkway overhead, and at least four more doors on both levels. One, directly across from where they were, was a fire door that had been secured with a chain. The place really was vast.

"Search everywhere," Kett told the two PCs. "And see if you can get that door open."

He made his way towards the stairs, meeting Gorski as she emerged from the machinery. Her radio bleeped, the message too laced with static for Kett to hear. She thumbed it.

"Say again?" she said.

Another message, this one worse than the last. Somehow, she understood it.

"Nothing yet," she reported, glancing at the stairs. "Which way?"

"Up?" he replied. "There's no power here, makes sense he'd need the light."

Gorski pushed past him, the metal staircase rattling as she headed for the first floor.

"Chester, check the doors on ground level," she said.

Andilet moved to the nearest one, bracing his rifle against his shoulder as he opened it. He vanished into the dark like he'd been sucked inside, his voice muffled.

"Armed police!"

Gorski was overhead, dust raining from the walkway as she clanged down it. The PCs were trying to get the chain off the fire door, but it was the size of an anaconda.

"Clear," said Andilet when he appeared again. "All yours."

Kett walked to the room as Andilet moved to the next, the tactical officer clipping his shoulder as they passed—a little too hard to have been an accident. Kett ignored it, peering through the door to find a storage space—nothing but a couple of filing cabinets, their doors open, their guts spread over the floor. He circled it dutifully before heading back out. When he followed Andilet into the next room, he saw that it was identical, and empty.

"This is pointless," he said. "They could be anywhere."

"Or nowhere," said Porter, as he joined him. The DI opened a large, solitary metal cabinet further down the wall, then closed it again. "What if we're wrong?"

It didn't bear thinking about.

They walked back onto the factory floor, watching Andilet as he ran up the stairs. The two PCs were trying to pry the bracket off the wall with a length of iron they'd found from somewhere.

"If you were this guy, where would you hide five lads?" asked Kett.

Porter thought about it.

"Place is enormous," he said. "Plenty of escape routes. Five victims, all young men, all injured, losing blood. But still fit, right? Fit enough to fight back. It would be like herding cats. Room like this, they could scatter a dozen different ways if they got loose."

"Right," said Kett. "He needs somewhere more secure, somewhere he can contain them. This guy doesn't want to reveal himself, he doesn't want the world to see him. He's not showing off, he's not after the headlines. He's all about being hidden."

He turned his eyes to the floor.

"You reckon this place has a basement?"

"Never met an old, abandoned, definitely haunted factory that doesn't," said Porter.

Gorski appeared on the walkway, shaking her head.

"Clear, sir," she called down. "Nothing up here but empty offices."

Kett was about to reply when there was a clang of metal from across the room, one of the coppers falling back from the door like he'd been shot. In the painful rush of adrenaline, it took Kett a moment to realise it had just been the sound of the bracket coming loose.

"Christ," he said, the room pulsing with the frantic beat of his heart.

He walked over, helping the fallen PC back to his feet. The man was studying a nasty gash on his hand which was now caked in filth from the floor.

"You alright?" asked Kett.

"Yeah, sir, it's nothing," he replied.

"Not nothing," said Porter. "This place is covered in dog shit."

"Not dog shit," said Kett.

"Well, whatever kind of shit it is, it's not going to do much good in an open wound. Probably best go get some Purell on that."

The PC looked to Kett for permission, then jogged out of the room, his hand held to his chest. Kett turned to the door as the remaining copper pushed the bar and opened it. The dark was chased away by Porter's torch, revealing another corridor, a door on either side and a second fire escape at the far end. A breath of cold, dead air washed over them, filled with the stench of smoke.

"Urgh," said Porter, a sound of genuine disgust. "Dibs not going in there."

He didn't have to. Gorski pushed between them and entered the corridor. Andilet covered her as she opened the door on the right, then again while she tried the one opposite.

"Clear," she said.

She moved to the fire door, this time holding her rifle while Andilet pressed the release bar. It wouldn't budge, chains rattling on the other side. Pale light strobed through the cracks as he tried to force it, and after a few seconds, he gave up.

"Locked," said Gorski. "Must lead back outside."

Kett walked to the door on the right, finding another storage room filled with mouldering boxes. The door on the left led into a much bigger space, one that was so long his torch didn't reach the far end. Like the rest of the factory, the floor here was covered in detritus, a carpet of metal and brick and paper and cardboard. Kett couldn't work out where it had all come from. Even as he watched, something big scuttled across the floor, squeaking.

Porter squeaked too.

"Bloody hell," the DI said when he'd recovered. "Was that a rat or a giraffe?"

Kett started to walk, but a voice from behind him made him stop in his tracks.

"Place is empty," said Andilet. "We should go help the others."

Kett ignored him, entering the room, his skin crawling at the thought of what might be hiding in the mounds of rubbish. The walls were covered with more pipes, some so big he could have crawled inside them. Old posters hung from the walls like corpses, warning of death and injury and mutilation.

If only they knew, he thought.

It was only when Andilet entered the room behind him, sweeping his powerful torch, that Kett saw the far wall. There was more machinery there, or so he thought, a scaffold of poles that looked like some kind of bike rack.

"What is that?" he asked.

"It's nothing," said Andilet. "Come on, this building's a bust."

Kett made his way over, one hand on a pipe to stop himself from tripping on the rubble. More things darted away from him, shadows that beetled into the dark corners of the room.

"Nope," said Porter, who was right behind him. "You can piss right off, you furry git."

Kett had almost reached the far wall when he finally worked out what he was looking at. The scaffold wasn't part of any machinery, it was a safety rail that fenced off the last section of the room. A hatch had been set into the floor here, maybe three metres long and half that wide, with a large metal handle. It was made of corrugated metal, and painted in the middle of it was a white lightning bolt and the words: *Authorised Entry Only.*

He took the handle and hefted the hatch up—only by a few inches, though, before his fingers gave out and it crashed down again.

"Ow," he said as his back twanged like a guitar string. "Heavy. Pete, can you do it?"

He got out of the way, watching Porter struggle to get the hatch up. The DI managed to raise it a foot or so before it slammed shut again, almost taking his toes off.

"Where's Duke when you need him?" asked Gorski, having followed them in.

"Duke?" said Porter, outraged. "I'm twice as strong as him."

He tried again, gurning like an Olympic weightlifter as he struggled with the hatch, his eyeballs almost ejecting themselves from their sockets. He looked a little like the Superintendent when he was raging, thought Kett.

He moved in to help, but Porter growled at him.

"I've... got it... sir."

He flipped the hatch over and it crashed against the wall. Porter hit the wall too, looking like he might be about to pass out. His cheeks were boiling, his chest ballooning in and out. Instead, he brushed his hands together and flashed a look at Gorski.

"Duke. As if."

Kett walked to his side, giving him a pat on the shoulder as they both looked at what lay beneath the hatch. It was a staircase, dropping into a dark that was so deep it could have been liquid. Even when Kett aimed his torch into the void, he couldn't see past the sixth or seventh step.

"Dibs not going down there," said Porter.

"I already told you, Pete," said Kett. "You're not an Edwardian schoolboy. Dibs doesn't work."

There was a bleep as Gorski thumbed her radio.

"We've found a basement just north of the main factory floor," she said. "We're going in."

She didn't look too happy about it, even with the assortment of weapons she carried. Neither did Andilet, who cradled his rifle to his chest, his face gaunt.

"Go on, Chester," said Gorski.

Andilet shot Kett another look—one he couldn't make much sense of—then dropped onto the top step. He slowly sank into the pitch, the tunnel working him down like a snake with its prey.

"Armed police," he called out.

Gorski followed, looking like a child against the impossible dark.

Kett watched them go, wanting nothing more than to run back into the day, into the light and the air.

Knowing that he couldn't.

"This bloody job," he muttered.

He turned to the PC.

"What's your name?"

"PC Sealy, sir," she said. "Tracy."

"Stay up here," he told her. "Make sure nobody comes up behind us, and keep this bloody trapdoor open. Understood?"

"Sir," she said with an audible sigh of relief.

"Go on, Pete," said Kett. "You're next."

"No," said Porter, and when Kett glared at him he wheezed out another word, "problem."

Porter slouched down the stairs, grumbling something beneath his breath. Kett hesitated for a moment more, reminding himself that he was with an armed tactical unit. If something was waiting for them down there, Gorski would handle it.

He dropped onto the first step, pausing again, taking out his phone. He texted Billie, not even sure why, just that he wanted to say something to her before he slipped into this coffin-shaped wedge of darkness.

I love you.

There was so much more he wanted to say, but he couldn't find the words. Besides, now wasn't the time.

"Do *not* let this thing close," he shouted to the copper at the top.

Then he grabbed the handrail and began his descent.

CHAPTER THIRTY-THREE

"CLEAR!"

Chris Sutagon emerged from one of the enormous storage silos that stood on the edge of the site, wiping her face with a gloved hand. She'd only been in there for a handful of seconds, but she was absolutely caked in filth—decades of unused beets turned to a soup of rot. She doubled up, spitting onto the cracked concrete path.

"That's got to be the worst thing I've ever smelled," she said. "Where's Joe? He's doing the next one."

Savage wasn't sure. Carmichael had vanished a minute or so ago, chasing phantom noises into the darkness between the towering structures.

"Nothing in there?" she asked. Sutagon shook her head.

"Nothing you want to see," she replied.

There was a scuff of footsteps as Carmichael appeared from behind the silo, his rifle in his hands but pointed at the ground.

"Could've sworn I heard something."

"Likely story," said Sutagon.

"Was a rat, I think," Carmichael said. "Place is infested with them."

It was, but that seemed to be the only thing it was infested with. There were no cars here, no vehicles of any kind, no evidence at all that anyone had set foot on the grounds since the fire. There was still a lot left to explore, but a terrible fear had been churning inside Savage's stomach for the last twenty minutes or so—the terror that she'd made a mistake.

Half of Norfolk Constabulary was right here, and they might have been looking in the wrong place.

"The last one's all yours, Joe," said Sutagon. "Unless one of you lot want to do it?"

"No thanks," said Duke.

Carmichael walked to the final silo. He opened the hatch, shining his torch inside before saying the word Savage knew was coming.

"Clear."

His radio bleeped as he stepped away, Gorski's voice.

"*We've found a basement just north of the main factory floor. We're going in.*"

"Roger," he said, clicking off the radio. He shook his head, his expression dark. "Last thing they should be doing, going into a basement in this place. Whole building looks like it could come down."

"We should go help," said Savage. "Right?"

Carmichael checked his watch, nodding.

"Nothing out here. Let's go."

They set off across the yard. It felt post-apocalyptic, nothing but rot and ruin for as far as Savage could see. The seagulls crowded the roofs, slipping on the smooth tops of the silos, their cries a never-ending wave of noise. Another group of coppers was emerging from a building on the right, and they shook their heads when Savage looked their way.

"Empty," yelled the tactical officer who led the pack—Goss, she thought. "Place is deserted."

They vanished into the next building along, serenaded by the birds.

Carmichael had found a narrow alley that ran behind the main building, and he stopped at a fire door that had been locked with a heavy chain. He gave it a rattle.

"We'll try the front," he said.

They circled the enormous body of the factory, the smell making Savage's head pound. It was as bad as a corpse, as if the building had once been a giant living thing that now lay decomposing. When they reached the front, she saw Superintendent Clare beside the parked vehicles, yelling into his phone.

Carmichael approached the main door of the factory, Sutagon right behind him. Savage was about to head after them when her phone started to ring.

She pulled it out of her pocket, seeing an unknown number.

"Oi!" Clare yelled. "Savage, Duke, get over here."

She slipped the phone back into her pocket, unanswered, and walked to where the Super was standing. He was still talking to whoever was on the other end of the line, his face flushed and sweaty, his big, yellow teeth bared in a growl.

"And if you do," he said to the phone, "I'll shove it up your tosshole so hard the tip will come out of your nose. Understood?"

"Sex line?" whispered Duke as they reached him.

Clare ended the call, flushed and panting hard.

"Definitely," replied Savage.

"Definitely what?" he said. "That was a unit in Dereham. They think they've just spotted Kett's mystery couple on the other side of the town, driving west."

"What? The fake Lynns?"

Clare nodded, wiping his face.

"Anyone got anything here?"

"Not yet, sir," she said, shaking her head. "Kett and Gorski found a basement, they're checking it now."

Clare thought about it for a second.

"I'm pulling us out," he said. "It was a good call, Kate, but I think you were wrong. The fake Lynns are in on this. Wherever they're going, I think we'll find the boys."

"Yeah," said Savage. "I guess."

"That's the problem, isn't it?" said Clare. "All we can bloody do is guess. What's your gut telling you?"

"Mine's telling me I'm hungry," said Duke.

"Tell me you're hungry one more time, Officer," said Clare. "And I'll give you something to eat."

"Oh, great," said Duke, missing the threat entirely. "I'm—"

"And it won't just be the tip!" screeched Clare.

"My gut's..." Savage started. "Ew, sir. That's too much..."

"I'm talking about a baton, Kate," said Clare, stamping his foot on the ground. "Keep your mind on the job, you pervert."

"I..." She took a breath. "I think you're probably right, sir. Whoever those two are, they're part of Maynard's plan. They might be able to lead us to the boys, or tell us where they are."

"But?" said Clare.

"But they might be a distraction. This place is too good to be true if you're a kidnapper, right? It's enormous, there are exits everywhere, we've been here half an hour and we've barely scratched the surface. Maynard's thing was all about the map, the pentagram. That's what he used to convince Berrycloth and the others that this was real, that this was the devil's work. This is the red right eye of the skull in the middle of his pentagram."

She paused for breath, the seagulls filling the silence.

"I think it's worth staying," she finished.

"Then stay," said Clare. "I'll leave your unit, and Gorski's tossed off somewhere underground, I can't reach her. But I'm pulling everyone else."

Savage nodded. Her phone was ringing again, and she pulled it out, seeing the same number.

"I'd better get this, sir," she said.

"Well God forbid I get in the way of your personal life, Kate!"

Clare thrust his hands into the air so hard his phone slipped out of his fingers, hitting the bonnet of an IRV before bouncing to the ground.

"Bloody arse twat!" he roared. "What did you make me do that for?"

He stormed off, and Savage answered the phone.

"This is DC Kate Savage," she said.

"The police officer?" came the reply. The voice was familiar, even though it was heavy with dread.

"Yes. Mrs Hipkin?"

"Have you found him yet?"

"No, but we're doing everything we can, we're out looking for Ian right now. He didn't mention anything about an old sugar factory, did he? Out near Yaxham?"

"A factory? No. Nothing like that. But you were looking for his phone, weren't you?"

"Yeah," said Savage. "He didn't have it when we found him at the paintball place."

"I've got it here," she said. "He'd hidden it in the shed, with some of his old paintball gear. Do you still need it? Will it help?"

"Maybe," said Savage.

She looked past Duke to the main factory building, seeing Sutagon half in and half out of the door. Past her was a darkness that felt too solid to be real.

"Can you come and get it?" asked Helen. "I don't fancy driving into the city."

"We can send somebody," she said. "Have you had a look at it? If you can check his messages, his emails, anything like that, it might help."

There was no reply, but Savage heard a rustling sound, then the click of a phone unlocking.

"What am I looking for?" she asked.

"Anything new," said Savage. "Anything strange. Messages from people you don't recognise, WhatsApps, Facebook, Instagram, all that stuff. Can you check his emails first? Anything from somebody with a numerical username. Uh..."

She put her free hand to her head, squeezing it.

"4522. Something like that."

She began to walk towards the main building, Duke slouching along beside her. Sutagon stepped aside so they could get through the door, a short corridor ahead leading into a larger space.

"Carmichael's gone to find the basement," she said. "I was waiting for you."

Sutagon walked on, debris crunching beneath her boots. Savage moved after her, Duke a comforting presence by her side. She clamped the phone to her ear as she went, hearing the occasional mutter from Helen on the other end. This section of the building had already been cleared, so they moved fast, entering the factory floor with its enormous collection of machinery and its high, windowed ceiling. Carmichael was standing in the middle of the impressive space, scratching his head.

"I have no idea where to look," he said. "I don't get why Jules wouldn't leave anyone to show us where to go. She had two officers with her, didn't she, as well as Kett and Porter? What happened to them all?"

He set off through a double door on the far side of the factory, his rifle up.

"Gorski!" he yelled. "Where are you?"

"Hello?" said the woman on the phone. "Mrs Savage?"

"I'm here, Helen. Have you found something?"

"I'm not sure. I've got his emails, and there are a few from that username you mentioned. 4522912?"

"That's right, can you have a look at the most recent one?"

She walked as she spoke, heading for the door that Carmichael had disappeared through. On the other side of it was a short corridor leading to a fire door, probably the one they'd seen outside. Carmichael was in a room to the left, a long, thin space that was packed so full of rubbish she could barely see him. He was struggling to get across it, sweeping his rifle madly left and right.

"Bloody rats," he said.

"It doesn't make much sense," said Helen. "I don't get it. What is it?"

"Can you read it out?"

Savage walked into the room, something crunching beneath her foot. It was a long-dead creature of some kind, she saw, its skull exploded to dust. A shiver ran through her.

"There's nothing to read," said Helen. "It's a link or something, just letters and numbers and then a dot com."

"Send it to me," said Savage. "Copy and paste it into a text. Can you do that?"

"I'm not sure," she said. "Do what and what into a what?"

"Hey," said Carmichael, a shout that made Savage flinch. He was on the far side of the room, his torch aimed downwards. "I think I've got something."

Savage slipped and tripped her way over, Duke beside her. Carmichael was standing by a metal railing that surrounded a large hatch on the floor. He stowed his rifle, grabbing the handle and trying to pull up the trapdoor. It didn't budge.

"Give me a hand with this," he said.

Duke grabbed the handle with him and they pulled together, but the hatch barely rattled.

"Locked," said Carmichael, straightening up. "Which is weird. Looks like an electrical access point, it wouldn't lock from below."

Savage's phone buzzed, and she pulled it away from her ear to see that a text had arrived.

"Just sent it," said Helen. "I think. Did it work?"

"It worked," she said. "Thank you. Listen, can you go through the rest of those emails, see if there's anything that might help us?"

"Yeah," she said. "I'll try. Please find him."

Savage hung up, thumbing the link on the screen. Carmichael and Duke were trying the hatch again, but they weren't having any luck.

"They must have gone another way," said Carmichael, using a gloved hand to wipe the sweat from his face.

"Or somebody locked the hatch behind them," said Duke.

Carmichael retreated to the door, kicking rubbish out of his way and almost going arse over tit. Savage left him to it, watching as the page loaded up on the screen. The only thing there was a text box, and Savage navigated back to the email to find the password. When she'd pasted it into the box, another page loaded. It was a video, and the person sitting there was the same one they'd seen before: Maynard, wearing his heavy robes and his horned mask.

He steepled his fingers, staring at the camera with dark eyes.

"Welcome to your final video."

Savage frowned.

"What is it?" Duke asked.

"I'm not sure," she said, and before she could say anything else, Carmichael's shout echoed down the corridor.

"Hey, we've found another way down."

She made her way across the room as best she could while watching the video, barely hearing Maynard over the crunch of her feet. She wasn't sure she would have understood him even if she had been able to hear him, his droning voice talking about Limination, about the inevitable disintegration of the human soul. He was making zero sense.

Carmichael was waiting for her on the factory floor, and he headed to the right-hand side of the room. Sutagon waited next to a large metal cabinet, which lay like a dead man where it had been toppled over. There was an open door behind it, a stairwell leading down.

"Somebody tried to hide it," said Sutagon.

"You done?" Carmichael asked Savage, nodding to her phone.

She nodded, slipping it into her pocket. It wouldn't work underground, and whatever Maynard was saying, it wouldn't help them now.

Still, something was nagging at her. The feeling that they'd missed something important.

Welcome to your final video.

"Stay behind us," said Carmichael. He checked his weapon, then braced it against his shoulder. "Chris, you take point."

Sutagon nodded, moving through the door.

"Armed police!" she called out, her voice echoing into the dark.

Carmichael followed, Duke waiting by the open door.

"What is it?" he asked.

"I'm not sure," she said.

She thought of Maynard in his hospital room. His smug grin. She thought about the amount of time he'd been planning this. He was dead, but Kett had been right: this was his legacy. This was what he was leaving the world.

Madness. Violence. Death.

She swallowed her fear as she walked to the door, giving Duke's arm a gentle squeeze.

"I've just got a horrible feeling we're walking into a trap."

CHAPTER THIRTY-FOUR

IT FELT MORE LIKE A PRISON THAN A FACTORY DOWN here.

Kett crept along the tunnel they'd found at the bottom of the steps, Porter treading on his heels, Gorski in front. Andilet had insisted on staying further back, just a puddle of torchlight fifty yards away as he made sure nobody crept up on them from behind.

The passage was narrow enough to trigger Kett's claustrophobia, his left shoulder brushing the concrete wall, his right rubbing against a forest of electrical boxes and plastic conduits. The ceiling was an inch or so over his head, and he swore it was getting lower with every step. There was no light down here other than their torches, no sound except for their panicked breaths and the scuff of their feet.

There was no oxygen, either, or so it felt. Kett heaved in deep, airless breaths, giddy with growing panic.

"Another door," said Gorski, her own voice weak with uncertainty.

They'd passed half a dozen rooms already, all empty. There had been a junction, too, which split off into more darkness. However big the factory had felt above ground, it was worse here—an endless warren of tunnels and corridors and rooms. Even though they'd been following a straight line, more or less, Kett wasn't sure he'd be able to find his way back.

Breathe, he told himself. *Just keep breathing.*

Easier said than done.

Gorski pushed through the open door, light exploding inside an empty room. It was the same size as the others, barely big enough for a person to lie down in.

"They look like cells," said Porter, so close that Kett could feel the words on the back of his neck. "Why would they need all these rooms?"

"I have no idea," he replied. Another wave of cold fear washed over him and he sucked in a lungful of stale air, hearing Porter do the same. He tugged at his tie to loosen it. "Back off a bit, Pete, will you?"

"Sorry," grumbled Porter, but he didn't give him any room.

"You alright, Chester?" Gorski yelled.

"Yeah," came the reply.

"Close the gap," Gorski went on. "I don't want to lose you."

She pressed forward, reaching another junction on the left. She shone her torch down it, revealing another tunnel that seemed to stretch to infinity. When she swung the light ahead, the featureless passage looked exactly the same. It would go on forever, Kett knew.

Because this was hell.

"This is insane," said Gorski.

There was a scuff of feet as Andilet caught up to them, the torch on his rifle illuminating the floor. Kett's light-starved eyes couldn't make any sense of his face behind the visor.

"Was hearing things back there," he said. "You hear it? Something rattling."

Kett shook his head.

"It'll be another unit," said Gorski. "We told them where we were going, they'll send somebody after us."

The thought of it brought a wash of relief until Kett realised there would be more people crushed into the corridor, more people taking all the air, more people between him and the exit if he needed to get out. This time the panic was white hot, enough to make lights dance against the dark. He braced a hand against the wall, feeling the ceiling press down on the top of his head like it meant to crush him.

"This bloody job," he said. It was just a whisper, but it carried through the quiet like a shout.

"I hear you," said Gorski. "Which way? Your call."

"Back?" said Porter, and Kett almost laughed.

"We keep going," he said. "Right? Clear this tunnel, then try the others."

Gorski nodded, setting off again. Kett had taken a couple of steps after her when he heard Andilet call out.

"Wait, you getting that?"

Kett stopped, trying to hear anything past the roar of his heart. Andilet had swept his torch down the tunnel to the left, the light trembling.

"What?" said Gorski, pushing against Kett.

"Footsteps," said Andilet. "Sounded like somebody running."

"You sure?" said Gorski. "Anyone else hear it?"

Kett shook his head, doing everything he could to keep calm. Gorski's shoulder was pushing against him, Porter so close behind he couldn't take a step back. If they didn't give him some space, he was going to scream a hole in the ceiling.

Everyone waited, everyone watched.

"There," said Andilet. "You must have heard that."

Kett hadn't heard a thing.

"We go this way," said Andilet. "Somebody's down there."

The officer didn't wait for Gorski to reply, setting off with his rifle to his shoulder.

"Armed police, if anyone's down here, make yourself known."

Kett glanced at Gorski to see her looking back at him, her expression unreadable.

"Go," she said after a moment.

Porter had moved into the tunnel, and Kett waited a few seconds before following him. More pipes and conduits hugged the right-hand wall here, some on the left, too, making it feel even more like he was working his way through the intestines of some vast industrial beast. There were times when he had to turn sideways to fit through the gaps, and even then it was tight. His stomach was a knot of anxiety, the acid burning his throat, and they'd been walking for thirty seconds or so before a thought suddenly struck him—another phosphorous-bright flash of panic.

"Wait," he said, planting his feet on the ground. "You don't think Maynard rigged this place, do you?"

"Rigged it?" said Porter. "Like a bomb?"

And the thought of it, of something detonating in the tunnel they'd just left, burying them alive down here, almost made him drop to his knees.

"No, sir," said Porter. "I mean, it's the sort of thing he'd do, I guess."

"Not helping," said Kett.

"And he did try to blow up that kid in the tank."

"*Really* not helping."

"Be a good way of getting rid of you," Porter said.

"Pete!"

"But that isn't what Maynard wants, is it? He's had a hundred chances to kill you. He could have asked Berrycloth to stab you. He'd have done it. And how would he even know you were here? He's dead. No, this is about his successor, the guy he's trained up. I don't think he'd choose anything as easy as a bomb."

Kett nodded, the sweat stinging his eyes. He scrubbed his face with his free hand.

"I hope you're right," he said. "Because if we all die down here, I'm going to beat your ghostly arse back and forth for the rest of time."

Porter laughed quietly.

"Sir, we all know you're going to be as broken in the next life as you are in this one."

"Hush," barked Andilet up ahead. He'd reached another junction. "I heard it again."

He swung his rifle from one side to the other, causing the shadows to dance. Kett edged past him, almost bursting into tears when he saw that the corridor was wider here, the ceiling taller. The passage was as straight as the one they'd first entered, running parallel with it. One way led back towards the factory, the other disappeared into more darkness. There were no pipes on the walls here, just the occasional fire escape sign.

Kett breathed hard, tasting something acrid and unpleasant in the air. He couldn't hear footsteps, but he could hear something: a low, growling hum from further up the tunnel.

"What is that?" Gorski asked as she closed in.

"Smells like exhaust fumes," said Porter. "Generator, maybe?"

He was right, and the realisation made Kett's stomach clench even harder.

"We're not alone down here," he said. "We were right."

Gorski pressed the button on her radio, but there was only static.

"How do you want to play it, sir?" she said. "We can go back, get the rest of the team?"

Kett checked his watch.

"We don't know how long we've got," he said. "The suspect knows we're here, he might have already started."

"He might have finished," said Porter.

"We go on," said Andilet. "He's outnumbered and outgunned. Right, Sarge?"

"He's only outnumbered if he's on his own," said Kett. "We don't know for sure how many of them we're dealing with."

"And Maynard will have armed him," said Porter.

Kett sighed, wiping his eyes again. Porter studied him, waiting for him to make the right call.

"Let's go. But Pete, you head back, let them know where we are."

Porter stared down the tunnel.

"On my own, sir?"

"Yeah."

He held up his Maglite.

"Just me and this little torch?"

"Yes, Pete."

The DI fidgeted for a second or two before nodding. One painfully slow step at a time, he set off down the narrow tunnel back to the one they'd entered through.

Andilet was already moving the other way, heading

deeper into the labyrinth. Kett hesitated a moment more before walking after him. The chemical stench became heavier as they went, the rumble growing louder. After a minute or so the tunnel ended in a T-junction, a faint light fluttering on the walls and the floor to the right. Andilet turned the corner, his rifle leading.

"Clear," he said, just a whisper. "But there's a genny up ahead."

There was, Kett saw when he turned the corner. A big one. It sat right in the middle of another stretch of corridor, rattling hard and spewing fumes into the air. He had to hold his jacket over his face to stop the poison from entering his lungs, but there was nothing he could do to stop his eyes from watering.

Beyond that was the end of the tunnel, lit up by a golden glow that poured through an open door. The generator was making so much noise that Kett couldn't hear a thing past it.

He moved forward, but Gorski grabbed his arm, hard enough to pinch his skin.

"Wait," she said. "Let us do our thing."

She took the lead, sidestepping the generator, never taking her rifle off that open door. Andilet followed, his own weapon aimed past Gorski's head at whatever might lie beyond.

Gorski moved through the door with a roar.

"Armed police! Get on the ground!"

Then it was Andilet's turn, the pair of them screaming out their warning—far too urgently for an empty room.

"Get down! Get—"

A gunshot. Gorski's voice was cut off mid-sentence.

Kett broke into a run, his spine full of broken glass as he reached the door. Ahead was a large room, baked in a light that was so fierce it burned his eyes. He lifted an arm to shield himself from the glow.

"Julia?" he called.

She was right there by Andilet's side, both of them shouting.

"Armed police! Get down!"

Kett had to move to the side to see past Andilet's shoulders, the noise and the fumes and the confusion making his head reel, making his body feel like it was an engine about to stall.

Then he saw what waited there on the far side of the room, and it almost broke him.

"No," he said.

He staggered forward, the tears stinging his eyes, not doing enough to blur the horror.

"We're too late."

CHAPTER THIRTY-FIVE

PORTER WASN'T SURE HOW HE'D MANAGED TO DO IT, but he was lost.

He'd made his way back down the tunnel to the junction they'd turned off before, and from there he'd gone right. But somehow he'd reached another split in the passage, one that he was certain they hadn't passed. Both passageways looked identical, although his torch was so weak he couldn't see much at all.

He gave it a pat on the palm of his hand to wake it up, only succeeding in cutting off the light entirely. The tunnel was plunged into a darkness so profound that it was like the eyes had been pulled from his skull, and he spun around in his panic, seeing shapes rise in the pitch, wild eyes and bared teeth and—

The torch flickered back on before he could find the air to scream with.

"Do *not* do that to me again," he told the Maglite. "Okay?"

The torch didn't answer, but the light stayed on as he made his way down the left-hand tunnel. It seemed the straighter of the two, and he recognised the tapestry of pipes. It took almost a minute before he reached the first doorway. It was on his left, which was the same side it had been on when they'd walked *up* this tunnel.

"What?" he said, turning one-eighty just to be sure.

The door was on the wrong side. This was a new passage.

He stood there, trying to work out what to do. The tactical team had cleared the first tunnel, but nobody had been down this way yet, which meant Maynard's Devil-man—or Devil-*men*—could be anywhere. It was all well and good exploring this place with two armed police, but all he had to defend himself with was his torch and his wits, and both of those were on the verge of sputtering out.

"So," he said, and for some reason he directed the words at his Maglite again. "Press on? Turn back?"

He lifted the torch, jiggling it.

"Go back," he said in a robotic voice. "It's not worth it."

He nodded.

"I agree, torch. Thanks for that."

He walked to the door, picturing the kidnapper on the other side, imagining his expression as he listened to Porter talking to his Maglite. The thought of it dragged a bark of insane laughter from deep inside him, one that only intensified as he thought about the suspect running scared from a mad copper.

The laughter died away as he turned the handle.

"Police," he squeaked. "I'm coming in."

The door opened with a squeal that filled the entire tunnel, revealing another small room—identical to the others they'd found in every way except one.

It wasn't empty.

He walked through the door, one hand on the frame, the

way a man in a boat might cling to the riverbank. Inside, picked out in torchlight, was a single mattress covered in stains, a sleeping bag crumpled on top. Next to this was a pile of rubbish, sweet wrappers, crisp packets, empty bottles and dozens of tissues—all stained with what had to be blood.

"The hell?" he said, moving as far into the room as he dared.

The smell suddenly hit him like a hammer to the face, piss and shit and the meaty aroma of blood. He gagged, searching the room until he found where it was coming from: a yellow bucket. Somebody had covered the top with a towel, but there was no mistaking the fact that it had been used for a toilet. The floor around it was drenched in filth.

He had to move all the way through the door to search the last wall. There was only one thing on this side of the room, a glass Kilner jar that was half-filled with blood. The lid had been clipped shut, the liquid inside thick and opaque. There were crimson prints all around the outside, maybe hundreds of them.

"Nope," said Porter, backing out of the room. "Nope, nope, nope."

It was proof, at least. They were in the right place.

The killer was here.

He pulled out his phone before remembering it was useless underground. He used it to take a couple of pictures instead, in case he forgot how to find his way to the room. Back in the tunnel, he set off to his right, then had to stop and think about it.

"Left," he said, turning slowly. "Right?"

The creeping shadows gobbled down his voice.

He wasn't sure what to do. He needed to find Kett, to warn him that they weren't alone down here. But if he did that, then who would get backup? What if there was more than one killer?

No, better to get the rest of the tactical team down here.

"Right?" he said. "So, *left*."

He moved quickly, feeling like the underground complex had shifted itself while he was inside the room: passageways changing, tunnels rotating like a Rubik's Cube. He had to keep glancing back as he walked because he thought he heard somebody running up behind him—just the echo of his own footsteps.

"Right?" he asked, almost a sob.

He upped his speed, almost tripping over his own shoes. There was another door ahead, on the left again.

This one was open.

He didn't want to look inside, but for all he knew there could be a teenage boy in there, bleeding out, pleading silently for help.

"Hello?" he croaked. "Police?"

The word sounded more like a question than a statement, and he cleared his throat, tried again.

"Police!"

He aimed his torch through the door, frowning.

A small room, a stained mattress, a crumpled sleeping bag and a carpet of rubbish. The air swam with the stench of human waste, and when he peeked a little further, he saw the yellow bucket, covered with a towel.

He saw the same Kilner jar, filled with blood.

"*What*?" he said.

He withdrew from the room, shining the torch back the way he'd come. How had he managed to do that? He'd only taken a couple of steps the other way before doubling back, and it had taken him a minute or so to get here. There was no chance this could be the same room.

He had to be sure.

With a heavy sigh, he walked back the way he'd come. The tunnel stretched, unbroken, no sign of a door, and he'd almost given up before he saw it peel itself from the shadows ahead. He looked through it.

The same room.

It was like somebody had thrown him into a pool of ice water, the dread unlike anything he'd experienced—worse even than when Aggie Clegg and her father had knocked him out and strung him up inside their bunker, ready to be sacrificed. That had been terrifying, of course, but it had been real.

This was just *impossible.*

He slapped himself gently on the cheek. Then again, not so gently.

"Pull it together, Pete. There has to be an explanation."

And there was. It wasn't the same room, it was *two* rooms, each one identical. He forced himself to believe it, until the bone-rattling hum of panic started to fade and his thoughts were able to settle.

But there was another thought in their place, and this one was scarier still.

Two rooms. Two *kidnappers.*

Maynard's man wasn't working alone.

"Shit on it," he said.

All the more reason to make it back to the surface, to get help.

He started moving, his legs like jelly as he jogged down the corridor. He made it to the first door again, peering inside for long enough to see the subtle differences he'd missed last time: the blue sleeping bag instead of purple, the bigger towel over the bucket.

"Idiot," he told himself.

Something answered him, the clang of metal on metal, loud enough to make him feel like somebody had slid a scalpel into his heart. He clutched at his chest with his free hand. The sound had been close, somewhere further down the tunnel. He opened his mouth to shout, then snapped it closed again, because if it was Mayard's Devil down there, then the last thing he wanted to do was call him over.

He waited, hearing another clang, then the scuff of feet. Ahead, at the far end of the corridor, a light appeared.

Nope.

He ducked back through the door, into the fog of shit and piss and blood. A third clang, then the definite scuff of somebody walking. Reluctantly, he clicked off his torch, sinking deeper into the room. The darkness wrapped itself around him like a pair of arms, a clammy hand over his eyes, pinching his nose shut, covering his mouth. He dropped down into a squat, fingers pressed to the wall to stop himself from toppling. He gripped the torch hard in case he needed to use it as a weapon.

Further down the tunnel, a high-pitched, awful scream echoed off the walls.

Followed by the hammer of footsteps as someone began to run this way.

SAVAGE HAD SUFFERED through countless nightmares of being trapped underground, but none of them lived up to the reality.

The underbelly of the factory wasn't just a basement, it was a labyrinth—a warren of interconnecting tunnels and corridors that seemed to have been designed by a madman.

And where another madman now hid.

"Careful," said Joe Carmichael, who led the way. His torch lit up a wide passageway pocked with fire escape signs. They'd passed a few rooms along the way, but there was no sign anyone had been down here.

Savage nodded, but she wasn't listening. She was still watching Maynard's video on her phone, which had partially downloaded before they'd gone underground. The old man was still prattling on, but making very little sense. She'd heard the word sacrifice a dozen times in the two minutes or so she'd been listening. It was pretty obvious what he was driving at.

What she didn't understand was why he'd sent the video to Ian.

Unless Ian *hadn't* been a victim, of course. He'd been working for Maynard at Cold Iron, one of his followers. Maybe he hadn't been kidnapped from the hospital after all, maybe Maynard had sent his men there to *rescue* him—to stop him from talking, or so he could help the kidnapper somehow.

Maybe he'd snatched him in order to punish him.

But if that was the case, and Ian had simply rejoined the ranks of Maynard's army, then who was the fifth victim?

"Anything useful?" said Duke by her side.

She held up the phone so he could see.

"... and by *his* holy eye your life will be deemed worthy, by *his* holy tongue your soul will be rendered unpure, your sacrifice will unleash something far worthier than your miserable life. Trust in *him* to make this true, to make something glorious from the filth of your existence..."

"Nice," said Duke.

"He's just going on and on and on about people sacrificing themselves," said Savage. "About giving up your life for something bigger, something better."

She kept the phone up, Maynard rattling through a few more paragraphs of cult-like manipulation until the video stopped. A wheel of death began to circle as it tried to buffer.

"That's all we're getting," she said, sliding it back into her pocket.

"Can you two make any more noise?" asked Sutagon. "If there's anyone down here, they'll hear us coming from a mile away."

"Sorry," whispered Savage.

Carmichael had reached the end of the tunnel, which was sealed with a double door. He gently opened one side, wedging it there while Sutagon walked through. Neither of them was calling out, and Savage didn't blame them. The atmosphere down here was oppressive, the darkness crowding in from all sides like a living thing, barely afraid of the torches. The silence was just as intimidating. It was the quiet of the grave, the threat of a soundless eternity.

"What I don't get is why Maynard sent Ian this video," she said. "What if he—"

"Quiet," hissed Sutagon. "This arsehole could be right behind us playing a tuba, and we wouldn't hear him coming."

She turned to Carmichael.

"You hear that, Joe?"

"A tuba?" said Duke.

The two tactical officers aimed their torches along the corridor together, but there was no sign of the end. Savage caught the faintest of sounds echoing off the walls, a soft hiss of movement.

Carmichael took one hand off his rifle in order to point forward. They crept onwards together, side by side, not making the slightest noise.

"Weren't even being that noisy," grumbled Duke. "It's like being back at—"

He seemed to choke on the words, like he'd got a chicken bone stuck in his throat. He jumped, his head almost hitting the ceiling, his arms flying to his face like he'd been shot.

"Aaron—" Savage started, but she was drowned out by a harrowing scream that tore from Duke's mouth.

He swung himself around, his arms flailing so wildly he almost hit her. She fell back against the wall, watching as he started running, almost taking out Carmichael and Sutagon on his way.

"Aaron!" Savage cried. "What is it?"

Duke ran another few paces and then stopped, smacking himself repeatedly in the face like one of the Marx brothers. Carmichael had fallen into a defensive squat, desperately trying to work out where the threat was coming from.

"Is it gone?" Duke said, practically dancing a jig on the spot. "Is it gone?"

"Is *what* gone?" said Savage, reaching Duke and grabbing hold of his hands. "What was it?"

"Spider," he said, his eyes as big as pickled eggs. "A big one."

"You have got to be shitting me," said Carmichael, standing up. "A *spider*?"

"This big," said Duke, stretching his hands about a foot apart. "Landed right on my face."

Both tactical officers fired a look at Duke that might as well have been a bullet. They set off down the tunnel again, tutting like disappointed teachers on a school trip. Duke stared at his hands, miserable.

"It was *really* big," he hissed.

"I bet it was," said Savage, giving him a gentle push in the right direction. "Big scary spider. Poor you."

Something clunked a little way down the corridor, a rattle of plastic. Carmichael and Sutagon must have heard it too because they started moving faster, their weapons trained at the right-hand wall of the corridor. There was a door, and it was open a crack.

The two officers readied themselves, nodding to each other.

Carmichael kicked open the door, allowing Sutagon to rush in.

"Armed police! On the ground! Now!"

Somebody else shouted, the sound of it drowned out by the thunder of feet as Savage and Duke raced for the room. She walked through the door to see Carmichael and Sutagon facing the far wall, their rifles aimed at a third man who squatted in the corner. Even with his hands over his face, she recognised him.

"Porter?" said Savage. "What are you doing, sir?"

"Kate?" he said, peeking through his fingers.

He stood up, brushing his hands down his trousers. The smell in the room was atrocious, like a Portaloo that had exploded, and Savage noticed an overturned yellow bucket by Porter's shoes.

"I was... *investigating*," he said, staring at his shoes. He lifted one foot, pulling a face.

"Looks like you were hiding, sir," said Duke, a glimmer of a smile on his face.

"I was investigating, Aaron," said Porter. "I found this room, somebody's been sleeping here. There's another one just like it. I heard voices, thought you might be the killer, so I waited in here ready to, you know."

He did a half-hearted Karate chop.

"Take you out."

"Hiding," said Duke, coughing the word into his sleeve.

"Well I was only bloody hiding because I heard a woman scream," said Porter. "I didn't know what was going on."

Everyone looked at Duke.

"That was a manly scream, sir," he said. "And the spider was bloody huge."

Porter had his mouth open, ready to sling back a reply, but Savage cut him off.

"Two rooms?" she asked. "Two kidnappers?"

He nodded.

"That's what I think. They've all got those jars."

He clicked on his torch and shone it against the wall to the left. Sure enough, there was a Kilner jar with a jelly of congealed blood inside it, ruby-bright in the torchlight. It was just like the ones they'd found before, only this was bigger. There had to be a pint or more in it.

"Shit," said Duke.

"Where are the others?" asked Savage.

"Up ahead," said Porter. "We found a generator, lights. He's here, the suspect. I came back this way to get help. Got lost instead."

"Can you show us the way back to them?" said Carmichael.

Porter puffed out a breath, staring through the door. He flapped his hands in a shrug.

"I can try. It's not far. Straight on, then left, then right."

Savage left the room, waiting in the corridor as the others filtered out behind her.

"You coming, sir?" she said.

"Somebody still needs to get help," Porter replied. "We'll go."

"We?" said Savage.

He lifted his Maglite, which fluttered uncertainly.

"Me and Mr Torchy."

Savage nodded, staring up the tunnel for a moment before she started walking.

"Straight, left, right?"

"Right," said Porter, watching them go.

"You got any idea what's waiting for us up there?" Savage asked.

She knew what he was going to say before he said it.

"Nothing good, Kate. Nothing good."

CHAPTER THIRTY-SIX

It wasn't a room, Kett realised, it was a shrine—a sacrificial chamber where five young men had lost their lives.

Each victim was chained to the far wall, heavy iron manacles secured around their wrists, their ankles bound in chains. They looked as if they'd been crucified, their arms outstretched. Masks covered their faces, although not the crimson monstrosities that their kidnapper had worn. These were pure white, each depicting a man's face with a serene expression—something Christ-like about them, other than the black holes of their eyes. They wore identical white robes, but there was barely an inch of fabric that hadn't been drenched in blood. More had spattered onto the floor around their feet, turning the concrete into a mosaic.

There was no hint of life at all in those sculpted figures, so much so that Kett wondered for a moment if they were real, or if they were merely scarecrows, empty mannequins like they'd found before.

Except he could see their hands. Skinny wrists, crooked fingers, filthy nails.

"We're too late," Kett said again, and the horror of it hit him like a train.

The large room was an artwork of wire and steel. Metal filaments stretched from wall to wall, hundreds of them, a woven carpet that ran between various pieces of machinery. More still hung overhead like spiderwebs, low enough to touch. A lantern had been fixed there too, blazing light. A single door stood open next to the five boys, darkness beyond.

"What were you shooting at?" he asked, speaking over the grumble of the generator in the hallway outside.

"Chester getting antsy," said Gorski, her eyes on the dead boys.

"Thought I saw something through the door," said Andilet. His expression was haunted, his eyes bulging. "A face."

Kett started to walk across the room, but Gorski grabbed his arm before he could plant his foot on any of the wires. She'd lowered her rifle, but she still looked wary.

"Not until we know it's safe," she said. "Not until we know it isn't rigged."

"We have to be sure, Julia," said Kett. "We might still be able to save them."

"They're dead," said Gorski. "They're—"

Across the room, one of the young men groaned. It was the boy on the far right, the mask concealing his identity. More wires had been twisted around his arms and his neck, disappearing into his hair, making him look like a marionette that had been tangled in its own strings. He moved his head and a curl of dark hair dropped over the mask, matted with blood. The eyes were voids, devoid of life.

"Shit," said Kett.

He tried to move again, but Gorski held him even tighter.

"Just wait," she said. "Let us check it out."

"Hey," said Kett. "We're police. You're going to be okay. Can you hear me?"

The kid moaned again, his hands clenching as he tried to reach the manacles that held him.

"It's going to be okay," Kett said. "Just keep listening to my voice. All of you, focus on my voice."

None of the other boys had moved, not even a rattle from their chains. Gorski stowed her weapon, crouching next to the nearest wire and following it to the wall. She trailed it up into a machine that looked like some kind of mechanical press, then shook her head.

"I can't figure it out," she said. "It could be an explosive, it could be *anything*."

Andilet wasn't moving at all. He continued to stare at the boys, his eyes red. He tongued his bottom lip like there was something he needed to say. His finger sat on the trigger of his rifle.

"You okay, Chester?" said Kett.

"No," he said.

"What did you see?" Kett asked. "Through the door."

Andilet didn't answer, not taking his gaze from the far wall where the boys hung. The one on the right was still groaning, his hands tugging at his chains. His head swung from side to side, a flutter of movement through the eyeholes of his mask. He saw Gorski first, then Kett, and when he finally turned his gaze to Andilet, he uttered a low moan of terror.

"No," he groaned, his voice muffled by the mask. "No, no, no."

It was like somebody had taken a chisel to Kett's heart. He spun around to see Andilet shaking his head.

"It's him," the boy cried out. "It's him, it's him!"

Gorski moved fast, her rifle snapping towards Andilet before he could react. He started to lift his own weapon, but she stepped in, close enough that she couldn't miss.

"Don't," she said. "What the fuck, Chester? What's he saying?"

Andilet opened his mouth, but nothing came out. He took a step back, still shaking his head.

"It's him!" the boy said again, almost a scream now. "Please, it's him! He did this!"

"Drop the gun, Chester," said Gorski.

The sound of footsteps hammered down the corridor outside, and Kett turned to see Joe Carmichael push through the door. When he saw where Gorski was aiming, he turned his own rifle to Andilet.

"It's Carmichael, Sarge," he said to Gorski's back. "Sutagon too. What's going on?"

Sutagon pushed in behind him, circling Kett so she could get a better line of sight on Andilet. Kett retreated, staying well out of the way in case anyone opened fire. Savage and Duke were at the door, and he waved them back. They retreated, struggling to breathe in the fume-filled air, struggling to hear past the rumble of the generator.

"Drop it, Chester," said Gorski. "I'm not going to ask again."

"Please!" howled the kid. He was tugging on his chains, desperate to free himself. "Don't let him hurt me."

Andilet let go of his rifle, which swung against his side. He held up his hands.

"Sarge," he said. "Jules, come on. It's me."

"Hell did you do, Chester?" said Sutagon.

"I didn't do anything," Andilet said, taking another step back. "Listen to me, I don't know what's going on here, but—"

"Don't listen to him," screamed the boy from behind his mask. "He did this to me. He did this to all of us. He's evil. Shoot him! Just shoot him!"

"I don't know what he's talking about," said Andilet, his voice breaking. "I've never seen that kid before. I've never been here before. I wouldn't do this. You *know* me, Julia. You've known me for five years. I wouldn't—"

A gunshot cracked the room in half, deafening in the small space. Andilet's head snapped back, a mist of blood filling the air in front of him. He stayed standing for all of a second before his body understood he was dead, his legs folding neatly beneath him as he crumpled to the ground.

"The fuck?" said Gorski, spinning around.

A second gunshot. Gorski tumbled, her rifle firing as she fell, taking a chunk from the ceiling.

Joe Carmichael swung his weapon towards the last member of the tactical team. Sutagon tried to manoeuvre her own rifle, but she wasn't fast enough. Carmichael pulled the trigger, and her throat exploded. She gargled, lifted her gun, only for another shot to strike her in the face.

She was dead before she hit the ground.

Kett staggered backwards, only the wall holding him up. The room was a chaos of smoke and blood, and through it he watched Carmichael move his weapon in a lazy circle. He aimed it at Gorski, who lay on the floor. She was trying to lift her gun with her injured arm, her eyes burning with fear, with hatred.

"Don't, Joe," said Kett, his voice coming from a million miles away. "She's pregnant. Don't do it."

"I'm not a monster," said Carmichael, grinning. He had

blood on his face, probably Sutagon's, and when he grinned, Kett saw that it was on his teeth, too. "Stop moving, Jules, or you die, and so does that thing inside you."

Gorski fumbled her weapon for a moment more, but her fingers were slick with blood, and after a second or two she stopped. She couldn't put her hands up, but she spread them to the side. Her face was warped with fury, but there was a sadness there too, a wounded disbelief.

"*You*?" she said.

"Yeah," Carmichael replied. "Me."

The boy across the room was groaning, unintelligible words trapped by the mask. Carmichael shouted back through the open door.

"Savage, Duke, you still out there?"

There was no sign of them, so he raised his voice, tried again.

"You've got five seconds to get back in here, or Gorski gets a bullet in the belly. One."

Nothing.

"Two. I'll do it, and you know I will."

Kett couldn't hear a thing past the generator. He wondered if they'd started running at the first shot, hoped that maybe they were long gone. Whatever happened in here, at least they'd be safe.

"Three."

"Okay," came a voice. "Okay, we're coming."

Savage appeared in the door, her hands on her head as she walked to Kett's side. Duke was there too, and he positioned himself in front of both of them. Across the room, the chained boy was sobbing hysterically behind his mask.

Carmichael still had his gun pointed at Gorski.

"Throw them, Jules," he told her. "All of them. The knife too."

Gorski pushed her rifle away with her good arm, then popped the button on her holster. She delicately pulled out the pistol and tossed it into the forest of wires. Carmichael didn't even flinch as he watched it hit the floor. She did the same with her Taser, then pulled a brutal-looking knife from its sheath.

"I won't bother asking you to get rid of the knuckle duster in your pocket," said Carmichael. "Because it's not like you can use it. But you, big man."

He nodded to Duke.

"Taser, spray, baton, on the floor."

Duke didn't look happy about it, but it wasn't like he had a choice. He dropped his weapons, stretching his hands out. He was still standing in front of Savage and Kett, but Carmichael jerked his weapon to the side.

"I can't see through you, you meaty bastard, so move."

Duke shuffled to Savage's side, his hands up.

"You three," said Carmichael. "Stay still, stay quiet, stay out of it. This isn't about you."

"What is it about?" said Kett, his frantic heartbeat drumming in his voice. His skin fizzed with adrenaline, his head pounding. He felt weirdly detached from his own body, like it wouldn't listen to him if he told it to move.

Carmichael pointed the rifle at Kett's heart. His finger was on the trigger, and when his face peeled open into another grin Kett thought he was going to shoot. Every muscle in his body tensed, his back screaming into a cramp. He had to lean against the wall, twisting his spine, before it throbbed away.

"A little on edge there, Robbie?" said Carmichael, watching him like a cat with its prey. "Because you should be. I honestly didn't think this would work, but there you go.

I should have trusted him. He said it would go down exactly like this."

"Maynard?" said Kett.

"Who else?" Carmichael answered.

"You're the guy he's been training? You're his successor?"

"Successor?" said Carmichael, with a snort of laughter. "Maynard's some rich old prick who got hard watching people get murdered. He was pathetic. He deserved to die. Me?"

He used his teeth to pull off his glove, his rifle never shifting. Then he grabbed his body armour, wrestling it up. He couldn't get it far, but enough of his stomach was visible for Kett to see the tattoo there, the lines of the pentagram, the crude outline of the skull.

"I'm something so much more than he ever was, more than any of those old farts dreamed of being."

"Hollenbeck?" said Kett.

Carmichael spat out another laugh.

"They were useless twats, all of them. Maynard was the worst. But I'll tell you something, he knew how to make a good plan. He was meticulous. He knew you'd find this place, he knew you'd send in a tactical team. He knew you'd be right in the middle of it. He knew that sooner or later, we'd end up down here, alone."

"We're not alone, Joe," said Kett. "There's a whole army of police up there, they'll be coming down any second."

"Except they won't, will they?" said Carmichael, looking at Savage. "You want to tell him, sweet cheeks, or shall I?"

"They got called away," said Savage. "Your Red Room couple were spotted in Dereham. Clare thought they'd be able to lead us to the boys."

"Handy, those two," said Carmichael. "Patricia and Patrick, that's their names. Weird as anything. Sick in the brain. Brother and sister, but there's a little more there, if you ask me. Maynard trained them up too. Turned them into this urban legend, follow the red line, find the red room, make a red wish, all that shit. That was all him. You know how much they believed it? You'll find out, when you finally catch up to them. Though they won't be able to tell you much."

"Dead?" said Kett.

"Part of their deal," said Carmichael. "They had their wish, this was the price. They provide a distraction for me, then they off themselves. Or each other. Maynard's orders."

"They're not going to—"

"You know they will, Robbie," said Carmichael. "Just like you know what's going to happen here, now. You have any idea what I will become when I complete this ceremony? When all five boys are sacrificed to the dark lord? I'm going to be master of them all. I'm going to be a God. I'm going to crush this world in my fist."

He clenched his hand to demonstrate.

"Maynard was right. The power, it's insane. You have to be in my skin to feel it, Robbie, you wouldn't believe it. It's like... I can't describe it; it's unimaginably good."

He groaned in pleasure.

"When the ceremony ends, I'm going to swallow your soul, I'm going to carve up your mind in this world and the next. I'm going to drag everyone you love down to hell, and make them my playthings..."

Carmichael dropped his head, his shoulders shaking. Kett couldn't figure out what was going on until he lifted it again, laughing so hard he could barely hold his gun.

"I'm sorry," he said, barely able to speak past his laughter. "Oh God, I tried. I really tried. I can't do it, it's too fucking stupid."

"*What?*" said Kett. He felt like he'd fallen out of reality and into a dream. As if any moment now he'd be woken by Billie, or by one of the girls jumping on the bed.

Carmichael was still laughing, the sound of it mixing with the sobs from the chained boy across the room, with the gurgling death rattles of Chris Sutagon on the floor, with Gorski's quiet groans. Kett looked at Savage, and at Duke, both as desperate and confused as he was.

Carmichael's laughter softened into a giggle, and he used his free hand to wipe the tears from his eyes.

"Man, that felt good," he said. "You should see your faces. I wish I had a camera. Wait..."

He dug into his pocket, pulling out a phone.

"Hang on."

He fumbled with it, taking his eye off them for the second or two it took to open the camera. Duke tensed, like he was going to lunge, and Kett took hold of his sleeve before he could move.

"Here," said Carmichael. "Say cheese. No, say *Satan*."

Nobody spoke.

He laughed again as he took the photo, then put the phone back into his pocket.

"I'm sorry," he said. "I had this whole thing planned out. Well, Maynard did. I was going to chase you through the tunnels, kill you one by one. I was going to make you think I believed it, that I was the new Devil. I was going to make you beg Satan for your lives, renounce God, whatever. I was going to make you question your own beliefs in order to save yourselves."

"Why?" said Kett.

Carmichael frowned like he'd never been asked the question before. Then he shrugged.

"Why not? Maynard hated you. I mean, the kind of hatred you see maybe once in a lifetime, the kind that burns you from the inside out. You're all he talked about, how you took down Hollenbeck, how you stopped all the fun. He was furious. You know, he actually blamed you for giving him brain cancer, because you stressed him out so much. Believe that? Now me, I couldn't give a shit about any of the twisted stuff they were into, but when a man like Maynard comes to your house one evening and says, 'Hey, Joe, you want to be heir to my kingdom? You want me to show you how to have some fun and fuck shit up along the way? You want to learn how to break rules, break people? Oh, and by the way, I'll pay you a tonne of money to do it.' I mean, you don't say no to that, do you?"

"How long?" said Gorski. She'd managed to prop herself up against the wall, her good hand resting on her belly. She was fading fast.

"Long as I've known you," he said with another shrug. "Came to me two years ago, right after Hell House. I'm just good at keeping secrets."

"You killed Ben, you piece of shit," she said, spitting at him. It fell short, landing on her own stomach. There was a river of blood dripping from the sleeve of her uniform. "He was your friend. He loved you."

"Yeah," said Carmichael. The smile dropped away, and he scuffed the floor with his boot. Once again, Duke tensed, but Kett kept hold of him. However fast the PC was, he couldn't outrun a bullet. "Feel a bit shitty about that, to be honest. I honestly didn't know about the..."

He pretended to wrap a noose around his throat, croaking.

"Mental, that. Maynard was planning to get caught, he wanted it, so that he could get this thing started. So that he could finally meet you."

He nodded to Kett.

"So yeah, didn't know Maynard was going to kill Ben, but that's the game, isn't it?"

"So there is no Devil?" said Kett. "No believers? No occult bullshit?"

Carmichael tutted at him like a disapproving parent.

"The Devil?" he said. "Come on, Robbie. Grow up. All of that was Maynard taking the piss. He never believed it, but he knew how to use it to make people do what he wanted. He always said that the only devils were people like him, people like me."

He jabbed the rifle at Kett.

"People like *you*, when you needed to be. There's no Devil, Robbie, just like there's no God. No heaven, no hell. There's just this. This stupid game called life. So fuck it, we might as well have some fun."

He laughed again, but there was an edge to it this time. He looked exhausted.

"You didn't have to hurt them," said Kett, looking across the room to the boys that hung from the wall. The survivor had fallen quiet, watching everything through the holes in his mask. "You didn't have to kill them."

Carmichael followed his gaze.

"Yeah, I know," he said. "But shit, I got carried away. For a little while there, I thought Maynard might be right, you know? For the tiniest of seconds, I thought he could be on to something. Five boys, five sacrifices, five pillars of consciousness. Divination, Exsanguination, Veneration, Invocation, Limbo... Limp dick... Ah shit, I can't even get that right."

He vomited more laughter, almost choking on it.

"Fuck's sake," he said. "They're never going to let me forget it. I'm supposed to be their master."

"What?" said Kett. "Who?"

Across the room, one of the dead boys snorted. It was the kid in the middle, his chains rattling as he started to laugh. He looked up, a glint of life through the eyeholes in his mask. The boy next to him started giggling too.

Then they were all moving—all five dead boys tugging at their chains, their eyes wild through the masks, a wave of screams and howls and laughter filling the room.

"Sorry," said Carmichael, weeping with delight, the tears actually running down his face. "I'm so shit at this. Maynard would kill me if he could see me right now."

The boys were still screeching like monkeys, deafening in the small space. Carmichael's face grew suddenly serious.

"That's enough, though," he said.

The noise continued, the boys lost in their delirium.

"I said *enough*!" he roared. "Let's not forget why we're here, lads. Let's not forget who's in fucking charge."

The boys fell silent, their hungry eyes watching Carmichael.

"Better," he said, scratching his head with his free hand.

"What's going on?" asked Kett. That sense of being inside a nightmare was worse than ever. "What are you doing, Joe?"

Carmichael looked at Kett, then at Duke and Savage, and finally at Gorski. Kett could see the mechanisms of his brain trying to process the emotions—a flicker of grief, of uncertainty, quickly vanishing beneath another lunatic smile.

"What are you doing with *them*?" said Kett, nodding to the boys.

"I'm not doing anything with them," he said. "Nothing they didn't ask for, anyway. Nothing they didn't want."

"Nobody wants this," said Savage.

Carmichael shrugged, the rifle bouncing.

"I mean, you'd think so, wouldn't you? What muppet asks to be kidnapped, stabbed, and strung up to a wall with a mask strapped to his face? When Maynard showed me his videos, when he told me what he was doing, I thought he was nuts. Nobody's going to fall for this. Nobody in their right mind would look at a masked man on YouTube and think that's what they want to do with their lives."

The boys were watching through their masks, listening intently.

"Shows what I know. These kids, they've been bowing down to the cult of the internet their whole lives. They're desperate for something to fill their empty heads, for somebody to tell them what to believe, what to be. How else do you think these influencers work? Some prick on YouTube tells them to ignore their teacher because she's a woman, and low and behold, they do it. Another one says the only way to properly control their girlfriend is to give her a slap. What happens? These lovely little teenage boys who wouldn't have said boo to a goose a few years ago are giving bitches black eyes and boasting about it on TikTok."

He looked at Savage.

"Not saying I agree with it, Kate. Ask me, anyone who lifts a hand to a woman should get their fingers bitten off. Just pointing it out, these piss-weak little boys are watching shit all day every day, and it's getting drummed into their stupid empty skulls. No wonder they start to believe it."

He sniffed, wiping his nose.

"Maynard told me it used to take years to recruit a proper killer. It took them months to properly corrupt their followers, to get them to kill. He only did the videos because he knew he didn't have the time to train somebody properly, and he knew it wouldn't be as good. I mean, all these dick-heads really did was put their email address into a form. But hey, a disciple is a disciple, I guess, even if they're a shit one."

"This is insane," said Kett.

"Thing is, the internet opens you up to so many more people," Carmichael went on. "There are, what, a hundred thousand teenage lads in Norfolk? I don't know. There are millions in the country, all on their phones, all looking for something to fill up their meaningless days, someone to show them how to live. All looking for a master. You only need a tiny fraction of them to be broken enough to believe."

He looked at the boys again.

"You only need five. Isn't that right, lads?"

"Yes, master," they said, a grumble that was almost too quiet to hear.

Carmichael laughed.

"Never gonna get used to that," he said, adjusting his gun.

"You don't have to do what he says," Kett told them. "You don't have to be a part of this."

The boys shuffled uncomfortably, their expressions hidden behind their masks.

"He's right," said Carmichael, aiming the rifle at them. "Hands up if you want to opt out and fuck off. I can end it for you right now."

Nobody moved, and he grinned.

"Right, I guess we'd better get on with it. Today isn't just a test for me, it's a test for all of us."

"A test?" said Kett.

"That's what the last video was, sir," Savage said. "Maynard was going on about sacrifices, I assumed he was talking about Ian dying, but..."

She turned to the boys.

"He was training you too, wasn't he? Everyone who did Maynard's course, they were all aiming for the same thing, they were all trying to get to that last video. That final test of loyalty."

"Maybe," said Carmichael, spitting yellow phlegm to the floor. "I don't know if any of them did it, I wasn't even sure what they were supposed to do. I didn't watch the videos, not all of them, anyway. Who's got time for that? Honestly, Maynard just wanted to prime them, put them in the right headspace. Make them his empty boys. He wanted them to prove their allegiance, even in the face of death."

"That's why you stabbed them?" said Kett.

"I barely touched them. A tiny jab, enough to get some blood for the stupid pentagrams he wanted me to leave everywhere. I mean, it probably hurt. But the wounds I gave them weren't enough to do much damage. Anyone too injured to go on?"

Again, he swung the rifle their way.

"Thought so," said Carmichael. "Maynard only wanted the strongest people to survive. You bleed out, you're not good enough. These twats completed their course, they survived their injuries, they stayed loyal to the end, didn't tell anyone. The sacrifice isn't their lives, not really. They were sacrificing the person they used to be, their old self. Embracing Maynard's version of them: a higher being that lives according to his needs, his desires, his greed. A true Devil, and all the more human for it."

"Do what you want, shall be the whole of the law," said one of the boys.

"*Wilt*, dickhead," said another. "Not want."

"Easy now," Carmichael told them. "Save that aggression for when it matters."

He looked at Kett again.

"Which is now, I guess, if we want to finish this and get out of here before all my old mates return. They are going to be *pissed* at what I did to you, Jules, and Chris and Chester."

He puffed out a breath as he glanced at the two dead tactical officers at his feet. Only for a second, though, before he returned his attention to the boys.

"So yeah, these five fine young fellows are almost done, but if they want to get their certificates of achievement or whatever, then they've got one last job. And that's you, Kett."

The room felt like it was growing colder, the fumes from the generator making Kett's body tremble. He knew what was coming. It was inevitable.

"The whole point of all this is that Maynard wanted you dead. He wanted you dead in the worst possible way. He asked for this part of the ceremony to be real, whether I believed it or not. *You* are the sacrifice."

Kett shook his head, the fear paralysing him. He tried not to think of Billie, of the girls, but they were right here with him in the room, their smiles, their laughter, their small hands in his.

"Do me a favour, Robbie, look in that box over there," said Carmichael.

Kett followed the man's finger to see a cardboard box against the wall a few feet away.

"No," he said.

Carmichael pouted.

"Don't be like that," he said. "It's a present, just for you. Open it, or Gorski's baby gets a bullet in the face."

He angled the gun towards her, and Gorski curled into herself in a futile attempt to protect her stomach.

"Sorry, Jules," Carmichael said. "Close your eyes, if it helps."

"Okay," said Kett. "I'm going."

It was like his feet were cased in cement, but he crossed the room one step at a time. He peeled open the damp cardboard, and when he saw what was inside, he almost cried out.

"Thought you might like it," said Carmichael. "Maynard taught me how to make them. Electric motor, steel wire, big battery. You don't get a lot of torque, but you don't really need it. Not like it's got to cut through steel, is it? Just flesh. Take it out."

Kett didn't move.

"I'm getting bored now, you stubborn cunt," said Carmichael.

He aimed his rifle at the wall over Gorski's head and pulled the trigger. Brick dust exploded, Gorski screaming as she buried her face in her hands. The bullet ricocheted, burying itself somewhere in the ceiling. The ring of a tuning fork whined inside Kett's ears.

"Pick. It. Up."

Kett reached into the box, grabbing the bulk of the item and lifting it. It was heavier than it looked, a solid mass of metal with a hangman's noose of wire dangling from it—big enough to loop around his head.

"No," he said again.

"Yes!" exclaimed Carmichael, grinning. "It's a ceremony, Robbie, a celebration. You need a tie."

"You kill him, you go to prison for the rest of your life," said Savage. "All of you."

"Yeah, I think that ship has sailed," said Carmichael.

"I've got it sorted, don't worry. We'll be okay. You see, they're going to kill you, Robbie. These kids. They're going to carve you up, cut off a few choice cuts, and bottle them. In jars, though, not bottles. They've been practising, over at the paintball place. You remember the sheep? They're all surgeons now. They were supposed to present their gifts to Maynard, but he's dead. So I'll guess we'll just hang onto them for a while, then maybe drop them off at his grave when it's all calmed down."

He shrugged.

"I'll have to have a proper think about it. You know what you're getting, lads?"

"Yes, master," said the kid on the right. "Divination. I get the eyes."

The boy tugged at his chains and they fell away from his wrists like a magician's trick, clattering against the wall. He shrugged off the robes to reveal a tracksuit underneath, still stained with blood. It took him a few seconds to pull the loose wires from his arms and neck, freeing himself. He stepped onto the carpet of wires, reaching into his tracksuit and pulling out a long, curved blade.

"*Eye*, singular," said Carmichael, sternly. "He'll need the other one to see what's coming next."

"Exsanguination," said the next boy along, pulling free. He lifted his mask for a second, then he must have realised he'd made a mistake because he pulled it down again. His face had been visible long enough for Kett to recognise Vincent Kinghorn from the photos on the Incident Room wall. "Gonna get me a finger."

He retrieved an identical knife, dropping it almost immediately.

"Twat," muttered one of the other boys as he picked it up.

"You're a fucking twat," said Vincent.

"I'm going to shoot all of you if you don't pack it in," said Carmichael. "Behave."

"Sorry, master," they said.

Kett realised he was shaking his head in an attempt at denial, pressing himself against the wall like he might be able to pass right through it. The garrotte was a lead weight, his arms trembling from the effort of holding it. This couldn't be happening, not again. He thought he'd left the horrors behind him in Hell House, he thought that night had been the end of it.

But somehow he'd landed here, inside an even worse nightmare.

"Limination," said another of the boys, a trace of an accent. "Still don't get why I have to touch *that*."

"Cock boy," said the kid on the right, sniggering.

"Doesn't matter, we get the idea," said Carmichael. He turned to Savage. "Sorry Kate, Aaron. Always liked you two. We might let you live. I haven't got that far yet."

He scratched his head.

"So I guess you'd better pop it on, then," he said, nodding to the garrotte. "Pretty simple. Noose goes around your neck, you flick the switch. Don't worry, I won't get it going until the lads have got what they need. Don't want you to miss the fun."

Savage shook her head.

"Don't do it, sir," she said.

"He has to," said Carmichael. "Or you die, and Aaron dies, and Julia dies. And then he dies anyway because I'll shoot him in the eye. So save us all some effort, yeah, Robbie. Can you do that for me?"

Carmichael shrugged his shoulders, the gun arcing outwards.

"Can you—"

Duke pushed himself off the wall like a sprinter from the blocks, closing the gap between him and Carmichael in three giant strides. He planted his hands on the man's chest before he could swing his rifle back, giving him an almighty shove.

Carmichael landed hard on the carpet of wires, his gun barking as it fired. A bullet cracked into a piece of machinery with a sound like a gong being struck. He tried to lift the weapon, but he was winded.

"Run!" Duke roared, doubling back. He grabbed Savage, dragging her towards the door.

Kett hurled the motorised garrotte at Carmichael, a lucky shot that hit the man in the shoulder just as he was aiming the rifle. He bolted after Savage and Duke, hearing a roar of fury from Carmichael and the five boys. More gunshots followed him through the door, a shrapnel of splintered wood ripping into his ear.

He fell into the corridor, almost slipping. He turned, seeing Gorski through the open door, reaching for her.

"Go!" she screamed.

She kicked out a foot, sending her knife skittering across the concrete floor. It struck the doorframe before spinning into the corridor.

"Go!" she shouted again.

Kett grabbed the door and slammed it shut. He picked up the knife.

Then he did the only thing he could do.

He ran.

CHAPTER THIRTY-SEVEN

TERROR DROVE HIM DOWN THE DARK CORRIDOR.

He bolted, almost crashing into the generator. He clutched Gorski's knife in his sweaty hand.

Behind him, the door opened, Carmichael stepping out in a wave of light. He had his rifle to his shoulder.

"Get back here, you fuck!" he screamed, and he pulled the trigger.

Something whipped past Kett's arm, ice cold but boiling hot. He dived around the corner as a second shot rang out, seeing Savage and Duke up ahead, waiting for him in the gloom. He legged it towards them, ignoring the pain in his back.

Duke grabbed hold of his jacket when he was close enough, dragging him towards another junction that cut right. This one was out of reach of the faint glow of the lights, the darkness like a living thing that coiled around his face.

"Kett!" screamed Carmichael. A clatter of feet as he chased them, another gunshot echoing like rolling thunder.

"Last chance, you piece of shit! Julia's dead if you don't come back!"

Kett stopped, but Duke dragged him deeper into the secret dark.

"He's going to kill Gorski whatever happens, sir," the PC whispered. "I promise you that."

Savage had taken the lead, moving swiftly. Kett couldn't see her in the dark, but he could hear her footsteps as she jogged down the corridor. He slipped the knife into his pocket so that he wouldn't stab himself if he fell, running his hand along the wall to keep his balance. A chorus of shouts and whoops and deranged laughter had risen behind them as the five boys followed their master into the labyrinth.

"Kett!" roared Carmichael.

Torchlight swept down the passage they'd just left, then chased them up the corridor. Kett pressed himself against the wall, Duke beside him, until the tactical officer moved on, heading the other way. Four shapes ran after him, crying out with excitement.

"Find him, you pricks!" Carmichael called out. "Kill him."

The light from their torches died away to almost nothing, then brightened again as a fifth boy entered the corridor they were standing in. He started walking towards them.

"Hurry," whispered Savage. "This way."

Kett moved as quickly and as quietly as he could, reaching a junction where Savage waited. He felt Duke's hand on his sleeve again, guiding him around the corner. Here, Savage pulled out her phone, the soft glow of the screen illuminating another identical tunnel which vanished almost immediately into darkness.

"Have you seen Pete?" he said quietly.

"He went the other way," Savage replied. "He went for help."

Hopefully, he'd found it.

"You there?" came a shout, echoing out of the tunnel they'd just left. It was the boy with the accent. "I've got a gun, so don't move, okay?"

"Yeah, sure, we'll stay right here," whispered Duke. "Prick. Come on."

The PC took the lead, using the dull glow of his phone screen to light the way. They moved as fast as they dared, passing half a dozen doors that wouldn't lead anywhere except a quick death when the boy found them. Somewhere ahead came a distant call, then a harsh bark of laughter.

"I have no idea where we're going," said Savage.

"Just keep moving," said Kett. "At the very least we try to separate them, take them out one at a time."

But even that would be almost impossible, if the boys had picked up Gorski's weapons on the way out of the room, or if Carmichael had shared his. Two rifles. Two sidearms. Two Tasers.

We don't stand a chance, thought Kett, patting the knife in his pocket to make sure it was still there.

They pressed on, turning right at the next junction. The sound of footsteps behind them had died away, and there was no light there any more. But the whoops and jeers sounded closer as the other boys made their way through the underground complex. Duke had picked up speed, the light from his phone barely visible.

"Shit," he said after a minute or so. "Dead end."

He turned back to them, his face ghostly in the near-dark. Sure enough, there was a wall behind him.

"Shit," echoed Kett.

There was a room to the left, and Kett tried the handle,

giving it a gentle rattle until it opened. Savage was trying the door opposite.

"There's no place to hide," she said. "We have to go—"

A gun went off, a flash of lightning and a peal of thunder. Kett fell through the door he'd just opened, blind and deaf. Another gunshot, a scream.

"Kate!" he shouted.

Savage and Duke had run through the door opposite, lit up by a third gunshot. Duke pulled it shut behind him, plunging the world into darkness for as long as it took their attacker to turn on his torch.

"They're here!" yelled the boy. "Hey, they're here! I found them!"

The torchlight wobbled as he ran, and Kett shrank into the shadows of the room. The kid appeared a second later, still wearing his mask. He tucked a slim torch into his armpit, freeing up his hand to grab the handle of the door that Savage and Duke had run through. In his other hand, he held Gorski's sidearm.

He seemed oblivious to the fact that Kett was ten feet behind him.

The kid turned the handle and gave the door a gentle push. It opened slowly, and he took the torch from his armpit, aiming the gun inside.

"We only want the old man."

Kett steadied himself with a breath, creeping forward. His boots scuffed the floor, deafening in the silence.

The kid wasn't listening. He was moving into the other room, sweeping the gun from side to side, speaking quietly.

"Fuck's sake. Where are you?"

He was answered by a shout from nearby, a rallying cry from the other boys. Kett took another couple of steps through the gloom, closing the gap.

"Here!" the kid shouted.

He started to turn, calling out again.

"They're—"

And he spotted Kett through the eyeholes of his mask.

"Fuck," he said.

He turned, pulling the trigger of the pistol far too early. The shot thudded into the wall, the sound of it deafening. Kett lunged, driving his fist into the boy's mask as hard as he could. It was made of porcelain, and it shattered on impact, revealing the startled face of Liam Uysal beneath.

Kett hit him again and the kid's head snapped back, the gun going off, a bullet burying itself into the concrete floor by their feet. Liam staggered, spitting blood. Kett grabbed his wrist and drove it against the wall, then again, the gun firing another bullet before he lost his grip on it.

"Fucker," growled Liam.

His head darted forward like a cobra's, his teeth finding Kett's eyebrow. The pain was worse than a bullet and Kett screamed his fury into the boy's throat, pulling away. He punched again, missing. Then he grabbed Liam's hair, rooting him to the spot, and drove his knee into the kid's crotch. Liam grunted, tumbling back, and Kett punched him again, square in the temple.

The boy dropped to the floor, smacking his head. He lay there, rocking from side to side, whimpering.

The pain flared inside Kett's arm, a fire that burned from his wrist to his shoulder. He tried to shake it out, only making it worse. He was making a noise, a low growl that sounded like a generator. When he tried to stop it, he found he couldn't.

He put his fingers to his eyebrow, the pain there like he was being branded. But there was no blood. The bite hadn't broken the skin.

Liam's torch was on the floor and he scooped it up in his good hand, tucking it under his armpit. The gun was there too, and as much as he hated the thought of it, he picked it up in his left hand, keeping his finger well away from the trigger. He could hear footsteps in the tunnel behind him, so he ducked through the door that Savage and Duke had gone through.

It wasn't a room at all, it was another corridor. There was no sign of them anywhere.

"Liam?" came a shout, one of the other lads. "Where are you?"

The corridor he'd just left lit up, a spotlight that illuminated Liam's body slumped against the wall. Kett clicked off his torch and hid behind the open door.

"Shit, Liam?"

Footsteps pounded his way. They stopped right outside the door, followed by panicked breathing.

"Hey, you alright? What happened?"

A gentle slap.

"Liam?"

Kett clamped his breath in his chest, sipping air. Fireworks danced across the dark corridor, the world tilting back and forth in a sudden wave of vertigo.

Light spilled through the door, the kid right there on the other side of it.

"Vin?" he said. "You in there?"

He took a couple of steps inside, his light stretching halfway down the corridor, revealing a tangle of pipes on the walls, unused whiteboards, more cardboard boxes.

And a shape in the darkness further down the corridor, a hulking form that quickly stepped out of sight.

"Oi!" said the boy, moving forward. He'd pulled his

mask onto the top of his head, where it rested on a tangle of curly hair. "Who's there? That you, old man?"

The boy took another couple of steps, and Kett charged. He lifted the pistol over his head and brought it down on the back of the kid's head. It struck like a hammer on a rock, shattering the mask and something beneath. He sprawled to the floor like his strings had been cut, his torch going out as it landed.

"Shit," said Kett, fumbling in the dark.

The boy wasn't making any sound at all, but Kett didn't trust his back enough to get down on one knee to check for a pulse. He turned his torch on again, seeing that it was Dennis Lynn who lay at his feet. His head was bleeding badly, but in the light of the torch, Kett saw that he was breathing.

"Sir?" came a voice from down the corridor.

Kett lifted the torch to see Duke, standing alone.

"You okay?" the PC asked.

"No," said Kett. "But I'm alive. Where's Kate?"

"Lost her," said Duke.

"You lost her?" said Kett, walking over and aiming his torch down the corridor. "How, Aaron? It's a straight line."

Duke scratched his head as he looked back.

"I'm not sure," he said. "There was a noise, I thought somebody was there, so I went into a room. She kept going."

A cry echoed down the corridor from the far end, a hyena bark of delight. Another followed, and then a distant shout.

"There's somebody here! There's somebody here!"

"Shit," said Kett. He gripped the gun in his good hand, held the torch in his bad, and started to run. "They've found her."

CHAPTER THIRTY-EIGHT

SAVAGE SKIDDED TO A HALT, SPINNING IN THE DARK like she was floating through space. She was so disorientated that she could barely tell which way was left or right, what was up and what was down. She reached out to find nothing but air, flailing to the side until her fingertips connected with something solid.

Only there, with the wall to hold her up, did she dare reach for her phone. She didn't turn on the torch, she just lifted the soft light of the screen, seeing the corridor she'd just run down.

There was no sign of Duke.

"Aaron?" she hissed.

He'd been right behind her when the gun had started firing, pushing her forward, doing what he always did—putting himself between her and danger. She'd thought he was right behind her, but somewhere in the cannon-blast of her adrenaline, she'd lost him.

"Aaron?" she said again, a little louder. "Where are you?"

There was no reply, no sound at all. The corridor she

was in seemed different to the others, two enormous pipes running along the wall to her left, one on top of the other, each big enough to hold a person. The ceiling was so low it brushed the top of her head. She couldn't see more than ten feet with her screen, so she risked the torch, discovering that the pipes ran for another fifty yards or so before disappearing into a tangle of pipework at the far end.

She aimed the torch back the way she'd come, seeing nothing but the clouds of dust that swirled in the glow.

She didn't know what to do. She didn't know where to go. She didn't know if Duke was alive, she didn't know if Kett had been hit by the bullets when the gun had started firing.

She didn't know *anything*.

Come on, Kate, she thought, trying to douse the fire of panic that burned inside her. *Stay calm.*

A shout echoed down the corridor. It reverberated off the walls. She couldn't even tell which direction it had come from. But was that a light behind her?

Yes, it was torchlight, getting brighter. She almost called Duke's name again before she heard somebody talking, a younger man's voice. One of the boys, approaching from a junction.

She clicked off her torch, but not before two of Maynard's followers stepped into the corridor, bathed in a bubble of yellow light. They were both wearing their masks, but one of them pulled his up in order to see better. It was Vincent Kinghorn, his eyes wide with shock.

"Hey!" he said. "Was that... Is that one of them?"

The second guy sucked in a breath and started screaming through his mask.

"There's somebody here! There's somebody here!"

Savage bolted, following the enormous pipes. The two

boys gave chase, baying like hunting dogs. They were faster than her, and they were hungry. Her own shadow swayed wildly as she ran, leading the way, blown into monstrous proportions by their torchlight.

There was nowhere to go.

Ahead, the corridor ended in a steel trap of pipework, a lattice of metal and plastic. The enormous pipes punched right through, with maybe enough space for her to squeeze alongside them.

She didn't have a choice.

She reached the wall, pressing her stomach against the curve of the pipes and pushing herself through the gap. Metal ground against the back of her skull, valves dug into her kidneys, but she kept going, sidestepping deeper into the dark. There wasn't even enough room for her to turn her head, she could only listen as the boys closed in, as they skidded to a halt. The light from their torch reached for her, a pair of fingers grasping at her clothes.

"Where are you going?" said one, a bark of laughter. "Nothing there, you bitch. Come back, we'll make it easy for you."

She advanced deeper into the configuration, the pipes feeling like they were tightening around her. She couldn't get a breath in, the pressure on her chest was too great.

"Get her with your knife," said one of the boys.

A squeal of metal on metal as they tried. Savage screamed through her gritted teeth, waiting for the blade to punch into her arm, her neck. She took another step, grabbing hold of pipes and cables to try to haul herself deeper into the mess.

"Can't reach her," said a voice. "Told you we should have brought the gun. Go in."

"You go in, Vin. You're skinnier than I am."

Savage couldn't look back to see what they were doing. The pressure on her skull was too much, her chest locked in a fist of steel. She tried to take another step, but the pipes held her tight, they wouldn't let her go.

"No," she grunted, thrusting against the barricade. "No!"

She was going to be trapped here forever, left to rot in the dark.

Another beam of light blazed on, right in front of her—on the far side of the pipes. It was bright enough that she felt like her eyes had been burned out of their sockets and she clamped them shut, screaming. A hand reached through, grabbing her throat, then the collar of her jacket.

"Stop!" she said, no air in her lungs to get the word out.

The hand wrenched hard and the pipes released her. There was a moment of agony as she was dragged through the gap, a blade of metal carving through the skin of her back.

Then she was free, falling to the ground, somebody pinning her there. She rolled, punching, kicking, trying to shake them off—the torch still blinding her. There was a grunt as her foot made contact with something solid and her attacker recoiled.

"Kate! Stop!"

"Pete?" she croaked, seeing Porter standing there, one hand to his thigh where she'd kicked him. He tilted the torch towards his own face, then back to the ground.

"Yeah, it's me. What the hell is going on?"

"Oi!" came a shout from the men on the other side of the pipes. Fingers of light reached for her. "Where are you?"

Porter offered his hand and she took it, letting him haul her back to her feet. He had to duck beneath the low ceiling, his back stooped, his head twisted uncomfortably. He used the torch to light up the steel forest she'd just escaped from, and she spotted one of the lads halfway through. It was Vincent, no longer wearing his mask. He was having as bad a time of it as Savage had, the machinery crushing him. He bared his teeth at them, like a rabbit in a trap, trying to jab the curved blade of his knife. He could barely move his arm.

"Fuck off," said Vincent when he saw them looking.

"Wait, Vincent?" said Porter. "You okay, mate?"

"No, he's not," said Savage. "And I don't just mean right now. The kids are in on it, sir, all of them."

"What? You're sure?"

She gestured at Vincent, at the knife.

"Pretty sure, yeah. Where were you?"

"Heard the shots," said Porter. "Came back. Everyone alright?"

"I don't know," said Savage. "I lost Kett and Aaron. The boys have got Gorski's guns, maybe more than one of them, and knives. It's Carmichael, sir. It's Joe. He's the kidnapper."

"*What*?" he said. "You're sure?"

"Yes, sir, I'm pretty bloody sure," she said. "They're all working together. Did you get help?"

"No," said Porter. "I got lost. This place gets bigger by the second. You know where you're going?"

Savage looked into the tangle of pipes, seeing Vincent's wide, frightened eyes, seeing the glint of his blade. He spat at her, his lips covered in white foam.

"As long as it's away from that guy, I don't care," she said. "What's down there?"

Porter swung the torch to light the corridor, which seemed to go on forever.

"Purgatory," he said. "Never ends. But I passed a junction. We can try there."

Savage broke into a jog, her body throbbing. Behind her, Vincent was screaming something, but she couldn't hear what. With any luck, he'd be stuck for a while, or he'd have to squeeze back through and find another way around.

"There," said Porter, aiming the torch to reveal a break in the left-hand wall.

She'd lost her bearings, but she thought it led back in the direction of the main access tunnel they'd entered the basement through.

Which meant it led back towards Carmichael, too.

"There's nothing up ahead?" she asked, looking further down the corridor.

"Empty rooms, no exits," Porter said with a shrug.

She took the left-hand turn into a narrower access tunnel. Here, at least, there were arrows on the walls, pointing towards the fire exit. She followed them, Porter's torch guiding them towards another junction at the far end. They had almost reached it when Savage heard a voice ahead.

"Cut the light," she said, and Porter switched off the torch. She was about to ask him if he could hear anything when the voice came again.

"Keep up, you prick. He's going to get away."

She jogged to the nearest door, slipping inside a small room. Porter followed her, and they peeked out together as the light at the end of the corridor grew brighter. Carmichael appeared, sweeping his torch down the corridor for a second before pulling it away.

"Jesus Christ," he said. "Maynard's an utter dickhead for picking this place. Still, he's only going one way. We'll hide by the stairs, shoot the cunt when he thinks he's home free."

It wasn't clear who he was talking to until he'd walked out of sight and one of the boys replaced him. The kid was still wearing his mask and robes, and he shuffled in his master's footsteps like he was on the way to his own execution. He held something in both hands, and it took Savage a moment to recognise the motorised noose that Carmichael had tried to get Kett to wear.

"I said hurry up!" Carmichael roared, and the boy trotted after him.

"This is bad," said Savage when she was positive they were out of earshot. "We've got to find Kett before Joe does."

"Yeah?" said Porter.

He clicked on his light, scanning the empty room before raising it to Savage's face. She held up a hand to stop it from blinding her.

"How are we going to do that, Kate?"

She didn't have an answer. She just started walking.

CHAPTER THIRTY-NINE

THE BASEMENT WAS A LABYRINTH, AND IT HAD MORE than its fair share of monsters.

Kett and Duke walked side by side, the twin light of their torches turning night into day, revealing the featureless corridor. It could have been the same one they'd walked down a dozen times, and Kett wondered again if this was hell, if he was doomed to traipse these endless passageways until somebody put a bullet in his skull—then again, and again, until the end of time.

At least they were armed now. Duke had taken the pistol, and he held it alongside his torch, close to his face like he was a trained member of the tactical team.

"You ever use one of those before, Aaron?" he asked quietly.

"The torch?" said Duke. "Yeah."

"The *gun*," said Kett, shooting him a look of disbelief.

"Oh, right, sure."

"I don't mean in video games."

"Then no," said Duke.

He hoped they wouldn't have to use it. But as awful as it

would be to shoot a teenage boy, they might need to. The five kids looked like they'd been utterly consumed by Maynard's madness, fully fledged members of his murderous cult. Kett didn't doubt for a second that they'd kill him the moment they saw him.

He felt infinitely grateful to have Duke by his side.

They reached a corner, Duke peeking around it first before stepping into another corridor. He had to duck to fit beneath the low ceiling. This tunnel was narrow, and almost completely filled by two enormous pipes that ran along the wall. They vanished into a grid of interconnected metal conduits maybe fifty yards to the left.

The PC turned the torch the other way to find nothing of note, just more of the same, stretching into infinity.

"Where is she?" said Duke.

They hadn't heard any more shouts, hadn't heard Savage's voice. Even if they had, it was impossible to pinpoint where sounds came from in this place, the maze of corridors confusing everything.

"Doesn't look like we can get through there," Kett said. "Try that way."

Duke aimed the gun to the right, and they moved on, taking a handful of steps before the big PC stopped. He cocked his head.

"You hear that?"

"What?" said Kett, who could barely hear anything over the ringing in his ears.

"Crying," said Duke.

He set off the other way, following the monstrous pipes.

"Kate?" he shouted. "You there?"

It wasn't crying so much as snivelling, a wretched whimper that was definitely coming from the end of the tunnel. They closed in on a web of valves and conduits that seemed to sprout in every direction from the walls and the floor and the ceiling. The giant pipes punched right through, one on top of the other. Kett would have put money on the gap being too small for anyone to fit inside, until they reached it and he saw that there *was* somebody in there.

"What the hell?" said Duke. "Is that..."

They leaned closer, lighting up the gap with their torches. A teenage boy was wedged into the cramped space, standing sideways. He wasn't wearing his mask, but he didn't seem to be able to turn his head towards them. Kett would have assumed he was dead, except he was still sobbing.

"You alright in there, mate?" said Duke, laughing gently. "Looks like you've got yourself into a bit of a pickle."

"Fuck off," said the boy.

"Sure," said Kett. "We're going. Have fun."

He moved away, only for the kid to unleash a desperate wail.

"Wait, please," he said. "Don't leave me in the dark. *Please*."

Duke shook his head.

"We get him out of there, he attacks us, sir," he said. "Guaranteed. We can come back for him when we're out."

"Please!" said the kid, struggling to speak. "I can't breathe."

"What's your name?" asked Kett.

"Vin," he said, sniffing.

"Vincent Kinghorn," said Kett. "You have any idea how much shit you're in?"

The kid groaned.

"I..." he started, but he didn't seem to have anything to follow it with.

"What's the plan, Vin? You're going to kill me, kill all of us, then what? You've got every police officer in the county looking for you now. Where are you going to go?"

"The master will get us out," said Vincent. "He promised."

"This is the same *master* who kidnapped you, yeah? Who cut you, then stuffed you into a hearse? *That* master is going to look after you?"

Vincent groaned.

"Right," said Kett. "Get your cuffs out, Aaron. Vin, we're going to pull you out, but I'm going to handcuff you to the pipe."

"Sir—" started Duke.

"I don't want a dead kid on my conscience," he said. "Vin, if you fight us, Duke here is going to knock you out. Okay?"

The kid didn't answer. Kett braced his shoulder against the pipes and reached in, grabbing Vincent's sweaty hand. He yanked hard, and the boy screamed. Duke slid the pistol into his equipment belt and pulled out his cuffs.

"I'm stuck!" said Vincent.

"No shit," said Kett, pulling harder. The kid squealed again, then something popped and he slid out of his prison like a link from a sausage machine. His legs gave way and he fell to the floor, a curved blade bouncing into the wall. He lunged for it, but Duke dropped onto his back like a tonne weight, flattening him.

"Leave it, mate," said the PC, snapping one side of the handcuffs around his skinny wrist. He clipped the other to a metal pipe, giving it a rattle to make sure it was secure. "Where's the woman you were chasing? You seen her?"

"Dead," spat Vincent. "Cut her up, didn't we?"

Duke pushed his knee into the kid's back, grinding it.

"Aaron," said Kett, a warning. But he felt it too, the fury.

Vincent screamed.

"She's alive! She's alive! I was messing with you. She went through there, through the gap, we lost her."

"We?" said Kett, looking back down the corridor.

Duke got off the boy, and he scrabbled back as far as the cuffs would allow. He propped himself against the pipes, baring his teeth at them like a cornered dog.

"Can't wait to see Joe carve you up," he said, his young face twisted into a mask of hate that made him look ancient. "You're finished, old man."

"I'm forty-six!" said Kett. "Why do you lot keep calling me an old man?"

"That's pretty old, to be fair, sir," said Duke.

"Where are they going, Vin?" Kett asked. "Joe and the others."

Vincent shrugged, staring at his feet.

"Where's the exit?"

The kid jerked his shoulders again, and Kett realised he wasn't getting anything else out of him. He set off the way they'd come, heading for the junction. They'd made it all of three steps before Vincent screamed out.

"No, don't leave me in the dark, please. Please!"

The kid looked tiny in the growing dark, hunkered into himself, his scrawny legs pulled up to his chest, his tracksuit trousers rucked up to reveal his mismatched socks. He had a bandage around his calf from the wound Carmichael had given him in the hearse, filthy with old blood.

He looked like a child.

He *was* a child.

Kett set his torch on the ground so that it lit up the tunnel around Vincent. Then he set off again, turning the corner.

"More than he deserved, sir," said Duke.

"I know. But he can't shoulder all the blame. Maynard was a manipulative bastard. He was very, very good at getting his teeth into people. Kid like Vin, he never stood a chance. None of them did."

"Still..." said Duke.

"We've got to win them back somehow," Kett added. "A little kindness is a good place to start. First thing we taught our girls. Messing up might feel like the end of the world, but there's always a way back."

"I don't remember you saying that when Alice put the cricket ball through your back window," said Duke. "Or when Moira pooped in your shoe."

"She didn't poop in my shoe, Aaron," said Kett. "She *put* poop in my shoe. It wasn't hers. Anyway, that's not the point. We need to show these kids they haven't burned all their bridges. They might not have been kidnapped, but that doesn't mean they're not victims."

"Wise words," said Duke. He flashed Kett a grin. "Old man."

Kett actually laughed, resisting the urge to give the big PC a clip around the back of the head. They'd reached the end of the corridor, and he took a right. This passage looked the same as the one they'd just left, a wave of déjà vu threatening to drown him. They only had one torch now, and the darkness seemed to know it. It trod on their heels, wanting nothing more than to devour them. The cold was settling inside Kett's bones, sapping the last of his strength.

"Exit," said Duke, pointing to a sign that was hanging limply from the wall. An arrow pointed the way they were going. "Can't be that far, we're—"

Duke's head snapped back, and he staggered into the

wall, gargling in pain. His torch fell from his hand, dying as it hit the floor.

The darkness swallowed them, absolute and terrifying.

Kett stumbled, reaching out for Duke. The PC was crying out, the noise harrowing.

"Aaron?" said Kett.

His foot kicked the torch, sending it rolling. The light flickered on for a second, revealing Duke slumped against the wall, reaching for something in his back. Then it snapped off again. Kett could hear footsteps running towards them, a guttural breath. Somebody thumped into him and he fell, landing hard. Duke was still screaming, the awful sound of it filling the corridor, filling Kett's skull.

"Where are you?" said a voice.

Kett started crawling.

"Where are you?"

His fingertips scuffed the torch and he picked it up, smacking it against the palm of his other hand to try to bring it back to life. He reached for the knife in his pocket, pulling it out.

"There you are," said the voice.

Duke's cry died out, a gasp of breath.

"Aaron!" Kett called.

He smacked the torch again, and it blazed on. The light blinded him, but not before he saw Duke wrestling with one of the boys—one hand on the kid's throat, the other gripping his wrist. The boy was holding another of those curved blades, his expression deranged as he tried to drive it into the PC's chest.

"Fucking die!" he screeched.

Kett got to his feet, running over to them, drawing the knife back as he went. He was only halfway there when Duke roared, lifting the kid off the ground like he was a feather pillow—hard enough to slam him into the ceiling. The boy's head hit one of the lights in a hail of glass, then the giant PC hurled him to the ground.

Kett kicked the kid hard in the wrist before he could get up, sending his knife flying. Duke dropped onto him, pushing his face into the ground. He reached for the pistol in his equipment belt like he was thinking about using it, then decided not to.

"Stay down," he growled.

"You alright?" Kett asked, slipping the blade back into his pocket, grateful that he hadn't had to use it.

"No," said Duke. "I think the little prick Tasered me."

Kett angled his head, seeing that he was right. Two barbs had jammed themselves into the back of Duke's neck, the wires trailing to the yellow Taser on the floor.

"Yep," said Kett. "He Tasered you."

The kid was still trying to get up, but Duke wasn't giving him any ground. He secured a zip tie around his wrists, pulling it tight.

"You Tasered me?"

"Yeah," the boy said, struggling to free himself. "Should be dead."

"Tasers don't kill people, you idiot," said Duke, trying to flex his neck.

"He's got a point, though," said Kett, leaning against the wall to stop himself from falling over. His heart was thrashing, his head faint. "How are you still standing?"

"Because I'm a machine, sir," said Duke. He grabbed the kid's hair, lifting his head. It was Ethan Mortimer—or at least a pale, wide-eyed spectre that might have been him. "Where's Kate? Where's the woman that was with us?"

"They were heading for the exit," said Ethan, utterly defeated. "The stairs."

Duke let go of him and his forehead cracked into the floor.

"What do you want to do with him?" asked the PC.

"I know what I *want* to do with him," said Kett. "Sadly, the Code of Ethics means I can't."

He glanced along the corridor, seeing the open door behind them. The kid must have been hiding in the room when they'd passed it.

"Put him in there," he said.

Duke hefted Ethan up by the back of his tracksuit and the seat of his trousers, walking to the door. The Taser rattled down the corridor after him like a reluctant dog. He threw the boy into the room like he was a sack of potatoes and Kett shut the door, ignoring the howls of panic from inside.

"How many's that?" he asked. "Four, right? Him, Liam and Dennis back there, Vincent in the pipes."

"Four," said Duke, nodding. "There's just Ian left."

"And Joe," said Kett.

Duke was trying to reach behind him, and it took Kett a second to realise the Taser barbs were still lodged in his back.

"Shit, sorry," he said.

He clamped the torch in his armpit, grabbing the first wire and pulling hard. Duke let out a scream that would have made Fay Wray blush.

"Sorry," Kett said again. "Hang on."

He pulled again, managing to free one of the barbs. He tried the other, Duke screeching and fidgeting—worse than one of Kett's girls when they had a splinter.

"I thought you said you were a machine," he said, plucking the second barb free.

"I am, sir," Duke pouted, arching his back. "Just a sensitive one."

Kett took a moment to collect his breath.

"You're alright, though?" he asked.

Duke nodded, but Kett could see the pain written into his expression, the fear too.

"I'll be alright when we find Kate," he said.

"We're going to get through this, Aaron," Kett told him. "Me, you, Pete and Kate. We're going to be okay."

"Yeah?"

"Yeah," said Kett. "I'm not going to let that arsehole win."

"So what's the plan, sir?"

"We find the others," Kett said as they started walking. "We find the exit, we find help. The tactical team will tear Carmichael apart when they see what he's done. Come on. It can't be much further. You smell that?"

The air here was a little less stale, the touch of a breeze on Kett's face. Duke shook his head, sniffed, frowned, then nodded.

"Fresh air," he said.

"Fresh air."

They pressed on, passing another exit sign, and then another. The basement was as silent as a tomb, no shouts, no gunshots, just the sound of their footsteps as they picked up speed.

"I recognise this," said Duke after a couple of minutes.

Kett swung the torch from left to right, revealing a collection of scarred whiteboards on the wall.

"The stairs are right there," Duke said.

There was a fire door on the left, and he ran towards it.

"Aaron, wait," said Kett.

Duke crashed through the door, plunging into the darkness beyond. Kett lumbered after him, flooding the stairwell with torchlight as he entered it. Duke had stopped moving, and Kett couldn't see anything past his broad shoulders.

"Come on, mate," he said, squeezing past. "We're nearly..."

And the words died in his throat.

Joe Carmichael stood above them at the bend in the stairs, leaning casually against the wall in a pocket of light. His rifle was pointed at Duke, but his grin was aimed squarely at Kett.

"Nearly," said Carmichael with a little laugh. "But not quite."

CHAPTER FORTY

So close.

But so *far*.

Duke reached for the pistol in his equipment belt, but Carmichael shook his head.

"You know better than that, Aaron. Get rid of it."

The PC did as he was told, throwing the weapon into the dark recess beneath the stairs. Carmichael swung the rifle towards Kett, aiming it low. The light was so bright Kett could barely look at it, but there was no missing the fact that his finger was on the trigger, his body tense.

"Stay right there," Carmichael said. "You're not getting away again, you slippery bastard. Take another step and you lose your kneecap. And that's only if I hit right, otherwise, it'll be your cock."

He dropped down a step, laughing to himself.

"And that'll be a real shame, because we need that for our jars. Right, Ian?"

He clattered down a little further and Ian Hipkin appeared around the bend in the stairwell. He'd shed his robes to reveal a bloody tracksuit, and without his mask his face was a portrait of misery. He was holding something heavy against his chest, and every ounce of warmth drained out of Kett when he realised what it was. The motorised garrotte looked even more monstrous in his small hands, the wire glinting in the torchlight.

"You seen any of my boys on your travels?" said Carmichael. "They're late."

"They're not coming," said Kett, trying to keep the tremor out of his voice.

"Dead?"

"No. They just realised they were in over their heads. Realised they were working for a piece of shit."

He looked at Ian when he spoke.

"I offered them a way out, and they took it."

It was a lie, and it didn't even seem to register on the boy's face.

"Don't feed me that bullshit," said Carmichael, dancing down another couple of steps, almost at the bottom. "Those lads were loyal. Maynard and I broke them, good and proper. Isn't that right, Ian?"

"Yes, master," said Ian.

"Can't hear you, you little twat."

"Yes, master," Ian shouted, the echo of his voice travelling up the stairwell. "Sorry, master."

Carmichael grinned.

"Like having my own private army," he said. "They'll do anything I tell them to. Maynard promised me that, and I never believed him. But watch."

He looked up at Ian. Duke tensed, but Kett hissed at him.

"Wait."

"No," said Carmichael, who must have thought Kett

was talking to him. "I'm done waiting. Ian, punch yourself in the face."

The kid hesitated for a second, unsure.

"Do it now," said Carmichael.

Ian braced the garrotte against his chest with one hand, then drove his fist into his own mouth. He hadn't pulled the punch, the impact rocking his head back. He staggered, almost falling, grabbing the handrail to keep himself up. Blood trickled past his lip, collecting between his teeth.

"Again," said Carmichael.

"Joe, that's enough," said Kett. "Stop."

Ian punched himself again, harder this time.

"Stop!" said Kett. "Ian, don't listen to him."

"Again," said Carmichael.

Ian drove his fist into his cheek. He dropped onto the step, gagging like he was about to throw up. His lip had started to swell.

"Good boy," said Carmichael. "You see, Robbie, this is the difference between us. This is why you'll never win. Maynard never believed in the power of the Devil, but he knew everything about the weakness of men. It's so easy now, because all they do is go online. Every other video on TikTok is telling them how to live their life, brainwashing them. You've got kids out there idolising all these pricks, following them, imitating them, trusting them. They've got..."

He used his free hand to tap himself on the side of the head.

"Empty fucking skulls, and every day they open up their phones and pour in all this shit, all this wickedness, all those lies, porn, violence. They're puppets, Robbie, empty-headed, dead little boys. You know how easy it is to fill an empty bucket with shit? It's so fucking easy."

Carmichael laughed.

"Is that what Maynard did to you, Joe?" said Kett. "Did he fill your empty head with shit?"

The smile fell away from Carmichael's face, and he licked his lips, staring at Kett. The rifle was still up, the barrel barely wavering.

"I'm not like them," he said. "Maynard didn't manipulate me. He *trained* me. He was my mentor, my teacher. He knew he was dying, he needed somebody to carry on his legacy. He was *my* master, Robbie, and now he's gone, I'm carrying on his work. I'm master now. Right, Ian?"

"Right, master."

"Master," Carmichael repeated, grinning again. "I love that."

"Why?" said Kett. "Bullying somebody into calling you master doesn't make you a master. It makes you a..."

His head was thumping, he couldn't think of the word.

"Prick," he finished. "It makes you a prick, Joe."

"Yeah? Who gives a shit? I can be a prick. I can be anything I want. Maynard showed me what real power is, when you're an alpha. A *true* alpha. It's freedom, Robbie. Freedom to be whatever you want, to do whatever you want. I'm off to a good start, wouldn't you say? The press are going to have a field day with all this. Maynard planned it, but I'm the one who carried it out. They've already got a name for it, from that stupid paintball place. The Cold Iron Kills. Not sure it's what I would have picked, but hey, what are you going to do? It's got a ring to it. There's a poem, you know? Cold Iron. You heard it?"

Kett shook his head. Duke was still bristling, his hands bunched into fists, but he had the good sense not to move.

"Maybe it's a military thing. '*Tears are for the craven,*

prayers for the clown—Halters for the silly neck that cannot keep a crown.' You must know it."

Kett didn't say anything. Carmichael was maybe ten yards away, three stairs from the bottom. There was a chance he could get to him, but all the man had to do was squeeze his finger and it would be game over. Ian was still sitting where he'd dropped, both hands resting on the garrotte on his lap like it was a cat.

"'*But Iron—Cold Iron—Is master of them all,*'" Carmichael went on, looking at Duke. "You believe in serendipity, Aaron? It's a beautiful thing. That's what Maynard always said. You make it happen by believing in it. You make it real by fucking manifesting."

"Manifest my cock, Joe," Duke said.

Carmichael laughed.

"It's a shame, what's about to happen to you," he said. "Thought you'd end up tactical. Thought maybe you'd have ended up right here with me at one point. You're an alpha if ever I saw one. Now you'll just be dead."

He shrugged, the gun bouncing.

"Anyway. Bored. Let's get this over with. Robbie, you pick up that knife Julia gave you?"

It would have been stupid to deny it. The hilt was poking out of his pocket.

"Grab that, would you, Aaron?"

Duke didn't move. Carmichael sighed as he turned the rifle towards him.

"You want to see what happens if I have to ask twice?"

"It's okay," said Kett. "Do it."

Duke pulled the knife out of Kett's pocket, pointing it up the steps.

"How about you come down here and we fight this out,

man to man?" he said to Carmichael. "Or are you too chicken?"

"Oh sure," said Carmichael. "Let me drop this *gun* and then fight you with a *knife*. You thick, Aaron? I'm not here to prove myself. I'm here because Maynard gave me a shitload of cash and a blueprint for living that's a lot of fun. I've been chasing highs all my life, only reason I'm in the unit. But this is something else. I'm going to point this out again, because you both seem to be completely missing the point. There are no rules any more, not for me. I can do whatever I want, it's the new law. Isn't that right, Ian?"

"Yes, master," said the boy.

"Stand up when you're talking to me," he snapped.

Ian stood, struggling with the weight of the garrotte. He swayed like he was about to pass out.

"So, Aaron, here's what I want you to do," Carmichael went on. "And you're going to do it exactly as I say, or I'm going to shoot you. And then I'm going to hunt down your girlfriend and shoot her too, just because I can. You listening?"

Duke nodded, still clenching the knife.

"I swore to Maynard I'd do his stupid ceremony," Carmichael said, adjusting the rifle strap over his shoulder. "He had such a hard-on for you, Robbie. He wanted you to die screaming, and he wanted to keep the juicy parts. Why? I have no idea. Trophies, probably. But I'm going to honour that wish, especially as it was his last one."

Kett swallowed, his throat dry. All he wanted was for the door at the top of the stairs to open, for the rest of the tactical team to come piling down it, for somebody to put a bullet in the back of Carmichael's head.

Please. Please. Please.

But the world above them was silent. Empty. There was no help coming.

"Lie down, Robbie," said Carmichael. "Right there on the floor. Bollocks up."

Kett didn't move. He didn't think he *could* move.

"Ian, put that thing around your neck," said Carmichael.

Ian's eyes opened wide, and he stared at his master, shaking his head.

"Do it, now."

"You don't have to do it," said Kett.

"Oh, but he does," said Carmichael. "Because I know you, Robbie. I've been watching you all these years. I know there's no way in hell you'll let a little scrote like Ian die, not even if it means giving up your own life. So..."

He looked back at Ian and screamed at him, the sound of his voice deafening in the stairwell.

"Put it on!"

Ian flinched so hard he nearly dropped the garrotte. He recovered, pushing his head through the loop of wire, sobbing quietly.

"You know how these work?" said Carmichael, talking to Kett. "You push the button and the wire starts retracting. Ten seconds and it's cutting into your neck. Twenty and your arteries are severed. Thirty, your head's on the floor. You saw Ben, didn't you?"

Carmichael drew his free hand across his throat.

"That was a thing of beauty. I'm going to use it on you, Robbie, but only if dickhead here doesn't fuck it up. And not until the end. Not until we've harvested what we need. By then, you'll probably be begging me for it. So I'm going to say it again. On the floor, or I flick the switch."

"Don't," said Duke.

But there was no way out of it, not with a rifle trained at their hearts, not with a teenage boy's life on the line. Kett eased himself onto his knees, the pain in his back like somebody was running a scalpel up and down his spine. He lay on the freezing floor, staring at the ceiling, feeling ridiculously vulnerable.

"Now, Aaron, how good were you at biology?" said Carmichael. "You should be okay. It's not like this is brain surgery."

He barked out a laugh.

"Eye surgery, sure. Ear, finger, cock. I can't even remember what the last one was. You remember, Ian?"

"Tongue," said the boy.

"That's right, well done, although you missed out the master again, didn't you? Tongue, how could I forget that? Maybe we'll start there, before I forget again. Aaron, cut out that prick's tongue for me."

His words reverberated around the small space. Kett's body was fizzing, the fear like an electric current.

"Don't," he croaked. "You don't have to do this."

"I know," said Carmichael. "I don't have to. I *want* to."

"Why?" said Kett. "Jesus Christ, Joe, this is insane. We've known each other for two years, we've worked together, drank together. You've got nowhere to go. Maynard isn't going to save you, Hollenbeck are gone. You do this and it's all over."

"Hollenbeck aren't gone," said Carmichael. "I'm Hollenbeck now. You thought you won, but you didn't destroy shit. I'm going to build it up again, with Maynard's money, with his connections. I told you already, there are thousands of kids out there looking for meaning in their life. Hollenbeck's just beginning, and I'm the fucking master of it all, master of *them* all. Now Aaron, do as you're told, cut out his tongue."

"No," said Duke. He dropped the knife, and it landed with a dull clang. "Fuck you, Joe."

"Wrong answer."

Carmichael pulled the trigger, and his rifle bucked. A bullet punched into the fire door an inch or so away from Duke's neck. The echo of it rumbled up the stairwell, Kett's ears breaking into a high-pitched whine again. Duke barely flinched.

"The next one will kill you," said Carmichael. "Then Ian dies too, and I cut Robbie open myself. Same result. So just do it."

"It's okay, Aaron," said Kett. "It's alright."

"Pick up the knife."

Duke did as he was told, his hand shaking so much he could barely hold it.

"The tongue," said Carmichael. "You do a good enough job and maybe I'll take you with me. Maybe we can empty up that big old head of yours and fill it with shit. There are plenty of cages where I'm going. Put a man through hell for long enough, keep him in the dark for a couple of years, and he'll do anything you tell him to. Isn't that right, Ian?"

"Right, master," said the kid, sobbing freely.

"You think you'll call me master one day, Aaron?"

Duke didn't reply, staring at Kett like he was waiting for a hidden message, like he thought there might be a plan.

But Kett had nothing. The exhaustion and the pain were overwhelming.

"It's okay," Kett said again. "Just say goodbye to the girls for me, yeah? Tell them I'll always be there."

Duke nodded. A tear rolled down his cheek, and he scrubbed it away with his sleeve.

"I'm sorry, sir," he said. "I don't know what to do."

"It doesn't matter," said Kett. "Just tell that to the girls, yeah? Tell them no matter how badly they've messed up, however many mistakes they've made, there's always a way to fix it. Tell them that even when they think they've gone too far, there's still hope. They can always turn around, they can always come back."

He glanced up the stairs, past Carmichael, to where Ian stood. The kid was shaking like a leaf, bowed beneath the weight of the garrotte that hung from his neck. His eyes were red raw, but he was watching. He was listening.

"Can you tell them that, Aaron?" said Kett. "Tell them no matter what happens next, I'm always on their side. It's going to be okay."

"I'll tell them," said Duke, wiping away another tear.

"Last chance," said Carmichael, and he aimed his gun at Duke. "One, two, th—"

His last word was cut off by a choked cry, then by the crack of the rifle as he fired a shot. The wall beside Kett's head exploded, dust hitting him in the eyes. Another shot, ricocheting off the footplate of the fire door. The light from Carmichael's torch strobed back and forth, a third bullet ringing off the metal handrail like a church bell.

Kett clambered to his feet, trying to work out what was going on. Duke grabbed him, pulling him towards the fire door as yet another gunshot split the world in two. He kicked Duke's torch as he went, the light spinning, lighting up the stairs like a spotlight, revealing the horror of what was happening there.

Carmichael crashed against the wall, dropping his rifle in order to put both hands to his throat. Around his neck was the motorised garrotte, a high-pitched whine as the wire contracted. Ian was scrabbling up the stairs on his backside, his eyes wild at the sight of what he'd done.

Carmichael opened his mouth, tried to speak. He groped at his throat, his fingertips drenched in blood. He took a step and slipped, something in his leg cracking as he tumbled down the stairs to the ground below. He lay there, thrashing, bucking, his back arched, his tongue thrusting towards the ceiling.

His eyes found Kett's, blistering as the vessels ruptured. He lifted a blood-drenched hand, reaching out, his lips forming unheard words.

Then Duke dragged Kett through the doors into the corridor beyond, and Carmichael vanished from sight.

It didn't stop the noises from filtering through, though. A wet crack. A final gasp. A drum of kicking feet.

And the whine of the garrotte's motor, long after everything else had fallen quiet.

CHAPTER FORTY-ONE

KETT WASN'T SURE HOW LONG HE STOOD THERE, shoulder to shoulder with Duke in the impossible quiet of the factory basement, in the unforgiving dark.

It could have been a minute, it could have been hours. If he made the slightest of movements he would shatter, scattering pieces of himself over the concrete floor. Even breathing felt like too much, as if his body had simply forgotten how to do it.

He had to keep telling himself he was alive, but it didn't bring the relief it should have. These last two days, these last two hours, these last twenty minutes, they had broken him. He was a shell.

He felt a strong hand on his shoulder. Duke, pulling him close.

"You alright, sir?" he said.

It seemed to take another eternity for him to find the words to reply, and they were a lie.

"I'm alright," he said. A trickle of light crept through the fire door from Carmichael's torch, no sound at all from the stairwell. "I'm okay," he said. "You?"

"Yeah," said Duke, and Kett heard the lie there too. "You think he's dead?"

"Yeah," said Kett.

"I'll check," said the PC.

Kett grabbed Duke's arm, rooting him in place.

"I'll do it," he said. "Wait here."

He pushed the fire door, but it wouldn't open. He had to put his shoulder to it and shunt hard before Carmichael's body rolled out of the way. Fortunately, the man lay face down, both hands touching his throat. There was a lake of blood around him, and Kett had to splash through it to get a better view of his face.

He didn't need to check for a pulse.

He pulled off his coat and draped it over Carmichael's head so that nobody would have to see what he saw, then he collected the torch and aimed it up the steps.

Ian Hipkin sat in the bend of the stairs, his knees pulled up to his face. He sobbed quietly, his big, red eyes watching Kett.

"I'm sorry," he said. "I'm sorry. I'm sorry."

"Hey," Kett said, stepping around Carmichael's rifle and climbing the stairs. "Hey, Ian, you're alright. You're alright. You've got nothing to be sorry for."

He sat down beside him and pulled him close, letting the boy cry into his chest. He was surprised to feel the tears in his own eyes, too many of them to scrub away. He let them fall.

"I didn't want to do it," Ian sobbed. "I didn't want to do any of it. You meant what you said?"

He peeled his face free, looking at Kett.

"There's always a way back? Right? You meant it? However bad I messed up, there's always a way back?"

"Yeah," said Kett. "I meant it. It's going to be okay."

That was another lie, of course. Whatever happened to Ian, he'd never escape today. No matter where he went, no matter how many years he lived for, he'd never leave this stairwell. He was a ghost, trapped down here as much as Kett was.

"There's always a way back," Kett told him, and he hated how hollow his voice sounded.

Below, Duke walked through the fire doors. He looked like he was about to say something when he was cut off by a thud from overhead. Kett's body almost buckled in fright. He got back to his feet, turning the corner and staring up the second flight of stairs just as another crunch echoed down from the doors at the top.

Somebody was trying to break through.

"Good news or bad news?" asked Duke as he climbed the steps.

Something slammed into the door again, followed by a voice.

"Aaron? Robbie?"

"That's Kate!" said Duke, bounding up the stairs. "Kate! It's me! Hang on!"

Duke wrestled with the heavy bolt, opening the door and lifting an arm against the sudden wash of daylight. Savage stood there, holding an extended police baton. Porter was beside her, a fire extinguisher in his hands. He threw it to the floor, annoyed.

"I was about to bust through," he said, gesturing to the door. "Just needed one more go."

"We'd have been waiting all week for you to knock that down, sir," said Duke.

"No you bloody wouldn't," said Porter. "One more, it was about to break."

Duke wasn't listening. He'd wrapped Savage in an enormous hug, her arms around his neck. The baton fell to the floor, rolling away.

"Ow!" said Duke, pulling free. "Sorry, got Tasered."

"No you didn't," said Porter.

"Yeah I did," said Duke, rubbing the nape of his neck. "Didn't even knock me to the floor."

"Yeah it did," said Porter.

"No, it didn't. Tell him, sir."

Kett limped up the stairs, pausing for breath at the top. Past Porter he saw the factory floor, swimming in green light from the skylights. He breathed deeply, the air beautifully fresh but not enough oxygen in it.

"Where did you two come from?" he asked.

"We saw Carmichael heading for the stairs, sir," said Savage. "So we went the other way, past the electrical stuff. We found PC Sealy at the bottom of the steps, she's out cold."

"How?" said Kett, still struggling to get enough air in. "We left her in the room, told her to keep the trapdoor open."

"Carmichael must have got to her," said Savage. "He came into the factory first, while we were talking to Clare outside. He must have knocked her out, then wedged the hatch shut from underneath. I have no idea how he got back up in time. Maybe one of the boys helped him."

She shrugged.

"We got out, we came round to see if we could surprise him from behind. But he'd locked the doors."

"They were about to give out, sir," Porter said. "I felt them about to go."

"I know, Pete," said Kett, sucking down more air. It didn't feel like enough, like his lungs couldn't fill themselves. "I know."

He reached out to pat Porter on the shoulder and felt the world tilt. The ground was ripped out from beneath his feet like a rug and he staggered forward.

Strong arms around him, a cry of panic.

Then nothing but the basement-dark quiet of unconsciousness.

"I'M GOING to toss it over him and there's nothing you can do about it!"

If there was one thing that Kett didn't want to wake up to, it was Superintendent Clare's voice. But there it was, breaking through the dreamless dark like a klaxon.

"I'm his senior officer," Clare went on. "I can toss anything I want over anyone I want, anytime I want."

"No you can't!" came another voice. "I won't let you. It's disgusting, and it will make a mess all over the bed."

"*You're* disgusting," said Clare. "Move out of the way, or I'll toss it over you instead."

Pure terror made Kett snap open his eyes. He had to screw them shut again almost immediately, the world too bright.

"Look what you've done," said the second voice. "You've woken him up."

"Good!" screeched Clare. "We can ask him if he wants it tossed on him."

"I don't!" said Kett, his voice weak. "I don't want anything tossed on me."

He tried to open his eyes again, wincing as the world swam slowly into focus. He was lying in a bed in the back of an ambulance, the Superintendent blocking the open doors and an exhausted paramedic standing between them like a bodyguard. It was bitterly cold in here.

"Please don't toss anything on me, sir," Kett said, feeling his teeth chatter.

"Why not?" said Clare. "It's nice and hot."

"It's *sticky*," said the paramedic.

"*What?*" said Kett, wondering if he was dreaming. There was a pain in his head unlike anything he'd experienced, like somebody had been let loose inside it with a chainsaw.

"It's not *that* sticky," said Clare. "And it will wash off."

"For the love of God, what are you talking about?" said Kett.

"This!" said Clare, and he held up a bundle of camel-coloured fabric that sent a shudder of horror through Kett's body. "My BTJ. Warmest coat you'll ever wear, and you know that, Kett, because you've already worn it."

"Christ no," said Kett, catching a whiff of the Big Tossing Jacket—a mix of dead cow, bacon grease, and something sickly sweet that actually *smelled* sticky. "That's even worse than what I thought you were talking about."

Clare blustered past the paramedic, and Kett almost screamed as he draped the awful coat over him like a blanket. The thing weighed a tonne, and the reek of it made him gag. But it did cut out some of the chill inside the ambulance.

"See," said Clare, patting the coat like it was a dog. "Nice and toasty."

"I think it's still alive, sir," said Kett, feeling the jacket squirm on his lap as gravity tried to pull it off the bed.

"That makes two of you," said Clare, deadly serious. He adjusted the jacket as he spoke, tucking it around Kett's legs.

"Duke told me what happened down there. I can't believe it."

He turned, staring through the doors of the ambulance. The front wall of the factory was right there, the door that Kett had run through a million years ago in search of five missing teenage boys. A dozen uniformed police stood around it in the twilight, reminding Kett of magpies. The memories were returning one by one, his brain reluctant to accept them.

"I *do* believe it, though," Clare went on. "You never think it can get any worse. And then it does."

"How long was I out?" said Kett.

"Not long," Clare replied.

"Not a concussion," said the paramedic. "I can't see any injuries. You fainted, I think."

"Is Julia okay, sir?" said Kett, trying to sit up in the bed. The BTJ made it hard, pinning him there like a hairy wrestler.

"Incredibly, she is," said the Super, turning back. "Bullet went clean through her shoulder. They're bringing her up now. As far as I know, the baby is okay."

That, at least, was great news.

"PC Sealy is recovering too, a nasty bump to the noggin. It could have been a lot worse."

"What about Ian?" said Kett. "The other lads?"

"Ian's on his way to hospital. He was out of his mind, asking for you. They had to sedate him. He killed Carmichael?"

Kett nodded, every vertebra in his neck protesting.

"Killed him with the same thing Ben Milford was murdered with. Ian turned against him."

He tried not to see it, but he couldn't stop the image of

Carmichael's face filling his mind—his bulging eyes, his black tongue.

"I won't say anyone deserved that," said Clare. "But he did. He turned against his own. He murdered Chester and Christine. He was going to kill you. Did he say why? Duke seemed confused on a few of the details. Most of the details, to be honest."

He sighed.

"*All* of the details. He doesn't have a clue what was going on."

Kett thought about it for a moment, trying to put the pieces together.

"Maynard," he said. "This is all him. He's had his hooks in Joe for years, brainwashing him, preparing him to be some kind of heir. This was his test, but it's Hollenbeck, so Maynard didn't want him to kidnap five victims, he wanted him to *recruit* them. He wanted Carmichael to prove he could be the new leader."

He breathed a humourless laugh through his nose.

"The new *master*."

"So Carmichael's our man in the hearse?" said Clare. "Our masked kidnapper? I don't see how. He was with us during the raid. He was with us all day."

"Carmichael left Cold Iron," said Kett. "He said he was escorting Milford's body, but he could have driven up to Fakenham to take Dennis. He had time."

"And Dennis was in on it," said Clare, nodding. "It's not like he would have resisted."

"I don't know, sir," said Kett. He'd gone from being too cold to too hot, the jacket ridiculously heavy. "I'm not sure exactly how it worked. I don't know if the lads knew what was happening. It was all about the videos they were watching. Maynard was corrupting them, one reel at a time, undermining their relationships, pulling them deeper into his madness, pushing them closer to the edge. He made them feel like they wanted it. There were a lot of kids watching those videos, but these five were the ones he broke."

He spluttered out a breath.

"I'm not sure we'll ever fully understand it."

"Maybe not," said Clare. "But we're going to shut it down. I've got a unit in Carmichael's place as we speak, tearing it apart. We'll find the other lads he's recruited, the ones at the hospital. All of them. That arsewipe Berrycloth is happily throwing his old master under the bus. He thought it was all real. He was counting on the Devil showing up. He's given us everything on Maynard, all his contacts, all his hiding places, all his secrets. It's finished."

"So there's not going to be a new Hollenbeck?" said Kett. "Because that's what Carmichael was hoping to do. He was starting it up again, in Maynard's memory."

"Hollenbeck are done," said Clare. "You pulled the whole plant out of the ground back in '21, and this."

He gestured out of the door to the factory.

"Is the fire that kills the roots. There's nothing left of them."

Kett took a breath, filling his lungs, feeling—for the first time in a long time—a beautiful rush of relief.

"The videos will be deleted, all evidence of Maynard's bulltoss will be hidden from public view. Will another group of psychopathic jizztrumpets rise up at some point and start tossing people off left, right and centre? Yes, I'm sure of it."

"Probably wouldn't be in *our* remit, sir," said Kett, trying not to let the Super's words form images in his head.

"But this particular group is dead and gone. They're finished."

Kett nodded, resting his head on the pillow.

"We've rounded up three of the boys, as well as Ian," Clare said. "Ethan Mortimer is still missing. The basement is huge."

"Yeah," said Kett. "I thought it was big on top, but the bottom half is enormous."

"What?" came a voice, and Spalding stepped into view.

"Completely out of proportion," Kett finished. "Oh, hey Alison."

"You're lucky you're already in an ambulance, sir," she said through gritted teeth.

"What?" he said, clueless. "*Why*?"

She glared at him for a moment more before turning to Clare.

"Sir, you need to see something."

"I'll be there in a minute," said Clare.

Spalding walked off, and the Super moved to the door.

"You should get some rest, Robbie," he said. "Take some time. What you went through today..."

He shook his head, his expression full of grief.

"It has to end, sooner or later."

"Sir?" said Kett.

"It can't go on like this forever. *You* can't go on like this."

He turned, staring out of the ambulance, struggling.

"Let's talk in a few days," he said. "When you're back on your feet. I've told Billie and the girls you're okay, they're heading to the hospital now. Go on, Robbie. You did good. All of you."

"Wait!" came a shout from outside.

Porter ran into sight, out of breath.

"I need your help, sir."

"Kett's out of commission," said Clare, stepping down from the ambulance. "What do you need?"

Duke appeared, Savage beside him.

"A witness, sir," said Porter. "I'm going to shoot Duke with a Taser to see if he falls over."

"You're going to *what*?" roared Clare.

"Because there's no way he's telling the truth," Porter went on. "One shot, if he stays standing, he wins, but he won't."

"Bloody will, sir," said Duke, slamming his hands to his chest like a gorilla. "I'm a machine. Bring it on."

"I'm going to shoot you both with Tasers," Clare said, furious. "Right in the todger, the baloney-pony, the battle banana, the undercover brother."

He grabbed Porter's arm, then Duke's, wrestling them away from the ambulance. His voice seemed to fill the entire car park.

"The Philly cheesesteak, the warden's goldfish, Uncle Bob's trumpet."

Savage leaned in, thankfully drowning him out.

"You going to be alright, sir?" she asked.

"Yeah," he said, nodding. "But only if somebody gets this coat off me."

Savage laughed, jumping nimbly into the ambulance. She pulled the BTJ off his legs, the cold air blowing in along with a rush of pins and needles as his circulation freed up. She held it to her chest for a moment.

"Thank you, for what you did for Aaron," she said. "For keeping him alive."

"You kidding?" he replied. "If it wasn't for him, I'd be dead."

She smiled, then jumped back down.

"See you soon, sir," she said, nodding to the jacket. "I'm going to find out if this place still has an incinerator."

He laughed, instantly regretting it as the pain in his head grew worse. The paramedic appeared in the door.

"You ready to go?" she asked.

Kett closed his eyes, thinking of Carmichael, and Maynard, and the five boys who had fallen under his spell. He thought about the job, so awful, so necessary.

He thought about Billie, about Alice and Evie and Moira, and how close he'd come to saying goodbye forever, how close they'd come to losing him.

Again.

Clare was right. It couldn't go on like this forever.

"Yeah," he said.

The paramedic closed the doors, and a few seconds later he heard the engine fire up. They pulled away slowly, the ambulance rocking on the uneven ground.

"I'm ready to go."

CHAPTER FORTY-TWO

Sunday

Kett basked in the sun at the top of the world.

Not quite the top of the world, maybe, but certainly the highest point he could get to in Norwich. Around him, in almost every direction, was woodland and meadow, bathed in the golden light of the cool afternoon. Below was the city, spread out at the bottom of the hill like a child's play mat, the buildings and cars and people no bigger than toys. Even the cathedral looked small enough to pick up.

He stood there, at the top of the world, and he *breathed*.

Back in the tunnels beneath the factory, in the claustrophobic, airless dark, he'd thought he'd never be able to fill his lungs again. He'd thought he'd taken his last breath. He'd thought it was going to be his grave.

But here he was, the city at his feet, nothing but fresh air and sunshine.

He'd survived.

It seemed perfectly fitting that this place, the highest point in the city, was called Kett's Heights.

"Put it in Dad's shoe!"

The silence was broken by Evie's voice, and he turned to see his daughters a little way down the path, Billie beside them. Moira had picked something up, something small and brown and distinctly poop-like, and the look she gave Kett was full of mischief.

"Please don't put poo in my shoe, Moira," Kett said.

His two youngest girls burst out laughing.

"Poo in his shoe!" said Evie. "It rhymes."

She broke into a little dance.

"Poo in your shoe, poo in your shoe, nothing makes you happier than poo in your shoe."

They burst into another round of giggles, Alice scowling at them over the top of her phone. Billie left them to it, walking over.

"Penny for your thoughts," she said, lifting a hand to shield her eyes from the sun.

"Just wondering if it's true," he said. When she frowned, he added, "That nothing makes you happier than poo in your shoe."

"I hate to break it to you, it's just a pinecone," she said.

She laced her arm through his, and he winced as they started walking again. His body was covered in bruises, every muscle aching even though the events in the factory had been three days ago. He was recovering, though, slowly but surely.

His body, that was.

It would take a lot longer for his mind to heal.

Every time he closed his eyes he was right back there, beneath the ground. Every time he closed his eyes he was being hunted through the tunnels, chased by Maynard's followers. Five boys, ready to serve him up in glass jars.

Every time he closed his eyes, Carmichael won.

"I'm okay," he said, sensing Billie's next question. He clutched her arm. "I'm here. You're here. They're here."

"And we're here, sir!"

He looked up ahead, seeing Savage and Duke sitting on a bench in the shade of the trees. They were both dressed in black tracksuits and trainers. Savage waved, and Kett wandered over.

"You made it," he said. "Where's Pete?"

"Bringing the picnic up from the car," said Savage. "He should be back by now."

"He's probably eaten it all," said Duke.

"No I bloody haven't," came a shout from behind them.

Porter was struggling up the steep slope, a picnic basket gripped in his hands. It wasn't exactly warm, but he was drenched in sweat, his face crimson.

"You sure you don't want a hand, sir?" said Duke.

"I'm sure," said Porter, wheezing. "You're not strong enough for this, mate."

He reached them, dumping the picnic basket on the ground. Something groaned like a wild beast, and they all turned to see Superintendent Clare stomping up the hill. He was wearing his BTJ, and he looked like some kind of angry yeti as he pushed through the trees.

"I thought you were going to get rid of that thing, Kate," said Kett.

"I did," she replied. "It must have crawled back to him."

"It's possessed," said Duke.

Clare looked possessed, red-faced and gurning as he reached them.

"Why are we here, Kett?" he barked. "I've got better things to be doing than tossing up this bastard hill."

"That explains the red face," muttered Kett. "You didn't have to come, sir. It was supposed to be family."

"I am your family," said the Super. "As much as I hate it, you're like the irritating son I didn't want and can't get rid of. Move your arses."

He flapped his hands at Savage and Duke until they got off the bench, then he collapsed onto it, extending his arms along the back. If he was hoping to have it to himself, though, he'd grossly misjudged Kett's daughters' awareness of personal space. Evie and Moira clambered up beside him, practically on his lap. Evie's nose wrinkled.

"What's that awful smell?" she said.

"Why are you dressed like a cow, Uncle Colin?" asked Moira.

"It's because he's wearing a cow," said Kett. "A whole one. And it's still alive."

Clare mooed at them, and they burst into giggles. So did Kett, the abundance of oxygen making him feel giddy.

It didn't last. Clare's face fell serious.

"Girls, give me a second with your father," he said. "Pete, get the picnic going. We'll be over in a second."

Porter hefted up the basket, lugging it to a table a little way down the path. The girls ran after him, clamouring for food. Billie stayed by his side, holding his hand in hers, giving him a reassuring squeeze.

Clare took a breath, and he must have seen Kett's expression, because he lifted his hands.

"It's nothing bad, Robbie. Nothing at all. Just some loose ends."

The Super glanced at Billie. Kett had told her most of what had occurred in the basement, of course. What he hadn't told her is what would have happened to him if Carmichael had won.

She didn't need that image in her head. Ever.

"She knows," said Kett.

"They're one hundred per cent finished," said Clare. "Hollenbeck. Maynard. It's over. We've rounded up everyone else who was working with them, all the kids they tried to coerce into being followers. Tracked them with their email addresses. They're just bored teenagers, they're not disciples. Not a single one of them was invested in Maynard's bullshit. We're pressing charges against some, but not many."

"What about the kids from the factory?" said Savage.

"They'll be charged," said Clare. "Although we're still not sure of the full extent of their crimes. Liam Uysal confessed to killing Maggie Poovey in the group home. He said it was part of Maynard's test. Emil was supposed to help, but he refused, which is why he ended up in the tank. Ethan Mortimer—we found him, by the way, dehydrated and delusional inside the basement—was supposed to kill his mother, too. He's the one who put her in the coal bunker and left her for dead."

"Christ," said Kett.

"Maynard's orders," said Clare. "He was trying to break them, mentally, so that they'd do anything he asked. It's not entirely their fault, but..."

"But they still did it," said Kett. "They still made that choice."

Clare nodded.

"I don't know how Maynard held so much power over them," he said. "I don't understand why people did what he told them to. That couple from the Red Room. Patricia and

Patrick Conlan. Brother and sister. We found them inside their car."

"Dead?" said Kett.

"They'd taped up the exhaust, and the windows, left the engine running."

"Maynard told them to kill themselves," said Kett. "After they'd distracted us. I didn't think they'd do it."

"It's almost like they worshipped him," said Clare. "It doesn't make any sense."

"Except it does," said Kett. "Because everyone needs something to believe in. Everyone needs a way of finding meaning."

Nobody answered him except the birds, who sung their joy from the trees.

"What about Ian?" asked Kett.

"He's coming around," Clare told him. "I don't think he remembers much. He's blacked it out. Carmichael was like a father to him. Ian was working with him for months, him and Maynard. He was their prototype, their experiment. He never stood a chance."

Clare's face creased with anger.

"I'm not sure how much of him is left in there. I'm not sure if he'll ever find his way back."

"He will," said Kett. "He saved me. Saved *us*. He'll find his way back."

"I hope so," said Clare. He leaned forward, releasing a fresh wave of musty stench from his ancient jacket. "We're releasing some of the details of the case to the press, but not all of them. No mention of Maynard, no mention of Hollenbeck. We're going to burn out the last of the roots, make sure nobody talks about him again, make sure nobody remembers his name, make sure there are no footprints for the next sick tossbag to follow."

He looked at Kett, his eyes red from the cold wind. He could have been a thousand years old.

"It's over."

"Thank you, sir," said Kett.

"No," Clare said. "Thank *you*."

The Super stood up, and for a terrifying second Kett thought he was going to try to hug him. Instead, he barged past, heading for the picnic table.

"For making my life bloody miserable!" he yelled as he went. "Thank you for giving me the worst case of constipation I've ever had. Thank you for sullying my dreams, you pervert!"

"I guess some things never change," said Savage as she watched him go. "You hungry, sir?"

"Yeah," he said. "You guys get started, I'll be there in a second."

Savage and Duke walked off after the Superintendent. Billie took Kett's other hand, pulling him close, looking him in the eye.

"It's over," she said. "I told you, Robbie. They came at us again and again, and we beat them every time. We won."

"You were right," he said.

He kissed her.

"So what now?" he asked.

"That's up to you," she told him, brushing his hair out of his face. He winced as she touched his eyebrow where he'd been bitten. "But we can't go on like this, Robbie."

He nodded, breathing in the fresh, cool air, shivering in the breeze.

"I know," he said.

"You've done your bit," she went on. "You've done more than enough."

"I know."

She kissed him.

"But you're the only one who can make the decision."

He didn't have to think about it for long.

"I hear the weather in Greece is pretty good," he told her, and her smile was brighter than the sun.

"Come on," she said, setting off, pulling him after her like they were young again, like their life was just beginning. "I'm starving."

He chased after her, laughing. Porter had spread the contents of the picnic basket over the table, a feast of Marks and Spencer sandwiches and scones and crisps and puddings and fizzy drinks that was being ravaged by the three girls—and by Duke, who was fighting Alice for a chocolate éclair.

Savage passed Kett a paper plate.

"Dig in, sir," she said.

He did just that, picking up a cheese scone and taking a bite. Porter emptied the last few things from the basket and walked over, a strange look on his face.

"I don't want to worry you, sir," he said, staring into the woods at the side of the path. "But I think we're being watched."

Kett squinted into the dark, seeing a slim tree that seemed to have grown shoulders. There was definitely somebody standing behind it, doing a terrible job at hiding his enormous belly. He was dressed all in white, like a portly ghost.

"We can see you, Norman," said Kett, speaking through a mouthful of scone.

Norman Balls peeked around the side of the tree.

"How?" he asked.

"X-ray vision, mate," said Porter. "What are you doing in there?"

"Nothing," said Balls. "I was just having a walk in the trees, minding my own business, not following you at all. What a coincidence."

"Very strange," said Kett.

There was a moment of awkward silence that the chattering birds tried to fill.

"I've brought tea," said Balls.

"Then get out here," Kett told him.

"More than welcome, mate!" Porter added.

Balls sprang out from behind the tree like an eager Labrador, clutching a thermos. He struggled through the undergrowth, and once again Kett braced himself for a hug. Instead, the strange little man ran past, heading for the table.

"Best friends forever!" he shouted as he went.

"Best friends for today," Kett offered.

"Good enough!"

Balls threw himself onto the sandwiches, almost barging Evie out of the way.

"Well, he did pretty much solve the case on his own," said Kett.

Porter laughed.

"That he did, sir."

Porter split off towards the edge of the hill where Moira was kicking pinecones. He pretended to tackle her and she screamed with delight, running away. Alice swept in to defend her sister, kicking Porter's shin so hard Kett heard it from where he was standing. The DI screamed too, although certainly not with delight.

"Nice one, Alice!" yelled Duke, earning a glare and a middle finger from Porter. "I'm on your team!"

The PC lumbered in, kicking the pinecone out of

Porter's reach, dribbling it towards the edge of the hill. Porter rushed at him.

"Give me that!"

"Kate, here," said Duke, scuffing the pinecone in Savage's direction. She collected it.

"Where's the goal?"

"Here!" said Evie, running to a tree.

"No, here!" said Moira, going the other way. "Give it to me!"

Savage tapped the pinecone and sent it rolling towards Moira, but Porter intercepted. He lined up a giant kick and punted it over the edge of the hill.

Unfortunately, his shoe went with it.

The DI watched as it spiralled down towards city, vanishing into the scrub.

"No!" he cried.

Duke was howling so hard he was almost on the floor, Savage hiding her own laughter with both hands.

"Do you not know how to tie your bloody laces, you oaf?" roared Clare.

"Can somebody get that for me?" Porter said, struggling to balance on one foot. "Please? I don't want a wet sock."

"You are a wet sock!" said Clare. "Toss off and get it yourself."

"I'll go," said Evie, heading down the hill.

"And me," said Moira. "Let's see how far we can throw it."

"No, wait!" said Porter, hopping after them. "They cost a fortune."

Kett watched them go, laughing so hard there were tears in his eyes.

"What a muppet," he said, when he'd recovered.

But he felt lucky to have Porter in his life. He felt lucky to have all of them.

Billie walked up, handing him a can of Diet Coke.

"All good," she said, and it was a statement rather than a question.

"All good," he echoed.

However bad the horrors of the last few days had been—the last few weeks, months, *years*—they'd still led him here, to this hill in the sun, to the cool breeze, to the sound of his laughter and the song of the birds.

To these people. His friends. His family.

"All good," he said again.

And it was.

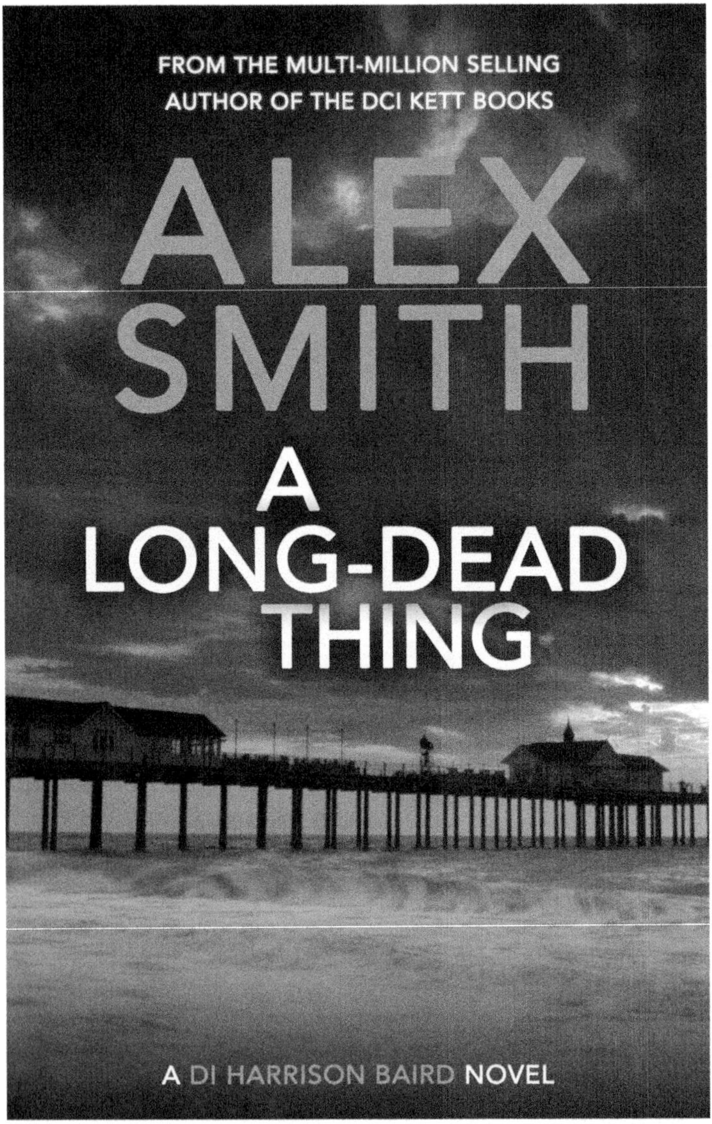
FROM THE MULTI-MILLION SELLING
AUTHOR OF THE DCI KETT BOOKS
ALEX
SMITH
A
LONG-DEAD
THING
A DI HARRISON BAIRD NOVEL

A LONG-DEAD THING

THE FIRST DI HARRISON THRILLER

It may be heaven on earth, but now hell has broken loose...

When a raid on a gang of people smugglers in Aberdeen goes wrong, impulsive Police Scotland detective DI Harrison Baird faces the worst punishment imaginable: relocation to England.

Posted in the sleepy seaside town of Southwold, and partnered with the apparently clueless DC Connie Connell, Baird finds himself in a world that's totally different to the gritty Scottish streets he's used to. Here, the biggest problem seems to be what topping to put on his ice cream, and how to avoid eating DI Henry Crump's awful fish pie.

But beneath the surface, the Suffolk coast hides a terrifying darkness. One night, a body is washed ashore—a long-dead thing—and in its eye is a silver coin.

When more bodies follow, each murdered more brutally than the last, Baird realises that he's arrived just in time to face a ruthless serial killer—one who seems to be targeting members of a powerful local crime family.

It's clear that things down south are not always what they seem. And sometimes, even in the most peaceful of places, you need to play hardball.

The first in a brand new series from multi-million copy bestseller Alex Smith, author of the DCI Kett books, A Long-Dead Thing has all the compulsive mystery, gripping action and hilarious comedy readers have come to love. Welcome to Southwold!

Available to buy now!

ABOUT THE AUTHOR

Alex Smith wrote his first book when he was six. It wasn't particularly good, but it did have some supernatural monsters in it. His latest books, the DCI Robert Kett thrillers, have monsters in them too, although these monsters are very human, and all the more terrifying for it. In between, he has published fourteen novels for children and teenagers under his full name, Alexander Gordon Smith—including the number one bestselling series Escape From Furnace, which is loved by millions of readers worldwide and which is soon to become a motion picture. He lives in Norwich with his wife and three young daughters.

Find out more at alexsmithbooks.com

RELENTLESS
MEDIA

Printed in Dunstable, United Kingdom

65185565R00282